"Sharon Souza's b⋯ into the embrace of an extrao⋯ ew adventure, the ⋯ of ⋯ ⋯, the anguish of unexpected sorrow, and the hard-won wisdom of faith and gratitude. When you have turned the last page and wiped your tears, the story will enchant you for days and weeks and maybe even years to come. This book is a treasure."

— KATHLEEN POPA, author of *To Dance in the Desert*

"*Every Good and Perfect Gift* swept me down memory lane to the joys and trials of starting a family. Sharon Souza uses her skilled hand to wipe away the fine line between friends and family and shows us that God has a loving plan, even when our faith is tested. A touching debut."

— NICOLE SEITZ, author of *Trouble the Water* and *The Spirit of Sweetgrass*

"*Every Good and Perfect Gift* captured my imagination from the first line, causing me to contemplate the bonds of such an extraordinary relationship. What would the world be like if more friendships were like Gabby and DeeDee's? Sharon Souza's debut novel is achingly beautiful and tender, often richly funny, and hauntingly memorable."

— JULIE CAROBINI, author of *Chocolate Beach* and *Truffles by the Sea*

"Sharon Souza's debut is chock-full of motherhood and grace, humor and friendship, wonderfully weaved with the strong cords of faith. Bravo!"

— RAY BLACKSTON, author of *Flabbergasted*

"In a crisp, upbeat style, Sharon Souza weaves an emotional tale of friendship and faith. She offers an insightful journey through complex issues. I came away touched."

— SALLY JOHN, author of *The Beach House*

A NOVEL

every good and perfect gift

SHARON K. SOUZA

OUR GUARANTEE TO YOU

For a free catalog
of NavPress books & Bible studies call
1-800-366-7788 (USA) or 1-800-839-4769 (Canada).

www.navpress.com

NavPress
P.O. Box 35001
Colorado Springs, Colorado 80935

© 2008 by Sharon K. Souza

ISBN-13: 978-1-60006-175-2
ISBN-10: 1-60006-175-3

Cover design by The DesignWorks Group, Jason Gabbert, www.thedesignworksgroup.com
Cover image by Getty
Author photo by Lisa Lesch
Creative Team: Jeff Gerke, Rachelle Gardner, Kathy Mosier, Arvid Wallen, Kathy Guist

This novel is a work of fiction. Names, characters, places, and incidents are either the product of the author's imagination or are used fictitiously. Any resemblance to actual events, locales, organizations, or persons, living or dead, is entirely coincidental and beyond the intent of either the author or publisher.

Published in association with the Books and Such Literary Agency, 52 Mission Circle, Suite 122, PMB 170, Santa Rosa, CA 95409-5370, www.booksandsuch.biz.

Scripture quotations in this publication are taken from the HOLY BIBLE: NEW INTERNATIONAL VERSION® (NIV®). Copyright © 1973, 1978, 1984 by International Bible Society. Used by permission of Zondervan Publishing House. All rights reserved; the *New American Standard Bible* (NASB), © The Lockman Foundation 1960, 1962, 1963, 1968, 1971, 1972, 1973, 1975, 1977, 1995; *The Living Bible* (TLB), Copyright © 1971, used by permission of Tyndale House Publishers, Inc., Wheaton, IL 60189, all rights reserved; and the *King James Version* (KJV).

Library of Congress Cataloging-in-Publication Data

Souza, Sharon K.
 Every good and perfect gift : a novel / Sharon K. Souza.
  p. cm.
 ISBN-13: 978-1-60006-175-2
 ISBN-10: 1-60006-175-3
 1. Female friendship--Fiction. 2. California, Northern--Fiction. 3.
Domestic fiction. I. Title.
 PS3619.O94E94 2008
 813'.6--dc22

                    2007028621

Printed in the United States of America

1 2 3 4 5 6 7 8 9 10 / 12 11 10 09 08

For Rick, sent to me by the Giver of all good gifts

Every good and perfect gift is from above, coming down from the Father of the heavenly lights, who does not change like shifting shadows.

JAMES 1:17

acknowledgments

Bub, "thank you" could never convey how much I appreciate your encouragement over the years. I would never have gotten here without you. Never. I'm so glad we're together on this journey.

Mindy and Deanne, my daughters, my cheerleaders. We made it. Rah! Thank you for reading, encouraging . . . ahem, *lecturing* . . . and for being women I'd want to pattern my characters after. To us, she'll always be Mike.

Brian, I know you're celebrating.

Wendy Lawton, agent extraordinaire and friend. I hope we have a long and satisfying ride.

Rod Morris, thank you for your kindness in this process. Rachelle Gardner and Kathy Mosier for your great editing; this truly is a better book because of you. Arvid Wallen for a wonderful cover design. And everyone at NavPress for a job well done.

Katy Popa, "As iron sharpens iron, so one [woman] sharpens another." Thank you for critiquing this book and the next and the next. . . . And for driving six hours for my celebration lunch. *Dance on!*

Gayle Roper, you were the first professional to give me hope. Do you know what a gift that is? Jeff Gerke, thank you for seeing the potential of this story and doing something about it. Judi Braddy, Jan Coleman, Debbie Thomas, and Laura Jensen Walker, thank you for making this writing life so much fun!

Lord Jesus, the greatest Gift of all, thank you for letting me write stories that bring glory to your name. I could do nothing without you.

This story is because of Evie. But the end will really be the beginning.

1

"Gabby, I want a baby."

I choked on my soda, grabbed the tissue DeeDee offered as I coughed up the liquid I'd inhaled, then looked to see if she was as serious as she sounded. She was.

"I want a baby," she said again, looking for all the world as if she'd uttered nothing more than, "Look at that, a hangnail."

I sat across from my best friend, DeeDee McAllister-Kent, at D'Angelo's, where we've had lunch every Tuesday since returning from college and marrying the men of our dreams, and that would soon be twenty years.

"We said we'd never have kids. You and Jonathan, and Sonny and me. We said that."

"I know." She dabbed at her mouth with a baby pink napkin, which up until that moment I had always considered mauve.

"You said this was not the kind of world to bring children into."

"I know."

"You said the world is fraught with too many dangers, temporal and spiritual. Those were your words. I remember."

"I know. I know everything I said. But now I want a child." Her eyes were wide and unflinching.

"You should have thought of this a long time ago, Dee. For heaven's sake, you're nearly forty."

Her eyes narrowed, but she managed not to frown. She was engaged in her own little war against wrinkles. "Thirty-eight and a third," she said with an indignant sniff. "And that's why."

"Oh, now there's a good reason to have a baby. Am I supposed to see logic in that?" This was a midlife crisis at its best, assuming women had midlife crises. "What did Jonathan say?" I raised an eyebrow and waited.

She straightened the flawless tablecloth with both hands. "I wanted to tell you first."

"Run it by me, you mean."

"But you know what he'll say."

"Yes. 'Anything you want, Dee.' That's what he'll say." I crossed my arms and looked beyond her. "You don't deserve him."

"Of course I don't."

Out of the corner of my eye I caught that taunting smile, the one that always disarmed me. But I was determined not to surrender my edge. DeeDee McAllister had been my best friend since the summer before sixth grade, and this was only the third time ever that I'd stood up to her. I'd forgotten how exhilarating it could be.

It wasn't that she was domineering, exactly. She was just, well, in charge. Of everything. Take my name, for instance. Gabby is not what I was christened, but since the day she careened into my life, nearly annihilating me with her brand-new Sting-Ray bike, that's what I've been called by everyone except my mother. She calls me Angel baby. Actually, she sings it. Angel baby, my Angel baby.

I hate to admit it, but I can see DeeDee's point. I would never tell her that, though, and hand deliver one more thing for her to be cocky about. As if she needed it. Not in this life. And about the bike? I know Sting-Rays were for boys, but they were cool, really cool, so naturally DeeDee had to have one. With a playing card in the spokes and a banana seat. The bike was a gift from the father who had just disentangled himself from her life. A consolation prize, I suppose.

She was new to the neighborhood, new to northern California, I learned, having moved from Orange County to our little town of Lodi in the San Joaquin Valley, best known for its cherries and tokay grapes. In the past decade we'd lost many of our orchards and most of our tokays to make room for the thousands of acres of zinfandel, chardonnay, and petite sirah that have a much more lucrative market.

Anyway, I was riding my own new bicycle on the street in front of my house when DeeDee came hurtling around the corner on her Sting-Ray, heading straight for me. We locked our brakes, losing a good deal of tire tread in the process, and came to a halt with inches to spare. I was shaken to the core, on the verge of hyperventilation as I thought about how close I'd just come to mangled bicycle and body parts. DeeDee wasn't the least bit fazed. In fact, she was laughing.

"Hi," she said, balancing herself on one bare foot. I had to lower my kickstand to keep from falling. "Nice bike."

I had certainly thought so up to that point. I'd gotten it — the exact one I'd asked for — on my eleventh birthday four months before, but suddenly I felt really uncool with my rainbow-tassled handlebar grips flapping in the wind. "Thanks," I meant to say, still trying to catch my breath, but only a puff of air came out.

She seemed unaware, more likely indifferent, to the fact that she'd shortened my life by a decade. "What's your name?"

"Angel Whitaker," I said, without the usual piety I used when informing a stranger of my hallowed name.

"Angel?" Her voice dripped with disbelief. "For real?"

For real? What did she mean, for real? Everyone had always loved my name.

"Oh, hey." She thunked her forehead. "I bet you were adopted, huh?"

"No," I said, in two defensive syllables. "Why would you think that?"

She shrugged. "It sounds like a name you'd give a kid you thought you'd never have. But, hey, don't worry, I'll call you Mike."

"Mike?" I felt my celestial ego come crashing down to earth. The word dropped off my tongue like liver.

"You know, like the angel."

"There's an angel named Mike?" I'd never heard *that* in Sunday school.

"He has a sword and everything."

"A sword?" I watched as she made a piercing jab with an outstretched arm. "You mean *Michael*, the *arch*angel?"

"That's what I said. Mike." She gave me a look as if I'd left my brain on top of my dresser before leaving the house. "Okay, okay. We'll go with Gabriel, if you insist. He's an angel too."

If I *insist?*

"And since you're obviously into the whole gender thing, we'll call you Gabriella. Gabby for short."

"Gabby." Was she kidding?

"Look, it's either that or Mike. But I am *not* calling you Angel. Got it?"

I stared with my mouth agape, wondering how God would deal with such impiety, then rolled my bicycle backward one giant step. If lightning struck, I wanted to be out of range of the ricochet. I didn't realize it at the moment, but from that day forward, that step backward would become the story of my life. Because there I stood at one of the most pivotal crossroads of my young existence, and I didn't have the wits to recognize my new identity or the adventure I was about to begin.

What I did recognize in that moment was that I had two choices. I could ask her name, as the manners my mother tried to teach me dictated, or I could get on my bike and ride away as fast as my wobbling legs would take me. Since they were still weak from my near-death experience, I abandoned my preferred choice.

"What's your name?"

She lifted the bill of her Los Angeles Dodgers baseball cap and glared. "Doris Day McAllister," she said. "But if you ever call me anything but DeeDee, I'll feed your tongue to my Doberman." I desperately hoped she was kidding. "You live around here?"

I motioned to the house behind us. It was a two-story colonial with a camphor tree in the front yard that had a crook of a branch where I loved to sit and read and think about the books I might write someday. There was a huge old walnut tree with a tire swing in one corner of the backyard too, but at eleven I was much too old for that.

"Nice," she said. "Got a pool?"

I nodded. "Do you?"

"Nope. Wanna swim?"

"You mean at my house?"

She gave me that look again as she pushed up the bill of her cap. "We can't very well swim at mine."

"I just meant — " What could I say? *My parents won't let me befriend a heathen?* That's how much *I* knew. Their arms were open to any and all, lost or otherwise, just like the Lord they served. I, on the other hand, was a little more cautious, having not yet embraced the message of the Great Commission, even though I had been the first to memorize it in my third grade Sunday school class.

DeeDee turned her cap so the white L.A. stitching faced three o'clock. "I suppose you have to ask your mom?"

"She'd say yes."

"Cool. I'll get my suit."

She did, and from that moment on we were inseparable, connected soul to soul — with DeeDee's soul having preeminence, of course.

Until that day I fully expected to be the most popular girl in Mr. Stevens' sixth grade class at Reese Elementary School, based on my popularity in Mrs. Shuckle's fifth grade class. I had also expected to be Queen Bee in the sixth grade Sunday school class at Faith Assembly, the church my father pastored. I had so looked forward to sixth grade Sunday school, which I would advance to in the fall. It was coed. Finally. And Bobby Shaw, the head deacon's son, would be in that class too. With me being the pastor's daughter and he being the head deacon's son, it was expected among our peers that we would gravitate toward one another. That's how things worked at Faith Assembly. And if there was a boy at our church I wanted to gravitate toward, it was Bobby Shaw.

But I made the mistake of inviting DeeDee McAllister to church the first Sunday after we met. I knew from that day on I'd have to settle for second most popular, in school and in church, because Bobby Shaw, along with every other eleven-year-old boy at Faith Assembly, couldn't take his eyes off DeeDee, and we weren't even in coed Sunday school yet. But it was worth it to have DeeDee McAllister as my best friend for the rest of our natural—if you could call them that—lives.

It was more than fate that brought us together on that memorable summer day. DeeDee could have plowed into any number of eleven-year-olds in my neighborhood and ended up as someone else's best friend, and who knows what might have become of her then? But it was destined to be me because DeeDee's spiritual life was about to take a major turn.

She would never have uttered the truth to any other soul on earth, but her heart had been shattered by her father's defection, as she called it, as thoroughly as if a fine china cup residing within her chest had been whacked with a Los Angeles Dodgers baseball bat. For some unfathomable reason, God allowed me to be the one to introduce her to a different kind of Father, one who knew how to put every shattered piece back in place, with only the faintest scar to show it had ever been broken.

She'd been ripe for the plucking, and with the prompting of my mother, who saw it so clearly, and the plain and simple preaching of my father, she was plucked the very next Sunday as effortlessly as the swan dive she made into my swimming pool that long-ago day. Things were usually just that easy for DeeDee.

The eleven-year-old in a Dodgers cap faded before my eyes. "I hope it's a boy," I said.

The thirty-eight-and-a-third-year-old smiled a mischievous smile, one that wrinkled her perfect little freckled nose, then shook her head. "It'll be a girl," she said.

Knowing DeeDee, I didn't doubt it for a moment.

DeeDee and I left our cars in the parking lot of Northern Exposures, the gallery she'd opened in a coveted piece of real estate in the heart of town soon after Jonathan and Sonny made the cover of *Fortune* magazine when WordWorks, their software company, became a leader in the industry. Granted, the heart of Lodi consisted of a mere six blocks on two streets, but they were the most sought-after pieces of commercial real estate in our community. DeeDee opened her doors Tuesday through Saturday from nine a.m. to one p.m., the prime time for shoppers and lookers. She was selective but kind when it came to the artisans she chose to consign, but all had to be from northern California. No exceptions. The cutoff line did, however, move farther south every year.

It was a pleasure to see the talent that proliferated in the communities that made up our little part of the world, particularly towns in the foothills of the Gold Country — towns like Sutter Creek and Jackson. Artists seemed to thrive at that elevation. Besides oils and charcoals and watercolors, DeeDee's shop displayed sculptures and carvings and pottery, some of the most unique works you could imagine.

She and I made our way on foot down School Street, looking in shop windows. It was part of our Tuesday routine. Fall fashions were already on display and it was just the middle of summer.

"April is the perfect month to have a baby." She patted her fifty-sit-ups-a-day tummy. "I won't have to be *out* of shape this summer, and I'll be *in* shape by next."

"That's only nine months away. You'd have to get pregnant—" I stopped and counted on my fingers—"in the next two weeks."

"Seventeen days," she said.

"Oh, *well*, then." I gave an exaggerated shrug.

"You don't think I can?" She cocked her head as if to say, *just watch me*, and I surrendered.

"I guess I'd better learn to knit."

"Crocheted blankets are much prettier," she called over her shoulder as she led me into, of all places, Lacey's Maternity Wear. We had made a sport on our Tuesday strolls of sniggering at women as they waddled in and out of Lacey's in their various trimesters of pregnancy, without a cupful of compassion between us.

"I thought you'd never be caught dead in a shop like this."

"Hush." She stopped in front of a mannequin whose midriff bulged beneath a bright pink form-fitting Spandex top. She looked long and hard at the bulge, and I was sure she would change her mind about pregnancy. But then she said, "Eighteen pounds, twenty at the most."

I gasped. "For the baby?"

"No, silly! For me. And I'll use plenty of that aloe cream we get at Dillard's. I can't see me with stretch marks." It was, of course, unthinkable.

"What do you suppose this is for?" I held up an item that looked like a wide elastic strap with Velcro on both ends.

"It keeps your belly button from bulging." She sounded every inch the expert.

I looked at her sideways. "For real?"

"Don't you remember Nina Simmons? She had to have been, I don't know, eleven months pregnant when we saw her the summer of our fifteenth reunion. Her belly looked like an overinflated balloon with the tied end protruding beneath her maternity smock."

My mouth dropped open. "That was her belly button?"

She laughed at my shock, snorting as a young salesgirl approached.

"Hey there," she said, greeting us with an expectant smile.

She was all teeth, the handiwork of an overpriced orthodontist if I were making a bet, and was, of course, as unpregnant as DeeDee or I. "Can I help you find something?" She had rings on both thumbs and several of her fingers and had a row of silver loops, descending in size, climbing up her left ear.

Filling in for her mom was my initial thought, she seemed so out of place. I shook my head as if to dismiss her. "We're just browsing."

DeeDee set the elastic thingy on the display table. "Actually, I need a few things."

Her eyes dropped to DeeDee's midsection. "You mean . . . for you?" The words came falteringly, as if she couldn't believe this ancient woman standing before her was in the family way.

"Well, certainly."

She arched a pierced brow. "Anything, you know, in particular?" DeeDee pointed a long, tapered finger in the direction of the mannequin with the Spandex. "Something that won't make me look like that."

The clerk looked in the direction of DeeDee's aim, then turned back to us. "We don't exactly do smocks anymore."

DeeDee's lips became a thin line. "There must be something in between."

The girl shook her head. "When are you, you know, expecting?"

"Actually, I'm expecting to be expecting," DeeDee said.

The eyebrow ring went up again. "Really?" She looked around as if searching for a hidden camera. "Maybe you should just, you know, keep looking." She gave us a sweet but dismissive smile, then went off to whisper with a coworker who was arranging maternity bras in the lingerie section of the little shop. The brassiere cups were large enough to hold the twin moons of Mars. Nothing DeeDee or I had on our chests would ever fill them.

"Thank you," I called as we stepped outside, the laughter already bubbling out of me. "Maternity lingerie?"

DeeDee snickered too. "Wow. Who'd have thought?"

We resumed our walk down School Street. DeeDee reached into her purse and brought out a pair of designer sunglasses, then slipped them into place to keep from squinting in the bright summer sunlight. "About dinner. We'll make a nice chicken salad or something light. It's much too hot to cook." She glanced at her watch. "Is seven okay with you?"

Seven? Tonight? "Did I forget something?"

She stopped and gave me The Look. "You don't expect me to tell Jonathan by myself, do you?"

"Oh, now wait a minute." I held up a hand to stop her. "Dee, this is your little project. You're on your own with this one. Besides, best friends or not, Sonny would never go for me getting involved in something so utterly private."

"Well, I don't expect you to tell *him*. Honestly, Gab, I don't know what you're thinking sometimes." She rolled her eyes and shook her head, setting her honey blonde tresses in motion. "We'll just bring up the subject casually, and one thing will lead to another. You know I can't do this by myself."

"Dee! Babies have never been a casual subject with us."

"There's a first time for everything. This will give you an opportunity to use that creativity of yours. Think of it as a plot for the novel you keep saying you'll write. It'll be such fun."

"I don't think I can." I honestly meant it.

She only smiled and led me toward the market. "Shall we have cantaloupe or strawberries with the salad?"

I sighed and accepted my defeat. "Strawberries. They're Jonathan's favorite. But let's get them from the stand across from the old hospital. You know they're the best."

She tucked her arm around mine and patted my hand. "See how I need you?"

❧

Sonny and I arrived at six forty-five. I headed right for the kitchen — a place in which DeeDee was not much at home — ready to slice strawberries or something, but, amazingly, everything was done. Sonny joined Jonathan in front of the tube for the start of the Dodgers/Mets game. DeeDee was the only southern California native in the bunch, but, true to form, she had turned the rest of us into Los Angeles Dodgers fans.

The guys were having a great time, and they were so, I don't know, *unsuspecting* that I almost felt ashamed of our little scheme, but DeeDee glowed with such expectancy I couldn't let her down. So, once dinner was over, the conspiracy began in earnest with coffee and crepes suzette with strawberries in front of the big-screen television in their living room.

The game was in the fourth inning. Jonathan found the remote in the pocket of his recliner and engaged the mute button. "What's the occasion?" He filled his mouth with a bite of the crepe, never averting his eyes from the screen.

"Oh man!" Sonny cried as the Dodgers' catcher was thrown out attempting to steal second base. They were trailing the Mets by two runs.

"Who sent him to second? Everyone knows he can't steal." Jonathan took another bite and washed it down with coffee. "Mmm. The last time I got crepes suzette it cost me a trip to Paris."

DeeDee closed her eyes and smiled. "And what a trip it was. We really should go again."

Jonathan dropped his fork with a clang onto his dessert plate.

DeeDee forced a laugh. "I'm kidding, sweetheart; don't be so nervous. I know you don't have time to get away, what with the new software coming out. While some of us live a life tinged with ennui," she said, bringing her wrist to her forehead with dramatic flair, "you and Sonny live the life of the American entrepreneur—never a dull moment."

He seemed a tiny bit relieved, but I don't think he enjoyed the rest of his crepe nearly so much as he might have.

After an adequate pause, DeeDee said, "You'll never guess who's having a baby." She threw the question into the air, supposedly for anyone to catch, but the guys weren't playing ball.

"Do tell," I said, taking up my cue.

She narrowed her eyes at me as a sign to behave. "Bonnie Singer. You remember, from our seventh grade Home Ec class."

"Bonnie Singer! No kidding! I haven't seen her since, gosh, I couldn't tell you when." Considering she didn't exist. "Is this her first?"

DeeDee nodded. "Isn't that precious?"

Precious? I forced a smile, feeling like we were reading from a really bad script.

"You were in seventh grade with her?" Jonathan's eyes were fixed on the television. "And she's having her first child? She has to be nearly forty."

"Thirty-eight and a—"

"I'm glad it's her and not you."

"I'll drink to that." Sonny offered his coffee mug for a toast.

"A lot of women are putting off motherhood until later."

"I'll have to admit," Jonathan said, "there was a time I hoped you'd change your mind about having a family, but you made it clear from the start, *no kids!*" He sliced his hand through the air for emphasis.

"I didn't put it quite like that."

He shrugged. "However you put it, that's what you meant."

DeeDee held her dessert plate in one hand, her fork in the other, her crepe untouched. "You should have said something."

"I went into marriage with my eyes wide open, sweetheart. You were honest about how you felt, and I respected that. Looking back, I see it was the right choice for us."

"Right choice?"

"You always said—"

"I *know* what I said." DeeDee toyed with a strawberry stuck on a tine of her fork. "I might have been hasty in my decision."

Jonathan laughed, and Sonny laughed too, but the laughter wasn't high spirited or jovial. No, it was laughter that said, *How did we ever get on this conversation?* It soon dissolved into nervous chuckles as Jonathan looked from Sonny to me to DeeDee. He was beginning to catch on.

Sonny was too. "Boy, I hate to call it a night, but—"

"It's only eight fifteen," our hostess said.

"Gee, is that all?" Sonny adjusted his glasses and looked at his watch again. "Must be fast."

With a glance, DeeDee passed me the ball, which I nearly fumbled. "Well . . ." I faltered right off the bat. "Did you know women over forty are becoming first-time mothers at an alarming rate? No, I mean *increasing*! The rate is *increasing*, not alarming."

"That depends on who you ask," Sonny murmured.

"You've got that right." Jonathan wasn't watching the game anymore.

Throwing caution to the wind, DeeDee actually frowned. This wasn't going well at all.

Jonathan moved out of his chair, sat down next to DeeDee, and put his arm around her. "Now, honey, I just read something about this, or maybe I saw it on *Dateline*. Anyway, it's one of those phases of life women your age go through."

I winced as soon as the words left his mouth. *Women your age?* He'd actually said that? To DeeDee McAllister-Kent?

"Your biological clock is winding down, and you're beginning to feel a twinge of maternal instinct as you see your chances at motherhood waning." He just didn't know when to quit. "I admit, I never would have expected it from *you*, but trust me, it will pass." He placed great emphasis on the last three words. "Why, I bet Gabby here is going through the exact same thing, aren't you, Gab?"

Sonny shot me a terrified look. "Are you?"

All eyes were on me.

"Well, *Gab*, are you?" DeeDee raised an eyebrow and waited.

This was so unfair.

"I didn't mean to put you on the spot," Jonathan said, and I began to breathe again.

Sonny stood in earnest and reached for my hand. "We really do have to go. Thanks for dinner, Dee. It was great. See you tomorrow, Jon."

I gave DeeDee an apologetic half smile. "Call me in the morning?"

"First thing," she said.

I had no doubt she would.

2

Sonny Nevin and Jonathan Kent were juniors at a small Christian college in northern California the year we met them. DeeDee and I were freshmen on the same campus. It was on the coast, three hours southwest of Lodi. They were on the water polo team and looked like poster boys for a California beach ad. Like us, they were best friends, inseparable. I couldn't believe they'd give us a second look, since we were merely freshmen. It had to have been DeeDee who attracted them, and not just because she was gorgeous — she was just so noticeable. Sonny says it had nothing to do with DeeDee, that it was me he singled out that night, but I wonder.

We were at a football game early in November, and I had the worst cold of my life. There wasn't a spot on my weary body that didn't ache. My nose was as red as a stop sign and painfully raw. I shivered over a cup of watery hot chocolate and tried not to sneeze on anyone, and it was only the first quarter.

"I should be in bed or at a hospital or something," I said with a moan. I poked my head out of my poncho, then withdrew it again, like a turtle, at a chill gust of wind.

"We couldn't miss our first college homecoming game." Compassion wasn't one of DeeDee's strong points.

"But I'm freezing. It's cold enough to snow."

She turned up her head to the star-studded sky. "It only feels like it."

"Dee, that was my point." I gave in to a shiver that began at the top of my head and worked its way down to my toes. I was certain I looked like my Labrador used to look when he'd emerge from our pool and shake himself to get the water out of his fur. I hadn't thought of Buddy in years.

In the bleachers behind us, three rows up, Sonny and Jonathan were cheering on their pals. "Harris, what's the matter, you got cement in your cleats?" one of them yelled—I didn't know which at the time—as a flag went down on the play, but I doubt Harris heard. He was buried beneath a mountain of shoulder pads. On another play, the other one cried, "Run, Doc, go!" as he rose to his feet and stomped on the bleacher for effect. "No! Stop! The other way!" Doc was tackled on the seven-yard line by one of *our* guys and, from what I hear, was taken by the coach the following Monday to get contact lenses. The fans were going nuts.

"I like the one in the blue sweater." DeeDee nodded her head back over her right shoulder.

Blue sweater? Was she kidding? Three-fourths of the crowd wore blue sweaters, ourselves included, blue and gold being our team colors.

"He was in the library the other day. Remember?"

"Ah. The one you're going to marry," I said, but it sounded like *bury* because of my stuffy nose.

"Now here he is again. It's fate. Ordained. I just feel it." She stood, turned, and surveyed the crowd, as if looking for someone in particular amid the sea of blue and gold, but it was only in hopes he'd notice her. I kept my face over my hot chocolate. I couldn't smell it and could barely taste it, but its warmth felt divine as it trickled down my throat. "The guy beside him isn't too bad either. Take a peek."

She handed me her compact, but as I caught my own reflection in the powder-coated mirror, I slapped it shut and groaned.

"What?"

"I need to get out of here."

She looked over her shoulder, then said, "Are you looking at the right guy?"

"It's not the guy, it's me. How could you let me go out looking like this?" I pulled my poncho lower over my face.

"It's your cold, that's all."

"I look like Deputy Dawg, for crying out loud."

She turned my face toward her and studied me for a second or two. "With or without the jowls?"

"I'm leaving."

"Kidding, Gabby. I'm just kidding." She pulled me back down to my seat. "Did you see him?"

"No."

She handed me the compact again. "Here, look. They're three bleachers up and just to your right."

Okay, he wasn't bad. He wasn't bad at all. "But what about the girls?" I said.

"What girls?"

"The ones they have their arms around."

She shrugged. "It's a passing thing."

"Oh, really? And how do you know that?"

"Honestly, Gabby, it has to be. How else are they going to marry *us*?"

"Us? Is this going to be a double ceremony?"

"Absolutely not. I'm going to be the only bride at my wedding."

"Tell *her* that." I snapped the compact closed again and dropped it into DeeDee's bag. "Can we go home now? Please?"

"Poor Gabby. Okay." She stood, tossed her bag over her shoulder, and let her eyes travel up the stands once more, while I hid inside my poncho. But as we climbed the steps, even I could see they were both looking our way. Okay, maybe the girls *were* just a passing thing.

DeeDee spent every afternoon in the library the following week but never caught sight of Blue Sweater Boy, as she called him. I guess it was easier than saying "the guy at the homecoming football game" whenever she referred to him, which was way too often. But considering the fact that blue sweaters were all over campus, it seemed a pretty generic term. Then, when I least expected it, there was his friend, Blue Sweater Boy 2, knocking me off my feet. Literally. We collided on the steps outside the student lounge, or rather he collided into me. I'd seen him coming and tried awfully hard to get out of his way, but he had his head down and was taking the steps two at a time. I could almost hear the theme from *Rocky* as he approached.

"Oh, wow, are you okay?" He reached for my hand and pulled me back to my feet. "I'm so sorry. Here." He began handing me my books and belongings. "Hey, didn't I see you at homecoming?"

Visions of Deputy Dawg flashed before my eyes and I know I turned red as a tomato. "Did you?"

He handed me the last of my books. "You sure you're okay?"

"Fine," I said, smarting from the ordeal and trying not to show it.

"Well, then." He took the last six steps in three easy bounds. When he got to the top he stopped, turned, and said, "Yeah, I did see you at the game."

I kept his smile with me the rest of the day.

I didn't mention the encounter to DeeDee. She'd have carried on about destiny and would have calculated the odds of *him* running into *me* with a student body of 5,200. And I'd have been forced to admit it did seem a bit odd, when it was actually just a tiny little coincidence. Even so, I found myself looking for him around campus—but it seemed Blue Sweater Boy 2 had dropped off the planet. Or maybe just out of school.

Not so for his pal.

"He works at The Red Onion!" DeeDee rushed into our dorm room one night after volleyball practice. "And he's a computer science major. Gorgeous and erudite, all in one neat package! Does it get any better?"

Erudite? Honestly, who uses words like *erudite*? College professors, that's who. And DeeDee. She went through dictionaries and thesauruses like I went through toothpaste. "I'm the writer, but you're the one with the vocabulary. Why is that?"

"'A man's language is an unerring index of his nature.' Laurence Binyon."

"Laurence who?"

"Which of us is the writer here? Laurence Binyon was an English poet. But for those who see the world in simpler terms, I'll just say he's a hunk with a brain!"

"Laurence Binyon?"

There it was again. The Look. *He*, of course, was Blue Sweater Boy. She dropped her jacket onto the chair by her desk. At least she meant to. It slithered off the seat into a heap on the floor. I knew from experience it would stay there until she needed it again. Organization wasn't one of her strong points either.

"You met him?" I set my book aside and slid my pencil behind my ear.

"Not yet."

"Then how do you know?"

"Jenny Lima's best friend's boyfriend is on the water polo team with him. She told me everything." She pulled off a *M*A*S*H* sweatshirt and replaced it with a turquoise sweater, the one that really set off her eyes. "We're indulging in pizza for dinner — just this once."

"From The Red Onion, I'll bet."

"He works Mondays and Thursdays, but only till nine." She looked at her watch. "So hurry up."

"Dee, I'm not hungry, and I've got this French test tomorrow. Besides, how do you know it's even the same guy?"

"I know. And I'll help you study later. Now come on. I'm not going alone. You want him to think I don't have a life?"

It was useless to argue. I grabbed my own jacket from the closet as she pulled me out the door.

We circled the block twice, then waited as a Honda loaded with cheerleaders backed out of the only space available in the parking lot of The Red Onion. I could have sworn I saw both of the girls who had been with the Blue Sweater Boys at homecoming, but DeeDee said I was imagining things. "If they were cheerleaders, they'd have been on the field leading cheers, not sitting in the stands with our future husbands."

Okay, she had a point.

We entered the restaurant, and sure enough, there they were, both of them in The Red Onion aprons, rolling out pizza dough with flour on their chins. Blue Sweater Boy 2 saw us first, and he actually nudged Blue Sweater Boy. Things were looking good. We slid into the only vacant booth, acting as if we'd never seen them before in our lives, and waited. It didn't take long. Red Onion Boy, formerly known as Blue Sweater Boy 2, was the first to reach our table. "We meet again," he said, handing me a menu and smiling the smile that I eventually learned had earned him the title of "Most Irresistible" his senior year at Brookfield High. It had only improved over time.

DeeDee gave me the most incredulous look ever. *"Again?"* She looked from me to him to me again. Her raised eyebrow said I had some explaining to do. But then, Blue Sweater Boy arrived with a wet towel and began to wash our table. It was still damp from a recent cleaning, but he wiped it anyway, then dried a hand on his apron, took the remaining menu from Red Onion Boy, and offered it to DeeDee. "Whatever you want, it's on the house."

Yes, indeed, things were looking good.

I hoped they would soon introduce themselves so we could refer to them in simpler terms from here on out. I wasn't disappointed. Blue Sweater Boy turned out to be Jonathan Kent. And Red Onion Boy? Well, his name was Stuart Oliver Nevin III. I groaned, thinking Red Onion Boy would be easier by far, until I learned that everyone called him Sonny.

"What's your name?" Sonny asked, and for the first time since sixth grade I didn't know what to say.

So DeeDee answered for me. "This is Gabby Whitaker," she said.

"Gabby? Is that short for something . . . or because you are?"

"Ha!" DeeDee said. "Good one."

"I mean, it's okay if you are . . . you know . . . *gabby.* I don't mind."

I still hadn't said a word.

"Ah. Well. It's probably short for something."

"It's a nickname," I said. "It's short for—well, for Angel actually."

"Angel? Really?" His voice fell to a whisper. "Were you adopted?"

"I'm working up the nerve to ask," I whispered back. "*Doris* here seems to think so." I had never spoken her name before. Not once in all of our years together. She looked as if I'd told him she was a serial killer.

"DeeDee," she said through teeth that were clenched. "McAllister." She smiled at Jonathan and handed back the menu. "What do you recommend?"

"The Red Onion special, with extra cheese. It's to die for."

"I love extra cheese."

"Since when?" I started to say, but figured I'd already said enough.

Their shift ended at nine, so they joined us for the finished product. It was a good thing they did—we couldn't have eaten that much pizza in a week. But Jonathan was right; it was to die for.

We exchanged basic information over dinner. Jonathan was from northern Washington, and Sonny was from Wichita, Kansas. They hadn't been friends as long as Dee and I, having met their first day of college, but if their bantering was any indication, their friendship was as solid as ours. They both were majoring in computer science, with an emphasis on software engineering, and minoring in phys ed.

"Just to keep in shape," Sonny said.

It was definitely working.

Before we left The Red Onion, the four of us had made plans

to get together the following evening.

Dee and I lay awake long into the night, fantasizing about the guys. Jonathan had the greenest eyes I'd ever seen and hair that was a shade or two short of black, but with hues of chestnut when the light hit it. He had Kurt Russell dimples that engaged when he spoke, and an expressive mouth. That was DeeDee's observation, an expressive mouth. Being an artist, she noticed things like that. He was definitely DeeDee's type—tall, two or three inches over six feet, a perfect complement to DeeDee's lithe figure. She had legs that went on forever and drew looks, regardless if she was wearing baggy jeans or a bathing suit. But if you asked her, she'd say, "What looks?"

Sonny could have been Jonathan's brother, except that his eyes were blue gray and his hair light brown. The only dimple he had was in his chin, but his smile was definitely a heart-stopper. He, too, was tall and gorgeously fit. I felt a little awkward beside him, as if I took away from his charisma.

"Will you stop saying that, Gab? Honestly, if you could see yourself as others see you, you'd be amazed. I'm going to paint you one day in all of your beauty. It will be my masterpiece."

I smiled in the darkness and wished I could believe her. "I want your relationship with Jonathan to stand on its own, you know, not be dependent on my relationship with Sonny. I mean, if it doesn't work out with us."

"I know exactly what you mean. But didn't you see the way he looked at you? Ooh la la!"

"Don't exaggerate. You know how I hate it when you do."

I could see the silhouette of her body as she raised up on one elbow. "Gabby, have I ever lied to you? *Ever?*"

I thought back over the years since the summer before sixth grade. DeeDee was extravagant, haughty, self-confident to extremes, but a liar? No. She had never lied to me. Not yet. "No," I answered.

"Then trust me. Sonny Nevin is crazy about you."

◈

Our first date with the guys was spent at the campus library. They did research while DeeDee and I sipped smuggled sodas hidden in our purses through straws and nibbled on red licorice. It's not that we were hungry or thirsty; it was simply the allure of the forbidden, much like the fruit in the Garden of Eden. We women are never too far removed from Eve, I suppose.

Our second date was much the same. And so was the third.

"What's with this?" I asked as DeeDee glanced through a novel she'd taken off the New Fiction shelf. It wasn't that I didn't like spending time at the library. I was an English major, and it was actually one of my favorite places to hang out, but I wasn't getting to know Sonny at a very rapid rate. If we were going to be married, I thought I should know something about him. I mean, what was I going to tell my folks? *This is Sonny. He makes pizza.* Just then he looked up from his note taking and waved from across the room.

"This is bizarre," I said to DeeDee as I tossed him a smile. "Are you sure they like girls?" I covered my mouth with my hand, just in case he read lips.

She rolled her eyes. "I told you before. They're developing some kind of computer software. It will make them rich and secure our futures. Give it time. It'll be worth it." DeeDee slapped the book closed.

"This is really appalling," she said. "Gabby, remember, when you're a writer, no cleavage. Write about things that matter. Write about us."

"Always and only?"

She looked off into the distance with deep concentration, as if looking into the future, then nodded. "For the most part."

"Okay. When we're old, really old and toothless, I'll write the story of us. It'll be *my* masterpiece."

Our fourth date was to church, the campus church that DeeDee and I had attended since arriving in the fall.

"This is the test," DeeDee said. "If they won't go or don't like it, then it's all been a mistake because I'm going to heaven and I won't love anyone who isn't going there too. It would be far too conflicting."

"Well, I'd say it's safe to assume they're Christians, Dee. This is, after all, a Christian college. Why else would they be here?"

"For the polo team, of course. You know what Pastor Tim says. Sitting in a pew doesn't make you a Christian any more than sitting in a garage makes you a car. So we can't safely assume anything."

I stopped applying my makeup in midstroke and set down my eye shadow. I looked from my face to DeeDee's in the bathroom mirror and wondered, *Why can't I think like she does?* She was so sensible, able to see the big picture without being distracted by peripheral images. If there was one of us who would allow herself to be entangled with an albatross who would pull her down spiritually, simply because he had blue eyes and a killer smile, it would be me, the pastor's kid. It was my nature; I was a soft touch. DeeDee, who was most definitely *not* a pastor's kid, would be the one to hold true. Life didn't always figure.

But they did like our church. And not just for us. Well, okay, maybe at first it was for us, but they were present every Sunday, unless there was a polo match. They took the preaching seriously and loved the music, but you could hardly help it. I'd gone to church since before I was born, literally, and had never enjoyed such terrific music. It made me want to get saved all over again. Every week. My dad said it was the anointing, and he should know.

For a young man, Pastor Tim sure understood about life, and he was able to apply the teachings of the Bible in such a way that it only made sense to follow it. If Jesus said, "You must be born again," well, okay then, that's what you did. Pastor Tim taught a Bible study on Tuesday nights, and because they liked his teaching so well, Sonny and Jonathan invited *us* to go. It was after one of those meetings that Tim led them both in a prayer that united their lives with the Lord.

I could never say that I became a Christian on such-and-such a day. I was raised in church as a PK—a pastor's kid—and while I have a strong commitment to Jesus, I really don't know the day it began. I just sort of grew into it. So I adopted DeeDee's spiritual birthday as my own.

"We'll be like sisters. Twins, spiritually speaking," DeeDee said.

So DeeDee and I shared a spiritual birthday, and Sonny and Jonathan shared a spiritual birthday. It really was beginning to look a lot like this was ordained, or something very close to it.

3

Jonathan didn't come around to the idea of fatherhood as quickly as DeeDee had hoped. "I ask him for one little thing, and this is what I get?" She scooted her chair up to the table at D'Angelo's and began rearranging the flowers and salt and pepper shakers to her liking. There was a pout on her perfect heart-shaped lips. She wasn't used to being denied.

I studied her for a moment, wondering how such a tomboy had turned into this lovely woman. "Dee, a baby is hardly *one little thing*." I did my best to lace my statement with sympathy. It didn't seem to matter.

"Whose side are you on?" She threw me an accusing look over the top of her menu.

"The baby's," I murmured, laying my menu aside. "I don't know why we bother to get a menu every week. We both know exactly what we're going to order." Caesar salad and soup du jour, which on Tuesday was creamy garlic potato.

"Quiche Lorraine," she said to our waitress, throwing me a curve.

"I'll have the same," I said, because that's what I always said.

DeeDee waited for the waitress to finish writing up our order. "I have the consummate name picked out." She quit pouting long enough to smile a dimply smile. "Want to hear?"

"Of course." I couldn't help but smile myself as I thought of how quickly DeeDee's moods could change. She didn't have time to hold a grudge or stay mad. There were more important things to get on to, and grudges only got in the way. Except, of course, for the grudge she held against her dad. That wasn't going anywhere, anytime soon.

"Macy McAllister Kent." She held up her hands as if to frame the words.

I repeated the name to myself. "Hmm. It has a nice ring."

"Nice ring? Are you kidding? She could be president with a name like that."

Funny, I thought, *DeeDee never played with dolls as a girl. Now here she is putting her hoped-for daughter in the White House.*

"What are you thinking over there?"

"Nothing," I said, but I swear, sometimes I was sure she could read my mind.

She speared an olive with a toothpick from the hors d'oeuvre plate and popped it into her mouth. "What does Sonny say? I know he and Jonathan must have talked about this."

"At length."

"Really?" Her eyes narrowed like a feline about to pounce. "How close am I?"

"Not very." I didn't tell her that Sonny had shared, almost verbatim, what Jonathan had said.

"It's the change," he had said, certain. "Her hormones have gone crazy. Absolutely nuts! Should it be happening so soon?" As if Sonny should know. "I need your help," he had begged. "You and Gabby have to help us through this."

"You have to help me." DeeDee's words mirrored those of her husband. "I've lost a whole week." She dropped her head into her hands, but I knew she wouldn't cry. She detested public displays of any kind, and she considered tears a last resort of silly women who didn't have the intelligence or imagination to get what they wanted any other way. I had seen her really cry only once in all the years I'd known her, and it was when my father died, not long after my wedding—but his death had astounded us all, and she simply hadn't had time to prepare for it. As if any of us had.

"Have you really thought about this? Really prayed about it?" I realized I sounded just like my dad.

She exhaled heavily and looked away. "I'd rather not go there."

"Dee!" I waited to continue while our lunch was served. "You can't make a decision like this in a vacuum. You need to ask the Lord about this and wait for an answer." That, too, was what my dad always said. "And trust Jonathan to be the spiritual leader God intended him to be," I added.

"I thought he would acquiesce."

"Acquiesce?" My eyebrows shot up. "He acquiesced when you wanted to get married in Paris—"

"You know that's what I'd always planned."

"—and when you wanted to open your gallery—"

"It's done well, as you know."

"—and he even acquiesced when you took him bungee jumping for his birthday last year."

"He's told me over and over what a thrill it was."

"Did he actually use the word *thrill*? Look at me, Dee. Did he say, 'Boy, that was a thrill'?"

She shrugged. "Maybe not exactly, but something to the effect."

"As I recall, he used the words *paralyzing fear*, and that was hours after the fact. Regardless, having a baby is a whole different ball game. It's a lifelong endeavor, not a one-shot excursion."

"I know that." She rolled her eyes. "Don't you think I *know* that?"

"He's just being cautious. He wants to be sure you're both making the right choice for the right reasons."

She placed her fork silently on her plate. "I thought you'd understand."

"I'm trying," I said, "but this was a jolt to us all."

She was thoughtful for a moment as she nibbled at her quiche. "I have prayed, Gabby. I really have."

"And?"

"I don't seem to get an answer."

"Maybe that *is* your answer." I gave her a *have-you-thought-about-that?* look.

"Our lunch is getting cold."

Yes, it was. Even so, it was delicious—enough for us to consider changing from our usual fare. All of a sudden we were emerging from our cocoons, and it was unnerving.

For as long as I'd known her, DeeDee had planned to spend her life in Paris in the shadow of the Eiffel Tower. She'd live on the Left Bank, of course, and paint after the fashion of her Impressionist idol, Camille Pissarro. I mean, what eleven-year-old even knows about Impressionism, let alone its shining stars?

I remember the first time I visited her house the summer we

met. Her bedroom walls were covered with magazine photos of the Seine, the Louvre, and Notre Dame, places I knew nothing about. Frameless poster-prints of Monet and Renoir with stark white borders were thumbtacked about her room at a variety of angles. She even managed to superimpose a full-body photograph of herself standing in front of the Eiffel Tower, but it was terribly out of scale. The top of her head reached nearly halfway up the structure. It reminded me of King Kong climbing his way up the Empire State Building. I bit the inside of my cheek to keep from laughing. "Your room looks like a travel guide." I couldn't keep from crinkling my nose.

"And yours looks like *Teen Beat*."

"Cool, huh?"

She hiked an eyebrow, a talent that would take me another seven years to master. "There's more to life than boy bands, Gabby."

That little comment, as well as my new name, caught me by surprise. What could I say to that? None of my other friends would have said something so strange. But DeeDee had her own phone, and, well, that trumped everything. I ran my finger over the yellow receiver and understood for the first time what "Do not covet" means.

DeeDee dropped onto her bed and folded her long legs Indian style. "I'm moving to Paris when I'm twenty."

"Why twenty?" I said. *Why Paris?* I wanted to add.

"Because until you're twenty you're just a child. And Paris is no place for children." She arched that eyebrow again, telling me there was more to her statement, but I didn't get it. "Besides, that'll give me two years of college art to really hone my talent."

"You're an artist?"

If looks could tell you just how juvenile you were, I'd have gone home sucking my thumb. "Of course. At least I will be once I start high school art. Along with French classes. In the mean-time—"she pointed to a tape recorder—"I'm doing the sublimi-nal thing."

Honestly, I didn't understand a third of what she said. But she was just so cool, and in the beginning that's what drew me.

"You're going, aren't you?"

I looked around for a clock. "Is it already five?"

DeeDee closed her eyes and pursed her lips. "Not home, Gabby. Paris. Hemingway wrote in Paris. All the great writers do."

"He did? They do?" Well, now I knew who my next biograph-ical report would be on. "How do you know so much?"

"L.A. schools are miles ahead of you northerners. I really should skip sixth grade altogether."

My nose crinkled again. "Oh."

"But that would put me at nineteen when I finish junior col-lege, and that would mess everything up."

"Right. Twenty."

"Exactly. So." She stuck out her hand. "Is it a deal?"

"Deal?"

She stopped herself halfway through an eye roll. "About Paris. You and me. Deal?" She gave me a moment, then added, "That's what best friends do, Gabby."

"Oh," I said again. "Well, um, okay."

She gave me a firm handshake to seal the deal.

But that was all before we ventured into The Red Onion. It soon became apparent that Sonny and Jonathan weren't leaving the

States, at least until they perfected and sold the software that would launch their career and make a name for them in this fledgling industry. And that was fine with me. I'd always gone along with DeeDee because it wasn't in me to do otherwise, but Paris had been *her* dream, and I fully expected she'd outgrow it one day. But it was far more than a dream to DeeDee, and she wasn't ready to let go of it. By the end of our sophomore year, we were well into our relationships with Sonny and Jonathan, and a choice had to be made.

I found her one spring day stretched out on her bed in our dorm room, deep in thought.

"Was your art class canceled?" I dropped my backpack onto the floor beside my desk, gladly relieving myself of its weight. She would never have missed that class willingly, or so I thought. But she looked troubled enough that I began to have second thoughts. "Hey, are you all right? Want to get some lunch?"

"No, no, and maybe," she said, answering all of my questions in order. "My class wasn't canceled, I'm not all right, and I'll think about lunch."

I sat on my bed and kicked off my shoes. "What's up?"

"What are we going to do about Paris, Gab?" She rolled onto her side so she could face me and propped herself up on one elbow. "I don't think Jonathan wants to leave California."

"Really?" I'd been waiting for this to come up.

"He's known all along. I made it clear from the beginning that I wanted to study art in Paris, so there was no point in going on and on about it. Right?" DeeDee sat up, crossed her legs, and rested her head in her hands. She was dressed in a T-shirt and sweatpants and hadn't put on any makeup. Obviously, she hadn't left the dorm room all day. "But last night when I told him you and I would be leaving after the semester, he looked at me as if I'd told him I'm an alien."

I felt myself growing tense. "We haven't talked about this for so long, Dee . . . haven't made any plans, about school or anything."

The faintest crease appeared in her forehead as she frowned. "What's there to talk about? We've planned this for nine years. We said we were going to live in Paris after two years of college."

"I know, but, well, I thought you might have changed your mind."

"About Paris? Whatever for?" She gave me the look Jonathan must have given her the night before.

"Well, the guys. I just figured things were different now."

"They graduate in May. The timing is ideal. They can work on their software anywhere. What better place than Paris? It's so inspirational." She shrugged as if to say, *So what's the problem?* "What does Sonny say?"

I began picking at my nail polish, a habit I fell into when I was nervous. "We've never really talked about it, actually."

"Not talked about Paris? I thought you and Sonny were serious."

"We are . . . I think. I just, well, I thought you'd change your mind."

"You said that," she said, then looked at me narrowly. "You've changed *your* mind?"

I shrugged, for lack of a better response.

DeeDee rose from her bed and walked to the window. The spring sun shining through the enormous budding elm on the other side of the glass bathed the room in dappled warmth, but DeeDee shivered. "You have."

"No. Not definitely." My nail polish was a mess. "I told you I'd go. I'll go."

"I wouldn't come between you and Sonny." She turned to face

me. "It's ordained, remember?" She tried to appear aloof, but I could see the disappointment in her eyes.

"What about you and Jonathan? Isn't that ordained?"

She shrugged as she turned back to the window. "I don't know anymore. How could it be?"

"Maybe we could go for the summer. They could do without us that long, couldn't they?" Inwardly I groaned. I didn't know how I could possibly go without seeing Sonny for three days, let alone three months, but I felt I owed DeeDee that much.

"If I go, it's forever, Gabby. You know that."

I felt overwhelmingly sad just then. "Maybe you won't like it."

"Not like Paris? You might as well say I won't like heaven."

Of course she was right. Her existence thus far had merely been a prelude to life, which would only begin in earnest in Paris. She was a woman of purpose, and that purpose was, and always had been, to lose herself in the unconventional world of Monet, Pissarro, and Renoir. She was made for the City of Lights, and it was made for her.

That I had not told Sonny about Paris was not an oversight, nor was it a willful omission of the inevitable. I just never expected it to become a reality, so, like DeeDee said, what was the point? Looking back, I guess it was a little odd that *he* never brought it up, since DeeDee had obviously spoken to Jonathan about our plans, and Jonathan undoubtedly would have shared that information with Sonny. But the concept of such a scheme was so far-fetched. If I didn't expect it to become a reality, why would Sonny?

So for weeks I agonized over the question of what to do about Paris. I was torn between my loyalty to DeeDee and my intense desire not to leave California or, more accurately, not to leave

Sonny. We hadn't discussed marriage in so many words, but we were definitely on the road to matrimony. Neither of us had dated anyone else since our unorthodox beginning at the library a year and a half before. It wasn't that we'd made a commitment not to do so; it simply never came up because we enjoyed being together, either as a couple or as a foursome with DeeDee and Jonathan. We talked about the future in terms of *us* and *we*. Nothing I said excluded Sonny, and nothing he said excluded me. It was understood that we'd always be together. And now that graduation was on the horizon, I fully expected that understanding to become something more tangible. What was I to do?

Find a phone booth and call home.

"Mom?"

"Angel baby! How are you?" Her cheerfulness quickly gave way to concern. "Is everything all right?"

"I'm fine, Mom. I just need some advice." I could almost see her stretch the phone cord across the kitchen and pull out a chair at the table. I'd seen her dozens, maybe hundreds, of times over the years pour herself a cup of tea, settle in at the round oak table on a matching chair with its faded blue calico seat cushion, and offer counsel to any number of women over the phone. As a pastor's wife, it came with the territory. But it truly was her gift. And now I needed her wisdom like never before. I emptied myself of my burden, holding back about Sonny and me as much as I could. I tried to convince myself that Sonny wasn't the issue, but in truth it was difficult to separate one from the other.

"Paris." I pictured Mother winding the phone cord around and around her finger. "I haven't heard you girls speak of that for ages."

"That's just it, Mom. We haven't. But DeeDee still plans to go, and she expects me to go with her."

"And you don't want to?"

"It's so impractical. I mean, how on earth could we afford to live in Paris? How would I finish my education?"

"Those things aside, sweetheart, do you want to go to Paris?"

The question hung between us as I groped for an answer, but nothing would come to me except the truth. "No," I finally said, feeling like the defector I was. "I honestly never thought it would come to this."

"Not come to this? With DeeDee? Oh, honey."

"Mom, did you really think I'd move to Paris? To live?"

"Of course not. I just thought you'd have settled that with DeeDee long before now."

"I should have." I groaned. "But how could I?"

"Let's talk about Sonny."

"Sonny?" She certainly knew how to get right to the heart of the matter. I felt my face grow hot, as if I'd been caught trying to slip one over on her. In a way, I guess I had.

"I suspect he's the reason for this change of heart? We like him, of course."

"You do?"

"Very much. Don't you?"

"Me?" How did she always know? I might as well come clean. "I do. Oh, Mom, I really do. I think DeeDee expected that she and Jonathan and Sonny and I would all go to Paris, get married, and live happily ever after in the shadow of the Eiffel Tower. I'm afraid to think what this could do to our relationship."

"Your relationship is solid, sweetheart. The only thing that could damage it is not being honest with each other."

"I can't stand to disappoint her."

"Just be honest. Things have a way of working out, especially when you pray about them."

"How do I pray about this one? Lord, change *her* mind . . . or *mine?*" *As if I didn't know.* "And what about Jonathan? They're so right for each other."

"Things have a way of working out," she said again. "Don't try to manipulate the outcome as you pray. Trust the Lord to know what's best. Simply pray for His will."

I honestly tried to follow my mother's advice, and most of the time I did manage to pray, *Thy will be done.* But there were times I couldn't help myself. I would beg and plead, *God, you have to help!*

"Your teeth are chattering."

I offered Sonny a smile with lips, I was willing to bet, as blue as a glacier. "I can't remember a colder Memorial Day."

"We should have canceled." He pulled me as close as our life vests would allow and looked around the whitewater raft, empty except for us and our guide. "I just kept thinking it would get warmer."

He'd obviously missed the weather report. The one that said, "Cold snap threatens holiday weekend revenue."

We'd planned this float down the American River weeks ago, for the four of us to ring in the summer. Nothing intense, no white water, no rapids, just an easy ride following the current downstream.

Right.

The wind howled through the canyon, and I moved in closer to Sonny's life vest. He didn't have much warmth to offer, but at least my right shoulder was blocked from the gusts blowing in off the icy Sierras.

"Who'da thought?" Sonny said, his lips close to my ear.

With bright orange paddles, our guide maneuvered the raft through the rocks and the tumbling water. "Not much farther," he shouted over the roar of the river.

Thank God. Thank God, thank God.

Jonathan had bowed out with a flu bug. I seriously envied him at that moment. And Dee, ever the smart one, had canceled without stating much of a reason. "Just things to do," she said, without further explanation. But in the frozen recesses of my mind I couldn't help wondering what she was up to.

It was after dark when we arrived home. Sonny and I were both so exhausted we called it a night. Dad was at his office at the church, involved in an emergency counseling session, and Mom was in the living room.

"I thought you'd be home long ago, as cold as it was," Mom said, getting up from the sofa. Then she actually got a look at me. "Oh, sweetheart, you look frozen solid. I was just making a cup of tea. I'll make two."

I chattered my thanks and followed her into the kitchen. Once the water was on to boil—Mom never made tea in the microwave—I held my hands over the pot, loving the warmth.

Mom brought a thick sweater and wrapped it around me. "DeeDee called. Twice."

"She probably wants to console me, knowing what a miserable day it was out there."

"Right," Mom said, and we both laughed.

I reached for the phone, punched in DeeDee's number, and got a busy signal. I watched Mom as she cut a lemon, poured boiling water into our mugs, then dipped a tea bag into each one. I followed her to the living room and dialed DeeDee's number again. Still busy.

Mom returned to her place on the sofa, picked up her Bible, and began to read again. I could tell from the materials scattered around her that she was preparing for the ladies' Bible study she taught every Wednesday night at church. I noted that she was reading from the fifth chapter of Matthew. One of the things I looked forward to the most during school breaks was being able to attend her Bible study.

"The Sermon on the Mount?" I asked.

"I love the Beatitudes and anything in red."

And because of her teaching, so did I. "You do them so well."

"Thank you, honey."

I held the phone on my lap, making myself wait another minute before dialing DeeDee's number again. "Did she sound okay?"

She looked up from her Bible. "Better than okay, actually."

I didn't know if that was good or bad. For weeks she'd been in such a funk about Paris, wrestling with what to do, torn between her life's passion and her feelings for Jonathan. I wanted desperately to help, but we both knew I was hopelessly biased. I had a bad feeling that she'd finally made her decision without me.

I dialed the phone again and waited as it rang. Finally, DeeDee answered. When she heard my voice she simply said, "I did it."

I held my breath, waiting for more.

"I bought my ticket."

Euphoria practically seeped through the receiver. I could have cried.

"Are you there?"

Not trusting my voice, I merely nodded.

"Gab? Oh, Gabby." She was precisely aware of how I was feeling. "Be happy for me."

"But . . . but . . ."

Mom caught my eye from across the room and offered a sympathetic smile. I didn't have to say a word—she knew. She closed her Bible, rose, and kissed my forehead, then carried her things upstairs, giving me the privacy I needed.

"I leave Friday," DeeDee said.

"Friday? Four-days-from-now Friday? I'm going with you," I said weakly.

"No, Gabby. It's my dream. I see that now. It wasn't fair to coerce you into it. You have your own dreams, your own life, your own calling. I can't expect you to live mine."

I was far from relieved. "Does Jonathan know?"

"We just got off the phone," she said, the exuberance waning. "I don't think he understands. But you do. I know *you* do. Will you help him?"

Me? Help *him?* Who was going to help me? "Friday?" I said again.

"I need to plunge right in. You'll drive me to the airport, won't you?"

"Are you sure, *really* sure, that this is what you want?"

"You know it is. Be happy for me."

"What on earth . . . ?"

I hardly recognized her on Friday. She had shed the college coed look and traded it in for pure Bohemian. Her long honey blonde hair was loosely plaited with a ribbon woven into the braid.

Large gold loops hung from her earlobes. She wore a broomstick skirt of undistinguishable print with a cute little rose-colored T-shirt that picked up the main color of the skirt. To complete the look, she had on a new pair of Birkenstocks—I remember when she said she'd go to the guillotine before she'd wear such a fashionless pair of sandals—and had removed the polish from her toenails. There was a toe ring on the second toe of each foot and a little chain around one ankle.

And she was braless. "DeeDee McAllister!"

She knew exactly what I was referring to. "It's the new me," she said, striking a pose. "The *libre-penseur*, the *artiste.*"

"The *vierge*," I reminded her.

She threw me a huffy look. "That's not going to change! But to be a virgin doesn't mean one has to *look* like a virgin—not when you're in Paris. Besides, you're missing the point." When my response was merely to raise an eyebrow, she added, "This isn't a sexual statement; it's an artistic one."

"All of a sudden you can't paint with a bra?"

"I prefer to use a brush." She laughed at her dumb little joke, then motioned to her bags. "Now help me with my stuff." She seemed eager to change the subject.

I didn't budge. "When you get there, the first thing you're going to do is find a church, right?"

"When I get there, the first thing I'm going to do is find a *room.*" She snatched up a duffel bag. Softening, she added, "*Then* I'll find a church. Now help me."

"Is this all you're taking?" I looked from the bag she held to the one I picked up.

"You'd be surprised at what one can do without."

"Like bras and razors and I'm afraid to think what else? Honestly, what *are* you taking?"

"This one has my painting supplies; that one has my clothes."

I lifted the suitcase with ease. "You've packed more just to spend the night at my house," I said and followed her out the door. "Where's your mom?"

"I made her go to the office. We said our *adieus* last night."

Suddenly, my heart was in my throat. "Did she cry?"

"You know my mom."

Yes, I knew her mom. Linda McAllister was the first divorced person I'd ever met. When DeeDee and I were kids, the divorce rate was much lower, and most families were still intact. By the time we were in high school, the statistics had made a drastic change and my family had become the anomaly, but in the early days DeeDee's mother was somewhat of a curiosity to me. I blush to admit that way back then words like *wanton* and *wayward* came to mind when I thought of her. I'd seen far too many old movies on TV. I'd never known a woman who smoked and occasionally drank a glass or two of wine. In all fairness, I'd never seen her drunk or even close to it, but she was different from anything my sheltered life had exposed me to. I soon learned she was simply a lonely woman who wanted a friend, and she relied heavily upon her daughter to be that friend. "You're all she has, Dee."

"You know I've spent years preparing her for just this moment."

And she had. She and her mother had gotten into role reversal right from the get-go. "I'll visit her," I said. "We'll cry on each other's shoulder." She threw me a scolding look, which I ignored. "What about Jonathan? Are we picking him up?"

"I asked him not to come." She tossed her bag into the backseat of my car, then slid into the front passenger seat.

I slid her suitcase onto the backseat from the driver's side of the vehicle, then stuck my head in after it. "You didn't break up, did you?"

She looked away from me and shrugged defensively. "It's not like we were engaged."

"What does that mean?"

"It means we broke up." Her voice was barely audible, and she refused to look at me.

My spirits were quickly faltering as I felt everything familiar begin to slip away.

We were silent as I wove my way through the streets of our town to get to the freeway that would take us to the San Francisco airport. I'm certain her thoughts were soaring, but mine, well, I struggled. If this Paris thing was meant to be, why did it feel so wrong? DeeDee was going off to fulfill her hopes and ambitions, but in her wake she was leaving a rash of wounded souls. Her mother's, Jonathan's, mine. *Lord, could that be right?*

An accident on the Bay Bridge cost us a good deal of time, so much so that when we got to the airport, passengers on her flight were already boarding the plane. She barely had time to check her bags and get to the proper gate. Clutching her boarding pass, she threw her arms around me and hugged me. It was the most affectionate act I'd ever seen her display, and it touched me deeply. She was usually so blasted independent.

"I'll call," she promised, then disappeared through the boarding gate without so much as a good-bye. But, of course, that was DeeDee's way.

I stood before the wall of glass that looked out on the tarmac, determined to watch her depart no matter how much it hurt, feeling as if my soul and spirit were leaving with her. It was like being suspended between heaven and earth, and the pressure on my physical self was crushing. What would I do without her? For nine long, wonderful years DeeDee and I had been inseparable, connected at the heart. She was the wind in my sails, helping me to soar. I was the anchor that kept her feet on the ground. In nine years we had not spent one day apart. On the few occasions my family went on vacation, DeeDee came along.

And she had refused to go without me the one awful time she went to visit her dad and his new wife, a.k.a. her stepmonster, in Long Beach. Amazingly, Mom had convinced my dad that I should be able to go for poor DeeDee's sake. The trip had been a ghastly disaster. DeeDee, never afraid to speak her mind, could not, *would* not, forgive her dad for the breakup of their family and had taken advantage of the opportunity to tell him so. At fourteen, DeeDee had more moxie than anyone I'd ever known. Not surprisingly, the weeklong visit had been cut drastically short.

At fifteen, when I had my appendix removed, DeeDee sat up all night with me in the hospital and cut school the next two days so I wouldn't spend one minute alone. Aside from the pain — and the scar — it was one of my most favorite ordeals.

And now she was going to Paris without me! How could I have let it happen? It was settled. I'd make my flight arrangements before I left the airport, then go home and pack. Mom, Dad, Sonny, they'd just have to understand.

Then, before I could put action to my resolution, she burst back through the boarding gate and called, "Gabby!" in a loud and desperate voice. She saw me at the window and rushed toward me with an inexplicable look on her face.

"What are you doing?" I stammered. "Your plane . . ." I motioned with an arm that seemed to float on its own as the 757 backed away from the terminal.

"Why didn't you tell me I can't paint?"

"What?"

"You're my best friend. You should have told me."

"It's *Impressionism*," I said. People around us were beginning to stare. "How did I know?" I had thought my lack of artistic knowledge had kept me from appreciating her skills. I mean, Impressionism is just that, it's . . . *impressionism*. You sort of think you know what you're seeing. If it doesn't look exactly as it should, well, isn't that the point? If it doesn't look at all like it should, maybe that told another story altogether. But what did I know?

"How could you let me go off to Paris knowing I'd fail?" Her eyes narrowed. "Or was that the plan all along?"

"Plan? There's no plan."

"In four semesters of college I barely managed a C in all my art classes combined, and in everything else I've gotten As. What does that tell you?"

"Nothing. You said yourself that art teachers are merely frustrated artists. What do they know?"

"Enough," DeeDee said. She was far too pragmatic to allow herself to be patronized. That in itself was proof that she wasn't made of the stuff artists are made of. There wasn't enough of the melancholy in her. In fact, there wasn't any. We knew that. We'd just never realized it mattered.

We watched as DeeDee's plane pulled away, and the reality of what she'd done began to register. She closed her eyes and made herself breathe deeply and slowly. At last she said, "My luggage is going to Paris and I'm not. Do you suppose I'll get it back?"

I'd never seen her look so pathetic—and it struck me as incredibly funny. I began to laugh, and when I snorted she laughed too. And we laughed until neither of us could stand and I was in grave danger of wetting myself. I ran for the bathroom. "At least your bras are safely tucked away in your top dresser drawer at home."

She slammed shut a stall door beside me. "No, actually, they're on a fast plane to Paris."

Suddenly I was an adolescent again, remembering the day I turned twelve. My mother had given me my first bra as a birthday gift. I was mortified and couldn't wait to share my horror with DeeDee.

"A bra?" Her eyes had gone straight to my perfectly concave chest. "That's it?"

I extended my right hand and showed her a birthstone ring, an aquamarine with two little diamond chips on the side.

"That's nice," she said, trying her best to be positive.

"I wanted that new album by—"

"I know."

"The one with—"

"I know. It's your favorite song. *My* mother wanted me to give you a packet of stationery. One with strawberries all over it. And scented."

I wrinkled my nose. "You didn't, did you?"

"Of course not. You'll die." She handed me a flat square package wrapped in bright red paper with holly leaves. I didn't care if it was leftover Christmas paper; I knew immediately what was inside. My album. She pointed me in the direction of my bedroom. "Let's go put it on."

"Thank you, thank you, thank you, thank you, thank you!"

As sounds of my favorite pop star filled the room, DeeDee went to my bureau and opened the top drawer. She pulled out the white, stretchy, cupless brassiere with the tag still attached. It was a 30 quadruple A. I turned a deep crimson. *Did they come any smaller?* Of course, DeeDee, six days younger than me but ahead of me in everything else, had been wearing one for weeks. And she actually needed it.

"You know," she said, wise beyond her years, "we *are* going into seventh grade. That means girls' phys ed. And *showers.* If

Janelle Matthews, who was practically *born* wearing a bra, found out you didn't wear one, there's no telling what mean and nasty things she'd say. Besides, if the guys don't have something to snap, it'll get around. You wouldn't want Bobby Shaw to hear *that*, would you?" She tossed the bra onto the bed beside me. "You'll get used to it. Most of the time I almost forget I have one on. But do cut the tags off, especially the one with the size."

Where had eight years gone? I glanced over at DeeDee's liberated bosom, humorously pronounced by the shoulder harness in the front seat of my car, now that we were safely on our way back home. It was all I could do not to laugh at the memory and the image beside me. True, she had developed earlier than me, but she'd stopped much earlier as well. Paris wasn't going to miss much.

"So what will you do?" I expected an answer like "Change my major, of course," but that was too benign for DeeDee.

"I'm going to marry Jonathan," she said.

I gasped. "He proposed?"

"This is the age of liberation, Gabby, and liberated men don't propose. Marriage is more of a till-death-do-us-part joint venture. It doesn't matter who initiates it . . . as long as the man thinks he did."

"And what about Paris?"

A look that expressed both the death of a dream and the hope of a new one played across her face. "Paris is for lovers and the gifted. And for honeymoons," she added with a sly smile.

My eyes filled with tears for DeeDee, but I didn't dare let her see. I lifted my sunglasses from the top of my head and pushed them onto my face. "You are the strongest person I know."

"It's a gift." She leaned back in her seat. "Mind if we stop at a pay phone? There's someone I want to call."

I offered up a prayer of thanksgiving and smiled until it hurt. All the way home.

4

Jonathan did propose, and quickly, before DeeDee could hire a painting tutor or in some other way attempt to change her mind about Paris. Not realizing he was a liberated male, his approach was sweetly traditional. There was nothing of the Bohemian in Jonathan. He actually got down on one knee and had a ring and everything. It was too much for DeeDee.

"I really have to think about this," she said to him.

To me, she gasped, "What have I done?"

She sat cross-legged on the floor of the spare bedroom my parents had turned into an office/study. I stifled a sigh, saved the story I was working on, minimized the screen, and joined DeeDee on the floor. "What do you mean, what have you done?"

"I've spent nearly two years with a man who's so . . . so . . . well, if he were a flavor he'd be vanilla!"

"Vanilla?" I tried not to chuckle. "And what are you?"

"Passion fruit! Oh, Gab, we're at opposite ends of the spice rack!"

She was absolutely right, of course, but so what? "Then think of your relationship as a rainbow," I said, well aware that we were both making a terrible mess of our metaphors. "Jonathan is the faintest hint of color and you're . . . vermilion! What's in between is a wonderful blend of who you both are."

She looked at me with an expression of wonder. "That's incredible," she whispered. "*You're* the artist, Gabby. I would never have seen that." She hugged me. "You're going to be a wonderful writer."

The wedding was set for September. In Paris, of course, but Dee and I would be back in time to begin classes at CSU–Sacramento, where we both had transferred and where Dee was now majoring in business.

I was delighted at how un-vanilla Jonathan was when it came to the wedding plans. He drew the line at wearing a beret and pantaloons, but otherwise DeeDee had carte blanche with the arrangements. Sonny and I and DeeDee's mother would be the only ones in attendance. Jonathan's parents were older and felt the trip would be too much for them. He had a sister, Janine, ten years older than he, but she had gone east to college when Jonathan was seven and had stayed several years after graduation. She was back in Washington now, but they rarely saw each other and weren't especially close. Sonny, of course, would be best man, and I was to be the maid of honor.

"I've been thinking," Sonny said as we walked through a quiet little park near my home one evening in June. "Paris would be quite the place for a honeymoon."

"I'm sure it will be glorious." I stopped to pick a daffodil. "They'll have a wonderful time."

"I was thinking of us," he said. He covered my hand with his and brought the flower to his nose and inhaled. Then he kissed my fingers one by one.

My legs felt like rubber, and I thought for a moment I'd collapse. I needed to sit down. Now. In the absence of a park bench I dropped onto the grass. "Us?" I whispered.

He cocked his head and smiled his lethal smile. "Why not?"

I nearly swooned. "What did you have in mind?"

"I'll leave the arrangements to you . . . so long as we're married when we land in France."

I looked long and hard into his magnificent eyes and saw no sign of teasing. "Okay, then." My lips turned up involuntarily in what felt like a silly grin.

"Okay, then." His kiss was unlike any he'd given before, and it sent tingles up and down my body. "Cold?" he asked.

"Not at all," I said, shivering again.

He smiled and pulled me close for another kiss. When at last I pulled back for air, Sonny produced a little white box and pulled up the lid in one smooth motion, as if he'd made the move a thousand times. A solitary diamond on a simple gold band caught the sunlight.

"Oh, Sonny." I couldn't think of another thing to say.

"If it's not what you like, we can find something else."

"Oh no. It's perfect. Just perfect."

He slipped the ring on my finger, then lifted my hand to his lips. I tingled at the touch.

Oh man, what a guy.

I was astounded at this turn of events and secretly amused that instead of being DeeDee's maid of honor, I would be her *matrone de honneur*. For once I was going to get the better of her. She was simply going to die.

We spent a mad and hectic summer preparing for weddings and showers and honeymoons and new living accommodations.

DeeDee had chosen September 5 for her wedding day, which meant that Sonny and I would be married on August 29. That gave us just over two months to put it all together. My wedding would be more involved than DeeDee's, but hers was a continent away. That made it a toss-up as to whose was more difficult to arrange. She helped with my invitations, since she had none to prepare for herself, and told me I wouldn't have to worry about her maid of honor gown—she'd handle it on her own.

"I'll look anywhere but a bridal shop. I'll wear anything but pastel."

That was fine with me.

I was in my bridal bra and panties when I heard DeeDee enter the bride's room of our church, where Mom was helping me dress.

"Where have you been?" I asked. "You're supposed to—" Then I saw her reflection in the full-length mirror that was supposed to highlight the bride. "Wow."

"What do you think?" She struck a pose and flashed me her very best smile.

She had on a Gatsbyish tea-length, backless sheath in shimmering cobalt blue that flared softly at the knee, and she wore a bone-colored, broad-rimmed hat with a flowing cobalt ribbon.

"Wow," I said again, and all I could think was, *Upstaged again*.

"You look beautiful," Mother said and touched her lips to DeeDee's cheek. "Divine."

DeeDee took the hat off and laid it on the table. "Well, thank you both for giving me my moment of glory, because once you put that on—"she pointed to my wedding dress—"not a soul is going to notice me."

Right.

"And look at you, Margie," DeeDee said to my mom. "You're gorgeous."

And she was. Mom's dress was far more conservative than DeeDee's and two or three shades lighter, nearly matching the eyes I had not inherited.

Mother beamed. "Wait till you see the flowers. You'll match the freesia to a tee."

And that was the idea. DeeDee had made sure that the fabric for her dress matched the freesia that would be in her bouquet, as well as in the flowers for the church. My bouquet was made up of roses, stargazer lilies, and trailing dendrobium orchids, all white as sugar.

Dee Dee slipped out of her shoes and wiggled her newly pedicured toes. "Okay. Where's the photographer?"

"Not yet!" I said. "I'm practically naked."

"Then put on your slip. We need pictures." She was out the door before I could stop her.

"I will kill her if she brings that man in here."

Mother only smiled. "She's right. There should be pictures of you getting dressed."

"But—"

She handed me my slip. "Better hurry."

DeeDee was back in a flash with the photographer's assistant. A woman, and she was all business.

"Get her garter," she said to Mother. "We'll start with that."

Well, there would be a few pages in my wedding album no one but Sonny was ever going to see.

❧

Trying on a wedding dress and actually wearing it for real was as different as hearing about Beethoven's Fifth and actually putting on the CD. Cliché or not, I felt like a princess the moment I stepped into my dress.

It was made of white silk with a soft lace overlay and was also designed in *Great Gatsby* style. The sleeveless bodice had no waistline but, like DeeDee's, flared softly at the knee as it fell to the floor. The hemline in front stopped at my toes, while in back it was longer and rounded, forming its own train. I wore a white lace hat with a silk ribbon that flowed down the back to my waist, and no veil. I wanted nothing obscured. DeeDee and I were perfectly coordinated. Like always.

I couldn't wait to see my Prince Charming and, more to the point, be alone with him. But we had to get through the day first. And what a day it was. I had no idea it would be so emotionally charged from the moment I tucked my arm around Dad's, as we waited to begin that long walk down the aisle. As he and I stood in the church foyer, listening for the organ to strike the first note of the "Wedding March," Dad could barely speak. His eyes shone with proud tears, and I was in danger of losing it right along with him.

"Daddy," I said, and that was my first mistake.

His breath caught in his throat and he looked to the ceiling, hoping to keep the tears from spilling onto his cheeks. He took out his handkerchief and wiped them away. "You'll always be my little girl, Gabby," he managed to say.

"I know," I said, "but we've got to get through this. Think you'll make it?"

He wiped at his nose, took a deep breath, and nodded. "You bet."

I wasn't convinced.

"Daddy? When you say the part about 'Will you take this woman?' and then you ask me, 'Will you take this man?' what are you going to call me?"

He was stumped and had to think for a moment. "What do you want me to call you?"

"I don't know." Just then the first chord sounded, summoning us to begin our walk down the aisle. I squeezed his arm a little tighter. "Surprise me," I said. "And, Daddy, whatever you do, don't cry!"

Who knew within a month he'd be in heaven?

Ah, Paris. If I fell in love at once, DeeDee was head over heels. From the moment we landed, she was enthralled. Overwhelmed. Conquered. I began to fear we'd never get her back to the States, but she promised me, on the QT, she'd at least think about it. She committed nothing to Jonathan, but I think he appeared to worry more than he actually did. He had all the travelers' checks—and her MasterCard, though she had yet to discover that.

After going through customs and retrieving our luggage, we piled into a single taxi—all five of us with all of our bags! DeeDee, in her flawless French, promised double the fare due to the extra passenger load, three being the usual limit. I was pretty certain we actually paid triple.

Hair-raising doesn't begin to describe the trip from the airport to our hotel. I was scrunched in between Sonny and Linda and had to press one white-knuckled hand firmly against the ceiling of the cab and the other against the seat in front of me to keep from being tossed about like a cork in the sea.

DeeDee rode shotgun, of course, and laughed all the way to

our hotel. "You look green," she said to me.

"I should have kept a barf bag," I said, and meant it. Linda flashed me a terrified look and did her best to lean away from me, but where in the world could she go? I pressed against Sonny and swallowed. *Please, please,* please, *God, do not let me throw up on my new husband.*

But, oh, the diesel fumes.

∞

Terri, our travel agent, had obviously never been to Paris, but in all fairness, DeeDee should have chosen an adjective other than *quaint* to describe the type of accommodations she wanted. Because in Paris, quaint apparently meant low-budget.

Sonny turned the key and opened the door to our room. He started to step aside to let me in but stopped midstep. "Bunk beds?"

"Bunk beds?" I repeated, stepping on tiptoe to look past his shoulder.

DeeDee, who was almost to the room next door, back-stepped until she reached my side. "Bunk beds. Wow."

She didn't laugh, but I saw one corner of her mouth turn up just a little. Sonny and I exchanged a whole conversation without words, while DeeDee hurried to unlock the door to her room. "Bunk beds," she said again. This time her lips were one straight line. She and Linda were slated to share this room till after the wedding, at which time Jonathan and Linda would exchange rooms.

"Beats a cot," Jonathan said from across the hall.

Linda paled. "A cot?"

"From the Great War, I think."

And then there was the bathroom—the one down the hall.

We shared a moment of silence, which was fitting, if you ask me. Then DeeDee turned on her heel. "I'll fix this."

We all followed like ducks on a pond. Ever dauntless, DeeDee explained to our innkeeper that Sonny and I were supposed to have the bridal suite—a wedding gift to us from Jonathan and her—to which he replied, *"No problème!"* with a broad smile and a wink. We followed him back up to the cluster of rooms and watched as he and an assistant took our bunk beds apart and placed them side by side. He flashed a huge, toothy smile and promised to send up a bottle of bubbly for our trouble.

"No. Wait. *Monsieur,*" DeeDee called to his retreating form.

He only waved and disappeared down the stairwell.

Fortunately it was the beginning of the off-season, so it didn't take long for us to find a real hotel with all the amenities we spoiled Americans have grown accustomed to, like a pool and a spa. And beds and bathrooms. It was *not* in the shadow of the Eiffel Tower, but DeeDee didn't take it too hard. The rest of us felt as if we had escaped from the Bastille.

The next morning DeeDee and Jonathan went off to pick up their marriage license and meet with the minister who was to perform the ceremony, while the rest of us got some extra sleep. Jet lag was always so much worse going from west to east, and we hadn't even begun to catch up. The five of us met over a late lunch in the hotel café.

"Well." DeeDee settled into her chair and picked up her menu. "Shall I order for everyone?"

Linda turned a wary eye on her daughter. "Nothing . . . *exotic*, okay?"

I didn't like the arch of DeeDee's eyebrow one bit. I kicked her under the table and sent her a look that said, *Behave!*

"Okay. Salads all around?"

"*Oui,*" we said in unison.

"Can you believe we're here?" DeeDee said. "This is so exciting. And the minister . . . isn't he charming, Jonathan?"

"One-stop shopping," Jonathan said.

"Meaning?" I asked.

"Not only does he do the wedding," DeeDee said, "but he provides a photographer, an organist, and witnesses if you need them."

"Each for an extra fee," Jonathan said.

"Of course, we don't need witnesses." DeeDee tossed a smile to Sonny and me. "But we did hire the photographer. He'll meet us in the garden late tomorrow afternoon."

The wedding was scheduled for sunset the next evening in the terraced gardens across the Seine from the Eiffel Tower. At night its fountains and statuary are grandly alight, and, of course, *la Tour Eiffel* would become the sparkling jewel of Paris once the sun went down.

"It's going to be incredible," I said.

In the early afternoon, DeeDee, Linda, and I went to pick up our flowers. Our *portier* procured a taxi and held the door open for the three of us.

"Couldn't we walk?" I implored, but DeeDee pushed me into the taxi, and she and Linda climbed in after me. DeeDee laughed and gave the address to the driver, who adjusted his beret and lunged into traffic. I marveled at DeeDee's mettle.

"She doesn't get it from me," Linda whispered, as if reading my thoughts.

We returned within an hour, but I was weak in the knees for at least that long again. The hotelman relieved us of our bouquets and stored them in the refrigerator until it was time to leave for the ceremony. We found the guys by the pool and, after changing, joined them for a swim. Linda went to her room for a little nap. While DeeDee and I didn't say so, we both knew she was becoming more nostalgic by the minute.

There had been times over the years when I felt a little sorry for Linda. She was not now and had never been happily divorced, and there were certain occasions when I knew she felt her singleness all too keenly. DeeDee's first date was one such occasion, which, quite truthfully, surprised us all. One day she was trying out for the boys' baseball team; the next she was sophomore homecoming princess. The metamorphosis was instant and complete. And when Adam D'Marco, the most gorgeous guy in the junior class, asked her to the dance, even I was sick with envy. I don't remember who my date was—in fact, I made a point of forgetting as quickly as I could—but I know that we doubled with DeeDee and Adam. When they picked us up at DeeDee's house, I saw a longing in Linda. Young as I was, I knew it was because she had no one, namely, DeeDee's father, to share the moment with.

At our high school graduation, Linda had no one to give her extra invitation to. She sat with my parents, feeling every bit the odd man out, like she always did. It's not that Linda didn't have friends; she did. She even dated once in a while, but she didn't have the one thing she wanted—a husband who was also her daughter's father to share all the milestones of their only child's life with. DeeDee never seemed to notice, not necessarily because she was callous or insensitive, but because her dad was a nonentity in her life. Her attitude was, who needs him? Now, faced with the prospect of giving her daughter away all by herself, I sensed Linda did. Except that Linda wouldn't be giving her daughter away. DeeDee was giving herself. Not *away*, but *to*. "I don't need any help for that," she said.

"You should spend some time alone with your mom today," I told her. "Just for a while."

"You think so?" She pulled herself out of the pool and began to towel dry her sun-streaked hair.

"You saw how she looked when we left her alone upstairs."

"I thought she wanted to rest before tonight. Lemonade?" She beckoned to a waiter.

I shook my head no. "She did. But she also wants to have some time alone with you."

She smiled as the waiter approached. *"Citron pressé, s'il vous plaît."*

"Et pour mademoiselle?" he said in reference to me.

"Madame," DeeDee corrected. She looked back at me. "You sure?"

I shrugged. "Why not."

"Deux, s'il vous plaît."

"Très bon." He bowed and backed away.

"How is it you know her so well?" DeeDee folded the towel and sat on it, letting her feet dangle in the water. "And I don't."

I shrugged again.

"Don't lie. We both know it's because you're so much more sensitive than I."

"Okay."

She looked at me with a wounded expression. "That hurt."

"You will, won't you?"

"I'll ask her to help me get dressed." She splashed a stream of water in the air with her manicured toes. "*You'll* have to wait and see me when my husband does."

"Husband-to-be," I corrected.

DeeDee smiled and gave a nod that said, *touché.*

At five o'clock we retired to our rooms to make ourselves ready for The Big Event.

"I had no idea you could just show up in Paris and get a marriage license, practically the same day," I said to Sonny as I prepared to shower.

He laid his clothes out on the bed. "Well, think about it. How many couples do you think come to Paris to get married? They have to be accommodating, don't you think?"

"I suppose. And DeeDee would certainly know. She's made dozens of phone calls in preparation." I stepped under a cool stream of water. "It's exciting being here, isn't it?" I called over the sound of the spray.

"And romantic." He stuck his head inside the bathroom doorway. "Aren't you glad we're married?"

I poked my head outside the shower curtain. "Are you?"

He gave a seductive smile that practically made my heart stop. "*Oui, mon ami.* Very, *very* glad."

I felt myself blush. "I didn't know you spoke French."

"Just enough," he replied.

Once dressed, Sonny and I waited in the lobby with Jonathan for the bride to descend. He paced like the nervous groom he was, wearing a handsome outfit that DeeDee had purchased, which made him look extremely continental. All of a sudden he stopped and looked at Sonny. "You have the ring?"

"Right here." Sonny patted his jacket pocket. "Relax, pal. It's not nearly as scary as you might think."

"Yeah," he said absently, then returned to his pacing.

I began to get butterflies in my stomach just watching him, remembering how nervous I'd been the week before. "Weren't you scared?" I asked Sonny in a whisper.

"Terrified," he said, "but that will be *our* little secret."

I was wrong to wonder how DeeDee could look any more beautiful as a bride than she had as a bridesmaid, because when she appeared at the top of the stairs, I gasped. Jonathan stood mesmerized, while the hotel guests milling about began to stare and whisper, probably wondering if she were royalty. Indeed, she looked as if she could be. She wore an ivory tea-length gown overlaid with Alençon lace, which shimmered with every willowy movement. It had a sweetheart neckline, accented by the sparkling diamond pendant she wore, and off-the-shoulder sleeves. A tiara glistened in her hair, which was swept up atop her head, with a few curling tendrils hanging loosely down her long and graceful neck. As she made her way down the red-carpeted stairway, she actually drew applause. Linda, just a few steps behind her daughter, glowed with pride and affection but kept her hankie clutched in a trembling hand. I nearly cried because the photographer wasn't here to capture the moment.

The hotelman met us with our flowers, bowing again and again to the bride and groom. I think he himself wondered who this elegant couple might be, and he gave us all the royal treatment from that time forward.

"Shall we?" DeeDee took the arm of her fiancé, as calm as could be. Linda, Sonny, and I followed them out the door.

Thankfully we took two taxis to the gardens. The photographer was already there setting up his equipment. Jonathan had barely renewed his pacing when the minister arrived. DeeDee conducted the introductions in a mixture of French and English, then allowed them to lead us to the spot where the wedding would occur. It was a scene right off a postcard, with a lighted fountain before us and the Eiffel Tower behind.

"This is everything I wished for," DeeDee whispered to me. It was almost magical in its splendor. The photographer arranged us with the sunset as a backdrop, then began his work while the sky was awash in color, capturing what was certain to be the most spectacular photographs imaginable. And then the ceremony began.

DeeDee handed me her bouquet, then turned to Jonathan. He took her hands in his. They both looked absolutely radiant. The minister opened the ceremony with an extemporaneous prayer of blessing in French, some of which I understood, then began to read from the script. "We are gathered here today in the presence of these witnesses to join this man and this woman in the holy estate of matrimony." He spoke in a heavy French accent, not unlike, I couldn't help but think, Inspector Clouseau.

Jonathan and DeeDee shared a sweet look of love, and I knew just how they felt. I caught Sonny's eye, and he gave me a wink.

"Who gives this woman to be married?" the minister asked, surprising me.

In a voice rife with emotion, Linda said, "I do," then dabbed at her eyes with her hankie. DeeDee, bless her heart, had given her mother a special gift in allowing her to say that little phrase.

The minister continued to read, stumbling over many of the words, while a small impromptu crowd, made up mostly of couples with hands intertwined, began to form around us.

"What a remarkable feat," I whispered to DeeDee. "You really pulled it off." She was actually being married in Paris, in the shadow of the Eiffel Tower.

Opening his Bible, the minister read from 1 Corinthians 13, first in French, then in English. "Love is very patient and kind, never jealous or envious, never boastful or proud, never haughty or selfish or rude. Love does not demand its own way. It is not irritable or touchy. It does not hold grudges. . . . If you love someone you will be loyal to him no matter what the cost. You will always believe in him, always expect the best of him, and always stand your ground in defending him. . . . There are three things that remain — faith, hope, and love — and the greatest of these is love." It was one of my favorite passages of Scripture and had been included in my marriage ceremony as well. I couldn't suppress the emotion rising within me. Why hadn't I thought to bring a hankie of my own?

Next they exchanged vows and wedding rings, then the ceremony concluded with Jonathan reading a poem he had written for his bride. It caught DeeDee completely by surprise and brought tears to her already shining eyes. She didn't actually cry, but it was only because she had such tremendous willpower. I felt my own tears trickle down my face and had to sniff to keep my nose from dripping.

When the minister announced, "You may now kiss the bride," Jonathan did with exuberance, while the crowd applauded and cheered. If all the world loves a lover, that goes double for the French. Finally, they were announced Mr. and Mrs. Jonathan Kent. The photographer took more pictures, this time with the Eiffel Tower in all its glory as the backdrop, as our audience began to wander away, offering their most lively congratulations. The five of us exchanged hugs and kisses, and I felt remarkably merry.

We strolled across the *Pont d'Iéna*, the bridge that crosses the Seine, where DeeDee tossed a white rose from her bouquet into the river. We spoke in hushed tones and watched until it drifted out of sight. Then we continued east to the Eiffel Tower, where we took the elevator to the top observation platform nearly a thousand feet above ground level. Each of us was speechless at the breathtaking views of the city at night, which included the *Arc de Triomphe* to the north and Notre Dame to the east. We dined in the restaurant high above the city. The reservations had been made as soon as the wedding date was set, and even at that, our table wasn't the best. But there was hardly a bad view from anywhere in the dining room. It was easy to understand DeeDee's fascination with Paris.

It was nearly midnight when we returned to the hotel. While the bridal suite had not been available for Sonny and me the night before, much to DeeDee's dismay, it was available for her and Jonathan's wedding night. As a gift and a surprise, we had the hotel staff move their belongings from their separate rooms into the suite while they were off being married. It was great fun to present them with the key at the end of the night.

"You didn't," DeeDee said. "This was supposed to be our gift to you."

"You tried, and we appreciate the effort."

"But we could only get it for one night, so don't waste any time," Sonny added, and everyone laughed.

"Sonny!" I punched his arm.

"*Bonsoir*," he said to the newlyweds and to Linda, then put his arm around my waist and led me off to our room.

We met for lunch the following day in the hotel's café to map out our sightseeing itinerary, which would begin in earnest now that the wedding was behind us. The Louvre was first on our list. It would be the only undertaking of the day. After placing our lunch order, we made small talk. I had warned Sonny ahead of time that he had better not say anything to embarrass the newlyweds — or me. Still, I held my breath until the most tempting moments had passed.

"DeeDee!" I said all of a sudden. "I thought about this in the middle of the night and had the most awful time going back to sleep! Sonny and I didn't sign the marriage license. I hope that doesn't mean, well, anything, you know . . . I'm really sorry."

DeeDee looked as if she'd been caught cheating on her finals.

It surprised me, and I hesitated before adding, "We'll have to go see the minister on our way to the Louvre. Hopefully he hasn't mailed it off yet."

DeeDee looked at Jonathan and then at her mother, who had the same guilty look on her face.

"What?" I looked from one to the other and waited. "What?"

The waiter brought our food as DeeDee appeared to search for an answer. She looked at Jonathan again with a look that said, *Help!*

"Actually," he began, then exhaled a heavy breath, "there wasn't a license to sign." The words came haltingly.

"No license?" I sucked in my breath. "You mean —"

"No!" DeeDee said, anticipating what I was about to say. "We *are* legally married."

"Then what?" I could see I was drawing looks from nearby tables, but I didn't care. My eyes were narrowed and fixed on DeeDee because suddenly I knew what she was going to say.

"France has the most . . . *moronic* marriage law," she began in a faltering voice. I'd never heard her stumble over her words like this before. "They actually require you to reside in the country for *forty* days before you can get a marriage license! Have you ever heard anything so absurd?"

"Forty days?" I said.

"That's exactly what I said, and just the way I said it, wasn't it, Jonathan?"

"Then you were" — I could hardly bring myself to say it — "you were married before you came to Paris?"

She closed her eyes and squeezed her lips tight, as if waiting for a blow. "We had to, Gab," she said at last.

"Without telling me?" She looked as pathetic as I'd ever seen her look, but I wasn't about to cut her any slack. Absolutely no mercy this time.

"We didn't want you to think of our wedding as a . . . as a . . . *formality*."

"It *was* a formality!"

"No!" she said. "The first ceremony was the formality. The wedding here was real."

"The first ceremony?" I shot back. "You mean the one without me?" I turned to Jonathan. "The one without Sonny?" He was going to share equally in the blame if I had anything to say about it. "And what about Linda?" One look in her direction and I knew she had not only known about it but had been present. "At least you had the decency not to deceive your mother." I sniffed and looked away.

"It wasn't meant to deceive," DeeDee said in a voice meant to soothe. "But forty days! And forty *nights*," she added in a whisper. "What were we to do?"

"How could you not have known? You, who know more about Paris than the locals?"

"I just assumed . . ."

I crossed my arms and glared at her. "When and where?"

DeeDee lowered her eyes, unable to look at me. "The

morning we left California. We went before a justice of the peace—"

"You weren't even married by a minister? DeeDee, how could you?"

"We *were* married by a minister." She dropped a fist onto the table. "Last night. You were there, remember?"

I felt about to cry and was not going to let them see it. I tossed aside my napkin and pushed back my chair. Without a word, I strode to the elevator—and then remembered Sonny had the key to our room. But I wasn't about to go back for it. Honestly, I couldn't even have a tantrum without messing it up! DeeDee wouldn't have let this happen. She was way too together for that. The brat.

I worked my way to the rear lobby and out to the pool. I found an empty chaise lounge, sat down, and stewed. A waiter approached but I waved him away. I was too flustered to communicate in a language I neither liked nor understood. I expected—and hoped—Sonny would find me at any moment, and when he did, I would insist we leave for home. I had no intention of sharing a honeymoon with DeeDee McAllister-Kent one more minute.

But Sonny didn't come. DeeDee did. And she was holding my room key.

"Sonny thought you might want this." She spoke as if nothing in the world was the matter.

I huffed and turned away from her. She sat on the end of the chaise lounge. I would have gotten up just to send her tumbling, but the arms were in the way.

"Gabby, what can I say? You weren't supposed to find out."

"Not supposed to find out?" I turned on her like a lioness about to pounce. "Since when do we keep secrets from each other?"

"This one couldn't be helped." She smiled a cajoling smile. "Honestly, I didn't know you had so much *sass* in you. You've been holding out."

"Don't you dare try to humor me."

"Oh, come on. Don't be angry. It really was just a formality. It didn't last ten minutes. But it made it possible to have the wedding I've always dreamed of. You of all people know how much this has meant to me."

Against my will I was giving in. "But why the secret? And why a justice of the peace? Why not Pastor Tim or my dad?"

"Your dad? You would *never* have forgiven me if I'd been married in secret by your dad!" She placed her hands on my cheeks and made me look at her. "Gab, the ceremony back home was just on my list of things to do, like getting my passport. It wasn't even consummated," she whispered. "It was simply a step in getting here for the most important event of my life. I would never have done this without you. You were part of the wonder, the magic. Think of it! Married in Paris!" She stood and held her hand out to help me up. "Forgive me?"

How could I not? *Love does not hold grudges*, came the words from 1 Corinthians. And we'd been closer than sisters for much too long.

I accepted her hand and even managed a weak smile. But as we walked alongside the pool on our way back to the lobby, where Sonny and Jonathan and Linda were waiting, I couldn't help myself. I pushed her in. It was the least she deserved.

5

"I checked out your blog last night," DeeDee said. We sat across from each other at our usual table at D'Angelo's. "Where do you get all your ideas? And how do you know so many writers?"

"Dee, it's what I do. And mostly we meet at conferences."

"Well, I loved the interview with, ah, um, you know."

"Melanie Marks?"

"Right." She snapped her fingers and pointed at me, then pressed her finger onto a small bit of crust left on her plate and put it to her mouth. "If it weren't for your book list I wouldn't know what on earth to read. Keep it coming. Especially—"

"Suspense," I said along with her.

"Right," she said again. She sat back and placed her napkin on the table. "Today I'm having that banana split."

Every week we threatened to go next door to The Frigid Scoop for a colossal banana split to top off our lunch, but, of course, we never did.

"What's the occasion?" I asked, knowing she'd change her

mind by the time our check arrived.

"You're going to be an aunt."

I nearly choked on my quiche. "You're pregnant?"

"Not quite yet, but Jonathan has finally come round to the idea." She glowed with wild emotion. "I threw away my pills this morning. Now I have to make up for lost time. April is out of the question, I know, but June is still a nice time to have a baby."

Not quite? Come round? Lost time? "Dee, are you sure about this?" I pushed aside my plate and folded my hands on the table before me. "You were always so adamant about—"

"No kids. I know." She rolled her eyes, slapped her forehead, and gave me a look that said, *What was I thinking?* "But it wasn't because I don't like children. You know I do. I was just afraid that if I brought a child into the world I might somehow fail her and, oh my gosh, the consequences would be . . . *eternal.*"

We had discussed this before, and I knew just how she felt. "And that's changed?"

"No," she admitted, "but Jonathan and I can provide an environment that will protect her. I realize that now. I mean, where would we be if our parents had been afraid to give us life?"

"You've done such a complete about-face. I don't know what to think. I mean, this could all be *hormonal*, Dee, and hormones change! You may feel entirely different a week from now."

"No. I won't. I simply have to have a baby."

This was not the self-centered, closed-minded DeeDee I knew and loved, the DeeDee who had to have her way or no way. Well, perhaps *that* part hadn't changed. But I now saw her as a DeeDee with befuddled hormones who was suddenly bent on mother-hood. A woman with *emotions*. She was a perfect stranger. I shook my baffled head. "How did you persuade Jonathan?"

"You know he's always indulged me," she said, reverting

abruptly to the spoiled DeeDee I knew all too well.

"But does he want to be a father? I mean really want to be? You don't go into something like this just to indulge someone."

"Gabby, I hate it when you lecture." She whipped her napkin, then smoothed it on her lap. "Of course he wants to be a father. Here," she whispered gleefully, "look what I bought." She reached into a sack I hadn't noticed from a little shop called Carousel and pulled out the teeniest pair of ballet slippers I'd ever seen. They were pink and satiny and tied with lacy ribbon. "She'll be a dancer. Aren't they precious?"

"Oh, Dee. I know you've lived a charmed life up till now. But what if it isn't a girl? What if you don't get pregnant?"

"Not get pregnant? I threw away my pills! Of course I'll get pregnant. Jonathan is quite virile."

I closed my eyes and held up a hand in traffic-cop fashion. "Dee, that is way more than I wanted to know about Jonathan Jeffrey Kent."

She laughed friskily and held up her iced tea glass in a salute. "Yes, I have lived a charmed life," she said, "and I intend to conceive. Tonight."

Four Tuesdays passed and DeeDee was not pregnant. "I don't know what's wrong," she lamented over a bowl of split pea soup. She had changed her lunch order in hopes of changing her luck. I reminded her she didn't believe in luck, but she said, "I have to do *something*."

"Maybe you're trying too hard. They say anxiety can really foul things up."

"I'm not anxious," she snapped.

I smiled and gave her a moment to rethink her response.

"Okay. Maybe I'm a *little* anxious. But time is getting away from me. I'm now thirty-eight and a *half.* I thought it would be so easy."

"We've both been on the pill for eighteen years, Dee. I think we've more than convinced our bodies we did not want to conceive. It's like we programmed our biological computers and there's no changing it now."

"You don't really think—" She put a hand over her mouth. "I'm going to see a doctor right away. And Jonathan, too. I'll simply die if there's something wrong."

DeeDee and Jonathan were scheduled to see Dr. Zoe Creager, a highly regarded fertility specialist, on January 8, but after a month, a last-minute cancellation gave them the opening they were praying for.

"Some wonderful woman went and got herself pregnant. We have an appointment Thursday afternoon!"

It was November 18, and DeeDee was ecstatic. That woman's good fortune saved them seven precious weeks. DeeDee expected after their visit with Dr. Creager to go home with the magic formula that would enable them to conceive. I know because she told me so in just those words. I warned her not to be so optimistic, that these things take time, but it was more than she could grasp. "This is a *specialist*. She'll know what to do."

Now, DeeDee was used to calling the shots in every aspect of her life, as anyone who knew her was well aware, but she met her match in Dr. Zoe Creager. "Relax and give it a year," Dr. Creager said after the consultation. "If you still haven't conceived, we'll have you both in for a workup."

Having imitated the doctor verbatim for my benefit, DeeDee paced in my living room like a pent-up tiger. We had gotten together to plan our Thanksgiving menu, though it rarely changed from the traditional turkey and stuffing fare. "Can you believe that? A year!"

"What did you say to her?" I offered her a chair. I hated when she paced.

"I told her we've already been trying for two months." DeeDee continued to stalk up and down the room. "And do you know what she said? She said, 'Yeeeeessssss,' as if to say, so, what's the problem?" DeeDee rolled her eyes and let out a huffy breath.

"And?"

"I told her in no uncertain terms that I had no intention of waiting a year!"

"What did she say to that?" I asked, with one eye on my Thanksgiving menu.

"We got it down to six months. She refused to budge beyond that." DeeDee's lips became tight with the recollection. "I'm only going to her because she's the best. But I did get her to do a sperm count on Jonathan."

"Ooh, I bet he just loved that." I thought about Sonny and knew exactly what his reaction would be. *No way!*

"I know it was humiliating, but he was a good sport."

"And?"

She frowned. "His sperm count is perfectly normal. That must mean—"

"Now, DeeDee, don't borrow trouble. If Dr. Creager said to relax and give it time, then that's what you have to do. Forget about making babies and enjoy yourself."

"Humph," she said, crossing her arms tightly. "That's what

Jonathan said. That's easy enough for him to say with the pressure on *me*. No, I can't look at this simply as a *pastime*. I have to get pregnant."

"And you will. Your mother is coming for Thanksgiving, right?"

She stopped midstride. "What does that have to do with me getting pregnant?"

I held up my list.

"Oh. Right." She nodded as she sat down on my sofa. "I'm so glad it's at your house this year. I don't think I could manage it. I can't seem to get my mind on anything but babies."

"We'll have her bring the relish tray." I wrote L-I-N-D-A next to that item on my list.

"I've begun to design the nursery. Only on paper, of course." She slipped off her shoes and tucked her feet up underneath her. "We'll use the bedroom next to ours, so she'll be close. Of course, we'll have one of those monitors in every room of the house, but this way she'll be nice and handy in the middle of the night."

"My mom will bring the pies. You know how she insists. Besides, I can't seem to get the knack of making the crust, try as I might." I wrote M-O-M next to the pies.

"It will be pink, of course. I think. But I can't decide on a motif. What do you think about lambs?"

I looked up sharply. "I've already ordered a turkey."

DeeDee gave me a blank look. "For the nursery."

"Oh, I thought—"

"I know." She slipped her shoes back on and began to collect her belongings. "Listen, my mind isn't into this today. But whatever you do, don't use that silly tissue paper accordion turkey as your centerpiece again this year. I'll bring my ceramic cornucopia. And put me down for the rolls. I just bought a bread machine.

Now I'm going to go home and make a baby. Oh—" she reached for the phone and punched the speed-dial button to the office our husbands shared—"I suppose I ought to have Jonathan join me."

"I suppose," I said absently, and wrote D-E-E next to the rolls.

⊱≈⊰

"Who knew conception could be such hard work?" DeeDee leaned back in my desk chair, her feet crossed at the ankles on the printer table. "Bless his heart, Jonathan is accommodating, but . . ." She ended with a shrug. She'd been trying for the rec-ommended six months to get pregnant. Nothing.

So in May, two months into our thirty-ninth year, doctor-monitored conception attempts began in earnest. And I was informed of every step along the way. If there was ever anything about DeeDee—and Jonathan—I didn't know, that changed abruptly. No longer were we simply the best of friends; I was now a tagalong on a grand and intimate journey in the quest of parenthood. Sonny and I, who had no interest in bearing chil-dren of our own, were suddenly thrust into the role of Supreme Cheerleaders for DeeDee and Jonathan.

Rah!

"What are you looking for?" DeeDee asked.

"My *AP Stylebook*." I tilted my head and scanned the spines of the books on the shelf in my home office. "I can never remem-ber if song titles are italicized or put in quotation marks. I should know that."

"Right. Doesn't everyone? Here." She handed me the book from a pile on my desk. "Right where you left it. What's your column about this week?"

I'd been writing columns for the *Lodi News-Sentinel* since graduating from college, as well as freelancing articles for women's magazines, both Christian and secular. I turned to "song titles" in the stylebook, which led me to "composition titles." And did my best to ignore DeeDee's question.

But she pressed me. "What's your column about?"

Mother's Day was less than two weeks away, and, typically, the week before Mother's Day my column was on some aspect of motherhood. This year, because of DeeDee's experience, my column was on childless women and how their childlessness affected them and their marriage. I used the story of Sarah and Abraham way back in Genesis for my opening, then went contemporary. I interviewed a couple of women I knew besides DeeDee who had no children by choice and a celebrity who had adopted two children from different countries, even though she and her husband were capable of having children of their own. I also included insights from the path I myself had chosen. Of course, DeeDee would see the article soon enough, but I wanted it to be complete before she read it.

"Quotation marks. That's what I thought." I slid the stylebook into its place on the shelf.

"Gabby." DeeDee took her feet off the desk and sat up straight in my chair. "You're stalling."

"You know. Mother's Day is just around the corner."

"And?"

"Well, I just thought . . . with your situation . . . well, maybe I'd—"

"Infertility? You're writing about infertility on Mother's Day? Good grief, Gabby!" She shook her head. "Not a good idea."

"Not infertility," I said, flustered. "Childlessness. Just wait till it's finished. You'll see where I'm going."

Her forehead crinkled. "You're writing about mothers who aren't? On Mother's Day? Does Pam know?"

Pamela James, with whom we'd gone to high school, was editor of the Panorama page, where my column appeared. "Of course."

"Oh, well, I'm sure it'll be a hit." She stood and picked up her bag. "If you need a quote, don't hesitate to call."

She was so good at sarcasm.

The first step in Dr. Creager's fertility guidance was to track DeeDee's menstrual cycle for regularity.

"You can help make the chart," DeeDee said, no longer upset about my article, which I'd received a number of positive e-mails about since the article ran. She handed me a sheet of pink linen paper and a sample chart to work from.

"You're the artist," I said.

"How hard is it to use a ruler? The other way." She made a motion for me to turn the paper to landscape rather than portrait.

"I know."

"And here." She handed me a package of neon-colored markers, and I went to work.

Since ovulation occurs approximately twelve to fourteen days before the next cycle, it was important to know the duration of DeeDee's menstruation and the number of days between the cycles. Four cycles had to be charted to establish an accurate pattern. And DeeDee was nothing if not accurate. "Man, I'd forgotten so much of this," I said. "But it's been, what, twenty-five years since high school biology?"

"Twenty-four," DeeDee corrected. "We were sophomores."

By the end of the summer, the pattern was established and DeeDee's most likely time of ovulation was determined. She decided to plan a romantic getaway for her and Jonathan for those two special days when she was most likely to conceive.

"We're going to Carmel Wednesday and Thursday. That's when I'll be at my peak."

Of course, I already knew that because of the chart.

"There's nothing like the ocean to relax and stimulate at the same time, don't you think? And, of course, *this* won't hurt." She held up a black nightie, or what would be considered a nightie if it had a little more fabric. "What do you think?"

"Whoa. Are you really going to wear that?" I felt my cheeks grow hot, and it was just the two of us in the room.

She sighed and plunked down onto the bed beside her suitcase. "It's been, well, difficult lately. All of a sudden the bedroom has become sort of a science lab. It's begun to . . . *affect* Jonathan. A change of pace—and *this*—will do him good." She held up the nightie again and let it drop into the suitcase, light as a feather. "I don't guess I'll need much else."

"Surely you're not going to spend your whole time in *that*! What about walks along the beach? And meals? You'll have to eat just to keep up your strength."

"Room service," she said. "We've got to make every minute count."

"Dee, don't you think a little more romance and a little less *assignment* would help?"

"Assignment?"

"You know, like, 'Okay, class, your assignment for Wednesday and Thursday is to go to Carmel and make a baby. If you don't come back pregnant, you fail.' That seems like a lot of pressure for a guy who's already, well, *affected*."

"I see what you mean." She sighed again. "But that *is* the assignment. Those are my peak days. You saw the chart."

"I know, but try to forget about the chart. And definitely make Jonathan forget about it. Just go and enjoy each other, without any other motive."

"You really think it will help, strolls along the beach and such?"

"That's what Dr. Creager says. It certainly can't hurt."

"Well, then." She went to her closet, brought out a few more items, and placed them in the suitcase. "But I don't think I'll need them."

On Wednesday and Thursday I sat down at my computer and tried to work on an outline for a devotional for writers I was thinking about writing. My working title was *A Ready Writer*, in reference to a line from Psalm 45: "My tongue is the pen of a ready writer." Amazingly, DeeDee had agreed to do the illustrations if I ever actually got something down on paper. It would be our first collaborative effort, and I was excited about it. But for nearly half an hour I sat and stared at a blank screen. All I could think about were the goings-on in Carmel-by-the-Sea. I tried not to blush.

I switched to a new page and began to write whatever came to mind, a trick that was supposed to get the creative juices flowing. But every word I wrote had to do with DeeDee's reproductive efforts. That was the beginning of the DeeDee-wants-a-baby journal. I wished I'd thought of it sooner. For nearly two hours

I wracked my brain to recall as many details, as many conversations, as I could and typed them all into the computer, thinking
it might be fun to look back over this someday. Especially if there
was a baby to celebrate.

DeeDee called the minute they got home. "Are you praying?"
she asked.

"I'm always praying."

"No, I mean *praying*. Because I have this really great feeling.
Oh. What a trip."

"Ooh! Enough!" I held up a hand she couldn't see.

DeeDee laughed. "Okay. Just pray, Gab. On your knees."

"You got it."

But while the ocean atmosphere may have relaxed and stimu-
lated, it didn't help produce a baby.

Jonathan and DeeDee spent her next peak period in a cabin
at Lake Tahoe. She did not come home pregnant. So the next
step was to chart DeeDee's basal body temperature to determine
a more exact time of ovulation. It was a real nuisance, but it was
a way to hone in even more on the time she would most likely
conceive. Every morning before getting out of bed, at exactly
seven o'clock, while Jonathan showered, DeeDee would take her
temperature with an ultrasensitive basal thermometer and call
me with the results before charting them on the graph. Since the
body temperature rises just after ovulation, she would be able to
clearly recognize the best time for future tries. The third time that
her body temperature peaked, Jonathan was late to the office. The
fourth and fifth times, too. Still, no baby.

But DeeDee was dauntless. Instead of giving up in despair as
I might have done, she persevered in the challenge of her life.

6

It was nearly Christmas again and one of the coldest winters I remember. Mother and I were doing some last-minute shopping and had run into Barnes & Noble for a book to use as Sonny's stocking stuffer. I found the computer section and began to scan the titles.

"What are we looking for?" Mother slipped on her reading glasses. They rested on the tip of her nose, so she had to bend her head backward to be able to read the spines of the books.

I referred to my list for accuracy. "*MACROmania*. He says it's a must-read."

Mother raised an eyebrow. "That ought to keep him on the edge of his seat."

"Trust me, it will," I said, and we laughed.

Even with both of us searching, it took ten minutes to find the volume amid all the technological titles, but at last it was located, purchased, bagged, and checked off my list. I sighed in relief. "One or two more stops, and this list is history. Now all I have to do is wrap everything. Ugh!"

"Let's get together for a wrapping party with DeeDee, like when you girls were in school. We'll make hot chocolate and play Bing Crosby records."

"That was always such fun—even if I did wrap my own Christmas presents."

"Only the boxes with clothes, which I had already taped shut," she reminded. "You never knew what was *inside* until Christmas morning."

"True. And I admit, it did add to the suspense. Hey, how about a latte?" I said as we passed the little café in the middle of the store. "Something to warm us on our way."

"I forget. Is that the strong one with chocolate or the nice milky one with whipped cream?"

"That one."

She made a sad little frown. "In that case, I should pass."

"Now, Mother, you could just as easily have a cup of hot tea, but it is almost Christmas. Treat yourself."

Her mouth turned upward. "Well, then . . ."

"Two decaffeinated lattes," I said to the girl behind the counter, "and two biscotti with almonds." I couldn't resist.

I tried to count the rings in the young girl's right ear, but her head bobbed to some indistinguishable tune playing throughout the store, and I gave up. *This must be the only place in town not playing the sounds of the season*, I thought. It seemed a little odd. Then again, maybe the indistinguishable tune was what they called an *alternative* sound of the season and I just didn't know it. I fished in my wallet for the exact amount I owed and followed Mother to a little round table with tall stools.

"Latte, biscotti. In my day it was simply coffee and cookies. But I admit, this sounds far more cosmopolitan." She picked up a biscotti, put it to her mouth, and crunched off a little corner. "Oh," she said, startled. "Is it supposed to be so . . . crisp?"

I couldn't help but laugh. "You can dunk it if you'd like."

"Do you?"

"No, I just nibble."

"Well, then." She took another little bite. After a minute or two of people watching, she said, "I'd like you and Sonny to have Christmas with me, at my house this year. DeeDee and Jonathan and Linda are invited too, of course."

"You're not going to Aunt Irene's after all?" That seemed a little strange since she'd made plans in the summer to spend Christmas in Idaho with her sister.

"She and Uncle Eddie are coming here." She sipped her latte. "My, this is good . . . and Ida can come too, of course. This is her year to come, isn't it?"

Sonny's mother, Ida Nevin, had been a widow nearly as long as my mother, but she was twelve years older than Mom, and her husband had been eight years older than she. He was seventy-two when he died, while my dad had been fifty-one.

Ida had flown out here from Wichita for Christmas every other year. The years she didn't come she spent the holiday with Sonny's sisters and their families. Mom was right; this would normally be Ida's year to join us. But she'd told Cindy, Sonny's older sister, that she didn't want to fly anymore. Now we would go to Wichita for Christmas on occasion. But not this year.

"So . . . hmm . . . that makes . . . eight? I suppose that won't be a problem. I'll bring the turkey—I have a twenty-five pounder on order."

Her eyes went wide. "For the four of you?"

"I was planning for five—you forgot Linda. Anyway, Sonny loves the leftovers."

"I know this is changing plans at the last minute, but I'd really love it if we could all be together at my house." She looked away and then back again. "Sort of a last hurrah."

My stomach began to churn. "A last hurrah?"

"I know this is bound to be a shock, dear, but, well, I've decided to sell the house. There, I've said it."

"You're going to sell Daddy's house?" A huge lump found its way into my throat. "I . . . I don't mean it like that. I know it's your house too, but . . . but . . ."

"I know, Angel baby." She offered a sympathetic smile and patted my hand. "All the memories. But, sweetheart, it's simply too much for me to handle by myself anymore. The roof needs replacing, the back stairs have turned to dry rot, the wallpaper is falling off in sheets." She held up a hand to squelch my objections. "I know I'm exaggerating, *a very little*, but I do need to sell while I can still get something out of it. So you all must come for Christmas. It'll be such fun. I haven't seen Linda in ages. And bring that card game I like so well. What's it called?"

"Uno?" My voice sounded as if I were about to be executed.

"That's the one."

Before Sonny and I were married I had spent every Christmas of my life in that house, and many since then. My family had never been able to go away for the holidays because Faith Assembly always had a Christmas night service. Since Dad was the pastor we couldn't leave town. But we often had visitors, Aunt Irene and Uncle Eddie the most frequent. My only cousin, a girl four years younger than me, would naturally, and unfortunately, accompany them. To say that Sonia was spoiled would be to say that King Kong was a monkey — somewhat of an understatement. She was a whiner and had the most perfect mouth for pouting. Her lips turned down like none I'd ever seen, and she'd cross her chubby little arms and stomp her patent leather shoe, always the right one, when she didn't get her way. Her parents had grown to fear her little tantrums, which embarrassed everyone but Sonia, and so they indulged her. But their indulgences only reinforced the behavior they disdained.

Mother always admonished me to be nice to Sonia, and I tried, but she was so horridly rotten. DeeDee had no patience whatsoever when it came to my cousin and insisted I come to her house to visit—alone—as long as my uncle's green Plymouth station wagon was parked in front of our house. But a week before Christmas when we were fourteen, DeeDee's mother went into the hospital to have a hump removed from the bridge of her nose (and came home with a profile remarkably like Bob Hope's), and so DeeDee spent Christmas vacation with us. By the day after Christmas, we were so fed up with Sonia's whining and stomping that we decided to do something mean and nasty to her, just for the sheer pleasure of it. But what? While we were in the kitchen trying to concoct an idea, Sonia came in to complain about all the toys she didn't get from Santa and what a sacrifice it had been to come to Cali*for*nia for the holidays and leave her toys and friends in *I*daho.

"What's that?" she demanded, pointing a stubby finger at a lovely fluted glass from which DeeDee drank.

"Eggnog," DeeDee replied with a glare.

She wrinkled her nose. "Gross."

"There's nothing gross about it," DeeDee hissed, then a devilish light began to gleam in her eyes. "In fact, it's delicious. Would you like a taste?" To my horror, DeeDee let her take a sip from her very own glass. "Isn't it yummy?"

"I want some!" Sonia said with a little stomp of her foot. "Fix it."

"Sure," DeeDee said, rising from the table. "Just sit there by Gabby and I'll get it for you." DeeDee gave me a pointed look that told me I was to keep Sonia occupied, so I revived the conversation about all the things she hadn't gotten for Christmas, which naturally did the trick. She whined and whimpered, and when DeeDee returned with a glass for the little imp, she didn't even say thank you. But DeeDee didn't seem to mind. In fact, she seemed jovial, which frightened me.

"What's that stuff?" Sonia demanded. "That wasn't in yours."

"It's nutmeg. And yes it was. I just happened to drink that part before you came in."

"It's good," I assured her, unsuspecting as I was. "I always sprinkle nutmeg in mine."

She looked at us both suspiciously.

"Really." I held my glass up in a toast.

"Drink it down and I'll fix you another glass. In fact, we'll race." DeeDee went to the refrigerator and brought back the half-gallon carton, then filled her glass and mine. "One, two, three."

We all downed our eggnog.

For a moment, we sat there without saying a word. I was looking at DeeDee, who was looking at Sonia, who suddenly began to cry and cough and wail all at the same time. She was making a horrible noise and wouldn't hush, even though I offered to give her my brand-new copy of *Anne of Green Gables*. She had coveted it since the moment I tore the Christmas paper away from its beautiful cover. Even that wouldn't silence her.

Aunt Irene came running from the den with my mother right behind her. Dad and Uncle Eddie were playing Chinese checkers and must have assumed the women could handle whatever was wrong because they didn't show up for the drama.

"What on earth is the matter?" Aunt Irene's voice sounded like a screech owl. But Sonia couldn't reply. She just continued to cry and cough and sputter.

"Angel?" Just Angel, and Mother's voice held a definite edge.

All I could do was shrug.

"We were just drinking eggnog," DeeDee said, innocent as you please.

"Water!" Sonia finally blurted. "Water!"

Aunt Irene ran to the sink, grabbed a glass out of the dish drainer, and filled it with water. "There, there," she said as Sonia bolted it down.

"You did something!" Sonia cried, pointing at DeeDee. "Mama, she *did* something!"

Aunt Irene gave Mother a look. "Margie?"

DeeDee offered an innocent shrug. "Maybe it was the nutmeg."

"Nutmeg?" Mother said. "I used all the nutmeg in the pumpkin pies."

"Really? I could have sworn . . ."

Mother walked to the spice rack and studied the little white jars that were decorated with blue windmills. She'd purchased them years before in Solvang, a beautiful Danish town in Santa Barbara County. She stopped cold, then looked back at DeeDee and me. Aunt Irene was so busy trying to calm the little devil that she missed the interchange.

"Maybe it was cinnamon?" DeeDee said.

"Maybe," my mother replied and then sneezed.

"Bless you," DeeDee and I said in unison, but Mother's only response was to raise an eyebrow at us both.

"Irene, is she all right? How about more water?" Mother filled another glass, then took the dishrag and wiped sprinkles off the counter before returning to the table.

"There, there," Aunt Irene said again. "Come with Mommy." She led her distraught child away to a place of refuge, while Mother remained in the kitchen with DeeDee and me.

"Strange," she said. "Cayenne pepper always makes me sneeze, but, of course, that wouldn't have been cayenne pepper I wiped off the counter." She walked by the table on her way out of the kitchen and said, "Matthew 7:12." I didn't have to look this one up. I knew it by heart. It was the Golden Rule.

"Cayenne?" I whispered to DeeDee.

"That isn't the worst of it," she whispered back, with another frightening grin. She walked to the cupboard and pulled out a bottle of milk of magnesia.

From what I understand, they had to stop at nearly every rest stop on their way home to Idaho.

If Mother sold the house, what would happen to my memories?

And where would she live?

"In a condo. On Orchard Drive. You know, over by the new visitors' center. I've put a deposit down."

"A deposit?"

"Before I had a chance to change my mind—or let you change it for me. It will be just right. Nice and cozy, no yard work. I know it's meant a lot to you to be able to come home at will, but I'm there, day in and day out, surrounded by memories. I'm ready for a change, sweetheart."

I sighed as my emotions took a dive. "I haven't meant to be selfish."

She touched my arm consolingly. "And you haven't been. But 'to everything there is a season.'"

There she was, throwing Scripture at me. But I had to be

brave, for her sake. "Well, then," I said as courageously as I could, "we'll make this the best Christmas ever."

"Thank you," she said, blinking away her tears. "I knew you'd understand."

I also knew the moment I got home I was going to have a meltdown.

7

I had the fright of my life just after New Year's Day. For the first time since I was twelve years old, I was late for my period. I opened my little round birth control pill holder, willing myself to be calm, but I could barely count the pills for the shaking of my hands. All of them were gone except five of the seven blue ones I took during the days of my menstrual cycle, which were simply there to keep me on track. Accordingly, I should have been on the third day of my period.

I wasn't.

I swallowed the third of the blue pills and realized I wasn't even the least bit bloated or crampy. So what was up? I hadn't forgotten even one of the yellow ones, and they were the ones that counted. Sonny came up behind me where I stood in the bathroom and gave me such a scare I thought my heart would stop.

"You okay?" He placed a hand over his own heart. I must have given him a fright as well.

"I . . . I didn't hear you coming."

"You look white as a sheet."

Downright bloodless was more like it.

"Here, sit down." He led me back to the bedroom. "Shall I get you some juice?"

"Yes . . . juice . . . something."

"I'll just be a minute." He reached a hand back toward me as if to keep me from falling off the bed in his absence. "Put your head between your legs. And breathe!"

I drained the orange juice he brought and gave him back the glass with a hand that continued to shake.

"There, now. Feeling better?" He looked as if he thought I would faint after all. "What is it, babe? A touch of the flu, you think?"

"I . . . I don't know. I'll be all right in a minute." *That* was a boldfaced lie.

"Maybe I shouldn't go to the office just yet." He touched my forehead to check for fever.

"No, really, I'll be fine. You just startled me is all." *If he only knew.*

He smiled a little apologetic smile. "I'll whistle next time. Let you know I'm coming."

I gave him a smile of my own in return, but my heart wasn't in it. I just wanted him to leave so I could count those pills again. And have a breakdown in peace.

"Well, then, I guess I'm off . . . if you're sure."

"I'm sure."

He kissed the top of my head. "Don't overexert. Get some rest. The holidays must have taken it out of you. You really do look peaked."

"I'll be fine," I said again. But really, I felt lightheaded and tingly all over. *Oh, Lord! Morning sickness?* "Sonny," I called after him, feebly, "you . . . you look great in your new tie."

He came back and kissed me lightly on the mouth. "You have great taste. Bye now."

When he was gone I fell back on my pillow. I'd heard of sympathy labor pains but never a sympathy pregnancy! If this was some kind of cosmic joke, it wasn't the least bit funny. "Lord, this is *Gabby*, remember?" I said out loud. "You have the wrong person! DeeDee and I may be connected at the hip, but she has her own womb!"

"Who has a womb?" DeeDee appeared at my door, dressed in jeans and an Old Navy T-shirt. "Sonny sent me back—said you're a bit under the weather."

"Hey," I said weakly. "You're out early."

"Gab." She drew it out to two syllables as only she could. "We're helping your mom today, remember? The attic."

"Oh, the attic. I forgot."

"Are you really sick?" She plopped herself down beside me. "Stick out your tongue."

"Whatever for?" I sat up and rolled off the other side of the bed.

"I don't know. I've just always wanted to say that. You know, like in the movies." She laughed as if there were actually something funny about it. "My, aren't you the grouch. Maybe you really are sick."

"I'm not sick. Just a little lightheaded. And I said *room*, not *womb*. Why would I be talking about wombs?" I was defensive and sounded it.

"Why would you be talking at all?" she asked. "There's no one here but you."

"I guess *you* don't count?"

"Of course I do, but you didn't know I was here, so technically

I don't. Or I didn't at the time."

"In fact, I did know you were here, and I said, 'I'm in the bedroom.'" I couldn't believe the lies that were rolling off my tongue! "I'm going to get dressed. There's a cup of coffee left in the pot. Help yourself."

"I'm off caffeine," she said, patting her tummy. "Just in case. But I'll get some juice."

I stood before the bathroom mirror, my eyes dropping to my abdomen. I couldn't really be . . . pregnant. Could I? I mean, wouldn't a woman *know* something like that? The minute it happened? Wouldn't she feel—oh! Like I'm feeling now? I grabbed the vanity to steady myself. Oh, what would Sonny say? And DeeDee? She'd hate me for this. She'd never speak to me again. I had to get a grip. And one of those home pregnancy tests. Right away. But, how—oh, the word itself was unthinkable—*pregnant* did one have to be for the test to be accurate? I'm sure DeeDee knew, but I couldn't just prance out to my kitchen and ask her!

"Are you about ready?" she called from the front of the house, not suspecting one little bit that I was about to betray her in the worst possible way.

"One minute," I called back. I might as well skip my shower since I'd be spending the day in my mother's attic, helping get the house ready to . . . to . . . All at once I began to cry in soul-wrenching sobs. This was all too much to handle.

"Gabby?" DeeDee hurried into the bathroom. "What on earth!" She put her arms around me and patted my back, as if she were consoling a *baby*. I sobbed even louder. "What is it?" she asked, in exactly the tone of a mother. "Is it the house? Oh, I knew this would be too hard for you."

I sniffed and reached for a Kleenex. "I'm okay, really."

"Right." She rolled her eyes sarcastically. "Should I call your mom? Tell her you're just not up to this?"

"No!" I blurted, then softened my tone. "No, she'll just hurry over with a pot of chicken soup." And with that uncanny mother's intuition she possessed, she'd know in a moment what I suspected. I dried my eyes and blew my nose. "Just give me a minute to get dressed."

"Sure thing," she said, then spied my open pill holder on the counter. "Well, it doesn't help that it's that time of the month." She rolled her eyes again. "Isn't it just the *worst*?"

Not the worst, I thought. No, not the worst by a long shot.

I pulled on a pair of jeans and a T-shirt and tied my hair back in a ponytail. Mom expected us half an hour ago, but until DeeDee showed up, I'd forgotten all about our commitment to help her go through the attic. "It's the most logical place to start," she'd said, "and the least pleasant. So we'll get it out of the way first thing and work our way down."

I realized suddenly where I got my logic.

She was upstairs when we arrived, sifting through the clutter. "What a mess!" Her red hair was tied up in an old blue bandana and she, too, wore jeans, only hers were rolled up halfway to her knees. I couldn't help but think she looked like Debbie Reynolds in *Tammy and the Bachelor*.

"Sorry we're late." I put forth a perky face but avoided her eyes, fearful she'd see right through me.

"I've only just come up myself. Where on earth do we begin?"

"No wonder they stopped putting attics in houses," DeeDee said with a grimace. "It's like a black hole up here."

"No telling what's been sucked into it. Won't this be an adventure?"

"What are you going to do with all these *National Geographic* magazines?" I asked. "There must be a hundred years' worth." They were stacked against the wall in wobbly towers five feet high and nearly that wide.

"No one ever threw them out, though I can't think why. I wonder if the library would take them. Or perhaps one of the grammar schools. Angel baby, be a dear. Run down and get that pad and pen I left by the coffeepot. I'll begin making a list of people and places to call to cart some of this stuff off. In the meantime, I suppose we should box them up. Oh, and, sweetheart," she called as I was halfway down the stairs, "bring back that big black marker so I can write on the boxes. Honestly," I could faintly hear her say to DeeDee, "if I didn't have my head tacked on, no telling where it might end up."

DeeDee's pleasant little laugh wafted down the stairwell and dissipated into the atmosphere, where four decades of Whitaker memories resided. It wasn't an original thought, I know, but if those walls could give up some of their treasured histories, they'd tell of Barbie dolls and boyfriends, algebra and acne, and the simple pleasure of growing up under this roof. I felt myself growing emotional again and forced myself to shake it off. If Mother could walk away, who was I to stop her?

When I returned, she and DeeDee were up to their elbows in nostalgia. I began taping boxes together and filling them up with the magazines.

"Don't make them too heavy," Mother said. "We'll never get them down the stairs."

"Oh," DeeDee suddenly called from her corner of the attic, "what a lovely cradle! Have you ever seen anything so gorgeous?"

Mother pushed herself up from the floor and wiped her forehead with her sleeve. "It was Angel baby's." She turned and gave me one of her sweet smiles. "Nobody uses them anymore. What a pity."

DeeDee rocked it lovingly, longingly, while my stomach rose and fell as if I were about to take a bungee dive.

"I know!" Mother said. "Would you like to have it?"

"Yes!" she cried.

"No!" I said at precisely the same instant.

They both looked at me with the most startled eyes.

"I mean . . . I mean . . ." My voice trailed off with nowhere to go.

Mother gave us both an apologetic look. "I suppose I should have asked you first, Angel. I just thought, well, DeeDee could put it to use." She said this delicately, not wanting to offend. She had never questioned my decision not to have a child, though I know she would have loved to be a grandmother.

Well, it's never too late, I thought. "Of course you can have it, Dee. I'll help you refinish it if you'd like." What irony. *You get the cradle. I get the baby.*

But DeeDee gave me a brave wink and shook her head. "That should stay in the family." She held up a hand as Mother and I began to object. "Really."

"Well, then."

We worked throughout the morning, packing some items and separating others for Goodwill and yet others for the dump. At one o'clock we trudged downstairs for some lunch. "I made tuna," Mother said, "everyone's favorite."

"With pickles, I hope," DeeDee said.

I did my best not to throw up.

Mother pulled the bread from the drawer and the mayonnaise from the fridge, then began putting sandwiches together. "There are chips in the cupboard there, Angel. DeeDee, you can fill the glasses with ice."

"Sweetheart, aren't you hungry?" Mother and DeeDee were

halfway finished with their sandwiches, and I hadn't touched mine.

"I guess not."

"She wasn't feeling well this morning," DeeDee said.

"Oh?" Mother frowned and went looking for her thermometer.

"It's nothing," I called after her. "Really."

She came back from the bathroom, shaking the thermometer, and stuck it in my mouth. "Let's hope it's not that Asian flu. People are dropping like flies." I felt ten years old again. "Well, it's normal," she declared after three minutes exactly. "Stick out your tongue."

DeeDee instantly broke into laughter. I admit, I couldn't help but chuckle myself. "Really, Mom, I'm fine."

We were back in the attic by quarter of two, and by four o'clock it actually looked as if we were getting somewhere. "Only one more box, then we'll call it a day." Mother lifted off a dusty lid and immediately drew in a breath. "Oh, sweetheart, it's your wedding box."

"My what?" I dropped the strapping tape onto a sack of Styrofoam packaging peanuts, stepped over a pile of crossword puzzle books from the sixties, and peered over her shoulder to see what on earth she was talking about.

"Your wedding box. You know, leftover invitations, cake napkins, and, look, here's your cake server."

"I always wondered what happened to that."

"There wasn't room in that first apartment you and Sonny moved into."

"The one on Mills," DeeDee said.

"So you boxed everything up and left it here, where we promptly forgot about it. Let's carry it downstairs and see what a treasure we've discovered. Give me a hand?"

I took one end while she took the other. It wasn't heavy, just bulky. Together we descended the stairs awkwardly but cautiously.

"Let's take it to the kitchen. We need a fresh pot of coffee. Decaffeinated, of course." Mother threw DeeDee a wink, and then she laughed. "In my day, women thought nothing of drinking coffee, tea, or Pepsi when they were pregnant, and look at how our children turned out. Why, my sister, Irene, drank coffee from sunup to sundown and delivered a nine-pound baby girl. You remember Sonia," she said to DeeDee.

"Exactly why we don't do such things today," DeeDee said.

Mother started to laugh, then seemed to think better of it. "I'll just get the decaf."

We took turns washing up at the kitchen sink while the coffee brewed. "Maybe I'll have half of my sandwich now," I said. "I'm hungry all of a sudden."

"I should think you would be, working all day on an empty stomach." Mother retrieved it from the refrigerator and put it on a saucer. "Are you feeling better?"

"Yes," I said, and meant it. I didn't feel sick anymore, just scared. Could I really prepare myself for motherhood? At nearly forty?

Mother filled three cups with coffee, then topped them off with vanilla toffee caramel coffee creamer. "Yum," she said with a wide-eyed smile. I didn't have the heart to tell her I preferred mine without. It gave her such pleasure to serve it. "Now." She pulled the wedding box into the little half circle our chairs formed. "Let's see what's inside."

There was a packet of a dozen or so invitations with their double envelopes and tissue paper, which had turned yellow and brittle over the years. We had exhausted our list of guests and simply had no one to send these last invitations to. There was no earthly use for them, but still we'd saved them because you couldn't just throw them away.

"I'd forgotten how lovely they were," I said, surprised to hear my own voice. I'd really just meant to think it. The ivory paper was embossed with a rose whose petals had just the hint of blush. Inside, in a delicate script, was written:

Rev. and Mrs. O. Riley Whitaker
invite you to the wedding of their daughter
Angel Joy Whitaker
as she is joined in holy matrimony to
Stuart Oliver Nevin III
on Saturday, August 29
in the year of our Lord . . .

Suddenly I began to sob. "I miss Dad," I managed to say, but nothing more.

"Angel. Honey." Mother was beside me in a moment with her arms around me.

"She was just like this before we came this morning," DeeDee whispered. "I think it's all a bit much for her."

"Of course it is." Mother pulled my head to her shoulder. "She's always been sentimental."

Why were they talking as if I couldn't hear? As if I weren't even in the room? I pulled myself away and reached for a napkin from the holder in the center of the table. I blew my nose and wiped my face, avoiding their inquiring eyes. "I'm fine," I said, but I could tell neither of them was convinced.

"I miss him too," Mother said, and I began to cry again.

"Then how can you do this?"

"It's *because* I miss him that I'm doing this. Sweetheart, I can't find one square inch of this house that isn't alive with his memory. I still have his cologne in the medicine chest, for crying out loud." She collapsed into a chair after her confession. "I've been stuck in a time warp for twenty years. I want to get on with my life. I need to get on with my life."

Why was I being so selfish? It had to be my hormones. My *pregnant* hormones. They had gone berserk. "Of course you do," I whispered. "I'm sorry, Mom."

"Nothing to be sorry for. It's understandable. I've had weeks, months actually, to think about this. To prepare myself. You've only had a few days. We'll take it more slowly."

"No. You've made the decision—you need to get on with it. There's a lot to do, and you can count on me to help."

"Me too," DeeDee said.

"So tomorrow we'll finish the attic, and after that, well, you just tell us what to do."

"That's brave of you," Mother said.

I smiled, but I didn't feel brave. I felt shaken to my shoes.

"Sonny, do you think it's a sin not to have kids—I mean, on purpose?"

He pressed the mute button on the TV remote and gave me a curious look. "Where did that come from?"

I gave an evasive shrug. "I just wondered how you felt."

"Well, now. Hmm." He pulled off his glasses and began to chew on the earpiece, the way he did when he was deep in thought, then said, "God told Noah to replenish the earth. Mission accomplished." He smiled and put his glasses back on.

"So you don't?" I felt a wash of relief.

He moved from his chair to mine and snuggled in beside me. "Think it's a sin? No, I don't think it's a sin."

"What if— " I said, and stopped. His look encouraged me to spit it out. "What if someone wanted a baby and couldn't have one, and someone else didn't but could?" I pressed myself against him.

"I'm afraid this baby thing is getting to you." He put his arm around me and squeezed. "Angel," he said, surprising us both. He hadn't called me that since our wedding day, when in response to Daddy's question he had said, "I, Sonny, take you, Angel Joy Gabriella Whitaker, to be my lawfully wedded wife."

"Angel, as much as DeeDee wants to have a baby, it's in God's hands. Let's leave it there. He knows what's best."

I looked up at him, my eyes locked on his. "Do you believe that, Sonny? Really believe it?"

"Absolutely."

"That it's in God's hands? That He knows what's best?"

"Absolutely," he said, more firmly than before.

I nestled into him again. "Okay, then."

I slept better that night than I expected to, but that wasn't saying much.

The next morning I called DeeDee first thing. "I'll pick you up in half an hour. I just have to make a stop first."

"Where?" she wanted to know.

"Where? Uh, doughnuts. You know how Mom loves doughnuts."

Now I'd really have to hurry if I was going to get to the drugstore and the bakery, too, and still get to DeeDee's when I said I would. But I had to find out if I was . . . was . . .

pregnant—without *anyone* knowing but me. That meant I needed a home pregnancy test. So I threw on my clothes, pulled a baseball cap over my ponytail, dabbed on a touch of lip gloss, and headed to Wal-Mart.

I knew right where they were. I'd been with DeeDee to this section of the store more than once as, wishfully, she determined which one she'd buy if the need should arise. I reached out my hand to get the one she thought was best.

"I knew it was either the change or this."

I turned slowly. "DeeDee." I felt as if I'd been caught reading her diary.

"How could you?" she demanded. "How *could* you?" Her eyes began to fill with tears. It was unthinkable, but she was going to cry. Right there in Wal-Mart. "It's your way of getting even, isn't it?"

"Even?" I stammered. I couldn't think what she meant.

"For Paris. You've never forgiven me."

"For Paris?"

"Don't play dumb." Her chin was quivering. *Quivering!* "For getting married without you. But this! Gabriella, how could you?"

We were drawing an audience, and the looks we were getting were extraordinary, to say the least.

"DeeDee," I said, trying to draw her away to some private, deserted aisle. "It's not what you think."

"Here! You forgot this!" She shoved the home pregnancy test into my chest. "Doughnuts!" Anyone following this conversation would have become pretty confused by now. "Have I ever lied to you?" she demanded.

"You mean besides about your wedding?" I shot back. I immediately regretted it.

"You see! You haven't forgiven me."

"And you think I would allow myself to get pregnant to get even? DeeDee! Yes, I was hurt that you got married without telling me, but I got over it the moment you went into the pool."

"No one's that easy! Not even you." She crossed her arms over her chest and threw her gaze at the floor.

"I am. Really. Look. Look at my face. What do you see?"

"Revenge!" she said with a glare.

I squinted into the glass that secured men's cologne from, well, I don't really know what it secured it from, and found my reflection. "Now be honest. That is *not* what you see. There are dark circles under worried eyes — and a little crease from sleeping on a wrinkle in my pillowcase," I said, touching my cheek, "but not a trace of revenge." I got just the hint of a smile. "There's a general appearance of panic that matches the feeling in my stomach, but no revenge! Look." I showed her every angle of my profile, which she begrudgingly peeked at. "See?"

"Okay. Maybe it isn't revenge, but how do you explain *that*?" She thumped the back of her hand against the box I held.

"I never miss a pill, Dee, but I've never been late either. I couldn't go another day without knowing one way or the other."

She drew in a deep breath. "Okay, let's go. If I can handle it, you can handle it." She nudged me toward the rear of the store. "We're in this together."

I gasped. "Here?"

"Right here, right now."

"But, but they don't allow merchandise in the restroom."

Dee snatched the box out of my hand, went straight to the express lane, and paid for the pregnancy test. Then she pointed to the front of the store. I felt as if I were walking the plank as we made our way to the restroom.

"Use the handicap stall," she instructed. "You'll have more room to faint."

The funny thing was, I'd already thought of that.

I locked myself in and began to read the instructions. "I have to pee on a stick?"

"We're not alone," DeeDee informed me. I heard the door open and close. "Ah, well, we are now. Yes, you have to pee on a stick. What else would you do?"

"Ooh," I moaned. "Can't I do this at home?"

"You're already in there. Just do it."

But I didn't have to. I closed the box and shoved it under the stall in her direction. "Got a quarter?"

8

"I'm in the middle of this ordeal and off she goes to Europe. Europe, for heaven's sake!" DeeDee paced in my kitchen while I put together a pot of spaghetti sauce to simmer.

"Dee, what are you talking about?"

"Dr. Creager. I told you, she was in Europe. We lost four whole weeks!"

It was February, just a few weeks short of DeeDee's fortieth birthday, and she was as unpregnant as ever.

"She has a life," I reminded DeeDee for the umpteenth time. "Besides, wasn't it nice to get through a few weeks without the hassle of tracking your cycle?"

"Jonathan tried that logic too, and the answer is no. I want to be pregnant before forty. That doesn't leave much time." She looked at her watch as if measuring the duration in seconds.

"I know, Dee, but don't put that kind of pressure on yourself. Or on Jonathan. It'll only make things more difficult."

"Jonathan isn't the problem, remember?"

"Maybe not technically, but even you said it's affected his, you know, *ability*." In spite of myself I blushed. "Now, what did Dr. Creager say? What's the next step now that she's back?"

She moaned. "We're looking for *structural* problems. Sounds like a termite inspection if you ask me."

"Which means?"

"I'm having an abdominal ultrasound on Wednesday. Not your usual type, but with a full bladder. Sounds fun, hmm? All that pressing and prodding."

I gave her a sympathetic look.

"Will you come?"

"Me? What about Jonathan?"

"I asked him not to. I'd rather he were part of the end result without having to be too involved with the intricate details."

Somehow I understood. "What time?"

"Nine thirty. I'll pick you up." On a whim, she grabbed me by the shoulders and kissed me on both cheeks, European style. "I don't deserve you," she said with passion.

"I know." I smiled and she smiled, but we both knew I meant it.

Dr. Creager was delayed due to surgery, so our nine thirty appointment didn't begin until nearly eleven o'clock. We spent more than an hour and a half in the waiting room with expectant women of all ages, shapes, and sizes. In a corner, huddled together, was a couple our age or older, who looked longingly at the bulging tummies around them. I found myself praying for them, and when they were called into the examining room, I even wrote down their names so I could continue to pray and not forget.

DeeDee was a nervous wreck by the time it was her turn. And since she'd been drinking water all morning for the test, she was grouchy and uncomfortable to boot. She disappeared behind a curtain to disrobe and reappeared wearing a hospital gown and nothing else.

"Wherever do they get this fabric? It's horrible."

The nurse came in to take DeeDee's blood pressure. "One thirty-nine over ninety-two," she said. "Nervous?"

"Considerably more than I was at nine thirty. And don't thank me for my patience. I ran out a year ago."

"Open your mouth." When DeeDee responded, the nurse said, "I just wanted to get my head out."

At that, DeeDee broke into a penitent smile, and I laughed outright. "I deserved that."

I couldn't have agreed more.

"Your pulse is elevated too. All typical. If you'll lie down on the table, the doctor will be with you shortly." To me she said, "You can move your chair this way a little if you'd like to watch the screen."

DeeDee avoided making eye contact with me as we waited. I wore my favorite chastening look just in case I caught her sneaking a glance my way.

Dr. Creager was a tall, thin woman in her fifties with a pleasant, expressive face. She had long salt-and-pepper hair that she twisted into a bun and secured with a leather clasp. She looked exactly as if she were stuck in a time warp from the sixties, and I'd have safely bet that she'd been at Woodstock. I liked her instantly. Half-glasses rested on the end of a long, patrician nose, leaving her ivy green eyes perfectly exposed. She spoke with a slight European accent I couldn't identify as she extended a warm, strong hand to me in greeting.

"DeeDee, forgive the delay. What should have been a simple delivery turned into a complicated C-section."

"Did everything come out all right?" DeeDee asked, then chuckled. "No pun intended."

"Twin girls. Mother and daughters are fine, though the father required five stitches from the fall. Seems Mommy wanted the twins to be a surprise. I don't recommend that." She smiled as she studied DeeDee's chart. "So, we're not pregnant."

"Not the teeniest little bit."

"Well, let's see if we can find out why." She made some adjustments on the computer in front of her and began to squeeze gel onto DeeDee's abdomen. "Mrs. Nevin, would you get the lights?"

I jumped off my chair and hit the light switch, feeling suddenly important, as if this were my contribution to seeing DeeDee happily pregnant. I'd already contributed once, of course, in a huge way—by not being pregnant myself.

Dr. Creager pressed the transducer firmly against DeeDee's abdomen. "I know this is uncomfortable. The bladder must be full to produce the right kind of echo sounds, which give us a nice little picture of your pelvic tract."

"What are we looking for?" DeeDee asked, trying not to grimace.

"Oh, enlargements, scarring, any type of abnormality that would explain your infertility."

There were several minutes of silence as Dr. Creager worked the instrument across DeeDee's belly. I studied the pulsating picture on the screen with squinted eyes, but it was pure nonsense to me. At last, Dr. Creager asked me to get the lights once again.

"So do I look as good on the inside as I do on the outside?"

Dr. Creager smiled. "Your uterus appears to be retroflexed,

or tipped backward," she explained, "but that doesn't have to equate to infertility. I don't see any other problems offhand, but our technician will give me a full report. I'll get the results to you right away."

"What's next? I mean, if this doesn't reveal anything."

"We'll check your hormones through blood samples to see what may or may not be present and try to determine if you're sperm-friendly."

"Sperm-friendly?"

Dr. Creager laughed. "You won't like it at all."

The technician verified that DeeDee's uterus was tipped, but otherwise the pelvic tract looked okay. Or, as DeeDee put it, "The plumbing is fine."

"So why isn't it working?" she asked.

Dr. Creager gave DeeDee a patient smile. "Our next test is to determine how well you and Jonathan are getting along, biologically speaking." She went into great detail about the relationship between sperm and cervical mucous. I sat in her office with DeeDee, wondering where in the world I'd been during sophomore biology.

"You'll need to come in twelve hours after intercourse so we can run a check."

I suddenly felt like a voyeur.

"What exactly are we checking for?" DeeDee asked.

"You need healthy mucous, and plenty of it, or sperm can't survive long enough to fertilize your ovum. It's just another step to rule out factors that aren't factors. Process of elimination, if you will. If we're lucky, it will be something as simple and benign as a lack of mucous."

"And if that's it?" DeeDee was hopeful.

"Cough syrup."

"I beg your pardon?"

I, too, was sure I'd heard incorrectly.

"It's simpler than estrogen and works just as well."

"Cough syrup? Do you . . . *swallow* it?"

Dr. Creager covered her mouth and nodded. It was obvious she was trying not to laugh. "The decongestant type, of course."

DeeDee and I looked at each other and shrugged. "Of course," we said in unison.

Two days later, at precisely ten a.m., DeeDee lay in Dr. Creager's examining room waiting to have her mucous appraised. I had stubbornly refused to leave the waiting room when DeeDee's name was called. "You're on your own this time." I picked up a magazine. "I'll just do a little catching up on my reading."

"*Popular Mechanics*?" she said with an eyebrow raised.

"I've taken up a new hobby. Go on. Take your time."

I'd learned more about carburetors than I ever thought possible when DeeDee emerged with a bottle of Robitussin Expectorant forty minutes later.

"Problems in paradise?" I asked.

"My mucous couldn't carry sperm to first base! If I've waited nearly two years to have a baby and all I needed was a bottle of cough syrup, I'll—" Her eyes grew narrow. "Don't you dare tell Jonathan."

"My lips are sealed."

"Honestly, I don't know whether to laugh or cry." She looked as if she were about to do both.

"I'll drive," I said, taking the keys right out of her hand. "Get in, buckle up, and take some deep breaths."

She followed my instructions to a tee, and by the time we

reached the freeway she was nearly herself again. "Could it really be this simple?" Her voice sounded weak and pathetic.

"If it is, you'll laugh about this someday." I wasn't convincing either one of us.

"See what being healthy has gotten me? Weak mucous."

I couldn't help it. I began to laugh, and I laughed until I was in danger of going off the road and had to pull off the freeway for safety's sake. Now *I* was the one on the verge of hysteria, but I wasn't about to give up the keys.

By the time DeeDee's fortieth birthday had come and gone, she was on her third bottle of Robitussin. According to Dr. Creager, it was doing the trick. Jonathan asked about the elixir more than once, but DeeDee would simply cough in reply.

"I think this whole pregnancy thing is getting to her," he said to me one day over the telephone. He called from the office so DeeDee wouldn't know. I could sense the worry in his voice. "She's *obsessed*, and I'm afraid to think what more of this could do to her. I don't know, Gab. I think it's time to face the facts and get back to normal life. We were perfectly happy without children. It seems obvious we just weren't meant to be parents. Why else wouldn't she be able to conceive?"

I didn't think he would understand the concept of weak mucous.

"I thought I would take her to Paris later this spring." He sounded desperate. "Sort of a fortieth birthday/twentieth anniversary/let's-get-on-with-life celebration. What do you think?"

"I'd keep her away from the top of the Eiffel Tower," I said, serious as a stroke.

"You think she'd take it that hard?" I could practically see his countenance drop.

"And then some."

"What should I do?" His voice was heavy with frustration. "I mean, this whole thing is out of our control. We just waited too long."

"Have you talked to Dr. Creager?"

"DeeDee hasn't exactly invited me along to her appointments."

"You could call her. She's very approachable."

"I'd feel like I was going behind DeeDee's back."

"That's only because you would be. Jonathan, I'd call the doctor. I'm not sure how much more DeeDee can handle, emotionally, I mean." *Or you either*, I wanted to add.

"All right then," he said. "But I'm not doing this in secret. I'll tell DeeDee I want to go with her to her appointment next week. Then she and I have a decision to make. We can't go on like this."

"Right. I think that's best. You go instead of me."

"Oh no, Gabby, you've been in the middle of this from day one. You need to be there too. We'll want your input."

"I don't know, Jonathan. Are you sure?"

"Absolutely sure."

Oh, Lord, I prayed when I hung up the phone, *you've promised never to give us more than we can bear. I'm afraid both DeeDee and Jonathan are at the breaking point. Please intervene, someway, somehow. And use me to help if I can.* My dad had always ended his prayers that way, so I did too. And not just out of habit—I meant it. Especially this time. Little did I realize how specifically God would take me at my word.

9

"I'd like you to chart your basal body temperature again for two months," Dr. Creager said at the conclusion of DeeDee's next visit. "I'd like to see what it shows before scheduling an endometrial biopsy."

"Biopsy? You think I have a tumor or something?" DeeDee shot a worried look at Jonathan and voiced my thoughts exactly.

"Oh, it's nothing like that. I'd like to examine your endometrial lining, but first I want to see what the BBT reveals. It's been some time since we charted it."

"What are you looking for? Honestly."

Dr. Creager scooted her stool back against the desk and crossed one leg over the other. She stuck her pencil into her French braid and folded her hands in her lap. "Okay," she said, "I suspect that you are no longer ovulating. The peaks on your previous charts were never strong. I'd like to see what they show now."

"Not ovulating? But my period is right on schedule. Always. I haven't even *begun* the change. I mean, I've never had a hot flash!"

Her cheeks were a bright pink and she fanned herself furiously.

Dr. Creager looked completely sympathetic. "It's possible to have a normal period without ovulating. It's called an anovulatory cycle."

A pained look crossed DeeDee's stressed-out features. "Are you saying I'm not producing any eggs?"

Jonathan reached across the distance and took hold of her hand.

"That's what I want to determine," Dr. Creager said. "By comparing current BBT charts with previous ones, we'll have an indication. If I'm wrong, it will save us from doing an uncomfortable and intrusive test unnecessarily."

"What if you're right—what if I'm not ovulating? Is there a treatment?"

"It depends on the cause. You may be entering menopause, in which case you simply may have run out of time. But let's not jump to conclusions." She retrieved her pencil and began to scribble in DeeDee's chart. "Record your BBT for two months and we'll compare results and take it from there."

Dr. Creager seemed to have an endless supply of compassion. Helping women conceive who otherwise might not be able to was definitely her calling.

"Do you have children?" I asked.

"Two girls." A happy smile crinkled the lines around her eyes. "Both adopted. So, you see, there are other ways to have a family."

"Then you're pretty sure?" DeeDee said. "I can't have children?" She and Jonathan shared a brief look.

"I wouldn't say it's certain. It seems obvious from your latest charts that you aren't producing many eggs. So your chances, as you've found out over the past couple of years, are greatly reduced.

But even if you aren't producing eggs, that doesn't mean you couldn't sustain a pregnancy if, for example, you were impregnated with an embryo created by your husband's sperm and a donor's eggs."

Two red blotches appeared in Jonathan's cheeks. I wished I'd stayed in the waiting room.

"Your uterus, though tipped, appears healthy," Dr. Creager continued, "so I think it would be possible, but the chances of miscarriage are much higher with this type of pregnancy, especially after forty.

"A surrogate pregnancy is another option, again using a donor's eggs and your husband's sperm. The embryo is placed in the surrogate's uterus rather than yours, making it much more possible to see the pregnancy through to term. Or there is adoption. Those are the options I see for you."

"Or, we simply remain childless," DeeDee said. She turned a serious face to Jonathan. He scooted his chair closer and put an arm around her shoulder.

Dr. Creager gave a slight nod of agreement. "Why don't you think about this?" she said to DeeDee and Jonathan. "Take some time, discuss the options. If you opt to be impregnated with a donor's eggs or choose to use a donor's eggs and uterus as a surrogate, we can help locate a donor who matches your genetic traits."

"Could you find a donor with, say, Meg Ryan's genetic traits?"

Jonathan chuckled and so did Dr. Creager. "That's possible. If you decide on adoption, I can recommend a wonderful agency. Or, if you choose, you can keep your family as it is."

DeeDee, serious once again, gave an understanding nod.

"She's right," Jonathan said. "It only takes two to be a family, and that's what we are. You and me."

"Yes," Dr. Creager said. "A complete family, just as you are."

DeeDee picked up her handbag and placed the strap over her shoulder. "Whatever we decide, I want you to know how much we appreciate your help. We'll be in touch." She extended her hand to Dr. Creager.

"It's been a pleasure," the doctor replied, then turned to me and said, "Everyone should have such a friend."

Jonathan left for a meeting once DeeDee convinced him she was fine. "More than fine," she said.

"Meg Ryan?" I asked, back in the car.

DeeDee shrugged. "She's just so cute."

I backed out of the parking lot and pulled into traffic.

"It's Tuesday, Gab," DeeDee said, "and we haven't had lunch at D'Angelo's in ages. What do you say?"

"We've just got time to beat the lunch crowd."

Our usual table was just being bused, so we waited for it. We took our seats, our menus closed on the table before us.

"Wow. How long ago it seems we sat at this very table and I said, 'Gabby, I want a baby.' I thought you'd die of shock." DeeDee laughed a simple laugh and opened her menu. "I'm going to have—"she laid the menu aside—"whatever you're having."

I reached across the table and took her hand. "I'm proud of you, Dee. Really."

"Jonathan wants to take me to Paris." There wasn't the fire in her eyes that just the mention of that magical city had always ignited.

"Paris? Wow." I tried to sound surprised, but my voice wasn't convincing.

"But I'm sure you already knew that. It's a trade-off, you know. Especially after today. No eggs. I never realized there was a limited supply."

"No eggs *maybe*," I said. But DeeDee only shrugged. "Maybe Paris is just what you need," I said as enthusiastically as I could. "Get away from everything. Forget about this whole biology lesson from hell and enjoy yourself, and each other. Come back refreshed, do exactly what Dr. Creager recommended, and then and only then, consider your options."

She sighed and looked away. "There aren't any options left."

"Maybe not," I said matter-of-factly, "but cross that bridge when you get to it." I tugged on her hand, coaxing her to look back at me. "Go, Dee. You and Jonathan. This obsession with pregnancy is coming between the two of you, and that would be the most tragic part of this whole affair."

"Will you pray for me? That I can leave this all behind?"

"Every minute of every day. Go. Fall in love again, with Jonathan, with Paris, with life. Trust the course that God has plotted for you, no matter what it is."

"I miss your dad so much at times, but it's obvious he bequeathed his wisdom to you. I don't know what I'd do without you." DeeDee squeezed my hand, then withdrew hers and straightened the napkin in her lap. "I'll call Jonathan when I get home and tell him to make the reservations."

The waiter approached, ready to take our order. He looked first to DeeDee, but she nodded to me.

I pushed past the lump in my throat. "We'll have . . . we'll have a banana split," I said on a whim. "The colossal. One for each of us."

The waiter frowned as he collected our menus. "I don't believe that's on our dessert tray, Madam. Perhaps," he said, "next door."

"Yes," I agreed, "next door." I reached in my wallet and handed him a five-dollar bill for his trouble.

DeeDee strapped on her purse and we made for the exit. "The colossal?"

"One for each of us. My treat."

"Well, then," she said as we entered The Frigid Scoop, "here's to new traditions!"

I dropped DeeDee off in her driveway, watched her disappear inside the house, then laid my head against the steering wheel. Without notice, a hot rush of tears poured down my face. *Wisdom? Me? What a joke.* "Dad," I whispered, "do you have any idea how much I miss you? How much I need you?"

I started my car and drove to the cemetery on the edge of town. When I was a child, the land surrounding the old part of the cemetery had been strawberry fields, before the expansion. I guess there was never an end to the need for more burial space. I could never come here without thinking of the Beatles song "Strawberry Fields Forever." I wondered if I should find that morbid or comical. If I told DeeDee, she would look at me as if I'd lost it. And then she'd laugh.

There had been a funeral recently near my dad's grave. There was no marker yet, so I didn't know anything about the life of the individual now buried there. I hoped it was someone who had lived a long, full life and had now gone on to an even better one. Seeing my dad's name on the marker always gave me a start. I had been used to seeing O. RILEY WHITAKER in a lot of places the first twenty years of my life: on the door of his office, on his parking space at the church, on our mailbox at home, on his ministerial license hanging over his desk in the den, where he often counseled troubled church members. But on a grave marker? No. I'd never gotten used to that.

His death had been startling, devastating. Who would have expected heart failure at fifty-one? Certainly not me. But then, he was my dad. I thought he'd never die.

It was the last Tuesday in September. Sonny and I had barely settled into our new apartment, barely adjusted to the incredible notion that we were married. Mom had invited us to dinner, I believe with the intention of making it a Tuesday night ritual. She liked to fill her life with habit and routine. At any given time, on any given day, I knew exactly where to find my mom and could pretty well predict what she'd be doing. It had added wonderful stability to my formative years. And now, it seemed, the Tuesday night niche was to become ours. Jonathan and DeeDee had been invited that first time too, but they hadn't been able to make it. It was startling to realize, as I stood there over my father's grave, that I no longer remembered why. I thought I'd never forget even the tiniest detail of the night my world had dimmed.

I was running out the door, uncharacteristically late, planning to meet Sonny at my parents' house. I remember thinking, *My parents' house. How odd that it's no longer home*, when the phone began to ring. I thought for a moment I'd just let it ring. I really had to go. But then, maybe it was Sonny. So I grabbed it and said hello with a voice as happy and carefree as you'd expect from a newly married twenty-year-old. It was Mom, and I knew right away something awful had happened.

"Angel?" Her voice was hesitant and frightened, not at all like the strong and steady woman she'd been all my life. "They're taking your dad to the hospital. In an ambulance. I don't think I can drive."

"Where are you, Mom?" Immediately, the adrenaline began to flow. "Where's Dad?"

"We're here. At home. He was slicing tomatoes. I don't think I can drive." Her voice was soft and sounded forlorn.

"I'm on my way!" I cried. "Don't worry!"

Don't worry? I worried all the way to their house, where Mom waited on the front porch with a puzzled look on her face. And I worried all the way to the hospital as we drove in silence, each caught up in our own fervent prayers.

How was I going to contact Sonny?

The emergency entrance was in the back of the hospital. I pulled into a parking space, and by the time I turned off the ignition Mom was halfway to the door. I ran to catch up. We were taken into the ER, where Dad was undergoing an initial exam, surrounded by a doctor and two nurses and someone drawing blood. He looked gray and gaunt. It terrified me to see him so weak and helpless.

As they were wheeling him upstairs to surgery, Sonny burst through the doors of the hospital. "Mrs. Williams said they'd taken your dad off in an ambulance." He was breathless, as if he'd run all the way. Mrs. Williams was as old as Methuselah and had lived next door since before we'd taken occupancy of the house. You could count on her to know what was going on in the neighborhood.

"It's his heart," I said, incredulous, trying not to panic, trying to be strong for my mom, and feeling as if my knees would buckle.

Sonny wrapped one arm around me and one arm around Mother, and I knew I didn't have to be the strong one. Sonny was there for me, for Mom.

"Let's pray," he said.

I felt him suck in a breath, then another, heard him swallow, knew he was waiting until he could trust his voice. My own tears fell onto the polished linoleum floor.

"God," Sonny said, his voice a strained whisper, "we need you. We need your strength. We need your touch. For Riley. Lord, you created that heart and you know how to fix it. We ask you to be with the doctors as they minister to him. But, Lord, in the end, we trust you and commit him to your perfect will. In Jesus' name."

It was exactly the prayer my dad would have prayed. But it's not what *I* was saying to the Lord. In my heart I was saying, *God, you have to fix him. You have to. We need him.* I *need him. Please don't take him home. Please. Don't.*

We waited more than two eternal hours, but Dad never came out of surgery. His heart had stopped and couldn't be made to start again. By the time we were informed of his death, DeeDee and Jonathan were with us. I still don't know who called them.

When it was all over, I allowed myself to think Dad had gotten a glimpse of heaven and decided there was no way he was coming back here—not even for us.

I knelt down and brushed away the leaves and dirt from the gravestone. Impossible to believe it had been two decades and that life had somehow carried on. Mom was nicely settled in a condo on the newly developed north side of town. The house sold almost immediately, and for full price. She had bought a condo-full of new furniture and had a newly leased Honda in the driveway, a portfolio at Dean Witter, and a membership at a health club. She had cut and colored her hair and looked and felt better and younger than she had at fifty. She'd worn the mantle of widowhood for twenty long years. Now she was a member of the singles' group at church.

Nothing stayed the same.

10

"Paris was just what the doctor ordered." DeeDee sat on my patio, sipping an iced tea and looking the most relaxed I'd seen her in two years. "I took all your advice. Threw the chart right out the window and just enjoyed my husband. For the first time in a long time I felt like we connected again."

"But you're ready to chart now, right?"

DeeDee threw me a curious look.

"I mean, I'm glad you and Jonathan had such a good time, but you're going to do this one last thing for Dr. Creager, aren't you?"

DeeDee was quiet for almost a minute, then she shook her head. "I'm through, Gabby. I want to get on with my life, with our lives. I've had Jonathan on the back burner for two years, and I suddenly realized I should be thanking my God that he's still with me. Sure, there was lots and *lots* of sex, but very little love-making. I just want to love my husband for a while."

Well. That was a side of DeeDee I'd never seen before, and

as much as I admired it, now was not the time for a change of character! "You have to find out what your options are before you decide to call it quits."

"There are no options, Gabby. Dr. Creager says we're born with a certain number of eggs, and mine are gone."

"You don't know that for sure," I reminded her. "Besides, we're the same age," I said, as if that made any difference.

Her shrug was one of resignation. "You might have gotten a flat, while I only got half a dozen."

"But, but, you're six days younger than me."

"And?"

"Well . . ." I shrugged. "It's just that . . ." What? If she was tottering over the brink of childbearing age, then so was I? Why on earth should that bother me? "Let's just see what Dr. Creager has to say."

But DeeDee shook her head. "I can't take any more disappointment."

Her words cut right through my heart.

Sonny and I spent our first real vacation in a decade touring the Oregon coastline, something we had meant to do for ages. We left early one golden Saturday morning the end of June for eight glorious days of relaxation and togetherness. I'd been tempted to bring my laptop so I could work on my latest piece for *Today's Christian Woman* while Sonny caught up on his reading and rest. At the last minute I stashed it back in the closet, determined to make this a truly work-free event. I was sure I'd regret that decision on the other side of the equation, but deadlines would just have to wait.

On our first morning out, Sonny and I wound our way toward

Oregon through the giant redwoods of northern California, in and out of the shadows created by the late-morning sunlight filtering through the ancient timbers. It was as if we were caught in a cosmic strobe light. I was hypnotized by the swift changes of dark to light. The subject brewing in my mind changed just as swiftly, from plausible one moment to unthinkable the next. I lowered my window enough to get a deep breath of the moist and pungent air, wanting to be drawn away from my own unsettling thoughts.

Sonny reached his hand across the seat and tickled my knee, something he seemed helpless to resist whenever I wore shorts. "I lost you somewhere back in the valley," he said. "Something on your mind?"

Boy, was there. But how to put it into words? I opened my mouth to try, but a sigh was as far as I got. He waited, expectantly, while I groped for just the right way to say it. When I came to the realization that there wasn't a right way, I simply said, "I want to give DeeDee my eggs."

He picked up the cell phone and scrolled down to their number. "If you don't think they'll last till we get home, tell her to stop by and get them out of the fridge." He pressed Send, then handed me the phone.

If this hadn't been so serious, I'd have giggled. We were not on the same page. Not by a long shot.

I turned off the cell phone and dropped it onto the seat between us. "I don't mean eggs, Sonny, I mean *eggs*."

I knew the instant he caught on. It was just before he nearly drove us off the side of the mountain.

He came to an abrupt stop on the edge of the highway, barely out of the way of a motorist spiraling his way up the mountainside behind us. He gaped at me wordlessly, with the most indefinable expression on his face, as the driver blasted an angry horn. "Eggs?" Sonny said at last. "As in *eggs*?"

"So she and Jonathan can have a child." I leaned toward him and away from the wooded cliff just outside my door. My eyes darted back and forth from the scene beyond my window to his face. I wasn't at all sure which was the more frightening.

"But, wouldn't that be like Jon and *you* having a child?" He looked as puzzled as I'd ever seen him.

"Only technically."

"Technically," he repeated, as if explaining it to himself. "I see." He put the car in gear and eased back onto the highway, looking dreadfully shaken.

"It would really be no different than if they used an anonymous donor, except I wouldn't be."

"Wouldn't be what?"

"Anonymous."

He pondered that awhile, mindless of the motorists piling up behind us on the unpassable two-lane highway as his speed dropped lower and lower.

"Do you think I should drive?"

He seemed not to hear. "Do women really share such things?" He kept his eyes on me as he waited for an answer.

"Th-they can," I said, watching the road more intently than he. "Really, Sonny, don't you think I should drive?"

"Drive?"

"You know, the car?"

He came to a turnout and used it, much to the relief of me and the drivers who accelerated their speeds and whizzed on by, but he didn't relinquish the driver's seat. "I suppose you and DeeDee have talked about this?"

"Actually, no. I wanted us to talk about it first."

I can't describe how relieved he looked. He very nearly smiled. "In that case, I suggest you never mention this to another living soul. Ever." My eyes stung with unexpected tears. "Oh, babe, please don't cry." He placed a hand against my cheek. "Don't get me wrong. I'd be the first person to help DeeDee have a baby if I could. No! Wait! That isn't what I meant." As I dabbed at my eyes I couldn't help but snicker at his ridiculous choice of words, which was good because it broke the tension between us. He visibly relaxed and let out the breath he'd inhaled. "I mean, your intentions are so . . . so . . . generous, but this goes way beyond the call of friendship."

"But why? You just said yourself that you'd help if you could. Although if you did, I'd personally—well, let's not go there."

"You know, I could use a cup of really strong coffee. Like from yesterday." He pulled back onto the highway and pretended I wasn't even present until we were safely seated in a booth at an almost-deserted diner.

The waitress greeted us with a near-empty coffeepot, undoubtedly left over from the morning rush, if indeed there was a morning rush in such a remote place. She filled Sonny's cup. Her long, tightly curled, bleached blonde hair was twisted, turned up, and clamped to the back of her head with a hot pink clip, while the ends of her hair shot out of the top of her head like a frizzled rooster tail. The clip, I noticed, matched her eye shadow to a tee, a fashion statement I wasn't sure how to decipher. I placed a hand over my cup, a definite sign that I wished to decline her offer of whatever was in the pot. "I'll take hot tea," I said, "with lemon and honey."

"Honey?" She laughed all the way to the counter. "I'll see if I can dig up a packet of lemon juice. There's sugar and Sweet'N Low behind the ketchup."

I gave Sonny my best *you-can-sure-pick-em* look and waited for him to start the conversation.

"So," he said, grimacing with his first gulp of the muddy brew, while I dunked a tea bag in a cup of tepid water. "Sweetheart, have you, you know, prayed about this?"

Sonny always knew just when to get spiritual on me, but this time I was ready for him. "I have," I said, nodding my head emphatically. "A great deal."

"And?" He seemed nervous about my answer.

"I don't feel a check, if that's what you mean."

"No?" He deflated like a tired balloon. "Not at all?"

I shook my head. "Of course, I wouldn't even consider this without your approval. After all, this is something that would affect all of us."

"I could see that." He nodded like a prescient sage. "Have you been thinking about this for a long time?"

"Not really. It's just something Dr. Creager mentioned."

"She mentioned that you should donate your eggs?"

"Not me specifically. It's just an option."

"Ah." He nodded again.

For a while we both looked out the window, which overlooked a mountain of redwoods. Ordinarily, we'd be talking nonstop about the view, snapping photos, loving the adventure. But Sonny worked at his horrid cup of coffee, and I forced down my lukewarm tea without further conversation.

His cup finally empty, Sonny held it up to the waitress, who was bent at the waist with her elbows on the counter, resting her head in her hands, watching a soap opera on a TV with the volume turned off. "Perhaps something fresh this time?" he asked hopefully.

She chuckled again without turning away from the screen.

"We don't make fresh till lunch." Just behind her was a revolving pie display. I wondered if the withered slice of pumpkin was a holdover from Thanksgiving. She looked back over her shoulder at me. "More hot water?"

"No, no, I think I'll pass."

Sonny reached for his wallet and withdrew a five. He let it fall to the table and motioned toward the door with his head. "Thanks," he called to the waitress.

"Anytime," was the reply.

Sonny fastened his seat belt and turned up the air conditioner. It couldn't have been more than seventy degrees outside in the clear mountain air, but a trickle of sweat ran down his temple. I shivered, closed my vent, and reached in the back for a sweatshirt.

"So." He cleared his throat and tried to sound nonchalant as he pulled back onto the highway. "If you haven't talked to DeeDee about this, do you think she'd even go for it? And Jon. I mean, what do you think he'd say?"

"I don't know about Jonathan," I confessed, "but DeeDee at least seemed willing to entertain the idea. Of a donor, I mean. Not that she asked me or anything." I left out the part about Meg Ryan. "I guess that's what got me thinking about it. But whether or not she'd accept me as a donor . . ." I concluded with a shrug.

"Why wouldn't she?" Suddenly Sonny sounded defensive.

"Well, I mean, there are emotional ramifications to consider."

"Yes, I can see that," he said again. "What would be involved in, uh, donating your, um, *eggs*?" He handled the word as delicately is if it would break with the usage.

"I checked out a book," I said, reaching in the back again.

I opened to the section on egg retrieval. "First, I'd be put on fertility drugs—"

"Fertility drugs? Isn't that, well, I mean, couldn't you—"

"Yes, fertility drugs often result in multiple embryos," I said, completing his thought, "but that's only an issue if the woman taking them is trying to get pregnant, which I'm not. Apparently, fertility drugs stimulate egg production, which is, after all, the whole idea. Then, let me see . . . 'under local anesthesia a needle aspirator attached to a transvaginal ultrasound transducer is inserted.'" I stopped reading when I noticed that the blood had drained from his face. "Well, you get the idea. It retrieves the follicles that contain the eggs that are placed in fluid, then *one* is mixed with the, ah, sperm—"

"That would be Jon's sperm."

"Presumably so."

"Uh-huh." He was gripping the steering wheel as tightly as a novice out for a driving test.

"And hopefully within, say, two days, fertilization takes place and the embryo is transferred into DeeDee's uterus, where it will spend the next nine months growing into a wonderful little baby."

"I see."

I reached over and patted his hand. "*Their* wonderful little baby. DeeDee and Jonathan's." He relaxed only slightly. "But, Sonny, you know Jonathan better than anyone, better even than DeeDee does." He nodded his agreement. "What do *you* think he'd say? Where is he with this whole fatherhood thing anyway?"

"You know he'd do anything for DeeDee. Like I'd do anything for you."

"Yes, Sonny, I know." It warmed my heart to hear him say it.

"Including having a child. And not just for Dee. I think Jon would really be a good dad if it comes to that. But I have to confess, *this* conversation never came up."

No. I had little doubt of that. "But what if it did?"

He gripped the wheel again. "I've got to tell you, babe, the whole thing seems very, well, like you and Jon would be making this baby," he said, diving right in. "That's what I think he would think."

Put in those words, it sounded scandalous. I closed the library book, laid it on my lap, and placed my folded hands on top of it.

"Besides," he continued, "wouldn't it mean that you and I couldn't . . . you know . . . *be together* during this process? How long would the whole thing take, anyway, with the fertility drugs and all?"

He was right. I looked out the passenger side window. "Well, then."

Immediately, he began to relent. "Sweetheart—"

I held up a hand to stop him. "No, Sonny, you're right. The idea is far too futuristic. At least for us. If DeeDee and Jonathan want a baby, they'll just have to find a way to have one on their own."

He relaxed a whole lot more at that. "Are you sure?"

Oh yes, I was sure. Honestly, what had I been thinking? This wasn't like giving someone a pint of blood or donating a kidney. This was exactly what Sonny said it was: making a baby with your best friend's husband. And he was right; it would be better if this was never mentioned again.

The Oregon coast was nothing like what I pictured when I thought of the beach. There were no barely clad bodies nestled in the sand, hungry for an unhealthy dose of UVs. No surfing, no volleyball, nothing like you'd see in southern California, where my parents had taken Dee and me for vacation in borrowed time-shares two years in a row. Once to Laguna, then to San Diego.

No, the Oregon coastline was not the place for sun worshipers and sand architects. The wind whipped at my jacket, my hair. And it was *cold*. But what the coastline lacked in beach appeal, it made up for in visual effects. It was spectacular in scope, awesome in power. Technicolor beauty unaffected by L.A. smog.

So one of us delighted in the following eight days, and one of us, I regret to say, only pretended to. In spite of the scenery, in spite of the company, my heart wouldn't stop hurting. I felt like a fragile little starfish at the mercy of the waves, helpless to control my own emotions. The sight of a baby could bring me to tears, and I didn't even want one! Not for myself. But I did want one for DeeDee. And if I could help make her wish come true, well, what was the harm in that? Perhaps plenty. I felt as if I was playing a mental game of ping-pong with myself, and no one was winning. It was all I could think of, night and day. Pro one moment, con the next.

And yet, here I was, forty myself. For all I knew, I could be as eggless as DeeDee. And then what? I could have gotten us all worked up for nothing. Or she might truly prefer the likes of Meg Ryan to someone like me.

Oh yes. Sonny was right. This was better left alone.

11

"Dinner? Tonight?" I had just gotten the suitcases unpacked and was about to tackle the chore of vacation laundry when DeeDee called to invite us over to eat. "I don't know, Dee, I'm exhausted. Maybe tomorrow?"

Her voice became enticing. "I'm making that wonderful little pasta dish you like so well. The one with all the cheeses—"

"And the basil and the cream?"

"And the pretty little shells."

This was one of exactly three dishes DeeDee could take pride in. So it was settled then. "What time?" As if I had to ask.

I could hear the smile in her voice. "Jonathan should be home by six."

"Sonny too. He barely helped me get the car unloaded before he headed for the office, *just to check the mail.* As if Jonathan would let it pile up."

"It's a guy thing. Whether they admit it or not, that business is their baby."

Oh, there was that word again!

"So don't wait to come. Sonny can follow Jonathan over and join you here. I've missed you." Her voice sounded as if she truly meant it.

"Me too."

Oh yes, we were connected at the hip. And the heart. But I hadn't called her once during my vacation. I know she took that to mean I was having a wonderful time, but in truth, I was afraid to call. She, like my mother, always knew immediately when something was wrong. And mean to or not, I'd end up telling her what was on my mind, and that was the last thing I wanted to do. For tonight, I hoped she would blame my melancholy mood on exhaustion. But somehow—and soon—I had to come to terms with my and Sonny's decision not to interfere with her and Jonathan's reproductive dilemma. My eggs, if I had any, would stay right where they were. End of story.

"Was it a long drive home?" DeeDee handed me a frosty glass of 7UP and cranberry juice with crushed ice, one of my favorite summer drinks. It looked lovely and inviting. I put the straw to my lips and took a long sip.

"Not terribly," I said, stifling a yawn, "but it's always so delicious coming home." We were out on her patio enjoying the mild June afternoon. Summer, it seemed, was not in a hurry to make an appearance. When it did, we would have a string of one-hundred-degree days that would zap the energy right out of me, but for now a breeze rustled the leaves of the pepper tree and wafted the scent of the neighbor's jasmine our way. "Oh, this is heaven," I said, feeling its feathery softness tickle my skin.

"Exactly." DeeDee lifted her glass in a little salute and raised it to her lips.

I laid my head back and closed my eyes. "Why is it that no

matter where I go, I love coming back to the valley? I mean, we've seen some of the most fabulous scenery the past few days. The red-woods, the ocean all shimmery and gold and smelling of brine, a sky so billowy and blue you wanted to crawl in and take a nap. Yet nothing compares."

"It's home."

She was right. Pure and simple. "You feel that way too?"

"Of course," she said, surprising me. DeeDee was so unsentimental most of the time that I didn't really think she would understand. "I love this valley, with all the vineyards, the farms, the orchards. In the spring especially, from overhead, it looks like a patchwork quilt, a lovely and priceless work of art. Whatever talents we think we have don't begin to compare with God's handiwork."

"The heavens declare the glory of God," I quoted from the Psalms.

"Yes, they do. And you're right. Nothing compares to home."

"Not even Paris?" I ventured.

DeeDee was silent for so long I thought she hadn't heard. Then she said, more to herself than to me, "I've had some disappointments."

I sat up and opened my eyes. Her eyes were turned away, toward the fountain with the lily pads, but I knew they were filled with longing. And not just for Paris. "Dee . . . Dee?"

"How could someone have such a change of heart?" she whispered. "Especially me?" She turned and looked at me with the strength I had always admired in her. "I always knew just what I wanted. What happened?"

"What did happen, Dee? You were always so adamant about not wanting to bring a child into this messed-up world. And when I really thought about it, it made perfect sense to me."

"Then it wasn't *my* conviction that kept you and Sonny from having a child?"

"Never."

"I've been so afraid lately that I may have interfered with the most important decision you and Sonny could ever make as a couple. And the awful part is, I never thought to ask if your decision was based on the way you felt or the way I thought you should feel."

I was touched by how guilty she looked. "We both know I've always been influenced by you, Dee, but only when it came to choices that *I* had to make. When those choices affected both Sonny and me, it was a whole different story. We talked about it and prayed about it and came to our own conclusion. So will you finally tell me why you so suddenly changed your mind?"

She looked away and seemed at last to focus on something a long way off. "My earliest memories from when I was, I don't know, maybe three were of my mom and dad arguing. Incessantly. They didn't yell or throw things or hurt each other in the physical sense, but I don't have a single memory of a kind exchange between them. Not one. I had no clue that marriage, *home*, was supposed to be peaceful, until I met your family."

My eyes filled with tears, which I furiously blinked away lest she see, but I needn't have bothered. DeeDee continued to stare off into the distance, as if it were a window to the past, and her face reflected the sorrow of the scene only she could see.

"When they separated, it was . . ." She shrugged. "A relief. Or it would have been, but my mom was so sad, and my dad was so *gone*. And I felt so cheated. It simply wasn't right that they brought me into this world and then refused to allow us to remain a family. They owed me that, don't you think? To have tried harder?" She looked over at me, and I quickly nodded. "It was their choice to stop loving each other. If I've learned anything in my life, I've learned that love is a choice. And I learned it from your dad."

I nodded, my eyes tearing up again. As far back as I could remember, he had taught me, and apparently DeeDee as well, that a person loved because he chose to love. Regardless of whether or not he was loved in return. Because that's how God loves. Unconditionally. It was the most valuable tool I'd brought to my marriage.

"But I'm the one who was cheated," DeeDee said with a mixture of sadness and resentment. The bitterness had waned over the years but wasn't entirely gone. "And so I was afraid. Afraid to create a child I might fail the way they failed me. And that's the sad and simple truth.

"But to answer your question, I began to realize I was more afraid of the empty little place I had left in this world by not creating that child. It was like I held the final piece of a beautiful puzzle and I wouldn't give it up. The picture still made sense, but it wasn't complete. And I could almost touch the void, it had become so real." She drew in a breath and let it out with a sad little laugh. "And now, two years later . . ." She shrugged.

I couldn't stand it anymore. "Dee, what would you say if I told you I wanted to give you my eggs?"

Her eyes grew enormous. "You mean as in *eggs*?"

"I know a donor is supposed to be younger. If you even wanted a donor. And I don't look at all like Meg Ryan. But it would be the joy of my life to help you and Jonathan have a baby." There. I'd said it, and there was no taking it back.

"Meg Ryan?"

"You told Dr. Creager—"

She looked totally confused, and then the light came on. "It was a joke, Gabby. Just a silly little joke."

I felt my face turn as red as a radish. "Then you wouldn't . . . you're not . . . well, I mean, interested?"

She gave me a look that touched a deep place in my heart. "You would do that for me?"

"Oh, Dee, you know I would." I moved to the edge of my chair and reached for her hands. "I'd do anything for you." My eyes filled up again and there was no stopping it.

"You would," she said, almost guiltily.

"And you'd do anything for me, whether you realize it or not."

"Would I? Would I really?" She withdrew her hands and sat back in her seat. "I'm selfish and willful and stubborn and spoiled. You're the giver; I'm the taker. It's always been that way, even when I don't mean it to be. Honestly, I don't deserve you or Jonathan or even my mother. Everyone's indulged me all my life."

"That's because you're a hard person to say no to." I smiled and blinked away my tears.

"That's what I mean. I'm a bully."

"Yes," I agreed, and almost laughed at how wounded she suddenly looked. "But what would I be without you?"

She looked away, dejected. "Unrepressed."

I stifled a smile. "Dee, you gave me my identity. Without you I'd just be plain old Angel Whitaker, and I wouldn't even know how pathetic that was."

She sniffed. "You were never pathetic. A little high and mighty, perhaps."

"A little? I was constantly checking the mirror to make sure my halo hadn't slipped. I walked around with an attitude that said, *Look at me, I'm an angel*. I reeked of pomposity."

"Okay, maybe you were a little pathetic, but at least you didn't bully people into giving up their individuality."

"Nor did you."

She raised an eyebrow and looked away.

"You didn't. Dee. Look at me." She took her time in responding. "You have a strong personality, yes. That doesn't make you overbearing, *exactly*."

"See? See there?"

"Oh, let's face it," I said matter-of-factly. "We are who we are. So what's the problem? I don't mind if you don't."

"You don't?"

I shook my head.

"And you'd really do this for me?" She looked hopeful, almost eager.

"I would. Gladly." I emphasized my answer with a nod.

"Have you prayed? No — "she held up a hand — "let me rephrase that. I know you've prayed, but have you waited for an answer?"

An answer? That was the tricky part.

Just then the phone rang, and DeeDee ran into the kitchen to fetch the cordless.

Yes, I had prayed. Earnestly. And, like my dad had taught me, I asked God to use me to help if I could. The next thing I know I'm heaven-bent on giving DeeDee my eggs. Was that an answer to prayer or a friend sticking her fertility ability in where it didn't belong? Her guess was as good as mine.

She returned with an inscrutable look on her face. "Can I give you my answer later?"

"Absolutely. I know you'll want to talk to Jonathan."

"Jonathan. Right."

And I was going to have to come up with a way to break this to Sonny. "What do you think Jonathan'll say?"

"About what?" Jonathan said from the open kitchen slider, startling me severely.

He walked to the back of DeeDee's chair, bent over, and kissed her on the nose. "Hey, beautiful." Then he wrapped an arm around me as I stood to receive his greeting. "Welcome home. Sonny said you two had a terrific time. You look—" He held me at arm's length and studied me. "Are you okay?"

"Great," I said, forcing a smile.

Sonny stood in the doorway. "Why wouldn't she be, after a week of R & R? Mmm. Something smells like real home cooking in here. Eight days of restaurant food was more than enough for me."

DeeDee rose from the patio chair. "We'll just toss the salad and stick the bread under the broiler, and dinner will be served. Follow me," she said, and I did.

As we worked in the kitchen, under the noses of our hungry husbands, DeeDee asked me with the look of her eyes, *Is it safe to discuss?* I gave her a definite *no* as I pulled the bread from the oven. She responded with the slightest nod, then placed the bubbly pasta dish in the center of the table. She left the oven mitt on her hand. "I'll serve your plates. This is far too hot to handle."

It's not the only thing. How do I get myself into these situations?

"Ooh," Sonny moaned as if he'd died and gone to heaven. "That smells out of this world. Jonathan, pray and let's eat."

We all took hands and bowed our heads as Jonathan thanked the Lord for His grace and provision. Then, as DeeDee began to dish up our plates, he rubbed his hands together. "Be generous. And speaking of generous . . ." He waited until he had our attention. "Sonny and I had the most remarkable conversation today." He smiled as if harboring a delicious secret. "Do you want to tell them, or should I?"

"Be my guest." Sonny dug his fork into his pasta and raised it to his lips. I saw that his face had taken on an expression that nearly matched Jonathan's.

DeeDee laid her fork beside her plate. "What's up?"

Jonathan shot Sonny a devious look. "Maybe we should save it for later. To go with dessert." He stuffed a fork full of cheesy pasta shells in his mouth.

"Nothing doing. Chew up and let's have it."

"Well," Jonathan said as Sonny reached over and laid his hand lightly on mine, "you remember back before Paris when I went with you to see Dr. Creager, and she said when it got right down to it we had three choices for our situation? We could A, adopt; B, use a donor or surrogate to instigate pregnancy—"

"Instigate?"

"Well, I'm not up on all the terminology, but you know what I mean. Or, C, we could be content with our family just the way it is. To be candid, I was perfectly happy to be content with our family just the way it is, just as I always have been, until today."

"What happened today?" I asked in a small voice, beginning to think I just might know the answer. The pressure of Sonny's hand increased ever so slightly.

"The meaning of friendship became more real than ever before. That's what happened today."

"Could you be a little more specific?" DeeDee held her thumb and forefinger up, as if registering the teeniest measurement. "For those of us with inquiring minds."

Jonathan turned to Sonny. "You sure you don't want to take it from here?"

"You're doing just fine." He reached for a toasty slice of garlic bread.

"Well, when Dr. Creager mentioned that you could possibly sustain a pregnancy—is that the right term? Sustain?"

"I believe so."

". . . where the embryo is a product of my sperm and a donor's egg, I thought there was only one person in the world we would ever consider for a donor, and, well, that was you, Gabby. But it's not the kind of thing you bring up in everyday conversation, if you know what I mean. Unless you're Sonny."

I shifted my eyes from Jonathan to my husband. "Unless you're Sonny?"

"He didn't have any problem bringing it up at all. He came into the office, sat down, and said, in these exact words, 'Jon, I had the shock of my life this week, but now that I've had time to think about it, I don't feel I can dismiss it summarily without talking to you about it first.' I said, 'Shoot, buddy.' He said—well, Gabby, you know perfectly well what he said. And, honestly, I'm—" He placed a hand over his heart and said no more.

Confusion spread across DeeDee's face. "How could she know what he said? She wasn't there; she was here with me. Jonathan, what *are* you talking about?"

Sonny cleared his throat, then laid his fork aside, looking as pleased as could be. "We want to give you our eggs."

We? We do?

I looked at Sonny, who looked at Jonathan, who looked at DeeDee, who looked at me. We were one mass of amazement.

"Well, this is one of the most interesting conversations I've had in my life." DeeDee's eyes said a huge thank you. "But—and I don't say this lightly—the answer has to be no."

No? The spell was broken and, with it, my spirits. "Don't you want to think about it?" I looked from her to Jonathan. "Talk about it? You know, together?"

Jonathan's brows joined together in a frown. His face, like mine, I'm sure, reflected a hundred questions. "I know we need to pray about this, babe. There are a lot of things to consider. And maybe it's not something we'll actually do. But like Gabby said, shouldn't we at least talk about it?" He left off with a shrug.

"Yes, it would certainly be something to pray about. I don't really know where I stand on the issue or, more important, what the biblical stance is."

Well, she might have told me that a half hour ago.

"But that isn't the main reason." DeeDee picked up her fork and took a bite of her pasta. She chewed it thoughtfully, then washed it down with a sip of tea. "The fact is, there's no room in the womb." She gave in to a little chuckle, as if enjoying her own private joke.

"Excuse me?" Jonathan said, as Sonny and I mumbled our own expressions of confusion.

"No room. I just got the call." She locked eyes with her husband and gave him a smile that said it all. "It seems the space is already occupied."

12

Jonathan coughed and pounded his chest as if to get his heart started again. "You're . . . we're pregnant?"

DeeDee smiled coyly at Jonathan, then gave me a wink. "Seems I won't have to borrow an egg after all."

All at once we were up, hugging each other and squealing. Sonny gave Jonathan a high five with one hand and then the other. "Way to go!"

For a second it looked as if they were playing patty-cake, not like children on the playground, but like Larry, Moe, and Curly. I half-expected them to do head butts. The sight of it pulled laughter from deep inside me. Pure, rich, and contagious. We laughed with such vigor we were in danger of hurting ourselves. Joy was so thick in the room it felt like clouds you could float on.

Pregnant!

Jonathan had DeeDee in his arms and was twirling her around the dining room. "We're gonna have a baby. We're gonna have a baby! When?"

She was laughing so hard she could barely reply. "Are you ready for this?"

We all stopped and waited.

"Valentine's Day! Do you believe that?"

I began counting on my fingers. "Then you're—"

"*Four* weeks pregnant." DeeDee waited for that to sink in.

I did the math. "You mean—"

"Paris?" Evidently Jonathan did the math too.

"Paris." DeeDee practically purred.

Sonny's face took on a crimson glow. "That's a little more than I wanted to know."

DeeDee just continued to laugh. Then she hugged me. "I couldn't say anything before Jonathan knew," she whispered into my ear. "Forgive me?"

"Of course." I stopped and drew in a much-needed breath, while my heart continued to do the bossa nova inside my chest. Only then did I comprehend DeeDee's words, *I won't have to borrow an egg after all*. Not have to borrow an egg? That meant—Oh. I reached for a chair, weak with relief and a little ashamed because of it. That meant no egg donation. Which meant no egg retrieval. Which meant *no needle aspirator attached to a transvaginal ultrasound transducer*. Ashamed or not, I could have turned cartwheels!

Pregnant!

My book was going back to the library first thing in the morning.

"Now we need to tell our parents. But I want to come up with something creative. I don't want our announcement to be boring."

That would be unthinkable.

She turned to me. "Do you remember Debbie Carter?"

I nodded. Unlike Bonnie Singer, Debbie was for real. And

I remembered the announcement. But DeeDee told about it for the benefit of the guys. "When they found out they were expecting—"she paused and touched Jonathan's arm—"it was so cool. They had their parents over for dinner, and then at the end of the meal they handed out these little prescription bottles."

Jonathan frowned. "Prescription bottles?"

Sonny looked equally confused. "Heart medicine? Just in case?"

DeeDee ignored them both. "Inside was a little note that said something to the effect that they were officially waiting for the arrival of Carter's Little Pill. Isn't that clever?"

"Carter's little pill?" Jonathan didn't get it. By the way Sonny was shaking his head, I could tell he didn't get it either.

"You know," I said, helping her out, "Carter's Little Pill." As if that would clear things right up.

"It was a commercial for—" DeeDee looked to me for help.

"Something," I said. "Well, I don't remember what it was for, but—"

"Liver! It was a liver pill."

I gave her a thumbs-up. "Right! Liver."

Now the guys looked really confused. "What on earth does a liver pill have to do with having a baby?"

"It's not the pill. You're missing the point here, Jonathan." DeeDee rubbed her forehead.

I stepped in again. "You know how children are sometimes referred to as pills? You know, like, 'Oh, what a little pill he is'?"

Sonny gave us a sideways glance. "Like birth control that didn't?"

Now I was rubbing my forehead. "Never mind."

"It was clever. Trust me."

"Well, since we don't have a *clever* name like Carter . . ."

Jonathan stopped and gave Sonny a conspiratorial wink, then turned back to DeeDee. "What do you propose?"

"We could change our name."

"And short of that?"

"Well, I do have a thought. We'll have a dinner for Mom, and Margie of course." She stopped and looked at Jonathan. "I suppose your parents won't be able to come?"

"It's a long drive from Bellingham. We'll have to come up with something clever from afar."

"I'll work on that, but back to the dinner. Here's the menu." She produced a piece of notepaper with a flourish. "We'll have *baby* back ribs, barbecued. *Baby* carrots. *Baby* red potatoes. On baby pink paper plates. And for dessert . . ." She actually giggled. "Baby Ruths! We'll see how long it takes them to figure it out. It'll be like Clue."

Sonny raised an eyebrow. "Somebody dies?"

"Well, then, I Have a Secret."

"Yeah. Better. Does someone get a prize for guessing? A trip or something?"

"Baby pink?" Jonathan said. "*Pink?* You're sure?"

"Is anyone taking this seriously?"

Sonny turned serious at that. "Hey, Jon. You're going to be a dad."

Jonathan lowered himself onto a chair, a dazed look on his face. Then he smiled. "Yeah. I am."

DeeDee sat on his lap, wrapped her arms around his neck, and kissed him on the lips. "A dad. Wow."

Then Jonathan crooked his head and gave DeeDee a thoughtful look. "Speaking of dads, are you going to tell yours?"

My breath caught in my throat. Could he really have said what I thought he said?

DeeDee pulled back, her face void of expression. All the festivity flapped out of the room like a balloon filled to capacity that was let go without being tied. "Why on earth would I do that?"

"I just thought, well, he is your dad."

"He stopped being my dad when I was eleven." She stood and moved away. "His choice, not mine."

"Sweetheart, you have to forgive him eventually."

"Yeah. I'll get to work on that. Right after I draft a Middle East peace plan." She returned to her notepad, her actions declaring the subject closed.

Jonathan's parents lived in Washington, near the Canadian border. They were in their late eighties, and while they were still relatively healthy and able to care for themselves, Jonathan was right, a drive down to California was out of the question. He placed a call to them early one Sunday morning before church.

"Just as I stepped into the shower," DeeDee told me quietly when the four of us were at lunch that afternoon. The guys were engaged in their own conversation. It was baseball season again. "Jonathan wanted to be sure he was the one to tell them."

"What did they say?"

"He said they were reservedly supportive."

"Reservedly?"

"The truth is, they would have liked to be grandparents twenty years ago. Now, because of their ages, there's a lot they'll miss."

Jonathan cut into our conversation. "They didn't *exactly* say that, but you could read between the lines. But they waited so long to get married and have kids that they were in their forties when I was born. If we followed suit, this was the logical outcome."

"In their forties." DeeDee became introspective all of a sudden. "Like we'll be. Was that a drawback, having parents on the older side?"

"No," he said with a shrug. "I guess this is really the first time that their age has become a factor, with grandparenthood on the horizon." He smiled and touched DeeDee's hand. "Don't turn serious on me now, goose. After the baby comes, we'll fly them down here and they can stay a month if they'd like. That should give them a good dose of grandparenting. Think you can stand it?"

Her eyes grew large. "A month? Of your mother's cooking? We'll both be as big as a house when it's all over."

"Maybe we can keep her out of the kitchen," Jonathan said, without conviction.

"Fat chance." DeeDee laughed at her little pun.

Sonny perked up. "You can send her over to our house. She sounds like my kind of woman."

I suddenly became defensive. "I feed you."

"Ye-ess. But when was the last time you baked homemade chocolate chip cookies with real butter?"

"Do women *do* that anymore?"

DeeDee rolled her eyes. "Only the ones who don't know we got the vote."

Sonny let her comment pass. "How come your sister never had kids?"

Jonathan shrugged. "Janine was always too busy, I guess. Professor of higher education, school board trustee, always sitting on some committee or another, and on and on and on. Plus, she and Colin were only married for three or four years, a casualty of their careers. It's too bad. Colin was a nice guy. I think. Actually, when you get right down to it, I didn't know him well at all."

13

On Monday morning I called my mother and invited her to join me for a late breakfast.

"What's on your mind?" she asked.

Honestly, if I believed in such things, I'd think she had a sixth sense. "Just breakfast." That wasn't the truth at all. I don't know why, but I wanted to be the one to tell her about DeeDee. "Say in an hour?"

I waited until the dishes were cleared and we were enjoying a cup of our favorite tea.

"What a lovely breakfast. I enjoyed it immensely. Now, tell me. What's the occasion?"

"Occasion?" It was only yogurt and granola and store-bought muffins the size of Connecticut, but she saw right through it. "Well, okay. You'll never guess."

"Must I try?"

"It's the most exciting thing." I took a deep breath and dove right in. "DeeDee's pregnant."

She was speechless for a moment, then she broke into the loveliest smile. "Linda's going to be a grandmother," she declared. "Oh gosh, Linda's going to be a *grand*mother." She set her cup down. "How do you think she'll take it?"

"You know Linda. Everything's a crisis before it's a celebration. She'll come around."

"Oh my. The changes this is going to bring." Mom picked up her teacup and stared into it thoughtfully. "Now, why don't you tell me what else is on your mind."

Busted. Like when I was fifteen and Brad Parker talked me into letting him come over to the house where I was babysitting. Both children were in bed asleep, and the Bagwells weren't due back until midnight. At nine thirty he knocked on the door, as planned. I led him into the den where I was watching *The Bad News Bears* on the Bagwells' big-screen TV. Big meaning larger than our twenty-one-inch Magnavox.

I could feel my pulse beating in my temples, not because Brad Parker was sitting on the couch beside me — though any other time that would have been the event of the century — but because I was immersed in guilt. It was positively against the rules — the Bagwells' and my mom's.

When Brad scooted over and put his arm around me, my scalp began to sweat. I turned to tell him I'd get us a root beer, just to put some space between us, when I saw his eyes close and his lips head for mine. He misjudged, and his mouth landed between my nose and upper lip. I pulled back with such force that his body got caught in the wake and his chin ended up on my chest. I yelped and pushed him away.

"No," he said, his voice a squeak. "It's not like . . . I didn't mean . . ."

"Out!"

"Honestly, Gab, I—"

"Go! Now!"

He snatched up his jacket and shrugged himself into it, his cheeks as red as cherry popsicles. "Well, what did you expect when you asked me over?"

What indeed? I had to grab the front door to keep it from slamming.

Shuddering, mostly from relief, I fell onto the sofa. The Bad News Bears had just struck out. And so had Brad Parker.

Mother always waited up till I got home, a fact that brought me nothing but angst that night. She knew the minute she saw me that I was holding something inside. Twenty-five years later, the same look was on her face as I sat across the table from her, playing with my teacup.

"Well." I shrugged, not knowing where to begin.

She sipped her tea and waited.

"You know what DeeDee's been through trying to conceive." We'd all trudged this road together, and it had fairly worn us out. "Well . . ." I didn't know how to put it into words. "You know Dad's signature prayer, 'Lord, intervene, someway, somehow. And use me to help if you can.'"

We said it in unison, she with a smile, and me barely able to choke the words out. My throat grew thick with tears, and I had to stop. She handed me a tissue and waited.

"Well," I said yet again. "I got this . . . idea." Why was this so incredibly hard? "That I should *do* something."

"Mmm-hmm."

"And so Sonny and I talked and it just seemed to make sense, though Sonny didn't think so at first, but he finally came around and I just couldn't believe it when he said we should, and I wondered how this would work when I don't look a thing like Meg Ryan."

She crossed her arms and cupped her chin in one hand. "Meg Ryan?"

I sighed deeply, then poured a second helping of boiling water into our cups and plunked a tea bag back and forth between them. "So what do you think?"

Her eyebrows disappeared behind her bangs. "About?"

I was going to have to do this again? My hands were suddenly icy. I rubbed them together and gave her what had to be a pathetic look.

"Um, sweetheart, I think you left something out."

"It must have been the part about the egg."

"The egg?"

My nod was noncommittal. "I was going to give her one." Suddenly it seemed like an extremely unconventional thing to do. Undoubtedly because it was.

She blinked once, slowly, then leaned back in her chair with the most unreadable look on her face. "Well." She reached for her mug, held it to her lips without drinking, then placed it back on the coaster. "Really."

"Sonny and I talked about it on our vacation. And at first he was like, 'No way.' Then all of a sudden he was like, 'Okay.' And so I thought I'll do this. I really will. And then DeeDee makes this grand announcement, 'No room in the womb.'"

"No room in the womb?"

I gave her a feeble, one-syllable laugh. "That's what she said, 'No room.' And so I thought, well, there's the answer to my prayer. And I couldn't help but wonder—"I reached for a tissue as my eyes filled with tears—"was my offer a good thing or a bad thing? In my mind I feel like a shuttlecock being whacked back and forth over the net."

Mother leaned into the table, resting her chin in the palm of her hand. "Mmm. Well. It's a new world, that's for sure."

"It is, isn't it? That's what I mean. It's so hard to know what's *right*. What do you think Dad would say? What do *you* say?"

She was silent so long I thought perhaps she meant not to answer. Then she said, "Of course, the real question is, what does God say?"

I held my breath in anticipation. Without knowing it, that's what I was waiting for. Wisdom from on high. And Mom was just the one to deliver it. She reached for her tote, as opposed to a purse, which she seldom carried, and pulled out her Bible. Instantly, the weight I'd been carrying lifted. Because Mom would open her Bible to just the right verse and declare, "Thus saith the Lord." And that would be that.

I determined then and there, for at least the hundredth time, that my Bible needed to look like her Bible. With a cover so worn you couldn't read the name she'd had engraved on it immediately after marrying my dad. Because breaking in a new Bible was completely out of the question. I needed to have pages falling out, even missing, because of use. And margins so full of notes that I'd have to break down and write my own commentary because there simply wasn't room on the pages for more.

As it was, my burgundy, genuine leather, gold-edged, red-letter edition had carefully underlined passages, like John 3:16 and Romans 8:28, made with black ink and a straight edge so the lines wouldn't look out of place on the page. They were passages that practically everyone could recite from memory. But the nuggets that Mother had excavated over the years remained hidden in my own well-preserved manual on life. I was like a baby robin, waiting in the nest for Mama to bring me the worm.

Pathetic.

Well, I'd take this worm gladly and then begin this very day my own excavation in earnest. It was certainly time.

I watched her lips, as if I'd actually see the words as they were spoken. As if I had a basket to put them in to carry them home.

"I have to tell you, I really don't know."

Don't know? That's not what I expected to hear. I shrank in my chair like a spoiled toddler, my shoulders caving in on my chest.

"Sweetheart, there are some things that aren't written in black and white, and I think this is one of them. So you take the accumulation of knowledge you manage to gain, mixed in with common sense, and you weigh it against that still, small voice you can only hear with your heart. Then you depend on grace to compensate for the mistakes." She gave a gentle shrug. "You know, David was called a man after God's own heart not because he got it right all the time but because he desired to get it right all the time. I believe the Lord gave us that example to show us that's all He asks of any of us."

The tears continued to trickle down my face.

"It's a remarkable world when one woman can help another couple have a child." Her voice caught in her throat, and this time it was her eyes that filled with tears. "That you would do that, give that kind of gift—I don't know what to say. There was a time I would have given anything to have a friend like you." Only her eyes conveyed the deep and enduring passion behind the words. As I looked at her, she read the question in my eyes. "I tried for the longest time to have a child, with no success. I had two miscarriages, one right after the other, after several years of trying to conceive. And, of course, in those days there were no fertility specialists or in vitro fertilization or any of the incredible things they can do today. At least none that we knew about or could have afforded if they were available. My doctor advised me to give up trying for the sake of my physical and emotional well-being. Your dad agreed, only because he was so concerned."

I held my breath and waited for the unthinkable truth to be told. "You mean . . . are you saying . . . I was—" DeeDee had been right!

My mother smiled and then chuckled as she shook her head. "No, sweetheart, you were not adopted, if that's what you mean."

I felt myself blush, even as relief rushed to slow my pounding heart.

"When I realized I was pregnant for a third time, I didn't tell anyone, not even your father. I didn't think I could stand any more pity if I were to miscarry again. So I kept my little secret all to myself. Then one night after church your dad had to meet with someone for counseling or something—I don't remember now. So I waited in the sanctuary, alone . . . except for the sweet presence of the Lord. I began to pray and to weep as if my heart would break, and suddenly I was overcome with the most divine peace. It felt as if an old quilt of my grandmother's had been placed over my shoulders, wrapping me in love and security. I could almost smell the cotton and feel the tiny stitches, and I actually reached up to see if it were there." She touched her shoulder as she might have done that night. "Well, there was no lightning bolt from heaven, but I knew—I *knew*—I would have that baby. And I did." She rested a strong and loving hand on mine. "I was all of twenty-five when you were born, but six years of barrenness had seemed an eternity."

"I never knew."

"I knew eventually there would be a right time to tell you."

All at once I began to sob. "Oh, Mother, have I been terribly selfish?"

"Selfish? Honey, whatever do you mean?"

"By not having a baby?"

"Oh, Angel. You don't have a child to please someone else. You did what was right for you and Sonny. And how could anyone think of you as selfish, considering this wonderful thing you were willing to do?"

I wiped my nose and dabbed at eyes that wouldn't stop crying. "Wonderful? Was it really?"

"Just ask DeeDee. She thinks you're an—" She stopped and smiled and patted my hand. "An angel."

I laughed through my tears and hiccuped. "Yes. With a sword and everything."

"With a sword and everything."

Her words were soothing and, as always, just what I needed to hear. When at last I trusted my voice, I said, "You would have made a remarkable grandmother."

"And I intend to now. In an extended sort of way, of course." She gave a wry smile. "You don't think DeeDee would mind, do you?"

"Mind? Just let her try." I stood and hugged her and thanked the Lord once again for making this unbelievable woman my mother. "Oh, and, Mom," I said, in an effort to change the emotionally charged atmosphere, "we're going to have the most preposterous announcement dinner you ever saw. Act surprised."

It took place at my house the evening of the day DeeDee had her first prenatal appointment with Dr. Creager, and it was the pinkest affair in history. My mother arrived early, as she always did, to help with last-minute preparations, like tearing salad greens and filling the saltshaker. I appreciated the extra set of hands, which always came in, well, handy. She wore a smile that simply wouldn't disappear, and twice I heard her humming "Brahms' Lullaby."

"Mom, that's a dead giveaway. I'm glad no one else is here yet."

As if on cue, DeeDee and Jonathan came through the front door. "We're here!"

"In the kitchen!" I called.

Jonathan carried a pan full of marinating ribs, which he handed off to me. I could smell the barbecue sauce even through the Saran wrap. Yum.

"Hey, Margie!" Jonathan and DeeDee took turns giving my mom a big hug.

"Sonny's out back firing up the grill," I said to Jonathan, as I frowned at the pink bakery box DeeDee carried.

She hiked her eyebrows a couple of times. "Something special."

My frown deepened. "You can put it on the refrigerator shelf. Right next to the lemon meringue pie I baked." *With lemons I picked from my very own tree.*

"Oh. You made the crust and everything?"

I nodded and shrugged at the same time.

"I guess I should have called."

"It's okay," I said in a tone meaning it was anything but. "If I know the guys, they won't mind two desserts. And I can send some pie home with everyone. So what's in the box?"

"It's a surprise." She slapped away my reaching hand. "Even for you." There was a gleam in her eye and something downright devilish about her smile. "So when's dinner? I'm starved." She stepped close and whispered, "I threw up my breakfast and my lunch." She said it as if it were an accomplishment. "Of course, it didn't help that all I wanted was olive loaf on toast."

"DeeDee, you hate olive loaf."

"And therein lies the problem. So when do we eat?"

I reached into the refrigerator and pulled out the dish. "I'll have Sonny start the ribs right now."

Linda arrived late, as usual. A real-estate closing had kept her far longer than she'd expected. She rushed in, then stopped dead in her tracks. Her purse, hanging from a shoulder strap at her side, swayed back and forth like a pendulum. She looked from the pink and white balloons to the pink and white carnations to the pink and white crepe paper streamers hung around the room, as if waiting for someone to yell, "Surprise!"

"Someone's birthday?" I could almost see her checking off a mental calendar to make sure she hadn't forgotten something really important. Like the commemoration of the day her only child had been born. But this was June, not March. I could see her take a breath of relief.

DeeDee handed her a cup of baby pink punch. "Hope you're hungry."

Linda murmured something intangible and slipped off her shoes. It appeared to have been a long day for her, and it wasn't over by a long shot. When she saw my mother, hidden behind a spray of balloons, she smiled a relieved kind of smile and made her way to where she stood. Linda whispered something as she gave her a little hug, but Mom's only reply was an almost imperceptible shrug. I had to hand it to her, she was playing along beautifully.

I called everyone to the dining room, and as we were being seated, DeeDee said, "Jonathan, *baby*, would you say the blessing?" I was still amazed that she had gotten the guys to go along with this truly ridiculous plan. "Mother, Margie." She purred their names as she pointed to their pink plastic plates. "Just start with what's in front of you."

"Ribs," Mother said as she picked up the platter. "Smothered in sauce. My favorite."

"*Baby* back ribs," DeeDee corrected. "Mom, you can start the carr—*baby* carrots."

"I'll start the potatoes." I plopped three jawbreaker-size spuds onto my plate, foiling DeeDee's plans, I know, but you could carry something like this only so far. If it wasn't obvious that these potatoes, all three of which I could fit into my mouth in one bite, were *baby* potatoes, then the whole exercise was destined to be lost on our one unsuspecting guest anyway.

Linda stabbed at a potato with her fork, then studied it as if it might self-destruct at any moment. "I usually put these in a stew."

Touché!

Linda reached for her drink to wash down the potato when she noticed the Baby Ruth. It lay at the head of her place setting in a horizontal position, like a headstone. I read confusion on her face and a dawning awareness that something *big* was happening. I followed her eyes around the table as she spied the other five candy bars.

I have no idea when DeeDee placed them there and, in fact, was surprised she'd gone ahead and brought them.

"Dessert," DeeDee said, noticing her mom's glance. So what was the pink box all about?

Linda laid her fork on her plate, then folded her hands in front of her. "Okay, what's going on?"

"Going on?"

Linda shifted her gaze to her son-in-law. "Jonathan, maybe you can—" She stopped and at the moment of understanding sucked in half the room's oxygen. "You're not—" She looked stunned to her toes. "I mean, *are* you?"

"What would you say if I told you I was?" DeeDee was smiling like the little devil she was.

"Well, I . . . I don't know. I'd, well, I mean, after all these years?" She looked from her daughter to her son-in-law, whose face didn't reveal a thing. "Is that what all the balloons are about?"

DeeDee continued to smile.

"You mean you're going to—" She touched her own tummy involuntarily. "Have a *baby*? At *forty*?"

"We thought you might catch on with all of the hints. Both of you." DeeDee turned to include my mother, who pretended to be completely at a loss. "Are you surprised?"

Linda looked from her daughter to my mother, her mouth working like a dying fish.

"Is that a yes? Mom?"

"Is she breathing?" Jonathan half-rose from his chair, licking barbecue sauce off his fingers. Seeing that Linda wasn't turning blue, he sat back down.

"Water," Linda choked out. Sonny ran to the kitchen and fetched a bottle of Evian from the fridge. Linda drank thirstily, dabbing at the perspiration on her forehead with her hot pink napkin.

". . . and so you see," DeeDee concluded fifteen minutes later, "Paris is all that and more." She reached for Jonathan's hand and squeezed. "So, whadaya think of our surprise, *Grandma*?"

The color drained from Linda's face. Oh boy. This was going to take some getting used to.

DeeDee seemed not to notice. "I hope you all saved room for dessert. Gabby, I'll help you with the coffee."

I followed her dutifully to my kitchen.

"Shall we use the dessert plates I gave you for your birthday? They'll be perfect."

Yes. I had thought so too and had them sitting on the counter—right next to my glass-handled pie server. "DeeDee, what's in the box?"

"I told you, it's a surprise." She smiled a smile that irritated me all the way to my toes.

"I hope you don't have anything shocking planned," I said snippily, not caring if she noticed. "Your mother is already about to hyperventilate."

"Shocking? Don't be silly." She threw me a look of complete innocence, but the tone of her voice was not one bit reassuring. She reached into the refrigerator and pulled out the pink box. "The cups are on the table, aren't they?"

"Right next to the Baby Ruths."

"Then don't forget the coffee." She left me standing in the kitchen.

I grabbed the plates and the pot and hurried back to the dining room. DeeDee was making a show of placing the pink box on the table. It was from The Nutcracker Sweet, our town's fabulous—and pricey—bakery. Apparently she'd spared no expense for whatever this was.

Linda put on a brave face. "Whatever it is, it smells delicious."

Personally, I couldn't smell anything but the coffee . . . except maybe a trace of lemon.

"Oh, Gab." DeeDee threw me an apologetic look. *Contrived*, if you asked me. "We forgot the pie server. Would you mind?"

Yes, to be perfectly honest, I did mind. I had a beautiful homemade lemon meringue pie—her favorite, by the way—sitting ignored in my refrigerator, and she wanted to use *my* pie server to serve up something . . . *mass produced*?

I went for it as quickly as I could.

When I returned, she was cutting the tape on the sides of the box. She offered a tantalizing smile to those seated around the table. She took the pie server, then paused. "Maybe you'd all like to see it before I cut into it, hmm?"

I looked at the box out of the corner of one eye, my arms folded across my chest, while Sonny and Jonathan and Mother and Linda filled in beside and behind us. DeeDee lifted the top of the box, carefully, so no one could see its contents until she was ready. Then, with great fanfare, she brought out her favorite cut-glass cake plate, and on it was a . . . a what? A fuzzy black-and-white, 8x10 photograph. For dessert? For a moment we all wore the same puzzled look while DeeDee continued to smile. Then she said, "I'd like you all to meet You-Know-Who."

My mother gasped and brought a hand to her mouth, Linda dropped deadweight onto a chair, Sonny slipped an arm around my shoulder, and Jonathan took the picture from DeeDee as gingerly as if it were the baby herself. We all had tears in our eyes.

"My first ultrasound," DeeDee said, radiant and proud.

"This is our baby? Our little girl?"

"Well, Dr. Creager insists it's too early to tell, but what does she know?"

Indeed!

We took turns looking at a little white spot in a sea of black. None of us could find words to describe what was in our hearts. When it came round to me, all I could think was, *what a perfect little baby girl*. I loved her instantly.

Jonathan took DeeDee's hand and nodded for all of us to take the hand of the person standing beside us. Mother took Linda's left hand and I took her right, allowing her to remain seated between us. She didn't appear to have the strength to stand at the moment. Then Jonathan bowed his head and began to pray. "Heavenly Father, we are inexpressibly grateful for this child you have given us. We will love, protect, and care for her—or him—with every-thing in us." I let go of Mother's hand long enough to wipe away the tears that trickled down my cheeks. "All of us will. I promise. I know this baby is a gift from you, and I ask that you keep your hand of protection on both DeeDee and the baby. We commit this entire pregnancy to you, Lord. This little child, whoever he or she may be, is yours. We won't ever forget that. In the name of your own precious Son, Jesus. Amen."

We stood in a hushed little circle, contemplating as we sol-emnly passed around the picture. When the photo came back to DeeDee, she laid it on the table and held up the pie server. "Gabby, would you please go and get that beautiful lemon pie? It really is time for dessert."

14

In the wee hours of Monday, July 22, eight weeks into DeeDee's pregnancy, the bedside phone startled me from a dreamless sleep. Jonathan's worried voice on the other end of the line immediately set my stomach to churning. "I'm taking Dee to the emergency room. She's been throwing up since midnight. I think something's really wrong."

"I'll meet you there." I hung up the phone and grabbed for my clothes in the dark. Sonny sat up in bed and shielded his eyes as I clicked on the nightstand light. "It's DeeDee. She's sick. I'm meeting Jonathan at the hospital." I pulled my hair into a ponytail and slipped on my sandals. "I'll call you when I know anything," I said, scrambling to find my car keys. They were probably right where they always were, but in my nervous haste I just couldn't find them.

"Take mine," Sonny said, trying to disguise a worried frown. "Wait a minute—shouldn't I come with you?" He was really awake now and starting to crawl out from under the covers.

"No, Sonny. Really. You'll need to be fresh for your meeting with Nor-Cal Developers. Jonathan won't be in any shape to be there."

"Maybe I should cancel." He brought the bedside clock close enough to read without his glasses. It was 4:37.

"Sonny, I know how much you want to design their software. Just pray for Dee. Pray that she doesn't—" My voice broke off in a choked sob.

Sonny scrambled over the bed and hopped out on my side. "It'll be okay." He wrapped his arms around me and drew me close.

"God, please," I whispered, my breath falling on Sonny's neck, "don't let her lose this baby."

"It's too early to reach anyone at church to get the prayer chain started, but I'll call your mom. She knows how to reach heaven better than anyone I know." He kissed the top of my head, then sent me on my way. "Call as soon as you know anything."

In spite of urging him to go back to bed, I knew there would be no more sleep for Sonny. He'd call my mom, then hit his knees until the alarm went off. No wonder I loved this man.

I made a mad dash out of our driveway, rolled through the stop sign at the corner of our street, and sped all the way to the hospital. If red lights had appeared in my rearview mirror I would have let them chase me all the way to the ER, but, thankfully, I didn't see one patrol car. As it happened, it was just about time for fresh pastries to come out of the ovens at Krispy Kreme, the favorite all-night haunt of our local police. In all fairness, nights were uneventful in our quiet little town. Eating doughnuts gave the graveyard shift a reason to go to work.

As I drove, I prayed with a passion I didn't know I had. And thought of my mother. Two miscarriages. One right after the other. That's what she'd said. What she'd endured. *Oh, God, not DeeDee. Please, not DeeDee.* "We need this baby," I whispered. "All of us."

The parking lot at the emergency entrance was nearly deserted on that early Monday morning. I parked next to Jonathan's black SUV in the well-lit lot and hurried up the ramp and through the double doors. He was just inside, nervously pacing before the receptionist's window. DeeDee was nowhere in sight.

Jonathan pulled me into a hug. "I'm so glad you came."

As if anything could have kept me away. "Where's Dee?"

"The doctor's examining her."

"Dr. Creager?"

"The ER doctor."

A young man in hospital greens approached us. "That would be me." He held out a hand to Jonathan. "I'm Dr. Garrett. And as far as examining her, that isn't quite accurate."

Puzzled, Jonathan took the doctor's hand and shook it briefly. "How is she?"

"Stubborn." A smile crossed his young face. "Says she won't be seen by anyone but Dr. — " he looked down at a piece of paper on which a name was scrawled — "Creager, I believe? Is that her ob-gyn?" He spoke with a Canadian accent and was obviously new to the area if he didn't know who Zoe Creager was.

"Fertility specialist. We're finally pregnant."

"Ah. I see."

And so did I. Dr. Garrett barely looked old enough to shave, let alone to have graduated from med school. In his hospital scrubs and shoe protectors — which looked remarkably like pajamas with feet — he looked like he belonged at a slumber party, not in a hospital emergency room. DeeDee wasn't about to subject her highly delicate self to this . . . teenybopper. And I didn't blame her for one second. I pulled my cell phone from my purse. "I'll call Dr. Creager's office." I pretended not to see Dr. Garrett's eyebrows come together in a surprised frown as I turned away to make my call in private.

The woman at the answering service proved nearly as stubborn as DeeDee. "The earliest we call the doctor is six a.m.," her nasally voice intoned. Her emphasis on *earliest* indicated she wasn't about to budge from that routine. I have no doubt she could have moonlighted as a drill instructor. But she'd probably never dealt with a fertility-chart-making, wannabe-egg-donating, warring angel named Gabby before. Adrenaline took control of me. More accurately, it possessed me.

"I don't think you quite understand," I said with a calm that was chilling even to me. "I expect this cell phone to ring in exactly sixty seconds, and when I answer it I expect to hear Dr. Creager's voice on the other end telling me she's halfway to the hospital. And by the time I push the little red *end* button on this same cell phone disconnecting me from Dr. Creager, I expect to hear her tires squealing into the emergency parking lot. I'm stepping outside, as we speak, just so I can hear them." I admit that wasn't entirely true. I was pacing like a madwoman in front of the sliding glass doors that led to the parking lot. But that was close enough. "So you need to hit the speed-dial button on *your* phone and inform Dr. Creager that DeeDee McAllister-Kent is in the emergency room of Memorial Hospital, throwing her guts up. Because if you don't, two things will happen. One, Dr. Creager will fire you *tout de suite*. And, two—" Two was my plan to find her, remove her liver without the benefit of anesthesia, and feed it to my rottweiler. Which didn't exist. "Well, you'll be much happier not knowing about number two. You have twelve seconds left." I disconnected the call and returned to Jonathan with a consoling smile. "She's on her way," I said sweetly.

Within fourteen minutes, Dr. Creager had arrived and been briefed by Jonathan. Then, swiping her name badge in the reader of the electronic security door, she disappeared into the examining area.

For the one and only time in my life, I regretted that I was a nonsmoker. I would have puffed on two cigarettes at once just to keep both hands occupied. Instead, I resorted, as usual, to picking off my nail polish. In no time, I had gone through all ten fingernails, leaving a little mound of Pink Passion flakes at my feet, and I began to contemplate the polish on my toenails, conveniently accessible thanks to my sandals. Jonathan, the picture of a desperate man, was leaning his forehead against the wall just outside the door through which Dr. Creager had vanished. We both interrupted our chosen activities from time to time only long enough to glance at the clock buzzing on the wall.

It was exactly like the clocks that had graced every classroom of every school I had ever attended: white-faced, black-rimmed, with black arrows to mark the time. And, just like in school, the hands seemed to be stuck. That was especially true when spring would finally give way to summer and June was the heading on the calendar above the teacher's desk. The last hours of a school year were interminable. Weeknight slumber parties, swimming at midnight, sleeping in till you wanted to get up. All these beckoned, but we were held captive by a second hand that refused to flow in a continuously fluid and forward motion, like, for example, the clock in our den, which all through grammar school had marked my bedtime. Instead, our classroom clock would stop with every tick, keeping you on the edge of your seat, wondering if it would ever make it to three o'clock. And three months of freedom.

Jonathan approached. "How *long* has she been in there?" He

had a red splotch on his forehead in the pattern of the plaid, tex-
tured paper that lined the hospital walls. I wasn't even tempted
to laugh. Instead, I squeezed his hand and tidied up the mound
of nail polish chips with my big toe. As if buoyed by my simple
action, he went back to his post.

The second hand ticked its way around the face of the clock
a dozen more times before Dr. Creager reappeared. Jonathan
looked up expectantly. I did my best to read her expression.

"Come with me. I'll take you back to see DeeDee."

She led us through the door from which she'd come. My heart
felt as if it were in my throat. I felt every irregular beat. Jonathan,
ahead of me, nervously clenched and unclenched his fists with
every alternating step. We couldn't have been more tense if we'd
been on our way to the firing squad.

"She has a bad case of the flu," Dr. Creager said.

I moaned my relief. "Thank God."

"We've given her something intravenously to help with the
vomiting, and we're putting fluids back into her." She stopped
and turned to Jonathan. "I'm going to admit her for at least a day
for observation and to keep her on the IV."

"Is there any chance . . ." Jonathan's voice faded away, but we
all knew what he was asking.

Dr. Creager nodded. "The first trimester is the most vulner-
able to miscarriage."

I winced at the word.

"I've examined her. There's no spotting, and the baby's heartbeat is strong. So I think we're okay. I'd like to keep it that way."

We stopped before a curtained cubbyhole. Dr. Creager pulled
back the curtain and stepped aside. DeeDee was lying on a gurney,
her head slightly elevated. Two sacks of clear liquid hung from an
IV stand, which pumped the fluids into her body. Jonathan went

to the side that didn't have the IV, leaned down, and kissed her forehead.

She opened her eyes and gave him a weak smile.

"You gave us a scare." He kissed her again.

She moved her free hand to her abdomen and nodded.

I took a silent step backward, inching my way toward the outer room to give them some privacy, but DeeDee stopped me. "Don't go anywhere."

"I was just—"

"I know." She lifted her right hand, with its medical paraphernalia, and motioned me toward her. Her hand was icy on mine. "I want you to pray. And don't stop."

Tears stung my eyes, but I blinked them away. I nodded. It was a frightening thought, but I had to be the strong one today.

❧

True to his word, Sonny had the prayer chain knocking at heaven's door the moment the church office opened. I know the fluids and antinausea medicine dripping into DeeDee's vein were beneficial, but the healing touch of God is what she needed most.

We'd never voiced it, but since the moment DeeDee made the announcement, we all knew hers was an at-risk pregnancy. This reminded us not to take anything for granted. I prayed without ceasing as DeeDee had asked. *Oh, God, please don't let DeeDee lose this baby. Dear Lord, it would be more than she could bear, and you've promised never to overburden us. Oh, Jesus, I'll do anything you ask, only protect them both.*

And as if someone had tapped me on the shoulder—and indeed Someone had—I was interrupted and made to think about my word choice. *Lose the baby... more than she could bear . . . anything you ask.* I prayed as if God were a schoolyard bully I had to bribe to keep from taking my lunch money instead of a loving heavenly Father who gives us every good and perfect gift. I could have wept with shame. Minus a Bible, and without recalling chapter and verse, I began to recall portions of Scripture that carried more hope than anything I'd prayed thus far. *I am the Lord that healeth thee. If you ask me anything in my name, I will do it. I have loved you with an everlasting love.* Suddenly, my trust factor soared. I spent the rest of the day thanking God and singing songs of praise.

15

L abor Day marked the sixteenth week of DeeDee's pregnancy.
Dr. Creager, who was handling this pregnancy personally,
had scheduled another ultrasound for the day after. While Sonny
held down the fort at the office, DeeDee, Jonathan, and I headed
off to our appointment. This would be the first time Jonathan
and I would see the baby and hear the heartbeat. It was the most
exciting moment of my life, but I felt like I was crashing a private
party. I had wanted DeeDee and Jonathan to go without me, but
DeeDee insisted that I come.

"This wouldn't be happening without you. You have to share
this experience."

"What do you mean?"

She touched her abdomen. "It was your prayers. I'm sure of
it."

Well, it was like turning on a faucet. And I thought she was
supposed to be the one with the crazy hormones.

"At least let Jonathan go in first," I said, and meant it.

So when DeeDee's name was called, she and Jonathan reluctantly left me sitting in the waiting room. It was a grueling quarter of an hour. I clutched a magazine but never turned a page. Instead, I began to imagine what it would be like when we got the call that DeeDee had gone into labor. I wiped my clammy palms across the thighs of my jeans and exhaled a quivering breath. I would absolutely fall apart, I just knew it.

"Mrs. Nevin?" A nurse stood in the doorway that led into the examination rooms.

I raised my hand like a timid schoolgirl. "I'm Mrs. Nevin." I stood and followed her into an examination room.

DeeDee lay on a narrow bed and smiled a greeting, while Jonathan sat in a chair, unable to tear his eyes away from the computer screen. "Go ahead. Show her," DeeDee said to the technician.

I felt that roller-coaster feeling in the pit of my stomach as I turned my eyes to the screen. Making sense of the pulsating picture before me was like reading Greek. I couldn't make heads or toes of it.

The technician drew an imaginary circle around the baby. "Here's the head. And this is its little bottom. And, look, here's a fist. I think we're disturbing the little dear."

I studied the screen, trying to see the features as she pointed them out.

DeeDee waved a hand at me. "You're trying too hard. Look away, then try again. It's like one of those trick pictures where you have to look for the negative to see the positive. And don't squint!"

I followed DeeDee's instructions and let my eyes focus naturally on the screen before me.

The technician pointed to the baby's head again. "See here? It sort of resembles something you'd see on *Close Encounters of the Third Kind*."

"Okay," I said, becoming excited again, "I see it now!"

"And here are the feet, and the — "

"Oh my." I felt dangerously faint. I touched my forehead with trembling fingertips and tried to shake away the cobwebs that were shrinking my vision.

Jonathan offered me his chair. "Here. Sit. It had the same effect on me."

"So what do you think, Gab? Does she have my profile?" DeeDee ran her index finger down the curve of her nose.

"It's too early to tell the sex," the technician said.

DeeDee chuckled as if that were the silliest thing someone could say. "Oh, it's a girl."

The technician took the challenge and looked back at the screen. "Let's see if I can find a — "

"Don't waste your time," I said. "If DeeDee says it's a girl, trust me, it's a girl."

"Well, regardless." The technician donned a mysterious smile. "I have a surprise for all of you."

With that, she turned up the speaker. A slushing sound and that of a rapidly beating heart filled the room. We all caught our breath, and I felt my own heart begin to accelerate. Tears filled my eyes and trickled down my cheeks. As Jonathan wiped at his own face with the back of his hand, I stood up and stepped away, trying in vain to give them a modicum of privacy. But DeeDee reached for my hand and pulled me back into the circle. "This baby is all of ours. And, honestly, I don't care who she looks like, Gab. I just want her to have your heart."

I was rapidly entering an emotional meltdown when the tech said, "The rate is 150. Usually that means a boy."

DeeDee sat up and began to wipe away the gel on her abdomen. "If you find a penis in there, I'll buy you lunch."

If you ask me, it was a safe bet.

⇛

If I thought the announcement dinner was extravagant, I hadn't seen anything yet. DeeDee insisted on a party to announce her pregnancy, and if there was a person she'd ever known since grammar school who wasn't invited, I didn't know who it could be. At least the menu didn't consist of every food with the word *baby* in it known to man.

The invitations, all 168 of them, which meant that more than three hundred individuals were invited, were shaped like fluffy white diapers secured with huge pink diaper pins and had to be specially made, because every baby-related invitation we could find was an invitation to a shower. But this wasn't a shower; it was a pronouncement: that the most intelligent, most talented, and loveliest child in the history of the world was going to be born. And she would be a girl. Nothing scientific validated that assumption, but DeeDee never doubted it for a moment. My bets were on her.

DeeDee wanted to fill the fluffy little diapers with melted Hershey's Kisses "to give them an authentic touch." But that's where I drew the line. I gave her a calligraphy pen and a bottle of baby pink ink and put her to work writing out the invitations.

The party was set for midafternoon on Sunday, October 19, at DeeDee and Jonathan's home. Even if only half of those invited actually attended, there wouldn't be enough room in both of our houses put together for that many guests. So outdoors was the only practical option available. Their backyard would easily accommodate the group, and while the afternoon would still be comfortable in October, by sundown it could turn quite cool. So two o'clock until seven were the hours we chose.

DeeDee and I visited Garibaldi's Fine Italian Dining, the premier caterers of our town, to select the menu for the party. We met with the owner herself. No subordinates for us. Mrs. Garibaldi was the living definition of the Italian matriarch: short and plump, with heavy dark hair twisted into a bun and secured in place with a score of hairpins. She wore an olive green chef's apron with *Garibaldi's* embroidered in white across the top in a lovely script. Underneath, she wore a white short-sleeved uniform-style dress and touched off her attire with thick-soled shoes that squeaked on the highly waxed black-and-white-checked linoleum floor. She spoke with a heavy Italian accent, even though, as she told us, she came to America when she was six. I couldn't help but wonder how much was for show.

We sat at a round table draped with one of Garibaldi's trademark olive green tablecloths. A white carnation in a clear vase sprouted from between the menus and the shaker of Parmesan cheese in the center of the table. Mrs. Garibaldi poured iced tea for both of us, then opened her planning booklet and touched the end of a pencil to her tongue. "Now, then. We begin. What type of party are we planning?"

"The party is a . . . well, it's not a . . . but then it's . . ." DeeDee shrugged. "What would you call it, Gab?"

"Well, let's see. It's not a birth announcement."

"No," she agreed. "Not yet."

"And it's not a shower."

"Not that either."

"Then I guess you'd call it . . . a pregnancy announcement."

"Yes, that's it. A pregnancy announcement." DeeDee beamed.

"You always have the right word for everything."

Maria Garibaldi beamed as well. "Ah, your first grandchild."

DeeDee's brow crumpled into a frown, and her lips became a thin red line. I knew the moment we left Garibaldi's we were going straight to Lacey's Maternity Wear for something that would make even the skinniest runway model look pregnant.

And it wasn't even Tuesday.

DeeDee made it through the planning meeting with more grace than I thought she could muster, having suffered way too many comments about the delights of being a grandmother. "And so young!" Maria had said. Well, that helped. But I was right. We'd no more than left the parking lot when DeeDee said, "We're going shopping." Her tone of voice was somewhere between that of Patton and Cruella de Vil.

I don't have time, I thought to myself. *I really have to finish my column*. Instead, I swallowed the words and sighed. My friend needed me. I could write tonight after Sonny went to bed. All night if that's what it took. So I buckled my seat belt, recognizing that my chauffeur was an incensed, forty-year-old, hormone-enriched, pregnant woman on a mission. I didn't dare rock the boat.

The invitations were mailed one week later, and DeeDee began readying her house with a vengeance. Every day after the gallery closed—which gave me all morning and early afternoon to write—we'd get to work. We took down draperies, which I carted off to be dry-cleaned, and had professionals come in to shampoo the carpets. Sonny and Jonathan spent a Saturday helping me wash windows, while DeeDee stood on the opposite side of the glass pointing out the streaks. This was teamwork at its finest. In fact, I was tempted to become pregnant myself if it meant getting help with my windows.

In a week's time the house was squeaky clean and the back-yard shrubs neatly trimmed, like boys getting a butch for summer. The pool tile glistened, and the filtered water shimmered a pale inviting blue. Not that anyone would actually swim in October, but overall, the Kent abode looked like something out of *House Beautiful*.

And I was exhausted. I hadn't missed a deadline for any of my columns nor disappointed DeeDee. I'd even written and sold two magazine articles in the last couple of weeks. But I felt my age like never before. Forty! How on earth had it happened so quickly?

As we sat one afternoon, admiring our handiwork and sipping cranberry juice and 7UP in the shade, DeeDee suddenly cried, "Gabby! The nursery!"

I expected to turn and see the house engulfed in flames, I was that startled by her outburst. Instinctively, I reached for the cordless phone, ready to dial 911, with my heart pounding in my throat. And then I remembered. "You don't have a nursery."

"Exactly!"

"So . . . what?"

"What if they want to see it?"

"Who?" I was afraid the juice had gone to her head.

"The guests," she said, looking at me as if *I* were the one losing it. "This is a pregnancy announcement, remember?" She might as well have added, "Duh!" at the end.

I was instantly defensive. "So?"

"Well, don't you think *someone* will ask to see the nursery? If I were going to a pregnancy announcement party, I would."

"Dee. You're barely five months along. No one will expect to see the nursery this soon. Trust me."

She looked straight at me with one eyebrow arched defiantly. "I say they will."

"Well, what if they do?" I hardly considered this a crisis. "Tell them to come back in four months."

Her eyes narrowed and her lips tightened. "That's cold, Gabby. And rude. I never expected such indifference from you of all people. You don't care if my baby has nowhere to sleep?"

I began to calculate again. One hundred twenty more days and I would have the old DeeDee back. Give or take a week. I smiled sweetly. "What do you suggest?"

"I think we should postpone the party until, say, January. That way I'll have time to design and complete the nursery. I'm trying to decide on a motif, but I'm stuck between Disney Babies and Noah's Ark. I mean, just think of the fun you could have with all the animals and—what?"

I inhaled deeply, counting to myself as I did. "Dee. One hundred and sixty-eight invitations have been sent. That's one *hundred* and sixty-*eight*. And they are for this coming Sunday, October 19. With or without a nursery—in fact, with or without you—the party is on."

"Well, you don't have to get huffy. It was just a suggestion."

And a bad one, I wanted to add. "Already we've had, I don't know, three dozen RSVPs. It's way too late to call it off."

"Three dozen? That's all?" She frowned. "Were there any regrets?"

"Mostly not."

"Then so far we have, what, maybe seventy people coming, and the party is just six days away?"

"We're getting more and more calls every day. Don't worry. Besides, we don't have to give Mrs. Garibaldi the final count until Friday."

"Well, three or three hundred," she said, putting her best foot forward, "we'll have a grand old time."

"That we will," I said, hugely relieved.

"Now, about the nursery . . ."

Sunday, October 19, dawned without a cloud in the sky, though a breeze that blew in from the south became stronger with each passing half hour. But that was okay. We could put up with a little wind. In fact, it might keep the temperature in a comfortable seventy- to seventy-five-degree range. Much better than the eighty-seven of the day before. We'd simply tack things down and not wear full skirts.

Maria Garibaldi and her crew arrived at ten a.m. right on the dot. Within two hours the backyard was made ready for two hundred guests, give or take a few, while DeeDee's kitchen was transformed into a satellite of Garibaldi's Fine Italian Dining. The aromas that emanated from within the house were irresistible and mouthwatering, and I'm certain I'd never smelled anything like them coming from DeeDee's kitchen before. Homemade ravioli, creamy Italian salad dressing, for which Garibaldi's was famous, garlic butter for homemade breadsticks. Oh, it was tantalizing. I hung around the kitchen looking hungry, hoping for a sample of something, *anything*, but Maria Garibaldi guarded her delectables like a jealous lover. No one had so much as a nibble until she said so. And so far, she hadn't.

By noon, that south wind had blown in a sky full of clouds. Not fluffy white cumulus clouds that children love to make pictures out of, mind you, but rain-laden clouds that grew darker and more threatening by the minute. Clouds that rumbled the atmosphere as they bumped together. A thunderstorm was gathering. The kind that washes away the grit of summer and brings out the sweaters and the lap quilts. The kind I long for after a long summer of temperatures that push the mercury to the century mark. But not today. *Dear Lord, not today.*

A frantic DeeDee clutched my hands. "Pray, Gab!"

As if I hadn't already.

By the time Sonny and Jonathan arrived from the morning's church service, which DeeDee and I had, of necessity, skipped, the clouds were no longer threatening—they were downright dangerous. They looked as if they couldn't hold one more drop of moisture without letting go a deluge. My father had always said he could detect the brewing of a storm just by the smell of the air. Today, the stuffiest nose on the planet could have foretold what was coming without ever looking up.

Dear Lord, I prayed again, *I know the rain falls on the just and the unjust . . . just don't let it fall on us.*

Sonny had sniffed the air hungrily before he'd even entered the house, and it had nothing to do with the approaching rain. "Oh! There should be a law against such tempting aromas when one is as hungry as I. When do we eat?"

"There's some fruit in the fridge," DeeDee said, her worried eyes still on the heavens.

"Can't I please just have one little slice of garlic bread? Maybe dunked in that pasta sauce and—"

DeeDee threw a look back over her shoulder. "Sonny, I've never considered you a wimp, *per se*, but it would take a bigger man than you to infiltrate Maria Garibaldi's kitchen. Trust me." She was well aware that she had lost possession of her kitchen the second Maria Garibaldi had arrived.

"Per se?" Sonny looked wounded.

"I'll tell you what." DeeDee glanced furtively toward the

kitchen and whispered, "You pray away those rain clouds, and I'll not only take it back but I'll personally get you a slice of garlic bread *dripping* with pasta sauce."

Now, Sonny was a man of faith, but this was an awfully tall order. "Not even Elijah could pray away those clouds."

"Well, then, the fruit's in the fridge."

I wouldn't swear to it, but I'm pretty sure I heard the word *wimp* come out of her mouth as she turned to walk away.

Sonny looked to Jonathan, who held up his hands defensively. "I'm going upstairs to change. Honey, where's my slicker?"

DeeDee turned a petulant eye upon him. "I fail to see the humor."

"Okay, okay." Sonny rolled up his shirtsleeves, figuratively speaking. "We'll pray. Who knows but for just such a time . . ."

"You're getting your Old Testament confused," I pointed out. "It was Esther, not Elijah, who was born for just such a time."

"That was then. This is now. And Maria Garibaldi's pasta sauce hangs in the balance."

So we prayed, Sonny, DeeDee, and I, holding hands under a heavy sky. And wouldn't you know it, a single sliver of silvery sunshine broke through the clouds, and there we stood with our shadows spilling onto the lawn as a testimony of God's grace.

True to her word, DeeDee embarked on a covert mission to get Sonny his pasta-drenched garlic bread. "Gab, you call Maria outside on some pretext, and I'll slip into the kitchen and grab the grub." She laughed at her wee alliteration. "I have such a way with words."

Honestly. She didn't have an ounce of modesty. "What about her helpers?"

DeeDee rolled her eyes and shook her head. "I'm not worried about *them*. You keep the boss busy and I'll do the rest."

So I went as far as the dining room and called to Mrs. Garibaldi, while Sonny and DeeDee slipped around the back and waited. "Mrs. Garibaldi?" I was certain guilt was written across my face. In Italian. "Might I show you something out back?" I couldn't help but notice a drop of the coveted sauce on her second chin as she appeared on the patio. She wiped her hands on her signature apron and followed me out to the gazebo. "The bakery is delivering a cake any minute, and I need your opinion. I'd like to set the cake table up here in the gazebo. It would make such a lovely setting. But, of course, we don't want anyone to see the cake until after the announcement is made. What do you suggest?"

She rested her chins on a chubby fist. "Letta me think. We could decorate the table with everything excepta the cake, which we will keep hidden in the kitchen. Then, when you're ready to make the blessed announcement, have your guests face thisa way." She pointed away from the gazebo and toward the house. "Then Luigi and I will slipa the cake into place without a soul ever seeing." She smiled with obvious pleasure. "What do you think?"

I think I'm a despicable sneak is what I wanted to say, but what I did say was, "I knew I could count on you."

"Well, then, backa to work." She carried herself off to the kitchen, where I hoped with all my heart that DeeDee had done her dirty deed without being detected. I would have felt horrible if Maria ever found out that I had been part of the great heist.

At two o'clock, when the first guests began to arrive, the sky was a canopy of blue, while Sacramento County just north of us got drenched by the first storm of the season. I didn't recognize half of the guests, though presumably I should have. There were business connections whose names I knew, if not the faces, and a number of individuals with whom DeeDee and I had attended school, from sixth grade to college graduation. I was startled at how *mature* they looked. The only guests I really knew well were the members of our church. But everyone, known or otherwise, seemed to have an air of expectation—which I suppose was the whole point.

I looked around for DeeDee, expecting to see her flitting like a butterfly from one cluster of guests to another, but I didn't find her. She was probably upstairs changing her outfit for the third time and putting every last hair in place. DeeDee would make the perfect impression, as she always did.

Things were going smoothly, with little groups of people huddled here and there, enjoying Maria's hors d'oeuvres and talking about the party. As I passed from one huddle to the next, I heard snippets of conversations that included such lines as, "Who do you suppose . . . ?" ". . . adopted, do you think?" ". . . symbolic, maybe not a baby at all." On the conversations went.

By two thirty it looked as if everyone had arrived, but DeeDee still had not made an appearance. I set my punch glass on a table and headed for the house when the band broke into a drumroll. Okay, now I got it. DeeDee was going to make her entrance, and probably the announcement, with a flourish. I moved with everyone else toward the French doors, where Jonathan stood just outside the formal living room. He cleared his throat a time or two as a member of the band handed him a microphone.

"Well," he said nervously, "I know you're all wondering why you were invited here today. We, uh, that is, my wife and I . . . well, we wanted to share with all of you that, um . . ."

"Spit it out!" someone called, and the crowd erupted with laughter.

Suddenly, from inside the house, DeeDee appeared at the top of the stairs. She was bathed in such a warm glow of light that she looked like an angel caught between two worlds. Whispers ran through the crowd as she descended the wide, sweeping stairway, as if it were Jacob's ladder. Even I, who knew DeeDee so well, half-expected to see a halo suspended atop her golden hair—slightly atilt, of course. She smiled like a princess bestowing her favor upon the masses. DeeDee knew how to work an audience. She joined her husband and slipped her little hand into his, her pregnant tummy accentuated by the stretchy pink dress that hugged her form. "What Jonathan is trying to say," she purred into the microphone, "is that we're in the family way."

The crowd erupted in applause, and then another drumroll sounded. We turned our attention to the gazebo, where Maria Garibaldi extended her arm toward the cake as if to say, *Ta da!* Pleasant little cries filled the air as guests began to get a glimpse of the five-tiered stork with a naked little baby doll cradled in the diaper hanging from its mouth.

I couldn't help it. Once the cake had been sliced and distributed, I inched my way to the back side of the gazebo and snuck a peak inside the diaper. Sure as the world, a melted, gooey Hershey's Kiss stained the white cotton diaper underneath the baby's bottom.

"Hope it didn't have almonds," DeeDee whispered into my ear, appearing out of nowhere and startling me half out of my skin. She laughed out loud, by herself I might add, until the tears flowed. Then she hugged me. "Gabby, you are such a sport."

Melting instantly, I returned her embrace and felt my own tears begin to flow. There we stood in one of the most solemn moments of nearly a lifetime of friendship when a woman neither of us recognized slipped up behind us. "DeeDee, Gabby, this is so exciting," she said, as if we knew exactly who she was, "and I just have to ask. Can I see the nursery?"

DeeDee and I burst into laughter, while our visitor, startled by our reaction, backed away and vanished into the crowd. And in a completely uncharacteristically selfless act, DeeDee refrained from saying, "I told you so."

16

With the second trimester behind us, our confidence in a successful pregnancy soared. DeeDee, who could never do anything conventionally, experienced *all-day* sickness rather than morning sickness right from the start. While she didn't mind for a moment, because, she said, it made her more aware of her pregnancy, the rest of us treated her as if she were a breakable doll. And it was exhausting. Jonathan hired a housekeeper to come in once a week, but I cooked a lot of their meals along with ours, did DeeDee's shopping along with mine, and ran her errands to boot. I really didn't mind. After all, they had gone to great lengths to conceive this child. Surely I could maintain the pace for three more months.

Jonathan was the worst of all. If he had viewed DeeDee as a woman who was self-sufficient and tireless before the pregnancy, he now saw her as the antithesis: a woman completely dependent. She barely was able to use the bathroom on her own when Jonathan was home. Bless his heart, he treated her as an invalid, and it was driving her nuts.

DeeDee still kept her hours at the gallery, but now she was looking for someone to hire during her maternity leave. She wanted someone in place by mid-December to help with the last-minute Christmas crunch. Then Dee would have time to train her, or him, so that she could take six weeks before her due date and eight weeks after for her maternity leave.

I was in the area, so I took a pumpkin spice latte—decaffein-ated, of course—by the gallery, now that Café Latte was gearing up for the holidays. "Have you placed the ad yet?"

"Just what I wanted, Gab. Thank you. And no, I told you I don't want to just open this up to anybody," she said.

"But, Dee, you're running out of time. You're going to have to train whoever you hire, and that can't be done in a day."

She gave me the look she wore whenever we had this discussion.

"No," I said. "We've been through this. I can't be your replace-ment. I have my column, the devotional we're supposed to be working on, an article to write for *Today's Christian Woman*." Not to mention a life with Sonny.

"And your laptop. It's probably quieter at the gallery than it is at your office."

"No. I don't want to be stuck at the gallery when I could be helping you with the baby."

"Stuck at the gallery? I see."

"Oh quit. You know what I mean." I sat down beside her. "Let's make a list."

That brought a smile. "You and your lists."

I pulled a notepad out of my purse. And a purple pen. I love purple ink. And lists. "Okay." I drew a vertical line down the middle of the page. "Who have you talked to? And who do you want to talk to?"

"You," she said. "Put that in both columns."

"Dee."

"It's only for a few weeks."

"Seventeen at the very least. The answer is no. Now help me out here. Have you talked to anyone? What about Mavis? Or Joanne."

Her eyes narrowed. "Which Joanne?"

"Dutra. Or even Baldwin. Either one would do a fine job."

"Joanne Dutra is faux painting every great room she can get her hands on from here to Sacramento, and Joanne Baldwin wears nothing but jeans. I will not have jeans in my gallery. Of course, I'd make an exception for you," she added, taking note of my outfit.

"What's wrong with jeans?"

"Practically anywhere else, nothing."

"And faux painting? Really? Isn't that a bit outdated?"

"She finally learned the technique. Now that's all she wants to do."

"Then I say you place an ad. Today."

"Why do you insist on being so mean to me?" She took a long sip of her latte. The one I, the mean one, had brought her.

I tucked my notepad back in my purse. "You're not going to believe this. I had lunch with Mother yesterday. She has a date tonight. A date! And she's added highlights to her hair."

"Well."

"Why are you smiling?"

"I think it's sweet."

"Sweet. Right. You wouldn't think it's sweet if your mother had the date."

"Are you kidding? I'd do handstands. It would mean she's finally, *finally*, over that loser, Roger McAllister."

"He's your dad, Dee."

She reached across the table and touched my hand. "You had a dad, Gabby. I had a DNA donor. Big difference. So who's the guy?"

"Someone she met in her singles' Sunday school class."

"Well, there you are. How bad could it be if she met him at church?"

"He could be a fraud, you know. It happens all the time."

"Give your mother some credit, Gab. She was a great judge of character the first time around, and she will be now." Suddenly DeeDee's eyes went wide. "Speaking of your mother! Why didn't I think of her before?"

"For what?"

She spread her arms wide and looked around the gallery. "For this. She's perfect."

I couldn't believe it. Mother was all for it.

The three of us sat in her condo, sipping mugs of spiced tea, while rain fell in buckets outside. Sonny and Jonathan had gone home to leftovers right after church to watch football, while DeeDee and I accepted Mother's offer of lunch. An hour later, with the dishes washed and put away, we sat around her kitchen table.

"You really should take your time thinking about it, Mom. It's five days a week, including Saturday, for at least four months. And through Christmas — the busiest time of the year."

"I'll be there to help through the beginning of January. After that, I'm only a phone call away," DeeDee said. She reached for an almond shortbread cookie and pointed it at me. "Don't you dare try to talk her out of this."

"I just want to be sure she knows what she's in for."

"That's very thoughtful," Mother said. "But I have thought about it." She nodded to DeeDee. "From the moment you said you needed to find someone. I just didn't want to impose myself on you."

"Impose? Margie, you could never impose yourself on me. You're like my second mother. I just don't know why I didn't think of it sooner. Of course, I'll pay you well, and I'll still help with the ordering. But there won't be much. I built my holiday inventory weeks ago."

"When should I start?"

"Tuesday," I said before DeeDee could respond. "You'll need all the time you can get for training."

Mother reached over and patted my hand. "Angel baby, I can handle it. Now chill."

"Chill?" DeeDee laughed until she choked over that one. "We'll work out the details later. Now, I want to hear all about your date."

Mother's cheeks turned red as holly berries. She grinned and lifted her shoulders. "Oh, I don't know. It was fine, I guess. Eugene was a gentleman, I'll say that. . . ." She let her voice trail off.

"I didn't see him at church this morning," I said. I was right; I knew it. He was a fraud.

"His gout flared up."

"Gout?"

"Last night. In his big toe. Rich food will do that," Mother said.

"I didn't know."

"So after dinner I drove his car to his house for him, then took a taxi home."

"A taxi?"

"I hope he paid," DeeDee said.

Mother's cheeks turned a little redder.

"Well, scratch *him* off the list," DeeDee said.

I frowned. "There's a list?"

"Hypothetical, Gab. Relax."

"Otherwise it was fine."

I knew Mother. She used the word *fine* when she really meant not even close to okay. Just like I did.

"So if he calls again?" DeeDee asked.

"I'll tell him I moved."

We all laughed at that.

"Linda should be here," I said. "She'd enjoy this."

"She could be if she'd come to church with us," DeeDee said. "But she schedules open houses every Sunday. It's her excuse. She doesn't think I see through her."

"I invite her all the time," Mother said. "I'll keep trying."

Linda was having a horrible time adjusting to the idea of becoming a grandmother.

"I want to come up with a *unique* name for the, you know, *baby* to call me." She tripped over the b-word every time it came up.

"How about Nana?" I suggested as we all enjoyed pie at our house on Thanksgiving night.

She wrinkled her nose and gave a quick little shake of her head. "Overused."

"What about Mimi?" Jonathan said. "That's what I called my grandmother."

She tried it a time or two, then again wrinkled her nose. "It's just not for me."

"Well, then," my mother ventured, "why not simply Grandmother?"

"That sounds a little *aristocratic*, don't you think?"

I think what she meant was *ancient*.

"Well," DeeDee said, as serious as you please, "I think she'll call you Granny. In fact, I think we should all call you Granny starting today, just so you have time to get used to it."

Linda looked horrified. "I'll think of something." She reached for a cigarette and her mother-of-pearl lighter and headed out to the backyard.

"You need to quit those!" DeeDee called after her. "I don't want any child of mine exposed to secondhand smoke."

Linda stuck her head back inside the doorway. "I'd never smoke around the *baby*!"

"Well, you certainly smoked around me, and for all I know I have cancer cells mutating all throughout my body this very minute because of it."

Linda looked utterly shocked, which wasn't the least bit unusual when it came to things her daughter said. "We didn't even know about secondhand smoke in those days. I told you I'm sorry."

"If you're really sorry, you'll quit."

"You know I've tried. It's not that easy."

"Sure it is. You simply never smoke another cigarette again."

Now, if DeeDee had ever been a smoker, I have no doubt she could have done just that, at any given time, no matter how long she'd smoked. Unlike most people, she had that kind of resolve. Linda, on the other hand, had none.

"You might try the patch," I offered.

"I did. Twice." She appeared the epitome of defeat.

"Well, the third time's a charm," DeeDee said matter-of-factly.

With that, Linda disappeared around the corner of the house and indulged in the guilty pleasure. My mother, bless her heart, followed her out into the cold November night for a little grandmother-to-grandmother conversation.

I gave DeeDee a chastening look. "You're so hard on her."

"I'm just getting back at her for not warning me about puberty."

Jonathan looked up from the game he'd TiVo'd for the evening. "She didn't warn you about puberty?"

"Not so much as a syllable. If it hadn't been for Wendy Greene bragging in seventh grade girls' phys ed that she'd gotten her period, I'd have been totally ignorant. I went home and asked my mother if she'd ever heard the phrase *gotten a period*, thinking I must have missed something in grammar class. She turned six shades of red and left for an open house."

Sonny ducked behind a section of the newspaper he was scanning in between penalty calls.

"It was hard for mothers in those days," I said. "People weren't so open about such topics."

". . . a lot to be said for the past," I heard my husband murmur.

"Not for your mother," DeeDee said. "Fortunately I was spending the night at your house when I got mine, or I might have called for an ambulance. She was perfectly perfect about explaining it."

"Who was perfectly perfect?" Linda trailed my mother into the house. She was fanning her face, as if that would eliminate the smell of smoke. "Explaining what?"

DeeDee looked about to answer when I gave her the most threatening look I could muster. She got my message loud and clear. "Nothing. We were just talking about grammar."

Linda reclaimed her favorite chair. "That never was my strong suit."

It was all I could do not to laugh out loud.

"We were talking outside," my mother said, "about this grandmother thing. Linda decided she loves the idea of being called Mémé."

DeeDee drew in a sharp and excited breath. "How positively French! Mémé Linda. And Mémé Margie. I insist!" she said, though my mother showed no signs of objecting. DeeDee bounced out of her chair and gave them both a hug. "I didn't know you knew French."

"It was Linda's idea."

"Mother?"

Linda shrugged and looked embarrassed, as she always did when all eyes were on her. "I glanced through your French books once in a while." She sounded as though she were apologizing.

Jonathan gave Sonny a puzzled look. "Isn't that what I said? Mimi?"

"No, Jonathan. Not Mimi," DeeDee corrected. "Mémé. The *e*'s sound like *a*'s, and the emphasis is on the second syllable."

"Mémé," Jonathan repeated, laughing, then mouthed the word *Mimi* to Sonny.

"Now that we've decided on our names," Mother said, "what about the baby's? Have you and Jonathan settled on anything?"

"We have. But it's a surprise."

Jonathan gave DeeDee a quizzical look with eyebrows raised, leading me to believe I alone knew the child she carried would be christened Macy McAllister Kent. And if it were a boy? Well, he'd get used to it.

Linda looked at her watch. "I'd better call it a day. I have an early showing tomorrow. Thank you for the wonderful dinner," she said to all of us. "It was lovely."

"Thank Gabby," DeeDee said. "She did it all."

"You're an angel," Linda said, then laughed. "But then I guess you always have been."

17

Our Tuesday lunches at D'Angelo's were never concluded now without a stroll down School Street that led us to Frills & Frocks, an upscale children's clothing store that had recently moved into town. DeeDee was convinced it had opened solely for her benefit and did her part to keep its tills well filled.

Okay, I did my part as well.

The drawers of the armoire that she'd moved into the still-unfinished nursery were filling up nicely. I was conservative in the selections I purchased, keeping them as gender neutral as possible. Not DeeDee. If our little bundle came out a boy, he was going to be well outfitted with lacy headbands and frilly little dresses that looked made for a doll.

DeeDee shared her pregnancy so intimately that I didn't miss a thing, from the first little flutter of movement she felt to the heartburn that accompanied nearly everything she ate. But it wasn't just us girls that were sharing this pregnancy. Jonathan gave Sonny a daily update of prenatal fatherhood, complete with dealing with mood swings and cravings. For their part, they enjoyed their data exchange as much as we did ours.

During her second trimester, DeeDee had produced little more than a pooch across her middle, and people were probably wondering if her pregnancy announcement was on the up and up. By December, there was no room for doubt. It seemed she went from concave to convex overnight. The eighteen pounds she had planned to gain were on the verge of doubling.

"All of a sudden," she said, measuring flour for a batch of double fudge brownies, "I can't stop eating. And I don't know whose mother to blame."

"Whose mother?"

"Well, if it's the woman's genetic structure that causes her to gain weight during pregnancy, then it's my mother's fault for passing it on to me. If it's the baby's genetic structure, then Jonathan's mother can step up and claim her share of the blame."

Somehow, I failed to grasp the logic.

"I walked by a mirror this morning and I was waddling! I'm being punished for all the years I laughed at pregnant women."

I took over mixing the batter. "Maybe you should try a carrot stick."

She narrowed her eyes and scowled at me. "That's cruel."

"It wasn't meant to be. Honest." I took a taste of the batter. "Oh, this is really good!"

"See?" She scooped a finger full of batter and licked it with intense pleasure.

"My advice? Lose the recipe."

She gave a pouty little frown, then smoothed the T-shirt across her belly. "Gabby, the most awful thing happened." She hesitated, as if reluctant to tell even me.

"What?" I stopped mixing the brownies and frowned as I

looked her up and down to make sure this most awful thing, whatever it was, hadn't happened to *them*.

She looked positively timid as she dropped her eyes to her midriff and slowly raised her top. A bandage three inches square was stuck to her belly.

"Dee! What on earth happened?" I reached toward her, then pulled my hand back as though she might break if I touched her. At the same instant, I was frantic to find the phone, thinking I should call, well, *someone*.

"All of a sudden it just popped out."

"Popped out?" The words nearly put me in cardiac arrest until I realized she couldn't possibly mean the baby. So what then? A hernia. Did pregnant women get hernias? "Does it hurt?"

"Not a bit. I just hoped this bandage would maybe, you know, push it back in."

"Where is Zoe Creager's number?" I frantically searched through the loose scraps of paper next to her phone. "I'm calling her right now. And Jonathan! Does he know?"

"I don't want him to see it. It's so . . . embarrassing. Maybe after the baby comes it'll pop back in."

Pop back in? "Dee, you can't wait for the baby to come. This could be serious. Now, where is Dr. Creager's number?"

DeeDee frowned and ran her hands over the bandage. "What can she possibly do about it?"

"She can take an X-ray or something."

She gasped. "Not when I'm pregnant."

"Oh. Well. Then let me see it." I braced myself. If it looked as frightful to my natural eye as it did to my mind's eye, I was taking her straight to the emergency room.

I held my breath and waited as she lifted one corner of the bandage and pulled ever so carefully. The bandage came off to reveal . . . "Your belly button?"

She looked away and squeezed her eyes shut. "What do you think?"

What did I think? I thought it looked like a garbanzo bean with an attitude, but I had the good sense not to say so.

"Will it go back, do you think?" She looked desperately hopeful.

"Oh, well, Dee," I said, smoothing the bandage back over the errant protrusion and taking a deep breath to calm myself, "one can only hope."

She looked hilariously pathetic, but if there was ever a time not to laugh, this was it.

"Sonny, want to come to Lamaze class with us? Jonathan's going."

We'd been through this conversation more than once, and the answer was still, "No way."

"But all the couples there will be, well, couples. Me there makes us the only trio, and I feel so out of place."

"If I went, that would make us a quartet, and that would be even worse."

"But one quartet equals two couples, and that's the whole point." I was pouting and didn't care. Obviously, neither did he.

"With me along, everyone would think we were a delusional couple who had wandered in off the streets since you're so conspicuously not pregnant. Without me, they would see you as a backup coach, which is exactly what you are."

I wrapped my arms around his neck and kissed the dimple in his chin. "But we're all in this together."

"With one notable difference." He removed his glasses to wipe away the steam caused by my breath on his face. "You're going to be in the delivery room, and I most definitely am not."

"Then who's going to run the camcorder?"

His eyes grew enormous. "Not me!"

I laughed and kissed him again. "Coward."

"Get going or you'll be late."

"Will you miss me?"

"Do you want me to?"

"I like it when you do."

"Then, yes, I'll miss you." He pulled me into a closer hug and began to kiss *that* spot on my neck. "Better yet, why not stay home?"

I was tempted . . . but no. "I missed last week because of my cold." I disentangled myself and promised I wouldn't be late. I smiled all the way to the garage and continued to smile as I backed out of the drive. What did I ever do to deserve Sonny? I'd been asking myself that question for more than twenty years, and still I had no answer. He was as wonderful as my dad, and what could you say beyond that?

DeeDee and Jonathan were waiting in front of their house when I pulled up. As she climbed into the front seat, she looked about to burst with a delicious secret. I was immediately suspicious. "What's up?"

"You'll see." She refused to say anything more, but I could see her mischievous smile even in the dark.

"Maybe you should tell her." I detected a definite note of condolence in Jonathan's voice.

"And spoil the surprise? Don't you say another word."

"Shall we grab a latte on our way?" I asked, because we usually did.

DeeDee gave me a sideways glance. "We'll be late. And tonight we don't want to be late."

"Okay. Maybe after."

Jonathan remained ominously silent.

The parking lot was full, not surprising since this was, after all, a hospital, so I let DeeDee and Jonathan off at the entrance and told them I'd catch up with them in class. I had to park in the overflow lot, and even though I hurried, the door to Room 204 was closed by the time I arrived. It was bad enough to be a third wheel, but to be a late third wheel made me feel even more conspicuous than usual. Not all the teams were necessarily couples—one girl had her mother for a coach, for example. But no one else had a backup coach—at least not one who attended the classes.

I turned the doorknob as quietly as I could and stepped into the room just as the lights went out. DeeDee whispered my name and waved a hand in the air, silhouetted by the light of a stark blue television screen, to guide me to my seat. Right in the front row.

"A movie?" I whispered as the video began to play.

She patted my knee. "Sort of."

Jonathan peered around her and gave me a weak thumbs-up.

The instructor adjusted the volume and said she'd be back later to answer any questions.

Immediately the blue of the screen changed to a brilliant white, and I squinted my eyes until they adjusted. Once they did, it took only a half second to realize I was about to view an actual delivery of an actual baby actually being born. No more simulation. This was the real McCoy! My eyes grew wide and round and I began to sweat. "You should have warned me," I whispered through clenched teeth.

"It was far too much fun this way," DeeDee whispered back. "Besides, you wouldn't have come. Am I right?"

"You're absolutely right. And if I weren't sitting in the front row I'd leave right now."

"Wimp," she said as a chorus of not-so-subtle shushing went up. She turned to me and mouthed, "Take notes."

The births—all three of them—were not shown in real time, of course, but were shown in time-lapse photography . . . until the actual moments of delivery. The first woman, who seemed to be suffering enough at the onset of labor, was to be pitied indeed by the time the baby began to *crown*. I had rather good command of the English language, if I did say so myself, but until that moment if someone had asked what a crown and a baby's birth had in common I would have replied a horrifically ignorant, "Absolutely nothing," adding a look that said *Duh!* for good measure.

As the camera began to zoom in on the . . . *action*, for lack of a better word, I had to look away. DeeDee, I noticed with some satisfaction, wasn't looking so smug anymore. In fact, with eyes glued to the screen, she was leaning forward in her seat as far as the bulge of her tummy would allow and biting her bottom lip. I honestly thought she was going to draw blood. Jonathan looked as if he didn't have any blood at all, even in the dark, and if he became even the teeniest bit more pallid, I was going to push his head down between his knees. I reached around the back of DeeDee's chair and whispered to Jonathan, "Breathe."

"I am," DeeDee whispered back, and she was. Right in time with the woman who was giving birth.

When the doctor announced, "Here she comes!" I made the mistake of glancing back at the screen. It was traumatic, to say the least. I had no idea that a newborn was so . . . well . . . let's just say it wasn't what I expected. Judging by what I saw on my compatriots' faces, we were all on the same page. And to think I had practically begged Sonny to come!

The second delivery was even worse. And the third, after way too many hours of labor, ended in a Cesarean section, in full living color.

I was breathless when it was finally over. "Well, then."

DeeDee did her best to appear unruffled, but I had a pretty good idea what she was thinking. *There's only one way out of this, and that's it!*

Jonathan was in a stupor, though I noticed with relief that his color was starting to return.

The drive home was, shall we say, reflective. I, for one, was wondering what excuse I could concoct to join Sonny in the waiting room and avoid this ordeal altogether. Of course, I would never allow myself to do that to DeeDee, but I was going to make absolutely certain that Sonny didn't reconsider his decision.

He was awake and reading when I came in. "Hey, how was class?"

I slipped onto the bed beside him and began to make little figure eights on his arm with my finger, a sure sign of nerves. "You know, Sonny—" I began, but he cut me off with a kiss.

"Babe, I'm sorry, but I can't do it, not even for you. When the time comes, I'll be there from start to finish, but only in the waiting room. It's the best I can do."

"Well, okay," I said, masking my relief. "If you insist."

18

DeeDee had finally decided on a theme for the nursery. Neverland! Featuring Peter Pan, Tinker Bell, Nana, the Darling children, the lost boys, and a reformed and affable Captain James Hook. She had gotten out her charcoal pencils late one night, taking full advantage of her pregnancy-induced insomnia, and sketched a wonderful scene on the bedroom walls. There were crocs and clocks and ships and fairy dust just waiting for a little color to bring them to life. She was on the phone early one Friday morning with the following words: "Throw on some old jeans and a T-shirt and meet me at the paint store in half an hour." She was way too gleeful, considering the sun had not yet peaked the wisteria.

"Half an hour?" I hadn't even finished my first cup of tea.

"Oh, and you might want to wear that old baseball cap of Sonny's, you know, to protect your hair."

My hair? "From what?"

"The paint, silly. Half an hour." That was it. She'd hung up the phone.

I looked at my half-eaten muffin and the newspaper waiting to be read, and sighed. This pregnancy was about to run me ragged. I wrapped up the muffin, dabbed on a touch of makeup, dressed exactly as instructed, and pulled into the parking lot right behind the newly inspired mother-to-be.

"This is going to be so much fun."

I had yet to learn what "this" was.

"And remember, bright and bold."

I followed her into the store. "DeeDee, what are you talking about?"

"The nursery. What else?"

"You've decided on a theme?" *For the dozenth time*, I added under my breath.

"Well, of course." She plopped down her drawing pad on a table, pushing books of wallpaper samples out of her way. "Look."

I thumbed through the first four pages of the drawing pad, each page representing one wall of the nursery.

"This is really good." The characters were so full of life you could almost feel the breeze on your face from the fairy wings. "Dee, you may have found your calling."

"We'll put Tink on the wall overlooking the crib, and we'll hang up a, you know, one of those things that hang over the crib—"

"A mobile?"

"That's it! A mobile made out of fairy dust."

"Fairy dust?"

"We'll improvise." She dismissed my question with a wave of her hand. "Peter Pan goes on the wall by the window, of course, right next to the Darling children. The lost boys will be on the wall with the closet, and Hook goes on the wall across from Peter, along with a croc or two." She turned to the page where she had sketched the happy captain.

"Where's his hook?"

"I put that hand in his pocket. Wouldn't want to traumatize the baby."

"Right," I said, as if a hookless Hook were the most natural thing in the world.

"Unless . . ."

I could practically see the wheels turning, like something from a cartoon. "Unless?"

"What if Captain Hook really had a hook?"

"He did really have a hook, Dee. That's where the name—"

"No, I mean, a real hook. You know, to hang things on. I'll raise his arm, like so." She found a pencil and began reworking the sketch. "We'll move him next to the closet, of course, and we'll make it a lovely brass hook. For now, I'll hang that darling polka-dot dress I found last week at Carousel on it, with a pretty little satin hanger. Can't you just see it? And then I can hang, well, just any number of things on it. He'll be like a butler. Butler Hook! Oh, Gab, I love the way you think!" She tucked the sketch pad under her arm. "Let's go check out the paint samples."

I followed her, thinking, *Okay, I don't mind taking credit for that one!*

DeeDee had said bright and bold, and that's exactly what we chose. This baby's room would be a rainbow of color—not a hint of pastel anywhere. We purchased a dozen quarts of paint, all in a different color; brushes in a variety of sizes; sponges; masking tape; and plenty of sticks for stirring. And we were ready to go to work.

I hauled our supplies up the stairs while DeeDee brought up mugs of fresh coffee. I was speechless when I entered the room.

Even without color, the characters and scenes she had sketched on the walls were wonderfully alive. A whimsical Pan stood bigger than life with his hands on his hips and his bowed legs ready to leap. "It's enchanting. I can't wait to begin."

DeeDee was delighted. "It just came to me. I jumped out of bed and went to work."

"You must have been up all night."

"You know how it is when inspiration hits."

"No, actually I don't. I can't seem to get started on this next article. It's due the first week of January."

"You're trying too hard." She talked as if she knew just what it was like. "Inspiration can't be forced or coaxed, and it doesn't like to be pressured. It thrives in an atmosphere that's, hmm . . ." She paused, looking for just the right word. *"Sans gêne."* Her accompanying gesture gave me the gist of the translation, which was loosely "trouble free." "Don't worry, you'll get back in the swing of things."

"Maybe once the baby comes," I said, knowing full well I didn't have that long.

"It has been an all-consuming event, I admit." She bent backward, with her hands on her hips, and moaned. Her belly protruded out in front of her. "What in the world are you doing in there?" She rubbed her tummy with one hand. "Hurdles?"

"Is she active today?"

"Come feel this."

Inwardly I groaned. I'd been avoiding this moment, on purpose and by design. I didn't exactly know why, but I was afraid of how it would affect me.

"Well, come here." She cast a questioning look my way, then placed my faltering hand over a bulge in her belly. Instantly it moved.

"Oh!" I pulled back, then timidly reached for the spot again. My hand came alive with the movement of the baby inside her abdomen.

"You should feel it from my perspective. Sometimes I think she's making popcorn in there."

As she turned to pick up her sketch pad, I knew I was about to lose it. I bolted from the nursery and headed for the powder room at the bottom of the stairs. Muffling my sobs with one of DeeDee's favorite guest towels, I cried until I emptied myself of the emotion that had been steadily building since the day DeeDee announced she wanted to have a child. I didn't realize just how affected I had been by this amazing odyssey until I felt that little kick in the palm of my hand. I had not wavered in my decision to remain childless, and I didn't waver now. But all at once I couldn't help but wonder what I had missed.

How had that first flutter of life felt to DeeDee? What was it like to find yourself humming lullabies and thinking it perfectly normal? What kind of wonderful intimacy had it brought to her and Jonathan's relationship? And would it be easy to expand that relationship to a circle of three? I would never know any of these things on a personal level, and I had never wondered about it before. But now . . .

A light tap sounded at the door as I wiped away the last of my tears. I blew my nose and splashed cold water on my face, but it did little to reduce the red blotches or soothe my puffy eyes. I was going to have to hide out for a while or face the music. Another little tap narrowed my options by one. I flushed the toilet, knowing full well she wasn't going to fall for *that* ploy, and opened the door as nonchalantly as I could.

She was propped against the wall on one elbow, smiling. "It has that effect on me, too, sometimes," she said, ignoring the condition of my face as only a real friend could do.

I followed her back to the nursery, muffling my sniffles as best I could. She tipped her head ever so slightly toward a box of tissues, then turned her rapt attention to the cans of paint, giving me time to regain my composure.

"Okay, then. We'll start over here." She motioned to the wall where wide-eyed John, Wendy, and Michael stood next to Peter. "We'll do the background first and then the characters. We might even get to Tinker Bell today. Then tonight I'll resketch Hook on that wall—" she pointed toward the closet— "and the lost boys over there." She picked up a brush as I opened the bedroom window and turned on the ceiling fan for ventilation.

"What are you doing? It's freezing outside."

"Protecting you—and her—from the fumes."

"Okay, I'll grab a sweatshirt, then wack to burk," she said, then laughed at herself for mixing up her words.

"You've been doing that a lot lately." I laughed with her, feeling the tension melt away.

"I tell you, my brain's gone on maternity leave . . . and my memory, too." She began to paint the sky, outlining huge, puffy clouds that she would fill in later. "It's the strangest thing. I went to call my mother yesterday, and I couldn't remember the number. I just stood there with the phone in my hand and thought, what do I do now?"

I laughed again and she did too. "Why didn't you use the speed dial?"

She stopped painting and looked at me with a quizzical look. "I don't know. I wondered that myself later in the day when I picked up the phone and dialed her number without even having to think about it. Hormones are funny things."

Hormones. That was DeeDee's answer to everything these days.

We made great progress that first day, finishing most of the background on all four walls. DeeDee showed me how to apply the basic colors of paint to the trees and the clouds and the sea. Then she followed behind, filling in the detail. I had no idea I could do such things. Of course, without her my handiwork would have been dull and one-dimensional. She added all the right touches that brought it to life. As I thought about it, that was a perfect illustration of our relationship.

I stopped by Mother's condo on my way back to DeeDee's the next Monday morning. I still wasn't used to the fact that Mother didn't live at home anymore. I no longer just walked in when I visited; I knocked. On my own mother's door.

"Sweetheart!" She was truly delighted that I had come, as if I hadn't seen her just the day before. "What a surprise." She had a bandana tied around her hair and a feather duster in her hand. "Getting things ready for the holidays," she explained.

Her condo still looked like a model home as far as I was concerned. "That shouldn't take long. How are things at the gallery?"

"I simply love being there. I've even been thinking that maybe after the baby comes DeeDee will still want me, at least part-time."

"You like it that much?"

"I do. It makes me feel so . . . cultured."

"You've always been cultured, Mother. You're the queen of culture."

"That's sweet, Angel baby. How about some tea?"

"No, thanks. I'm on my way to DeeDee's. We're painting the nursery. Finally."

"She decided on a theme. Good for her."

"I won't tell you what it is because it's a surprise. But I will say, this is so much fun. I didn't know I had it in me. Of course, DeeDee's doing the real artwork—I'm just putting color on the walls."

"I can't wait to see it."

I was on the brink of telling her about my emotional melt-down at DeeDee's on Friday, since that's really why I had come, but I found I couldn't. And I wasn't sure why. I had thought about my reaction to that simple little touch all through the weekend but couldn't articulate how I was feeling even to myself, let alone someone else. Not even Mom. Maybe DeeDee was right and it all boiled down to hormones.

"Enjoy the fun part," Mother said, drawing me back to the moment at hand, "because next comes the nesting."

"Nesting? What's that?"

"That's when the work begins. DeeDee will turn that house inside out getting it ready for the baby."

"Like you when you're spring cleaning?"

"Like me on steroids when I'm spring cleaning. It happens without fail when it gets this close. Just watch. You'll see DeeDee become more domesticated than you ever thought possible. She'll clean out everything from the attic to the basement—neither of which she has, but that isn't the point. She'll have the carpets cleaned, and she'll even rearrange the cans in the cupboard. It's the most predictable thing in the world."

"But we did all of that for the announcement party—except the cupboards."

"Doesn't count."

I moaned because I knew it meant I would be drafted to do more than help paint the nursery walls. And I was already worn out.

"Don't worry; I'll help. And Linda will too. She's just dying to be asked to do something."

"Really? She's so busy with work." I ended my thought with a shrug.

"She's excited, you know, but then we all are."

There it was again, that little pang in the pit of my stomach. Not regret, I was quick to note, but . . . what? "Mom," I began, not really knowing what I wanted to say, "something is happening in me."

A look of perfect understanding spread across her face. She laid down the duster and led me into the kitchen. She turned the burner on under her teakettle and nudged me in the direction of the table. It wasn't the one I'd seen her settle into so many times over the years, offering wise counsel as the wife of a pastor. That one was in my kitchen now. I simply hadn't been able to let it go in the moving sale. But though this table was glass-topped instead of oak, the wisdom and compassion hadn't changed. She fixed our tea, then sat down across from me. After a sip or two, I told her what had happened in DeeDee's powder room.

"I feel so fickle, as if I don't know my own mind. All of a sudden I'm afraid I'm missing out on so much."

"Well, having a child certainly brings a new dimension to a couple's lives."

"But it's not even that, Mom. Today you talked about nesting, as if it were the most natural thing in the world, which I guess it is, but I've been your daughter for forty years now, and we've never had that conversation before."

"There was no occasion for it."

"Exactly. There's a dimension even in our relationship that's been affected because I decided not to have a child, things we'll never share because there was no occasion for it." I drew in a breath and let it out slowly. "All of a sudden I'm afraid my life will never be complete, sort of like a photograph not fully developed."

"No." She reached across to pat my hand. "Just developed with a different exposure."

"Black-and-white instead of color? Matte instead of glossy?"

"There are courses we can choose for our lives, one equally as right as another. As long as we understand and are true to the absolutes, the most important of which is the lordship of Jesus Christ in our lives, we have the flexibility to make decisions that fit our personalities. Up until now you've been perfectly content to remain childless. You may be at a place where you're rethinking that decision."

That was it exactly. "I'm terrified, Mom."

"Have you talked to Sonny?"

"I wouldn't know what to say to him. Besides, there's no point in throwing his world into a tailspin when I may come to my senses at any moment."

Mother smiled. "You may have a point. And you know, I was thinking, why not have a shower? It might help to get your mind on other things. Then, when you readdress your feelings, they might seem a whole lot clearer."

"A shower? Now? I'm on my way to a painting soiree."

She rolled her eyes and shook her head. "Not for you. For DeeDee. A baby shower."

I thumped my forehead with the palm of my hand. "A baby shower! Of course. I meant to talk to you and Linda about that very thing. Somehow I got sidetracked."

"Yes. With Lamaze classes and nursery designs, et cetera, et cetera. You've been consumed with this pregnancy. No wonder your emotions are so raw."

"Will we have time? The baby is due in, what, eight weeks?

And what do we say about the sex? DeeDee's convinced it's a girl, but what if she's wrong?"

"Yes, there's time, but we should make a list and get the invitations ready to mail by the end of December. And as far as not knowing the sex, that's the way it was for thousands of years. It only adds to the fun."

"Shall we make the shower a surprise?"

"Absolutely."

"Then we'd better not have it at my house. Or Linda's. That would be too obvious."

"Then I'd better get back to my cleaning." Mother gathered up the cups and took them to the sink.

"You wouldn't mind having it here? Honestly?"

"Mind? I'd be delighted."

"Then I'll start putting a list together this evening."

"And I'll call Linda. I know she'll have some names to add. Maybe the three of us could get together tomorrow night to make all the plans."

"Sounds great. Now I'd better be on my way or DeeDee will think I've abandoned her."

She walked me to the door and we hugged. "Thank you, Mom."

She held me a little tighter in response. "When the shower is behind us, before the baby comes, it would do you good to get away for a couple of days. Just you and Sonny, somewhere romantic and restful. If you're still having these second thoughts, talk to him."

"I'd give him a heart attack and come home a widow." I threw my hand over my mouth. "Oh, Mother, I'm so sorry. That was thoughtless." I could have crawled into a hole.

She gave a quiet little chuckle. "Honey, I know I'm a widow.

Trust me, I'm over the shock. Now think about what I said. It really would do you good."

❧

By late Thursday afternoon we had put the finishing touches on all the characters, and the room had come alive. DeeDee chose sunshine yellow as the main color for the bedding and accessories, which complemented the theme beautifully. The crib, changing table, and armoire were painted a glossy white, as was all the woodwork around the windows and doors. I'd never seen a room with such dimension. For the finishing touch, DeeDee hung a mobile from the top of the crib, and, sure enough, the colorful shapes were covered in fairy dust . . . or maybe it was sugar.

"This is enchanting, Dee. If I ever write a children's book I know who I'll get to illustrate it."

She took in the whole of our handiwork with her eyes. "It has been fun." She rubbed her belly and sighed contentedly. "Little one," she said in a soft, whispery voice I'd never heard her use before, "we're ready when you are."

19

The baby shower was set for a Saturday afternoon, one month before DeeDee's due date, and I knew exactly what I was going to give her. Since Mother had moved into her condo, losing the attic space she'd had for years, she was storing a few special items at our house. One of them was the cradle that DeeDee had fallen so in love with, even before she was pregnant. From the moment I heard there would be a baby, I planned to get it ready for her.

Whenever I had a spare hour I would sand the wood smooth of all its peeling paint until the tips of my fingers felt rough as a scouring pad. I was amazed to find such beautiful wood under the coats of white paint. Sure, white was nice for a cradle, but the maple was so beautiful I hated to hide it again. I really had to think about how I was going to finish it.

I was almost certain we'd managed to keep the shower a surprise. I'd registered DeeDee at one of the local shopping chains that had a large nursery department, listing items I'd heard

DeeDee mention, then filling in the gaps with the obvious: diapers, sleepers, blankets, et cetera. Hopefully I had covered most of the bases. Mom and Linda went in together on a stroller that did everything but babysit.

We called upon Maria Garibaldi to cater hors d'oeuvres for thirty-five and had The Nutcracker Sweet design a three-tiered musical carousel cake that revolved on a mirrored base and played a medley of lullabies. The carousel horses were made of crystal and threw off a rainbow of colors from the reflected sunlight as the cake revolved. It was a unique design. Perhaps I hadn't lost my inspiration after all.

I was eager for DeeDee to see it—and to find out if we had truly pulled off the surprise. It was a little past two. Everything was ready and everyone had arrived. Everyone, that is, but DeeDee. She was a few minutes late, but that was not unusual. I mingled with the guests, making small talk with one little group and then another, while Linda, out of view of the guests, paced in front of the dining room window with a worried look on her face.

"She should have been here by now," she whispered as I advanced.

My mother served another round of punch, then joined us. "Maybe you should call. It's nearly half past two."

I went into the kitchen and dialed their home number. Jonathan answered on the third ring. "Hey, it's me." As if he wouldn't know.

"Hey," he said cheerfully, then his voice dropped to a whisper. "Did you pull it off?"

I couldn't help but smile. Did he think he'd ruin the surprise if he spoke too loudly over the telephone? "Well, that's just it," I said. "DeeDee isn't here yet. Do you know what time she left?"

"Well, yeah. I walked her out to the car myself about a quarter of two. She's had plenty of time to get there."

"Okay," I said, trying to keep my voice from betraying the worry that was setting in. "I'll try her cell phone. But isn't it just like her to get the last laugh, even when she doesn't know the joke?"

"Yeah, it is, but have her call me when she gets there, would you?"

"You bet."

I ended the call, then immediately dialed her cell number. My hands were clammy, a sure sign of my anxiety. I thought of all the reasons she might be late as I waited for her to answer. If she came up Elm Street, which would have been the most direct route here, she might have been stopped by a train. They could go on forever at times. Which is why I usually took Turner Road. It was less direct but had an underpass. If she had taken Turner, that would add an extra five minutes, which meant she should have made it here in twenty minutes at the most. But according to Jonathan she left forty-five minutes ago.

Or she might have stopped for flowers. She always brought something for her hostess, and since she thought this was a luncheon for our mothers and us, I could see her stopping for yellow daisies. They would complement my mother's table perfectly, and she knew it. Okay, if she went by the florist's, that would add another ten minutes. She still would have been here fifteen minutes ago. "Answer," I said, not realizing she already had.

"Gabby?"

"Dee?" I went weak with relief. "Where are you?"

"What do you mean where am I? Where are you? I'm here at your mom's house and no one's home."

"What do you mean no one's home? I'm here, my mom's here, and your mom's here." Not to mention the other thirty or so guests.

"Knock it off." I could hear the irritation rising in her voice. "There's not a car in sight, and no one answered when I knocked at the door."

I laughed, certain she was pulling my leg. "Right."

"I'm not kidding, Gabby. I've been waiting half an hour and no one's here, *and my bladder's about to burst,*" she added in a whisper.

Okay, now I was really puzzled. "Maybe you have the wrong condo. I've almost done that myself a time or two."

"Condo?" Her voice went flat all of a sudden. "Oh wow. I've been sitting in front of your house since two o'clock. Well, not *your* house, your *old* house."

"On Crescent?"

"I'll be there in ten minutes." Her phone instantly went dead.

"She's on her way," I announced, wondering what in the world she was doing on Crescent Way. "Everybody get in place."

"Tell me you were surprised." I stood at the sink, scraping the cake plates clean of any leftovers, then rinsing and arranging them in the dishwasher. "At least a little."

DeeDee sat at the kitchen table with her feet propped up on a chair to elevate her swollen ankles. "Okay, a little, but mostly that it took you so long to have the shower." She smiled and winked. "No, really, it was a blast."

"Now there's a word from the past," I said, "but it was, wasn't it? I didn't know I could laugh so much over diapers and colic."

"At the next shower we'll have our own stories to tell, won't we?" She rested her hands across her belly and looked as content as a cat on a sunny windowsill.

My stomach fluttered as I thought back over the baby shower. Yes, it was fun — but I'd found myself becoming increasingly worried as I watched DeeDee interact with our guests. It was like she didn't know who they were, or like she knew the faces but, try as she might, the names wouldn't come to her. She seemed confused. And after having gone to the wrong house . . . well, I just didn't know what to think.

I shook my head and tried to put it out of my mind for now. Hormones, right? "Are you scared, Dee?"

"Yes," she said, and now she wasn't teasing. "Those women today all sounded so confident about motherhood, but I'm terrified. That I won't do it right. That somehow I'll fail."

My mother came into the kitchen with a bagful of discarded gift wrapping and bows. "And they were terrified too when they were sitting where you are." She pushed the paper farther down into the bag to make room for the wad that Linda brought in behind her. "We all were. Isn't that right, Linda?"

She nodded and managed to look terrified still. "Frightfully."

"Well, if I'd been *my* mother, I'd have been frightfully terrified as well," DeeDee said, pushing away her qualms, and mine, too, with one of her famous smiles.

"You received so many nice things today," my mother said. "But the fun part is putting them all away."

"Now that you have the nursery finished," Linda added. "It's as darling as any I've seen."

"That's quite a compliment coming from a real-estate agent." DeeDee didn't bother to mask her pride.

"I can't tell you how many times I folded and refolded sleepers and diapers before Angel came, just so I could feel them in my hands." Mother closed her eyes as if reliving the experience. "Of course, you don't have diapers to fold and refold these days, but you have plenty of other adorable things."

It came again, just then. The sense that I had missed out on a whole dimension of relational experience with my mother. It was my own choice, I know, but that didn't lend much comfort. "I never knew that." I hoped I didn't sound as envious as I felt.

"We all do it," Linda admitted, as if confessing that she, too, was a closet baby-clothes folder.

My mother caught the look in my eye and sent a wink and just the hint of a smile meant for my eyes only. Her expression, in a comforting language all its own, said, *We'll talk.*

"But speaking of gifts . . ." DeeDee looked sideways at me and crossed her arms. "Where's yours?"

"Mine?"

"You have something up your sleeve and you know it. This isn't the only surprise you've been trying to keep from me."

"*Trying* to keep? You mean you really weren't surprised?"

"I said I was." She tossed me a cryptic smile and refused to go any further. "So, about my gift?"

"It's here," I said, "but I wanted to give it to you when it was just the four of us . . . after everyone else left. It's kind of personal."

She raised an eyebrow. "Okay. I'm intrigued."

"Good." I gave her one of my own cryptic smiles and went back to loading the dishwasher.

"Gabriella!"

Gabriella? She rarely called me anything but Gabby or Gab. Ha! I really had gotten to her. I looked over my shoulder at Mom and Linda. "What do you think, girls? Has she waited long enough?"

"I don't know about *her*," Mother said, "but I know I have. I'm dying to see what it is."

"Well, then, wait here and close your eyes. All of you."

I dried my hands on a paper towel, snatched my keys out of my purse, and headed out the front door, leaving it fully open. I lifted the rear door of my SUV and carefully slid out the bulky item from beneath the blanket covering it, then closed and locked the vehicle again. When I reached the front door I called out, "Are your eyes closed?"

From the kitchen I heard a chorus of yesses. I stepped into the living room and placed my burden in the center of the room. "Okay. Mom, Linda, bring DeeDee in, but make sure she keeps her eyes closed."

"Can *we* look?" Linda called back hesitantly.

"That would probably be a good idea," I replied, smiling to myself. I wondered sometimes how Linda functioned as well as she did all by herself in the real world.

"Okay, then, we're coming."

I stood waiting, eagerly, proudly . . . hoping I wasn't making too big a deal out of it.

"Oh," my mother said. It was more a sigh than a word, and I knew I wasn't.

"How lovely," Linda said at almost the same moment.

But when DeeDee opened her eyes, I knew I'd achieved the surprise and the delight that I had hoped for. "Oh, Gab." She knelt to better inspect it. "What a special, special gift." She gently rocked the cradle, *my* cradle, as if her baby were already in it. "Is it really the same cradle?"

"It is. In all of its natural beauty."

Mother put an arm around my shoulder. "You refinished it yourself?"

"I did, and I have the raw fingers to prove it."

"And the ruffle thing? You made it?" DeeDee ran her fingers along the edge of the fabric.

I nodded. "I was beginning to get really worried that you wouldn't decide on a theme in time for me to get this finished. When you finally did and then selected that wonderful yellow fabric for the window topper, I bought some extra for this. I didn't know sewing could be so easy. Of course, when you have a sewing machine with a smart card, how hard can it be?"

"And this doll? It matches everything. How adorable."

"I found the pattern in the fabric store and couldn't resist. All it took was a little muslin added to the other cloth I bought and some stuffing. And it's baby proof." I pointed a finger at her. "That's very important."

"Who drew the face? You?"

"Remember, I'm not the artist, but I did the best—"

"It's beautiful." DeeDee picked up the doll and brought it to her cheek. "I don't know what to say." She looked up from where she knelt and gave me a smile too tender for words. "I know this cradle is special to you. I'll take good care of it. And the baby, too." Her voice became a whisper. "The real one."

"Okay, enough," I declared, after I swallowed the lump in my throat. The day had been too nice to end it with tears. "Everyone is invited to my house for a barbecue." I reached for the phone to call Sonny. "But I suppose I should inform the chef."

"Tell him to make it hamburgers," DeeDee said, "with pickles and onions and lots of cheese."

"In January?" Linda said.

"That's what covered patios are for."

❧

"So tell me, what were you doing on Crescent Way?" We had finished a delightful barbecue way ahead of the season—

hamburgers just the way DeeDee liked them, baked beans, potato salad, and canned peaches. Now the two of us were on the patio enjoying a clear January sunset. Mom and Linda had called it a day, and it had been a full one. Sonny and Jonathan were engaged in a game of chess that had thus far lasted three weekends.

She gave me a bewildered look that I had become used to seeing as of late, but this time there was nothing playful about it. "I never gave it a second thought. I left home at quarter of two and headed straight for Crescent. I pulled up in front of the house, wondering where all the cars were." She covered her mouth. "Oops."

"You knew?"

"Let's say I suspected. Anyway, I knocked at the door, then I rang the bell, then I actually tried the knob. It was locked."

My eyes went wide. "Aren't you glad? You might have been arrested for breaking and entering."

"If the door had been unlocked, *technically* it would have just been entering. But, yes, I'm glad it was locked. So I went back to my car and . . . waited."

"You were just sitting there when I called?"

"It never occurred to me that I was at the wrong house. I didn't know what else to do."

"This is scary, Dee."

She waved a dismissive hand. "It's hormones."

"Okay, it's scary hormones. But I think you should talk to Dr. Creager. Don't you see her on Monday?"

"Tuesday. At three. But what am I supposed to say? I had a temporary brain freeze? I'm sure this is completely normal. After all—" she looked down at her tummy—"I have been a little preoccupied. And, by the way, I've been meaning to ask, would you mind helping me get the house in order, you know, before the baby comes?"

"In order? Dee, your house is—" I started to say *immaculate*, then remembered my mother's warning. This was the nesting she was talking about. I smiled and choked back the word. "Sure, Dee, I'd be happy to."

❧

I waited for everyone to go home that night before telling Sonny about DeeDee going to the house I'd grown up in instead of the condo my mother had lived in for nearly a year. "It was the strangest thing. Not only did she go to the wrong house, but she didn't seem to know who all the guests were when she finally got to the right one."

Sonny dried the last of the cookware that wouldn't fit in the dishwasher, then took my place at the sink to clean his barbecue utensils. "Well, who were they? Did she know them all?"

"Certainly. They were friends from church and women from your office and a few we've kept in touch with from college."

"Honey, I hate to tell you this, but that happens to me more and more with people I don't see every day. It's just, well, we're not thirty anymore."

"No. You're not getting it. If you could have seen the struggle that was going on inside, it was, I don't know, almost frightening. There was an element of confusion that simply isn't DeeDee."

At that he became thoughtful for a moment, as if debating whether or not to say what was on his mind. "You know, Jonathan mentioned something a while back. I don't remember all the details, but ultimately, he said the same thing you just said about an element of confusion. At the time we chalked it up to hormones," he concluded with a helpless kind of shrug.

"And that's what DeeDee has been saying for months now.

But I'm beginning to think it doesn't have anything to do with hormones."

"Then what?"

"I don't know, Sonny. Maybe it's nothing more than funny little occurrences that don't mean anything, but if I get a chance, I'm going to talk to Dr. Creager. See if she has any ideas."

"Maybe you should just make an appointment and go in, without DeeDee, of course, and see what she has to say."

"I'll talk to Jonathan first. Maybe if we compare notes we'll realize it really is nothing. I could just be overreacting. I mean, I've driven halfway to the old house myself more than once before realizing Mom lives on the other side of town."

"And I have too," he admitted. "Funny how we can be such creatures of habit."

"Funny," I echoed, trying to ignore the churning feeling that stirred in the pit of my stomach because it wasn't really funny at all.

20

My mother and Sonny conspired to get me out of town the first weekend of February for a few days of rest before The Big Event. Knowing how I loved the sea, Sonny took me to a wonderful bed-and-breakfast in Mendocino, two hours north of San Francisco on Highway 1. As we crested a hill, and the endless Pacific came into view, I rolled down my window and breathed deeply of the salty air. "It doesn't get any better than this," I murmured, to myself more than to Sonny.

I had agreed to this getaway only because it was still eight days until DeeDee's due date. "And throw in an extra week for good measure," Mother had added in her most authoritative voice. "First babies are always late."

So I was absolutely confident we had fifteen days at least, and I was going to be gone for just three of them. Still, I charged the battery on my cell phone to the max and decided against buying a pager for added precaution only because Sonny assured me that cell towers had sprung up like California poppies all along the coast and that we would have perfect reception there and back.

If the towers were there, they were hiding, I noted, as we drove beneath a sky filled with wispy clouds, but Sonny was absolutely certain we were in range of anyone trying to reach us from DC to Maui. Just to be sure, I phoned DeeDee and insisted she call me right back. It was with great relief that I saw her name and number appear on the little screen of my cell phone and heard her voice loud and clear on the other end, telling me I wouldn't hear a word from her all weekend—unless, of course, there was an emergency. I breathed a little easier—then checked to make sure the volume on the ringer was as high as it would go.

"Okay?" Sonny said, with his most understanding smile and the patience of Job.

"Okay." I was determined, for three days, to put everything out of my mind except Sonny and this glorious little spot he'd brought us to. "However did you find this place?"

"A new client owns it. Wyn Dawson. Purchased it last summer and just finished renovations. I've been wanting to check it out. Thought this would be the perfect time."

I formed my mouth into a little pout as he pulled into the parking lot of Dawson House. "You're not here to work, are you?"

He took my hand and brought it to his lips. "Not a chance."

"Well, all right then." A little shiver went up and down my arm.

From the before and after photographs on display in the lobby, Dawson House had been a neglected Victorian turned into a lovely inn with all the charm and elegance money could buy. There were six bedroom suites, all decorated differently but in keeping with the Victorian theme; a cozy dining room with an enormous fireplace at one end; and a waiting list six months long.

"You must have scored some points with Mr. Dawson to have

jumped to the head of the line like this." I smiled and slipped my hand into the crook of his elbow, thinking how proud I was of his business acumen.

He was on the verge of saying something in reply when a woman, moving like molten lava, approached. Her long red-gold hair was draped over one shoulder in a most provocative way, as if the toga-type, body-fitting gown she wore wasn't provocative enough. Her eyes were the color of emeralds. *Has to be contacts*, I thought to myself. As she stopped before us, we were engulfed with a scent that was subtle yet alluring. And expensive. She could have been a double for Nicole Kidman. No doubt about it, this woman was dangerous.

"Sonny," she purred, touching him with those eyes in a way that made me positively bristle. "You came." Then she extended to me an exquisite alabaster hand with long, tapered fingers and perfect natural nails that glistened with a transparent pink gloss as soft as a blush. "Wyn Dawson." There was a challenge in her voice a man would never recognize.

Wyn Dawson? My left eyebrow arched, and I found myself at a definite loss for words.

"My Gabby. Wife. My wife, Gabby." Sonny emitted a nervous little laugh that I found only slightly less mortifying than his introduction. "She thought you were a man."

With a little laugh of her own, Wyn tossed her hair behind her bare shoulder and sent another cloud of perfume into the air. "I get that a lot."

Given enough time, the writer in me could have formulated a really good comeback, but in the pressure of the moment all I could do was curse DeeDee for saddling me with a nickname like Gabby, for heaven's sake. *At least it isn't Mike*, I thought, for the first time in all these years.

"I'll show you to your suite, then give you a tour of the house." Personally, I'd seen enough, but before I could find a way to graciously decline, she took Sonny's other elbow and led us up the stairs. I had to admit Dawson House was five-star enchantment, but chances were slim to none that the Nevins would be repeat customers.

Alone in the Victoria, the grandest of all the rooms in Dawson House, I folded back the Queen Anne's lace comforter on the antique four-poster feather bed, fluffed a pillow, and stretched out. "So, Sonny, tell me about Wyn Dawson."

"Wyn?" He shrugged as he slipped off his shoes and sat beside me on the bed. He leaned on one elbow, looking as blasé as he could manage. "She's rich, beautiful, single—for the third time, if I remember correctly—determined, intelligent, tell me when to stop."

I slowly rolled my head in his direction. "Now would be a good time."

He smiled and then laughed and scooted a little closer. "Would that be jealousy I see in those lovely gray eyes?"

"Are all of your clients so . . ." I stopped and shrugged. "Words fail me."

He laughed again and covered my lips with a warm, wonderful kiss. "Did I mention she's not my type?"

"Oh? Does that mean you go for poor, homely, dull-witted women?"

He scooted closer yet. "Only if they look like you."

Should I push him off the bed or surrender to his kiss? His next statement made my decision a simple one.

"Have I ever told you," he said, kissing my nose, chin, earlobes, and eyelids in strategically placed pauses, "that since the moment I saw your little red nose sticking out of your poncho hood as you climbed the stadium stairs at homecoming, there's been no one for me but you? Not even Winifred Dawson."

Winifred?

"Every woman I see is measured against your beauty, your grace, your charm, and, quite truthfully, there's no comparison. Do you really think my running into you on the steps of the student lounge was an accident? You, Angel Joy Gabriella Whitaker Nevin, are the real deal. I wasn't about to let you get away."

Okay, I didn't push him off the bed. In fact, I let him get a little closer. The room had grown chilled with the late afternoon sea breeze gusting in through the open window, and the warmth of his arms was as delightful as a fire in December. A foghorn sounded from somewhere far away, and the sound of the breakers hitting the shore spilled into the room. I had hit it right on the head—it didn't get any better than this. Before I could say so, a shrill blast filled the room, breaking the spell we'd cast. My cell phone. Sonny and I exchanged a look mingled with dread and disappointment in the split second it took me to grab it off the night table. "Dee?"

"It's Jonathan. Her water broke." There was a distinct edge of panic in his voice. "We're on our way to the hospital."

"Now? But Mother said—it's only February 6."

"Get here as quick as you can."

I slid off the bed and into my shoes as we spoke and motioned for Sonny to do the same. "We're on our way. But, Jonathan, don't you dare let her have that baby till we get there!"

Sonny needed no further explanation. He grabbed our bags while I gathered up our other belongings. "This is it?"

"Her water broke. That's as *it* as it gets." My heart was racing and I had to tell myself to breathe. "Sonny, we have to hurry."

We were met with some startled expressions when Sonny

stopped at the desk to check us out, the most startled of which belonged to Winifred Dawson. "We're having a baby," Sonny said.

It was Wyn's eyebrow that arched this time as she scrutinized my midsection. "Did you say a baby?"

"Her water broke," Sonny said, as if that made it abundantly clear.

For my part, I said nothing to clear up the confusion that was swimming beneath Wyn Dawson's emerald green contact lenses. "Love the room, but we'll have to take a rain check." I took Sonny's arm and sashayed out of the inn.

❦

It took three and a half hours to get back to town, most of which were spent on my cell phone getting a moment-by-moment account from Jonathan. No doubt about it, those cellular towers were being tested to the limit.

When we arrived at the hospital, we found Linda and Mother wandering the halls of the maternity ward, two grandmothers sympathetically reliving their own deliveries. "Oh, Gabby." Linda threw her arms around me and sniffled. "I'm so glad you're here. I can't bear to see her in so much pain."

"Pain? Are they giving her something?"

My mother smiled consolingly. "Sweetheart, it doesn't work that way. Pain is part of the process."

To me, that sounded like the title for a lecture on acupuncture. "Where is she?"

Mother pointed to the second door on the right as she wrapped an arm around Linda's shoulder.

Sonny aimed a thumb at Linda. "I'll just stay out here."

I tiptoed into the room, as if loud footfalls would exacerbate DeeDee's distress, and when I spoke, it was in whispers. There has to be some psychological phenomenon that causes us to approach suffering with a gentle posture, as if sneaking up on it will somehow help the sufferer. It didn't.

"Gabby!" DeeDee wailed when she saw me. "I can't do this!" Jonathan rubbed her hand and threw me a desperate look. *What happened?* I mouthed, but DeeDee read my lips. "I should have told you, but I didn't want to mess up your weekend."

"Told me what?"

"I thought it was false labor. Doesn't *everyone* have false labor?"

She was asking me?

"But no. You're barely out of town and I turn into Niagara Falls." She grimaced with a contraction and squeezed the life out of Jonathan's hand, while I tried to erase the mental picture her words had conjured.

"Where?" I asked. It was all I could think to say.

"On the threshold of Kentucky Fried Chicken. It was horrible. I stood there like a lummox wetting myself."

"Kentucky Fried Chicken?" I repeated doltishly. It was a question thrown out for anyone's consumption.

"I was craving mashed potatoes and gravy." DeeDee sucked in her breath as another contraction hit.

"What does Dr. Creager say? I mean, isn't it too early?"

"Ready or not, here we go. That's what I say." Dr. Creager approached the bed wearing a comfortable smile. "The baby is in position, the heartbeat is strong, and DeeDee here is cooperating just as if she knew what she was doing. By that I mean contractions are coming quickly, she's dilating at an amazing rate, and I expect that baby to pop right out without a hitch." She threw

DeeDee a wink and moved to the end of the bed. "Let's see how you're doing."

I turned to leave the room while Dr. Creager conducted her examination, more for my comfort than anyone else's, but DeeDee grabbed onto my arm. "You're not going anywhere," she said. "We're in this together."

Obediently, I moved into position at her right shoulder, while Jonathan moved to her left, but I stubbornly averted my eyes during the examination. I scrutinized an Impressionist watercolor print hanging on the wall just to the left of where Jonathan stood. It was surrounded by matting the exact color of the wallpaper, not mauve or lavender but something in between, and framed with a white acrylic frame. The window, dressed in vertical blinds and sealed shut under countless coats of paint, was an old wooden crank window, such as you would find in the really old houses on the east side of town. The recent remodel of the maternity wing had been cosmetic rather than structural. Beneath the window was an air conditioning system that blew out tepid air and rustled the blinds. Even so, my forehead was beaded with perspiration.

"You're already up to seven," Dr. Creager announced. "It won't be long. Perhaps before midnight. Just go with the contractions, DeeDee. Breathe through them. Don't try to fight them. I'll be back in a while."

It was eight p.m., twelve hours since Sonny and I had left town for the coast. DeeDee had been in early labor without even knowing it. Since Jonathan had called to say they were on their way to the hospital, the contractions had steadily grown closer together and the pain more intense. According to snippets of whispered conversation I had with Jonathan, DeeDee had gone from sarcastic wisecracks early on to snappish rebukes aimed at whoever was handy as the pain increased. Now when the contractions came she was absorbed by them, curling up like a potato bug, holding her breath against the pain.

"Try to breathe," I'd say, reminding her what we'd learned in Lamaze class. "Maybe it'll help." Some coach I turned out to be.

Mother and Linda wandered in and out of DeeDee's room as the evening progressed. Mother brought coffee and bottled water for Jonathan and me like the angel of mercy she was. I saw that her lips constantly moved in a silent, never-ending prayer. Linda wore the pitiful expression of a mother helplessly watching her child suffer. It didn't matter that DeeDee was forty years old. She was Linda's baby, and, judging by the look in Linda's eyes, she was remembering her own birthing experience more keenly as the evening wore on.

True to his word, Sonny hid out in the waiting room with the latest *Newsweek* magazine, though I doubt that he absorbed much of its contents. All things considered, it was the best place for him. Mother kept him updated, and I ventured out a time or two myself, just to get a break from the mounting tension. Jonathan could not be prevailed upon to leave DeeDee's side for even a minute. I found that hugely commendable.

I kept DeeDee stocked with ice chips throughout the ordeal. It was all they'd allow her to have besides water.

"I've had nothing to eat since dinner last night. I'm starved."

But as the evening wore on, she stopped asking Jonathan to smuggle her in a Big Mac and fries. The only thing she craved now was relief.

I had no knowledge of the discomfort she was in, other than by observation, but I hurt for her. More than once I had to turn away as I blotted my tears and wiped my dripping nose.

Linda was on the verge of tackling the first person she saw with a cigarette, though it had been weeks since her last puff. Mother helped her retain her resolve with soothing words of encouragement, but it was a challenge for both of them.

By eleven fifteen DeeDee was feeling the urge to push. I quickly fetched the nurse, whose shift had begun only a few minutes before, and filled her in on DeeDee's progress, to the best of my limited ability.

"Let's take a look." She pulled on a pair of latex gloves, as if she had all the time in the world. She reminded me of Snow White, with her dark hair and white uniform, and I half-expected a whistling dwarf to jump out of the closet. "Okay, Mrs. Kent, try to relax."

DeeDee clutched the sides of the bed, her body tense with another contraction. Her teeth were clenched together. "I have to push!"

"No, no. Don't push, Mrs. Kent. We have to wait for Dr. Creager."

She may as well have instructed her to hold back a tidal wave. And personally, I wouldn't have gotten within kicking distance.

"I. Have. To. Push!" Every muscle in her body strained under the impulse.

Jonathan grasped DeeDee's hand as all the color drained from his face. "Is it coming?"

The nurse finished her examination. "You must wait," she declared. "I'm getting the doctor now."

"I can't wait!"

The nurse hurried out of the room. "Doctor," we heard her say, "she's crowning."

Dr. Creager entered with a *let's-get-down-to-business* air but managed to calm us with one of her easygoing smiles. Ms. White began to help DeeDee get into position for delivery.

Mother and Linda had also been close enough to hear the call for Dr. Creager and entered the room on the doctor's heels. Linda gasped. "Is it time?"

Dr. Creager laid a comforting hand on DeeDee's arm and nodded to Linda. "DeeDee, the baby's coming and I need you to listen to me. When a contraction comes, I want you to push with it. The baby is in good position, and it shouldn't take much longer. Are you ready?"

Everyone got in place: the doctor and nurse at the foot of the bed, the rest of us as far away from *that* vantage point as we could get. No bird's-eye view for us, thank you very much.

"This is so different," my mother whispered from behind my shoulder. "When you were born, there were no such things as birthing rooms. Everything was sterile and not even the father could be in the delivery room. To be honest, I'm a little nervous." I turned and gave her a worried look. "I've never seen a real live birth before," she said in her own defense. "A mirror hung over the delivery table when I was having you, but I didn't dare look."

"Would you rather wait with Sonny? I mean, you're not going to faint or anything, are you?"

She shook her head no, a bit weakly I thought. "I'd better stay with Linda. She looks as if her knees could buckle at any moment."

Remembering the video we'd seen in Lamaze, I felt my own legs grow weak. Well, if DeeDee could do her part, surely I could do mine. But there was one thing I would never understand. I turned to Mother. "Why would anyone go through this more than once?"

A strong contraction gripped Dee just then. She groaned loudly as she pushed, bearing down with everything in her to make the most of the contraction.

"That's good," Dr. Creager coached. "Just like that."

DeeDee relaxed and lay back as the pain subsided. She was covered in sweat. Jonathan took a cloth and dried her face, then bent over and kissed her forehead. He whispered something for her ears alone, then kissed her again. If I didn't already love this guy as a friend and a brother, I certainly would have after seeing his tenderness throughout her ordeal.

The doctor kept a close eye on the monitor that gauged the baby's heart rate and other vitals. "DeeDee, we're looking good and we're almost there. I want you to push with everything in you during the next contraction."

DeeDee moaned pitifully. "I can't do this anymore." She looked thoroughly exhausted. My fingers were cramped from DeeDee squeezing them, as I'm sure Jonathan's were on the other side of the bed, but I wasn't about to complain. Instead, I was ready to call the whole thing off.

"Yes, you can," Dr. Creager said. "Okay, here we go. Push. Push hard!"

I don't know about everyone else, but I was pushing right along with DeeDee.

Behind me, just under her breath, my mother was praying like crazy.

I counted off the seconds as I watched the clock and the monitor, forgetting even to breathe. "You can do it, Dee," I whispered, as her body began to respond to that last critical contraction. "Push. Push!"

She gritted her teeth and pushed with all her might, groaning loudly with the effort.

"Keep it up, the baby's coming! Good, good!"

"Push, DeeDee, push!"

"Come on, sweetheart, you can do it!"

"Oh my Lord." Linda's words. Just before she hit the ground.

DeeDee's groaning became a wail, as if that would somehow provide the strength she needed to push this baby free.

"Good! The head is out. Now for the shoulders. DeeDee, we can't wait. I need you to push again."

DeeDee groaned and drew in a ragged breath. I didn't see how she could have enough strength left to finish the job, but gripping our hands even tighter, she repeated her previous effort, straining with everything in her to deliver this child. "Ooooooh!" One shoulder and then the other became visible. Finally, with a gush of fluid, the tiny body slid free of the birth canal. It was 11:35.

And all was well.

DeeDee fell back onto the bed and drew in gulps of air between her sobs. Jonathan dropped his head in silent prayer, grimacing with emotion. My mother wiped at her eyes, while Linda tried to stand up on legs as weak as willow shoots. I stood in awe of what was yet to come, namely the moment when we would actually see the newest of God's creations. Collectively, we held our breath waiting for the pronouncement.

Dr. Creager held up the infant. "We have a girl." She positively beamed with the news, while the rest of us broke into cheers, not because she was a girl, but simply because she was. The baby lay flailing in the doctor's hands, naked except for the milky white mucous that coated her skin. We all began talking at once, saying how beautiful she was, and what a miracle, and can you believe it, when DeeDee raised her head to get her first glimpse of her daughter.

"What do you think of her?" Dr. Creager asked, proud as could be. She passed the baby to a nurse, who placed her in a hospital bassinet and began to suction her nose and mouth.

"Wow," DeeDee said, looking at me with eyes barely focused.

"She looks just like your uncle Eddie." She dropped onto her pillow, for all intents and purposes dead to the world.

21

In the wee small hours of morning, as the song goes, we managed to go home to get some sleep. Even Jonathan agreed that DeeDee would allow herself to rest if none of us hung around. And she definitely needed her rest. But, of course, we stayed long enough for each of us to hold our new baby girl. Jonathan was first, and I could have kicked myself to Baghdad and back for not having my camera. And the sad thing was, I had put my own little bag together, just as DeeDee had in preparation for her trip to the hospital. It contained, among other things, a book for Sonny to read in the waiting room, a notepad and pencil to record highlights of DeeDee's labor and delivery from a writer's perspective (I laugh now that I thought I might actually have the presence of mind to do that), a box of granola bars, and my digital camera with a fully charged battery and an empty one-gig memory card that would hold five hundred photos or more. The canvas bag hung by its strap to the coat tree at our front door, ready to grab on our way to the hospital.

In the days leading up to the delivery, I had assured Mom and Linda that they needn't bother trying to remember their own cameras when the moment finally arrived. All they need do was get to the hospital. I had even decided not to take my camera out of the bag to take along on our weekend getaway for fear I'd forget to put it back and not have it for just this moment. And, as if that weren't enough, in all the hours of labor while we waited and paced and prayed, I never even thought about my camera. If I had, I could have sent Sonny to get it. Ah well. I, for one, would never forget this extraordinary day.

The baby found her voice as the nurse, finished with the suctioning, wrapped her in a thin blanket and handed her to Jonathan. Startled, the baby tensed her little body, then began to squall as she was passed from one set of hands to the other. Without a hint of consternation, as if he had been doing this for years, Jonathan wrapped her tiny body in his arms and held her close to his chest. Instantly she stopped crying and tried valiantly, but in vain, to open her eyes to see who was kissing her perfect little fingers. He had a look of wonder on his face that somehow took me by surprise. My breath caught in my throat, and I had to swallow again and again to keep my tears from gushing. It was a look I would have given all I had for DeeDee to see.

Jonathan handed her off to me just as Sonny popped his head into the room. "Oh" was the most profound thing I could think to say as I took her in my arms, and I said it repeatedly. "Come look."

Sonny stepped to my side and reached, hesitantly, with one finger to touch the downy soft hair on her perfect little head. My heart thumped, and I couldn't stop cooing at her. Her eyelids fluttered as she tried again to get her first glimpse of the world, while her little bowed legs continued to flail. I looked at her perfect little face and felt my heart expand, hugely, to make room for this little life, thinking, *This is no ordinary child*. I didn't realize at the time there was no such thing.

I didn't want to give her up, but, reluctantly, I made a motion to hand her to Sonny. He held up his hands and took a step back, a look of terror crossing his face. "Not yet," he whispered.

So Mémé Margie eagerly took her turn. She was calm and confident, as if she, too, had been handling babies every day for the last forty-plus years. For her, it was like riding a bike — some things you never forgot. Mémé Linda was the complete opposite. Mother stayed close, her arms poised and ready to support Linda if she so much as wobbled a knee.

While their lives had, for so many years, been connected because of the deep bond that DeeDee and I shared, they had suddenly been linked more profoundly and permanently than either of them would ever have dreamed. From this day forward, the little child they so carefully cuddled was bound to knit their hearts together with hers until you couldn't tell where one stopped and another started. And I was sure that would be true of all of us. Baby Girl Kent, as her hospital bracelet identified her, was the newfound nucleus of our little world.

DeeDee's eyes were open now, taking in the scene as the baby went from one grandmother to the next. "My turn." Her voice was raspy and strained. As Linda laid the child in her daughter's waiting arms, the baby let out a single cry, showing off dimples that matched her father's to a tee. "Well, that was hardly worth the effort." DeeDee ran her finger down the slope of her daughter's perfect little nose. With that, Baby Girl Kent made one final effort and opened her eyes to look into the smiling face of her mother as her first view of life.

It was only right.

We said good night to DeeDee and followed as the baby was wheeled to the nursery in her bassinet to join her tiny compatriots, who had also come into the world on this special day. We stayed long enough to watch her get her first bath and her first diaper put on. Her skinny little legs looked almost purple sticking out of the white disposable diaper. She kicked and wailed like a banshee until the nurse wrapped her up nice and tight in a pink hospital blanket and pulled on a matching stocking cap to keep her head warm.

Baby Girl Kent. She was six pounds, two ounces, and nineteen inches of perfection.

We were all back after a short nap and a quick bite to eat, looking as if we'd taken a tumble in the Maytag. DeeDee, on the other hand, had showered and applied the teeniest bit of makeup and was dressed in a pink T-shirt that said, "I'm the Mommy."

The baby lay asleep in her bassinet next to DeeDee's bed, making adorable sucking motions with her perfect little mouth. Jonathan knelt beside the child, a look of awe and trepidation on his face, thinking thoughts unfathomable, no doubt. He proudly wore a pink T-shirt of his own that said, "I'm the Daddy." Only DeeDee could have pulled off such a feat. I started to ask if she had any baby blue T-shirts tucked away, just in case, but I already knew the answer. In this phase of her life, she had proven herself to be a woman of sure and unwavering faith.

"Okay, the moment has come. Tell everyone her name." I waited, anxious to hear the name I'd come to love since before the child was conceived, one I loved even more now that it was attached to such a perfect little girl. Macy McAllister Kent. Future president of the United States of America.

DeeDee reached into the bassinet and picked up the child, who moved her head like a windup doll, then settled back into a peaceful sleep in the crook of her mother's arm. There was a look I'd never seen before shining in DeeDee's eyes. "Angel," she said. "Her name is Angel."

The silence was broken only by my sharp intake of air. "No! It's not!"

"It's not?" Linda said at the same moment Jonathan said, "It is?"

"No," I said at the same moment DeeDee said, "Yes."

Mother's face mirrored the confusion that abounded in that little hospital room.

"Dee," I said desperately, "tell them. About Macy. About the White House. Don't you remember?"

"Don't *you* remember," she said right back at me, "what I said when you told me your name the day we met?"

"Yes," I snapped. "You said, 'It sounds like a name you'd give a kid—'" I was suddenly unable to finish.

So she finished for me. "You thought you'd never have."

Tears burned my tired eyes as the room settled back into a solemn hush.

"But just for you, we'll give it a French twist. Her name is Angel, mind you, but we'll call her Angelique."

"She'll never be president," I whispered. "Not with a name like Angel Kent."

"Maybe not, but she'll be everything God created her to be. We'll all make sure of that."

Okay, leave it to the preacher's kid to blow it. Again.

❧

Thirty years earlier, DeeDee gave me a nickname that all but eradicated my given name. We now did the same to my little namesake. Not corporately and not officially, but we each managed to give her our own special moniker. To Jonathan, she was Sunshine. To my mom, she was Sweet Baby Girl. Linda called her Dumplin', Sonny called her Sport, and I called her Gelée, the sound of the third, fourth, fifth, and sixth letters of her name. Translated to English it meant *jelly*, but I chose to overlook that.

Whatever her name, this little child was about to bring the most extreme changes into our lives. While the guys did their best to keep a measure of normalcy to their schedules, DeeDee and I threw ours right out the window. Mother was doing a fine job with the gallery. And though I'd scrambled to finish the text of our devotional before DeeDee delivered, I missed it by three chapters. I'd work on those chapters in the early morning, then go over to DeeDee's, because I was quickly learning that if you so much as closed your eyes for one moment you were bound to miss something.

I hadn't intended for this to happen. I expected to be far more detached. I knew DeeDee would need help, especially in the first few weeks, and I was prepared to do my part. What I wasn't prepared for was the fact that I couldn't wait to do it. I'd rise early in the morning, work on my devotional, and hurry through my household duties in a perfunctory manner, without even reading my morning newspaper over a cup of tea, as had been my habit for more than two decades. Then I'd quickly shower, throw my hair in a ponytail, and rush over to DeeDee and Jonathan's house — usually before the baby even woke from her early morning nap — because the ten o'clock feedings were mine, using breast milk that DeeDee had pumped, and I wouldn't have missed them for the world.

DeeDee craved her own special time with Angelique, and the middle of the night was it. I was almost envious to hear her tell how much she enjoyed it.

"The world is small and secure at two in the morning with just the baby, a rocking chair, and me. There's nothing to distract, and I don't have to share." She wore a private, faraway look when she spoke those last few words.

I could envision her in the nursery in her favorite pj's, curled up in her rocking chair nursing the baby, singing lullabies in French, and running her finger over that soft, newborn skin, while an eternal bond grew between them. It touched my heart in a wistful sort of way.

Jonathan took the six a.m. feedings, using the milk that DeeDee pumped, so she could get a few hours of uninterrupted rest after her night's vigil.

I reluctantly dragged myself home in the late afternoon to fix dinner for Sonny and me and throw in a load or two of laundry, but I couldn't help but wonder what I was missing while I was away from the baby. Would she roll over for the first time? Or discover her toes? Or laugh out loud? Or perform some other first in the innumerable list of firsts that new babies delight their parents with?

But within a few weeks our lives were, once again, more normal than not. Strangely, none of us could remember what life had been like without Angelique.

DeeDee turned into a doting and adoring mother, positively a new person in my eyes. I would never have believed she could be so maternal, not even when she became adamant about having a baby. If I were to be honest, I think in the beginning I expected that she would hire a full-time nanny and dote from a distance, rather like the Queen Mother. I mean, everything in her history led to that assessment. But to see her now, she was the quintessence of motherhood, and this was a side of DeeDee's many-faceted nature that truly amazed me.

And Jonathan? Well, he was a daddy through and through, that's all there was to it. No one could make Gelée laugh like him, and the pleasure of it positively brought tears to his eyes. And if his plans and intentions counted for anything, this child would be fearless, because he was going to show her the world in a hands-on kind of way. Starting now. Nearly every morning he would put her in her stroller — not the *frumpy* one our mothers bought for the baby shower that DeeDee and I used on our walks with the baby, but a sleek jogger-model Jonathan had purchased himself — and take her with him on his two-mile run. Or he'd strap on his Rollerblades and push the stroller at a nice brisk pace, stopping to show off his beautiful baby girl to anyone who gave him the slightest provocation. I knew by the time she was four, Gelée would have a pair of her own. Along with a helmet and knee and elbow pads.

He began to compile a list of things he planned for them to do at one time or another before she went off to Harvard, his methodical mind ever at work. It was a list that gave DeeDee and me nightmares, with things like skydiving, rock climbing, white-water rafting, and spelunking. Spelunking! And this from a guy who was rendered speechless by his one and only bungee jump. I regretted having ever defended the man.

"This is a side of Jonathan I've never seen before," I said to Sonny on one of our Saturday morning walks. It was the last of March, and the trees were starting to awake from their long winter nap. Tiny buds appeared on barren limbs, the promise of new life. A few homes had tendrils of smoke curling from their chimneys, adding an acrid aroma to the air, indicating that someone besides us had stirred on this damp morning. But most of the houses still had blinds closed and curtains drawn and newspapers lying at odd angles on the porches. I breathed in deeply, then exhaled a visible puff of breath. "I mean, spelunking of all things. Do you think he means it?"

"He's excited. It'll wear off." When I gave him a raised eyebrow and my severest *you-really-believe-that?* look, Sonny added, "Probably not completely."

Suddenly I was struck with a thought not at all pleasant. "Do you think he's sorry she's not a boy?"

"A boy? No way. He's the happiest man I know—when it comes to fathers," he said, catching himself. "He just wants her to really experience life, and he wants to experience it with her. I doubt they'll ever get to spelunking. It's pretty far down on the list."

"You've seen it? I'd hoped DeeDee was exaggerating."

"No, no. The list is real all right. But he revises it almost daily. He's tamed it down, in fact."

"Tamed it down?"

"You wouldn't have wanted to see the first draft."

I raised an eyebrow and slowed my walking. "Do you suppose all new fathers are this . . . dangerous?"

"Well, let's just say God knew what He was doing when He made mothers. They're a nice counterbalance." He smiled, but I wasn't so sure he was teasing.

22

Gelée was dedicated at six weeks of age on a Sunday morning in the church where my father had dedicated me. There were times when I felt his absence deeply, and this was certainly one of them. I couldn't help but think what a remarkable thing it would have been to have Dad dedicate this special child. I fully intended not to cry. After all, this was a joyous occasion. But my thoughts were taking me places I didn't wish to go, and my emotions got the best of me. Sonny slipped me his handkerchief, which I tried to use as surreptitiously as possible, while crouching in front of the church with my camera.

My mother, usually the solid one, must have been thinking thoughts similar to mine, because she struggled for composure as I'd never seen her struggle before. She bit her lip in an effort to keep her chin from quivering, and not just because of the occasion. There were just so many memories. After all, she had been the pastor's wife at this very church for a quarter of a century. She had come here as a young woman, scared but in love, and had given herself wholeheartedly to her husband and to the ministry. She had played "Jesus Loves Me" during countless baby dedications, through one miscarriage and then another, fearing she'd never have the child she longed for. And to think I never knew this. The dedication of Angelique must have stirred up a world of recollection for her.

Linda, poor thing, was scared to death. She wasn't used to being *in* church, let alone *in front of* the church, and it showed. She rocked from her toes to her heels and couldn't figure out what to do with her hands during the entire dedication, then practically sprinted off the stage when it was over, relieved, I know, to become just another face in the crowd. I half-expected her to keep walking right down the aisle and out the back doors, but she followed Jonathan into the pew and sat down, keeping her eyes front and center for the rest of the service, unconsciously twisting a hankie around and around her fingers.

Our little group was approached by half the church when the service was over, many of them getting their first look at Angelique. She was dressed in a cotton candy pink pinafore with white socks and booties and wore a ruffly white headband around her nearly bald head. She was positively adorable. She had enjoyed a bottleful of formula just before church, so she slept contentedly through all the oohs and aahs that I soon learned were part and parcel of admiring a baby.

While DeeDee didn't know all the well-wishers who approached, she did know most of them—or should have anyway. Except for during college, she had attended this church nearly every Sunday since the age of eleven, not to mention youth nights and summer camps. Yet, when she attempted to introduce her mother to people who were by no means strangers, she faltered and failed the first five times out of six. Finally, to spare anyone any more embarrassment, Jonathan and I took over the introductions, while DeeDee proudly showed off her baby and thanked each visitor for the compliments they gave.

If I hadn't known DeeDee as thoroughly as I did, I might have missed the faint trace of confusion in her eyes as she tried to bring to mind the names of people she had known for years. Granted, she didn't see these people every day or speak to them on an ongoing basis. Ours was a large church, especially considering the size of our little town. But we attended social functions with many of them, and a number had frequented her gallery over the years. She shouldn't have struggled for recall as she did. I'd seen exactly the same confusion in her eyes on the day of her baby shower. Something really wasn't right. And all of us knew it.

"Did you see it, Sonny?" I asked as he and I drove home that afternoon. "That odd look on her face, as if she were groping for something just out of reach? I tell you, there's something wrong. I don't know how else to say it."

He nodded almost imperceptibly. "Didn't Sally Griffin go on that retreat with the two of you a couple of years ago? Where was it, over on the coast somewhere?"

"Both she and her sister-in-law Megan. The four of us shared a cabin. We had a ball."

"DeeDee didn't seem to know her. Rather, she did, but she didn't." He caught himself as he reiterated word for word what I had said to him just over two months ago.

I clutched his shoulder. "Exactly. It was almost painful to watch her groping for a name she should have been able to spit right out. She keeps saying it's hormones, but I think even she's beginning to wonder what's going on."

"Did you ever talk to Jon, you know, after the shower?"

"I meant to. I tried to." I looked out my window. "I didn't know what to say."

He pulled the car into the garage as we reached home, then leaned over and kissed the worry from my forehead. "Come by the office tomorrow and we'll have lunch with Jon. Somewhere we can talk privately."

I gave him a smile spiked with concern in spite of the kiss. "I think that's a good idea."

He lifted my chin with a gentle touch and kissed me again. "We'll figure out what's going on. I'm sure it's nothing."

A niggling little something—more than worry, less than fear—had taken residence in the pit of my stomach, and every time I thought about DeeDee it surfaced. I would do anything for her, make any sacrifice. Again and again. But how do you fight something you can't see? Or name?

"I'm going to call Mother." I stepped into the kitchen from the garage with Sonny right behind me. "If it's hormones, she'll know. All this worry may be much ado about nothing. Let's pray it is, Sonny. Really, really pray."

I was right. Mother had noticed DeeDee's confusion, for lack of a better word, and was trying to call me as I was calling her. "I noticed it to a small degree at the baby shower, but I attributed it to her being flustered by the surprise factor. Now I'm not so sure."

"Could it be hormonal, or simply that she's tired? She's been through so much the last two years trying to have this baby."

"It certainly could be fatigue. The first few weeks following childbirth are exhausting, even with all the help DeeDee's getting. But hormonal? I don't know. Maybe having a baby at the same time your body is preparing for menopause can throw your hormones into a tailspin. That would be a question for her doctor."

"Then you didn't experience anything similar when I was born? I know you were much younger than Dee, but I was hoping to hear you say this kind of thing isn't at all uncommon." I paced nervously as I spoke.

"I wish I could, honey. Have you talked to Linda?"

"I didn't want to worry her if this really is nothing. She tends to look at the dark side of things, even when there isn't one. Besides, she's done so well giving up smoking, and I don't want to rock the boat."

"Good point. What about Jonathan? Has he mentioned any of this to you?"

"No, but Sonny thinks we should take him to lunch and talk about it."

"I think that's a good idea. Call me afterward."

I hung up the phone with that gnawing, sickly feeling in the pit of my stomach. "God," I whispered, "whatever is wrong, please let it be simple. Better yet, let it be nothing."

We went to a café on Pine Street that was famous for its crepes. Sonny and Jonathan ordered the special of the day, but all I could manage was a glass of iced tea. My stomach had churned most of the night, and I knew it would rebel if I tried to put anything in it.

"This is a nice surprise," Jonathan said to me, then caught the look that Sonny and I exchanged. I had hoped Sonny would at least mention the reason for this get-together, but like me, he probably had no idea what to say.

Jonathan sat back in his chair, his expression going from upbeat to concerned. "Everything okay?"

I toyed with my bundle of silverware, picking at the raffia that held the napkin in place, not sure how to put my thoughts into words. Jonathan folded his hands and waited for me to begin. "Have you noticed anything unusual about DeeDee lately?" I asked.

"Unusual?" He shrugged a shoulder. "You mean like preoccupied, ultrasensitive, forgetful?" He smiled, trying to break the tension, letting me know that whatever DeeDee was, he did and always would adore her.

Jonathan paused as the waiter served his plate, then Sonny's. We joined hands and Sonny prayed, then looked up at me. "You sure you won't have something?" he asked.

I shook my head.

"So, Gabby, you obviously have something on your mind."

I should have waited for them to eat, I decided, thinking I might be blowing everything out of proportion.

"Go ahead," Jonathan said.

"Maybe it's nothing, but DeeDee doesn't seem herself these days."

"You mean yesterday at church?" When I nodded, he continued. "I agree she was a little off her mark, yet she seemed perfectly fine once we got home."

"Did she?" I asked hopefully.

He nodded as he took a large bite of a chicken and broccoli crepe. "Good," he said to Sonny. "Yes?"

Sonny agreed. "Did she mention anything about it? About how she was feeling or what happened?"

"Nothing specific. Just said she was tired and took a nap with the baby."

"Had you noticed anything unusual before yesterday?" I asked.

He shrugged. "Like I said, she's been forgetful, but she seems perfectly fine at home."

I had to agree with him there. I spent almost as much time with her as he did, and I hadn't really noticed anything unusual except when she was in a crowd. "But crowds have never affected DeeDee before."

"She's never had a baby before. She's pretty wrapped up in that little girl. But then, aren't we all?"

Well, that was the truth. I couldn't help but respond to the smile that crossed his face with one of my own. "I guess that means you're enjoying fatherhood?"

"Oh man, it's . . . I don't think I can describe it. Take the best experience you've ever had and multiply it to the nth degree." He finished off his second crepe.

Sonny asked the waiter for a box, which was unusual. He and Jonathan never had problems cleaning their plates. But this time Sonny placed his leftovers inside the Styrofoam container, then slid it over to me. "For later," he said, giving me a wink.

I let out a breath. "I'm probably blowing this whole thing out of proportion. You're right, Jonathan. Except for a little forgetfulness, DeeDee seems just fine. I'll try to quit being such a worrier." I snatched up the lunch tab before either of the guys could reach for it.

"But you didn't even eat," Jonathan said.

I picked up the container. "I will. Besides, I invited you." That was the rule. Regardless.

Jonathan wrapped an arm around my shoulders as the three of us walked to our car. "Thanks for your concern and your friendship. DeeDee's a blessed woman to have someone like you in her life. I suppose you could say you're her"—he gave me a crooked smile—"guardian Angel."

I groaned. "That was really bad."

He laughed. "It was, wasn't it?"

23

DeeDee returned as the manager of her gallery the Tuesday after Easter. I helped her set up a mini-nursery in one corner, with a portable crib, a small rocker, and a freestanding cupboard to hold diapers and baby supplies.

"Glad to be back?" I asked.

"I am," DeeDee said. "I didn't realize how much I had missed it." She spread her arms and looked around. "Now I have it all. Your mother did an excellent job, by the way."

"I knew she would," I said smartly.

Dee hiked her eyebrow. "Right. So what can I do to really thank her? Where would she like to go?"

"Go?"

"For a long weekend, or even a week. A vacation. On me. With a friend, of course. It's no fun going off alone."

"You mean, like get on a plane and go somewhere?"

"Exactly."

"Gee, I don't know. She likes . . . well, she likes . . . home."

That was the truth.

DeeDee brushed that off with a wave of her hand. "Let's think. I know there must be someplace she'd like to go. And I really want this to be a surprise. I don't want to ask her."

"Well, there is something she's talked about, but not for a long time."

"What? What?"

"I won't tell you unless you let me pay the friend's way. Your share for Mother will be quite enough."

"Oh no, this is on me all the way. I want the full blessing."

"Well, then, never mind." I went back to stacking Huggies in the diaper holder.

"Gab! Come on. Out with it."

I shook my head. "Nope. Just send her to Tahoe for the weekend."

"Not on your life." DeeDee's hands were on her hips. It always made me laugh when she did that because her hips were so not there. "Tell me."

"Not unless — "

"When did you get so spunky?" she said, and then she smiled. "I like it."

That made me laugh for real. "Do we have a deal?"

DeeDee shrugged a shoulder, then nodded. "Okay." I stuck my hand out and she crossed her arms. "I said okay."

"Shake or it's no deal."

She took a step backward. "You're positively sassy."

"You've been rubbing off on me for years."

This time she laughed as she shook my hand. "I have, haven't I? So, where are your mom and some lucky friend off to?"

"Alaska. On a cruise ship."

"Oh, Gab! That's perfect."

We went to work on the reservations right away.

❦

On the Fourth of July we gathered at our house for a barbecue, minus our mothers—unfortunately. Linda was flying home from a seminar in Vegas, and Mother was at a play in Sacramento. With a man! After dinner our plan was to go to the local fireworks display at Lodi Lake like we did every year. It was directly across from the General Mills Plant. And if they made Cheerios today, anyone within a one-mile radius would know it. Personally, I liked being in the area on those days.

Angelique awoke from her nap in a fussy mood. Nothing anyone did could soothe her. DeeDee tried, Jonathan tried, I tried, even Sonny tried—and he usually preferred to be in another state if she so much as whimpered. It wasn't that her crying got on his nerves, at least not entirely, but like the rest of us it killed him to see her unhappy.

By late afternoon she had cried until her voice was nearly gone and all she could produce was a pathetic squeak, and still she cried, breaking all of our hearts in the process and making her mother frantic. Her cheeks were as red as radishes, and the thermometer showed her temperature to be 101.3.

"That does it," DeeDee said, "we're taking her to the emergency room."

So we strapped her in her car seat and headed to the hospital.

A crying baby who will not be consoled is the worst form of torture for a new mother. DeeDee paced the halls of the hospital, waiting for her child's name to be called by the triage nurse. Finally, with tears streaming down her own cheeks, she handed Angelique off to Jonathan, who gave me the signal to comfort DeeDee while he took another turn with the baby. I stuffed some Kleenex into DeeDee's hand and waited for her to blow her nose.

"Why don't they *call* her? If anything happens—"

"Nothing's going to happen." I said it bravely, but my own heart raced with fear.

"Angelique Kent." Finally. "Only one of you in the triage station," the nurse said when Jonathan and DeeDee moved toward the door.

Jonathan saw the *you're-not-about-to-keep-me-out* look on DeeDee's face and handed the baby back to his wife. He nodded in our direction. "I'll just wait with them," he said. As if he had a choice.

Once the triage nurse had taken Gelée's brief and uneventful history, the baby was taken back to a little cubby in the emergency room. Mercifully, we were allowed to go along.

We didn't have to wait long for the doctor. He stepped into the room, pulled the curtain closed behind him, and introduced himself all in the same moment. He bent down and looked directly into Gelée's tear-filled eyes. "What seems to be the problem, little one?" His voice rang with compassion. I liked him instantly. When we all started talking at once, he said, "Why don't we hear from Mommy first."

In the bravest voice she could muster, DeeDee explained the events of the day, not omitting a single detail. Fever. Cranky. Not herself at all.

He examined her eyes, ears, and nose; felt the glands on both sides of her neck; and pressed on her tummy, humming a calming little tune as he worked.

"How long has her temperature been elevated?"

"Since she got up from her nap, about two thirty."

"Has she taken fluids?"

"She won't take her bottle and she wouldn't even eat her strained bananas."

"And bananas are her favorite." This from Sonny.

"Hmm," the doctor said. Then, as if from a sudden burst of inspiration, he ran a gloved finger along Gelée's lower gums. Immediately she stopped crying and began gnawing on the intrusive finger. "Aha."

"What?" we all said at once.

He peered into Gelée's mouth and smiled. "Here's the problem. She's cutting a tooth."

"Tooth?" DeeDee said, unbelieving. "We knew it was coming in, but—"

"It hurts to have teeth?" I said.

"Like the dickens when you're five months old."

I was stunned by this revelation.

"How long will it last?" Jonathan asked.

"It's almost through now. We'll give her something to reduce the fever, rub on a little Baby Orajel, and give you a sample to take with you. You'll be good to go." Gelée continued to gnaw on the doctor's finger with a look of extreme gratitude on her face, as a puddle of drool collected on the plastic-sheeted gurney. "By the way, an ice-cold teething ring is like manna from heaven when they're teething. I'd keep a couple on hand. This is just the beginning."

All this because of one little tooth? That did it. I was enrolling DeeDee and myself in an Early Childhood Development class at the local junior college. Posthaste.

One week later I showed up at my usual time for Gelée's morning feeding. "I did it," I said. "We're enrolled. And, ta-da, I finished the second-to-last chapter in the devotional. One more to go. Which means you need to get busy with the illustrations."

"Enrolled?" DeeDee was in an old T-shirt, a pair of army green sweats, and white athletic socks. Her hair was gathered up in a clip, and she wore no makeup.

"In the class, Dee. Early Childhood Development?" There it was again. That look of confusion. "We talked—"

She smothered a string of sneezes in a wad of tissue.

"About it. Bless you," I said. "And again."

She moaned a thank you. "How can the same nostril be stuffed up and running all at the same time?"

"You don't look so good." What I really wanted to say was, *You don't remember?*

She leaned a weary shoulder into the back of the sofa and rested her chin on her knees. "It's just a cold."

"It came on awfully sudden. Maybe you should call the doctor."

She reached for more tissue and shook her head. "Just a cold," she said again.

"Well, at least go upstairs and take a nap. I'll stay with the baby until Jonathan gets home."

DeeDee threw me a *bless-you* look. "A nap would be good, but I think I'll stay right here. I don't have the energy to climb the stairs." She spread a chenille throw over herself and was out before I could vacate my end of the couch. I covered her feet and carried my laptop to the kitchen to work on the final chapter of the devotional.

Gelée gave me fifty minutes of productive work time before she stirred from her nap. I changed a messy diaper without so much as an *"Eeewww"* and got a dimpled smile for my trouble. Then I warmed a bottle and settled into the feeding chair, as the family room rocker had come to be called.

Before Gelée was born I'd have sworn I didn't know any lullabies. But somewhere in the recesses of my memory, they were there. I hummed away as Gelée consumed her lunch, keeping eyes the color of liquid cobalt focused on my face. Then she reached a tiny fist toward the bottle, grabbed hold of my little finger as if it were her connection to this world, and sighed contentedly as she sucked.

My eyes blurred with tears, and I almost laughed when I heard myself echo her sigh. I swear I didn't know I had such capacity to love.

After the last good burp I carried her with me to the kitchen. I placed her in her cradle, *my* cradle, intending to get back to work. But I couldn't take my eyes off her. She was thirteen pounds of perfection, everything about her utterly right. We talked, she and I, for the longest time. I provided the words; she provided the sounds that bubbled out of her like pure joy. What was that line from *Peter Pan*? Or maybe it was the movie *Hook*? Something about fairies and laughter . . . I went online, typed in a few key words, and found it. "When the first baby laughed for the first time, the laugh broke into a thousand pieces and they all went skipping about, and that was the beginning of fairies."

I understood it completely now.

And loved the baby's Neverland room more than ever.

All too soon Gelée drifted off to dreamland, her breath coming evenly from parted lips that looked like a kiss from heaven. Every one of my senses arced, as if electric joy ran through my veins at the sight of her.

Gelée gave me new insights into the Fatherhood of the God I

thought I'd known my whole life. He was no longer the Lawgiver and the Judge of the Old Testament. He was the Father whose deep love for us . . . for *me* . . . had moved Him to give the most precious thing of all. Suddenly the passage from the third chapter of John took on profound meaning. *For God so loved the world that he gave his one and only Son . . .*

And for the first time in my life I got it, God's love. Sent in the form of a Baby. So that we'd get it.

DeeDee's cold lasted nearly a week. And not for one moment did I mind the extra time it cost me caring for her and Gelée.

I did try to stop worrying, as Jonathan encouraged, but over the remainder of the summer I saw little things that alone might have gone unnoticed but when combined were adding up to something bigger. Besides the forgetfulness, something was fading right out of DeeDee's eyes. The sharpness, the focus, just wasn't there. Always on the cutting edge before, she had become withdrawn and indecisive, and it had nothing to do with the baby, of that I was certain. I started a new journal that summer, a DeeDee's-episodes journal, color coded by symptom. DeeDee would have loved the chart I came up with, but it was not for her eyes.

More and more, she struggled with recall. Not just with names, but with words as well. DeeDee had a vocabulary greater than the average person, but it was slipping away at a noticeable rate. She clung to familiar words and phrases and employed repetition as if it were a crutch, particularly at church. "She's such a nice girl." "They're a nice couple." "A nice sermon." I could almost predict what she'd say in any given situation.

But her French remained flawless. Oddly. And she reverted to it as if it were her native tongue, whipping out phrases now and again for sport.

"*Angelique et peux-je déjeuner, s'il vous plait.*"

Angelique. Please. That much I got. I frowned hard as I tried to remember the rest.

And DeeDee would laugh like the DeeDee of old. But only for a moment. "Lunch, Gab. We'd like lunch."

And the joy, as fleeting as a forgotten dream, would give way to the fear that was brewing in all our hearts.

On the afternoon of August 19, Mom stopped by the Kent house to see DeeDee and Gelée before she left for her cruise. "I just want to say thank you again, Dee, and give Sweet Baby Girl a kiss before I go." She reached for the baby, who was rocking in her Baby Papasan, a great little invention to lay the baby in that rocked, vibrated, and played lullabies.

"Go?" DeeDee looked surprised. "Where are you going?"

"To Alaska. With your mom." I could see she already regretted saying anything.

"My mom? Linda?"

Mom held the baby and looked to me for help.

"A cruise," I said. "They're taking a cruise. Together."

DeeDee gave a slight nod. "And you're thanking me? Then I guess I should say you're welcome. So, you're welcome."

"It was a thank-you gift," I said, "for Mom's help with the gallery."

"Ah. And Linda?" DeeDee said.

"My treat."

She bit her lip and looked as if she was trying so hard to remember. "What fun."

"Well, I need to finish packing." Mom kissed Gelée and handed her to me, then walked to DeeDee and gave her a long hug. I saw the tears in her eyes, saw her blink them away. "The Lord bless and keep you," she said, a blessing straight from the heart. Then she kissed DeeDee's cheek.

"I want to lie down," DeeDee said after Mother left.

"Go on ahead, Dee. I'll be here."

24

When Mother returned from her cruise, she asked DeeDee if she could resume helping at Northern Exposures. Not to replace DeeDee, just to help as a volunteer. She said it was because she enjoyed being there so much, but we understood it was to oversee the daily operation of the gallery. It was getting to be too much for Dee, but she strongly resisted Jonathan's hints that they find a full-time manager. So she could spend her time with Angelique, he said. DeeDee firmly said no.

There was nothing major to add to the journal until Sonny's birthday in early November. DeeDee came to my house to help prepare dinner. Gelée, now nine months old, took an afternoon nap while we worked in the kitchen preparing a new pasta dish I'd gotten off a cooking show on The Food Channel. I retrieved my ingredients from the refrigerator and the pantry, carefully comparing them against the recipe, while DeeDee worked on a superb-looking salad.

"Oh no. How did I manage that?"

DeeDee turned from the sink, where she was draining a jar of artichoke hearts. "Manage what?"

"I missed the Gorgonzola cheese on the recipe when I was shopping. I'll have to run back to the store."

"You can't get out—I'm parked in the driveway behind you. I'll go."

"You don't mind?"

She shook her head as she reached over and pulled off a sheet from the note cube I kept by the phone. "Anything else?"

"Let me double-check, just in case. No, I think that's all."

"Gorgon . . . gorgon . . ."

"Zola. G-o-r-g-o-n-z-o-l-a." I spelled slowly, as if to a ten-year-old, every letter a stab in my heart. "It should be in the deli/produce section where the fresh cheeses are in the new market up the street. I love having such a gourmet store so close. Don't you?"

"New market?"

"You know, we went to the grand opening a few weeks ago." When she didn't respond, I added, "We stuffed ourselves on all those wonderful canapés."

Finally she nodded, though her face remained blank.

"You remember?" I wanted to make sure. When she nodded again, I reluctantly said okay and told her I'd keep an eye on the baby while she was gone.

The monitor resting on my counter assured me that Gelée was still sleeping soundly, so I shredded the other cheeses the recipe called for and chopped the vegetables. I filled a large pot with salted water in which to boil the pasta and added some ingredients to the salad DeeDee had begun. I set the table for six, since both of our mothers would be joining us, and made the garlic butter for the bread. All this, and DeeDee had not yet returned.

When I heard Gelée begin to stir, I washed my hands, then

went upstairs to get her. Our guest room had become a guest nursery so Gelée would have her own room at our house. And central to the décor was a painting of DeeDee's I'd found in a storeroom of her gallery—one she'd painted several years ago of a child's playground in winter with a swing that was empty. Well, if that picture wasn't worth a thousand words. It hung directly over the crib. Which wasn't empty.

Gelée lay on her back in the crib, playing with her toes and cooing. The little cloth doll I'd made lay at her side. It was turning out to be her favorite toy, which delighted me to no end. She smiled the instant she saw me, sending a flutter through my heart, as it always did, and I thought once again, *She's undoubtedly the most remarkable child ever conceived.*

As I changed her diaper, I tickled her tummy, and she laughed out loud. She let out a huge burp when I picked her up, then smiled a broad smile, revealing four milk-white teeth. "Well now, that must have felt good. Did that make room for another bottle? Hmm? Are you hungry?" Drooling, she grabbed my nose. I kissed her plump, dimpled cheek. "Let's go down and see if Mommy's back."

She wasn't.

The clock showed that she'd been gone forty minutes on a ten-minute errand. But I wasn't going to worry. For crying out loud, DeeDee was a grown woman. She was probably perusing the shelves of the new market, which were stocked with items not common to most grocery stores. I didn't blame her for taking a look around . . . but it *was* nearly five o'clock. I needed to get my meal prepared.

A little rap sounded at the front door, and I knew right away it was my mother. She let herself in. "Angel baby?"

"In the kitchen, Mom."

"Oh, there's my Sweet Baby Girl." She dropped Sonny's gift on the kitchen counter and took the baby from my arms in one fluid motion. "Look at how you've grown." Gelée drooled down the front of Mother's blouse and kicked her feet excitedly. "Ah, we're going to have another toofy any day, yes we are. Hi, darling." She gave me a kiss in greeting. "Where's DeeDee?"

"At the new market up the street." I looked at the clock again, trying not to broadcast my worry. "Have you been there yet? They carry the most exotic products. Their produce is completely organic, and their fresh salad bar is incredible."

"I saw the ad for the grand opening, but I never think about it when I'm on this side of town."

"Come by one day this week and we'll make a day of it." I glanced at the clock again. "Speaking of making a day of it, DeeDee's been gone forever. She must be having a good time."

Just then, I heard the front door open again. DeeDee came into the kitchen, placed her purchase on the counter without a word of explanation, then went and gave Angelique a hug. "Hold her while I finish the salad?" she said to Mother, then kissed her baby's toes.

"There's nothing I'd like better."

I picked up the grocery bag and removed the cheese. It was exactly what I wanted, but the sheer plastic bag bore the name of the market across town — the one DeeDee was used to shopping at. "Did they not have Gorgonzola at the new market? I was certain they would."

DeeDee kept her eyes on the salad she was tossing. "New market?" A frown creased her forehead as she repeated the words to herself a second time. She seemed to be straining to understand them.

I felt as if my heart had literally dropped to my toes. "Never mind, Dee." I gave her a little hug. "Thank you for getting the cheese."

As Mother looked up from the baby and caught my worried eye, I shook my head ever so slightly. I'd explain later.

❧

After dinner I took Jonathan and Sonny aside and told them what had happened, while Mother helped DeeDee give the baby a bath. "She needs to see a doctor, Jonathan. Right away."

"Does it matter what market she went to?" Sonny asked.

"That isn't the point, babe. We were at the grand opening of that market and she went on and on about how fabulous it is, and now she doesn't remember it's there."

For the first time I saw real concern in Jonathan's eyes. "I just kept hoping it was hormonal or, I don't know, something easy to explain away. But . . ." He shrugged. "It's getting worse. And I don't even know what *it* is."

"Then you agree she needs to see a doctor?"

He nodded. "I'll call tomorrow."

❧

The afternoon of November 11, Jonathan took DeeDee to see her doctor, who ordered a complete blood workup and other kinds of lab work we knew nothing about. Her follow-up appointment was for the week after Thanksgiving.

And speaking of Thanksgiving, Jonathan and DeeDee were taking Angelique to visit Jonathan's parents in Washington, since they'd only seen the baby in photos and videos.

"We want you to come along," DeeDee said. Her arms were

outstretched on either side of Angelique, who'd begun to pull herself up to their sofa, her little legs bowed like a broncobuster. "Jonathan's renting an RV. It'll be so much fun."

I loved the idea of being with Gelée on her first Thanksgiving, but I was having a hard time committing. "I'll think about it," I promised.

That night at home I said to Sonny, "What will Mom and Linda do if we go to Washington?" I sat with my back against the arm of our sofa, my legs crossed over Sonny's lap.

"Survive," he said. He ran his hand back and forth over my foot.

"So you think we should go?"

He gave an easy shrug. "Why not? It might be a fun trip in an RV, and I could help Jon with the driving."

That surprised me. I expected Sonny to be more reluctant than I was. "They're planning a whole week, you know."

"It's a long way to Bellingham. Any less wouldn't make sense."

I scratched a smudge of something off my jeans. "I kind of thought about trying one of those deep-fried turkeys this year."

"Deep-fried? You?"

"Well, I hear they're —"

He reached over and took my hand. "Why don't you tell me what's really on your mind."

I gave him a suspicious look. Just how well *could* he see into my soul? "Well . . . it's just that . . . I don't know, I guess I feel that, you know . . ." My words collapsed into a shrug.

"Wow. That's some bush you're beating around."

I couldn't help but smile, knowing I was busted. "It is, isn't it?"

"Enormous. So what's the problem?"

I had no choice but to come clean. "Maybe it's just me, but I feel that the first time DeeDee and Jonathan take the baby to see his parents, they should go as a family. Without anyone else."

"Funny. That's exactly what DeeDee said you would say, but before I tell you what she told me to tell you, shall I tell you what I think?"

"Okay," I said, not sure I really wanted to know.

"I think you're afraid people will think you're becoming too attached to your best friend's baby and that you're enjoying motherhood vicariously through DeeDee. *And*—"he held a finger up to stop me from interrupting—"that by staying home you'll prove them wrong. Did I hit that psychological nail squarely on the head or what?"

My eyes stung with unexpected tears.

"Sweetheart." He pulled me into his arms and kissed the top of my head. "Nothing could be further from the truth. The vicarious part, that is—not the proving them wrong part. Besides, with the way things have been, DeeDee might need your help."

In spite of my resolve not to cry, the tears trickled down my cheeks. "Sonny, I'm having such a hard time finding my place. I'm just Auntie Gab and I know that. But I . . . I . . ."

"Love being with her? And watching her change on a daily basis?"

I nodded.

"That's perfectly okay."

I clutched his arms as he began to pull away. "There's . . . there's more." My heart felt like a punching bag inside my chest, leaving me almost too breathless for words. But I sucked in a breath and spilled my guts on the exhale. "I honestly couldn't go through what DeeDee did with the charts and the getaways and the Robitussin and thermometers, but, Sonny, I think I'd like—"I gasped for more oxygen—"to try."

He leaned back and looked at me with eyes as big as nickels. "Are you . . . saying . . . ?"

I nodded and pulled him close, hanging on as if my life depended on it.

We held on like magnets too charged to separate, then his words came in a whisper. "Okay. Yeah, that's okay."

I looked to see if he was kidding, because if he thought this was some kind of joke, well, it just wasn't funny. But honesty oozed from every pore. "Okay? It's okay?"

"Would I lie to you about something like that?" He used the sleeve of his shirt to blot my tears.

Whoever said chivalry was dead didn't know Stuart Oliver Nevin III. *No, he wouldn't lie. About anything.* I laid my head against his chest. His heart beat faster than my own, and that made me smile. Here we were, two forty-plus-year-olds on the brink of a life-changing decision. And scared as tomb raiders. "Are you sure?"

"Well, the results belong to the Lord, but I wouldn't mind giving it a good try."

I smiled again. "That's sporting of you."

He smiled back. "Did you really mean no getaways?"

"Well . . ."

"And that Robitussin thing. What was that about?"

Robitussin? Did I really say Robitussin? "Oh, it's just . . ." I brought a hand to my mouth and coughed. I mean, it couldn't hurt to keep a bottle on hand. Could it? I pulled him closer. "This will be our secret. For now. Okay?" And then I kissed him to seal the deal. He kissed me back, and I couldn't help but think, *This is going to be fun.* "So what did DeeDee tell you to tell me?"

He made an honest attempt at mimicking DeeDee's

I'm-the-boss face, managing only to look like a Jack Benny impersonator, and a bad one at that. He said, "We leave Monday morning at seven. Sharp."

And we did.

25

The San Joaquin Valley was mired in fog as we pulled out of town, having loaded the RV with enough supplies to stock a Babies"R"Us outlet, but by the time we reached Siskiyou County, we had risen above it. The sun was in its winter mode, not radiant enough to warm the chill November air, but luminous enough to warm our spirits and light us on our way as it reflected off yesterday's snowfall.

We stopped at Mount Shasta for an indoor picnic lunch, then bundled up ourselves and the baby to venture out for the first major photo op of our Northwest Adventure, as we had dubbed our trip. The winter air painted apple red cheeks on Gelée, who smiled like a pro for the camera as she ate her very first snowball. She gnawed and drooled as she chomped on nature's own teething ring, loving every melting flake.

Played out and comfortably dry, she went right down for a nice long nap as soon as DeeDee tucked her into her travel crib, leaving the guys conducting us on our way while her mother and I engaged in a game of Shanghai Rummy. This had been a favorite game of ours since junior high. There was some debate as to who the better player was—I had my opinion; she had hers. Together we were unbeatable, which is why the guys refused to let us be partners when we played as teams. Individually, we were competitive and ruthless.

But DeeDee wasn't on her game this day.

"Um, Dee, that's a heart." I pointed to the red ten stuck between the nine and Jack of diamonds that she had just put down on the table.

She pondered that for a moment, then looked at me, seeming not to grasp my meaning. I gave her a look that said no matter how glad I was she'd insisted I make this trip, I wasn't going to let her cheat. We were beginning a marathon match that would last us the seven days of vacation, and I had no intention of giving her an edge—not with a trip to a day spa at stake. Frowning, she reached for the erring card, then pulled her hand back hesitantly.

"The ten," I said, pointing again. She quietly retrieved it and placed it back in her hand, then looked to see if that would satisfy me. "Dee, you can't simply leave the nine and the Jack. Do you have a ten of diamonds or don't you?" I knew very well she didn't because I had both of them in my own hand. As she riffled through her cards, I saw that look of confusion come into her eyes, and I felt suddenly as if I were falling.

She turned her hand, as a child might do, to show me her cards. "Which one?"

I folded my own hand and laid the cards on the table. "Never mind. We were up awfully early. Why don't we rest while the baby takes her nap?"

As DeeDee made her way to the bed in the back of the RV, I looked up to see Jonathan's eyes staring at me in the rearview mirror. He looked exactly how I felt: submerged in panic, on the verge of drowning.

Aside from moving a little slower and appearing the teeniest bit fragile, Jonathan's parents were exactly as I remembered them from our one and only meeting fifteen years before, with one or two minor changes. His mother's skin had become transparent over the years, and there were large blue veins running like mole tunnels across the tops of her hands. And his father's hair, well, it just wasn't there anymore. Otherwise, they looked to be in pretty good health. Suddenly it was important to me that Jonathan came from good parental stock. Health and longevity were in his genes, and I liked the thought of that.

"Oh," Eleanor Kent said, the utterance more a breath than a word as Gelée lifted her sleepy head from DeeDee's shoulder. "Here she is." She reached out her hand and caressed the baby's back as tenderly as a new mother.

Gelée offered this stranger a shy, dimpled smile but clung to her mother's sweater. With her little hooded jacket trimmed in faux fur, she looked like a koala hanging on for dear life.

"That's okay; she'll warm up to us soon enough."

Jonathan gave both his parents an enormous hug. "You remember Gabby and Sonny." It wasn't a question.

"Of course. How nice to see you again." This from Jonathan's mother. "How was your trip? Are you hungry?"

They welcomed Sonny and me as if we were part of the family, and I realized how unfounded my fears had been. Sonny gave me a sideways glance, accompanied by a *what-did-I-tell-you?* smile. I shrugged one shoulder ever so slightly. *Okay, you were right.*

Amazing how it no longer took words for us to communicate.

"We had dinner in Vancouver," Jonathan said.

"Pie then? I baked your favorite."

"Not pecan!" Jonathan nudged Sonny. "You'll think you died and went to heaven."

"I made two," Eleanor said. "One for now, one for Thanksgiving."

DeeDee caught my eye and puffed out her cheeks. I saw right off that the stories of Eleanor's cooking were not exaggerated. And pecan, well, who could resist pecan?

Their home appeared to have been built about the time Jonathan came into the world. As I soon discovered, they had purchased it new just before his birth. It had solid plaster walls with a texture you just wanted to touch, high domed ceilings, and ornamental casing around all the windows and doors. The hardwood floors showed years of use, telling their own kind of tales, as such a home should.

Suddenly I saw my six-year-old self in my stockinged feet sliding down the hardwood-floored hallway of my parents' home on Crescent Way, with a pillowcase-turned-cape pinned around my neck and flying in the breeze behind me. I wondered where Gelée would find to do such things in our wall-to-wall carpeted houses, and it made me sad to think she might not.

My mother's floor had looked just as worn until we rolled up the faded rug that had lain sprawled under the dining room table for decades. There, the wood glistened with the luster of poured-out honey, smooth and scratchless. I had a feeling Eleanor's house would reveal similar finds.

"Why have you never told me about this place?" I whispered to DeeDee. "This was built when homes had personality!"

She looked around her, as if realizing what a treasure it was for the first time herself. "I dunno."

"You can put your things in Jonathan's old room," Eleanor said. DeeDee motioned for me to follow.

The room was furnished nearly as it had been the day Jonathan left for college, Eleanor told me. The red satin spread and cro-cheted coverlet were the only changes. "Footballs just didn't seem the proper theme for guests," she said, though sports-lover wall-paper still lined the walls. Everywhere you looked, little red and white figures were tossing footballs, slugging homers, and scoring hockey goals on a warm ecru background. "This is where you and Jonathan will stay," she told DeeDee. We can make a pallet here for the baby." She indicated a little corner of the room. "If that would be okay."

"We brought a travel crib. It should fit just perfectly."

Eleanor looked pleased as could be. "Well, then."

Sonny and I were going to sleep in the RV since their only other spare bedroom—the one that had belonged to Jonathan's sister, Janine—was doubling as the attic they didn't have. Eleanor let us venture a peek into the room, which looked as if you could hang an Antiques sign over the door and open for business the next morning. There were tarnished treasures collecting dust in that little room and throughout the house valuable enough to make a dent in the national debt. Eleanor had pieces of furniture, dishes, and glassware brought from Scotland that had belonged not only to her mother but her mother's mother, too.

Jonathan's father came up behind us. "Eleanor is what you call a pack rat." He shook his head as if he didn't know how he tolerated such a nuisance, but the smile on his lips said he could indulge his wife as well as the next man. Could it be that neither of them realized what a valuable collection was stored under their roof? "Mother, the boys can't wait another minute for their pie."

"Well, then," she said for the second time.

If I'd ever seen a lovelier pie, I don't know when it would have been. The golden pecan filling came up to the brim of a pie shell that could only be described as a work of art. It seemed a crime to cut into it, but after the first bite I was ecstatic that she did. That glorious pie was homemade perfection. The pecans, chopped to just the right size, were crunchy and warm, and the filling was sweet like corn syrup, but bold, with just a hint of molasses. I savored every tiny bite — tiny, for I wanted to make it last as long as I possibly could — giddy to know there was another one like it waiting to be cut on Thanksgiving Day.

"I'd give a year's salary and a kidney besides to bake a pie like this just once before I die."

Eleanor looked as if my little compliment had made her day.

"This week is going to be dangerous for my waistline," I told Sonny after we'd turned in for the night. "And yours, too. We're walking every morning and every night! Rain or, well, rain!"

This was the Northwest, after all.

This Thanksgiving was like every Thanksgiving I could remember. I awoke early, dressed without disturbing Sonny, hurried through the misty rain from the RV to the house, and hungrily breathed in the aroma of roasting turkey as I stepped through the door. Eleanor, covered in a stained and faded apron, greeted me with a smile and a hot cup of coffee, then went back to tearing loaves of French bread for the dressing.

"That looks easy enough even for me. Can I help?"

She thanked me as she passed off the bread and went to

chopping celery, olives, and onions. All I could think was how good this was going to be.

"My mother uses cornbread. Everything else looks the same."

Eleanor gave me a sidelong glance, then whispered her reply. "My mother did too, but my mother-in-law, well, let's just say Quinlan loved her cooking. I learned to adapt early on." She went back to chopping. "But cornbread dressing, now that would be a treat."

"Why not make both?"

Eleanor and I turned to see DeeDee standing in the doorway with Gelée in her arms. Both looked as if they weren't ready to face the bright kitchen lights. DeeDee walked to the fridge and retrieved a bottle of formula.

"Both. I never thought of that." Eleanor stopped her chopping. "But with all of you plus us . . ." She snapped up the second loaf of French bread and stuffed it in the freezer. "Why not?"

I took over the chopping, my eyes tearing severely as I diced the huge yellow onion, while Eleanor pulled out the ingredients for two large pans of cornbread.

"No salt," we said in unison, then laughed.

DeeDee sat at the table, feeding a contented Gelée her bottle. "No salt?"

"The broth. It's salty enough."

"But lots of pepper," I ventured.

"Absolutely."

I'd have high-fived her for that if I thought she knew what a high five was. Instead, I gave her a thumbs-up. She winked and looked as happy as Gelée with her teething ring. "Cornbread dressing," she murmured. "My."

Jonathan's sister, Janine, drove up from Seattle on

Thanksgiving Day, arriving midmorning and ready to do what she could to help. She was older than Jonathan by ten years, and though she didn't physically look older than her actual age, she appeared older in an academic sort of way. She was a tenured English professor at Seattle Pacific College, and if there was ever a person who embodied her chosen profession, Janine was that person. If you looked up *English professor* in the dictionary, you'd find her picture alongside the definition. She was created to be an English professor, plain and simple.

I picked up early on that Janine was comfortable in her life without Colin, and that surprised me. Because of what I knew about Linda, I assumed that most divorced women were miserable without their former mates, but Janine showed me how narrow my thinking could be.

Then I thought of Sonny and the richness he added to my life, and I wondered if Janine knew just what she was missing. And it hit me again. Had *I* any idea what I'd missed by not having a child?

Was that about to change?

It rained throughout the day, which was no surprise, but Quinlan Kent kept a fire crackling in the old brick fireplace. The house was not only toasty, but the blend of aromas from the roasting turkey, the sage-laden dressing, and the blazing oak logs was almost more than a sane person could stand. By the time dinner was announced, I wasn't sure I could have waited another minute.

We found our places at the table, grasped hands, and listened as Quinlan thanked our "good and gracious God" in simple but moving words. I felt as if I were eavesdropping on a private conversation, one that had to bring a smile to the lips of the Lord, as he expressed gratitude for blessings that I too often overlooked.

When he finished, Eleanor looked to her son and said, "Johnny, will you begin?"

Johnny? That was sweet. I liked it. Even if it didn't suit him, and that was only because to me he was Jonathan and always would be. But Sonny stifled a smirk, and I knew what Jonathan was in for once we were on the road back to California. It would be "Johnny" this and "Johnny" that, and he'd probably like it as much as I liked to be called Angel. All at once "Johnny" wasn't so sweet.

My eyes went to his hands because I expected him to dish out a scoop of the mashed potatoes, then pass them on to me, since I was to his left. But no, he kept his hands folded on the table before him and began to offer a list of things for which he was thankful. Suddenly I understood. This was Thanksgiving, and we were going around the table recounting our blessings. I was next.

That was unfortunate. Because when Jonathan got to the end of his list, he lifted Gelée out of her chair, raised her toward heaven, and said, "Lord, I thank you for the Sunshine you sent us the day our daughter was born. She's brought something wonderful to our lives we didn't know was missing. Now, happily, nothing's the same. And I thank you for giving me a father's heart, something I didn't know existed till I discovered I had one. I will love and protect her and teach her to know you. All I ask is for your help." He lowered her to his chest and kissed her feathery soft hair.

And I was supposed to follow that?

I choked back my tears, squeaked out something about friends, and passed the baton to Sonny.

Finally, we came full circle to DeeDee. "Well," she said, looking as benign as I'd ever seen her in such a setting—and that put fear in my heart. "I'm thankful for . . . eggs." She flashed a smile to everyone at the table and bent over to kiss her daughter's cheek.

"Eggs?" Quinlan whispered and turned to his wife. "What does that mean?"

Eleanor cocked her head exactly like a house finch and threw the question to Johnny with her eyes.

Who looked as if he'd swallowed the turkey. Whole.

There was an awkward moment of silence, then DeeDee cleared her throat in an exaggerated manner. "Hmm-hmm." All eyes turned back to her. "Did I say eggs?" She laughed as if she'd made a great joke. "What I meant was *legs*. I'm thankful for legs. As in, how about a drumstick?"

A sudden squeal from Gelée told me the child was not only adorable but had great timing. DeeDee took her from Jonathan and strapped her into an antique high chair Eleanor had found in the storage room, then plopped a helping of mashed potatoes on a Winnie-the-Pooh saucer and placed it in front of her. Gelée pounded the metal with an open hand and grinned, happy as a puppy with an old shoe.

DeeDee filled a little spoon with the fluffy, buttery potatoes and offered Gelée a bite, but she had other ideas. She turned her face away from her mother's offering and used a chubby, dimpled hand to scoop up a helping and stick it in her mouth — or at least she tried. Most of it ended up on her face, but the little bit she managed to taste obviously appealed to her because she went back for more. And more. And more.

It was such a delight to watch her eat her first mashed potatoes on her first Thanksgiving that we all got to laughing, and the more we laughed, the more she performed. She had mashed potatoes in her ears, her hair, her nose, and she even managed to get a little in her mouth. But eating mashed potatoes was nothing compared to her first taste of whipped cream scooped off of DeeDee's slice of pumpkin pie. It was more fun than we'd had in ages.

Janine left for home after the dishes were washed, though Eleanor offered to make her a snuggly bed on the sofa if she preferred to stay. Gelée went down for the night, the men turned on another football game and immediately fell to snoring, and Eleanor sat before the fire, working her knitting needles as deftly as if they were an extension of her fingers. DeeDee and I pulled out the playing cards. We each took a stack to shuffle, then I dealt from the reassembled deck. I watched as DeeDee arranged her cards, holding my breath as I looked for any signs of confusion as the game began. But she seemed right as rain, and she beat the socks off me on the first round of play.

I wanted to ask what on earth had happened in the RV on our way up to Washington, wanted to know what was going on inside her head, but I couldn't find a way to put the question to her. One thing I knew, I'd give her a mud facial and a pedicure to boot if she'd promise never to scare me like that again.

And I prayed. That it was hormones. Or fatigue. Or any other stressor that comes with being a new mother. But more than once I found myself chewing on my bottom lip until it hurt. Worry wasn't something you could just turn off.

By Monday I was ready to be home and eager for my own bed. My bones didn't adapt to change as readily as they once had, I reluctantly admitted, but only to myself. The visit had been delightful, but Christmas was looming large on the horizon, and I had a feeling it was going to be a doozy. I hadn't so much as purchased a Christmas card, so I had my work cut out for me.

Plus—and my heart flittered every time I thought about this—I was going off the pill after my next cycle, which was due on Thursday. Home was the place to be for such a momentous step.

We took our leave of the Kents at seven sharp, disappointing Eleanor. She was bent on fixing us a breakfast of ham and eggs, potatoes and English muffins, and fresh-squeezed orange juice to send us on our way. It was no easy feat getting out of there with only toast and coffee.

Her forehead wrinkled in worry. "You'll all waste away to nothing."

Fat chance. I, for one, could have fasted forty days and forty nights and *maybe* could have fit back into my pre-Washington jeans. Another of Eleanor's meals would have put me over the edge for sure.

I had to know. "However do you stay so petite?"

"Oh, dear, I eat very little of my own cooking."

Well, I should have asked *that* little question days ago.

Sonny manned the wheel after lunch, while Jonathan dozed in the front seat beside him. I was making my way through *David Copperfield* for the third time in a decade, enjoying every delightful word, when DeeDee emerged from the sleeping quarters, where she'd been napping with her daughter. She looked half asleep as she sat down in the captain's chair next to mine, pulling her hair into a ponytail. "I can't find my dad's number."

My head jerked up from my book. I was certain I had not heard her correctly.

But no, she said it again. "I can't find my dad's number."

I glanced at Jonathan, who had come fully awake at his wife's words.

"He told me I should call sometime."

"He told—when?" I laid *David Copperfield* on my lap.

"Before he left. The day he gave me my bike." She yawned

hugely. "Let me know if you find it," she said, then went back to lie down beside her sleeping daughter.

Sonny, Jonathan, and I sat in a fog of confused silence for a minute or two. "She must have been dreaming." This from Jonathan, who looked as though he didn't believe it for a second.

And neither did Sonny or I. But we nodded like a couple of bobblehead dolls.

"Yeah."

"Dreaming."

I could almost hear the crash as my heart broke into a thousand unfixable pieces.

26

Jonathan took DeeDee to her appointment on Tuesday morning to go over the results of all her lab work, while I kept the baby. My stomach churned the whole time they were gone, and I paced like a pent-up puppy. My concentration had taken leave. I was there in body, but my heart and soul were at the doctor's office with DeeDee.

Gelée was her own sweet self and bobbed up and down on her chubby legs while clinging to the sofa, the coffee table, my knee, whatever was handy. Her legs were getting stronger and she was getting braver by the day. At any moment she might let go and take that first step. We were all excited at the prospect, but there was no way I was going to let that happen with her mommy and daddy away.

I picked her up and put her on my lap. "How about a story, sweet girl?"

She reached for my earring. I dodged her fingers while I picked up the Mother Goose storybook made entirely of cloth. I'd found it at our church's craft sale.

"What shall we read first?" I held the book just out of her reach and turned the pages with my free hand. "Ah, how about Little Bo Peep?"

She smiled, showing me four teeth.

"She lost her sheep. Oh, see how sad she looks?"

Gelée continued to smile and reached for the book.

"She doesn't know where to find them. I know! Let's help her look." I put the book aside and stood with the baby. "Shall we look behind the chair? Oh, not there." I bounced her as we walked. She loved to bounce. "Maybe they're under the table." I bent as low as I could with her in my arms. "Nope. Not there either. How about the closet? Think they might be in the closet?"

Of course they weren't, but it helped me walk off my nervous energy.

When DeeDee and Jonathan hadn't returned by noon, I fed Gelée her lunch and put her down for a nap. Finally at one fifteen they arrived.

"Tuna sandwich?" I asked.

"We ate," Jonathan said. "But thanks." He looked grim enough to make my stomach clench with fear. I was glad I hadn't eaten.

DeeDee didn't look any better. She dropped her purse onto the coffee table. "Where's Angelique?"

"She's about an hour into her nap." I motioned to a pair of living room chairs. "Come sit down. What did the doctor say?" I kept my voice upbeat.

Jonathan sat, leaned forward in his chair, and rubbed his hands together. DeeDee stood at the window, looking into my backyard, her hands balled into fists.

"The lab work was pretty normal," Jonathan said. "Her iron's a little low, but that's easy enough to correct." He looked up at

DeeDee and then back at me. "He's thinking it could be, well, sort of like postpartum depression."

"I'm not depressed," DeeDee snapped, turning from the window. "I've never been happier in my life."

"Honey, he doesn't mean that you're not happy — it's just that there may be a chemical imbalance somewhere. You heard what he said. It's not at all uncommon."

"I'm not depressed," she said again. "I wasn't before this appointment anyway."

Just then, Angelique let out a cry from the bedroom.

"I'll go," DeeDee said.

I waited till she was halfway up the stairs. "Wouldn't she know if she's depressed?" I asked Jonathan.

He held up his hands as if to say, *I don't have a clue.* "He's putting her on a couple of prescriptions. If there's not a noticeable improvement in a month or so, he'll do an MRI of the brain."

"What would he be looking for?"

"He didn't say specifically." The look on Jonathan's face told me what he thought, though.

"A tumor? It could be a tumor?"

"Let's see if these medications help. It might just be hormones after all."

"I don't know, Jonathan. Should they wait a whole month before they do an MRI? Maybe you should insist they do it now."

"Dr. Biddle seems to think it's worth giving the meds a chance. Dee and I talked. We're willing to give it a month."

The inside of me quivered from head to foot. "A month. Well, okay. Okay. That takes us to December 21."

"And we're going to find a permanent manager for the gallery."

Instantly my eyes stung with tears. Northern Exposures meant so much to DeeDee.

"We talked about that, too, Gabby. She can't handle it anymore."

"Oooh-weee," DeeDee said as she carried Gelée down the stairs. I hurried to wipe the moisture from my eyes. "She had one poopy diaper! She's a happy girl now."

Jonathan stood. "I'll take it." He took the diaper from DeeDee and carried it outside to the trash container.

DeeDee put the baby into her winter coat. "It's hormones," she said, giving me a sideways look. "Just like I've been saying."

I nodded. "Just like you've been saying." And still I trembled.

As soon as they left, I went online and looked up postpartum depression. Up to 20 percent of women deal with it at one level or another following pregnancy. But as I read the factors that often contribute to postpartum depression, such as low self-esteem or a problem marriage, not one of them applied to DeeDee, and only one of the symptoms seemed to fit: trouble concentrating or thinking. And I wasn't even sure that's how I'd describe what had been happening. It was more a memory problem than a concentration problem.

If the doctor said a month, then okay, but I wasn't giving him one extra day.

If it hadn't been for Gelée, Christmas would have been low on my priorities, and not just because of DeeDee's health. I'd finally finished the devotional, but any collaboration with DeeDee was no longer feasible. I turned it in to my publisher the second week of December, without illustrations, knowing they would have a good illustrator available to them. But it was a disappointment. DeeDee and I had talked about doing this for so long. I kicked myself for putting it off.

For the next six days I did little else than pace and pray, waiting for DeeDee's follow-up appointment.

Jonathan and I were in Dr. Biddle's office the day after the month was up. I went because DeeDee simply wouldn't go, so Jonathan asked me to come. I was more than happy to hear from the doctor firsthand.

As we sat in the waiting room, I prompted myself not to be afraid but to pray. Yet in my heart I was terrified. Something dreadful was happening, and I was pretty sure it had nothing to do with postpartum depression. I found myself quoting a verse from Psalm 46 to myself over and over again. *God is our refuge and strength, an ever-present help in trouble.*

And this was trouble.

"It's nice to see you again," Dr. Biddle said to Jonathan, who then introduced me.

"She's a very close friend of DeeDee's."

"Like sisters."

Still, he seemed surprised that I was there. He spent a couple of minutes reading through DeeDee's chart. "Has there been any improvement in your wife's condition?"

"Not at all," Jonathan said. "I think we should go ahead with the MRI."

He wrote something in the chart and said, "Sometimes it takes a while for a patient to respond to medication. I did give her a refill, I believe."

"You did, but you also said if things weren't better in a month, you'd schedule the test. I'd like you to do that."

He gave a slight nod. "I did say that, but aren't we talking about a few isolated incidents of memory lapse? Fatigue can certainly bring that on, and anyone with a new baby is undoubtedly fatigued."

"Memory lapse doesn't really do justice to the seriousness of the situation," I said. "Anyone who knows DeeDee needs only to spend an hour with her to see there's a problem." I looked over at Jonathan. "Did you tell him about the baby shower?"

"The baby shower?" Dr. Biddle asked.

"She went to the wrong house and then just waited and waited, not even realizing it until I tracked her down on her cell phone. We were all so worried, and then when she finally showed up she laughed it off, but—"

"It wasn't so funny," Jonathan said.

"And then there was the baby dedication at church. All the people she knew, but didn't."

"And the simplest words she can't recall in conversation, and the odd things she says out of the blue."

"Such as?" Dr. Biddle asked.

We told him about the phone number incident. Then, between the two of us, we did our best to describe the strange behavior, the bewildered looks, the forgetfulness. All the while, Dr. Biddle scribbled notes in the chart.

"For a while when something odd would occur, DeeDee would say, 'It's hormones.' Now she doesn't say anything at all." Flakes of nail polish were falling around my feet.

"Sometimes she looks frightened," Jonathan added, "like even she doesn't understand what's happening. Last night I brought up the trip we made to Washington over Thanksgiving. I don't even remember now why I brought it up, but this blank look came over her face, and I could almost see her brain straining to recall what trip—" Jonathan's voice cracked and he swallowed hard. He turned his head away and blinked furiously.

That's all it took for me. The dam burst and I couldn't stop the tears. Embarrassed though I was, I cried, as if a wellspring had been opened. I'd suppressed so many emotions in the three years of our odyssey, far more than I realized. I tried to remind myself that this wasn't about me. But it didn't help. Because I wasn't crying for me. I was crying for us.

I'd have left the room, but Jonathan's chair blocked me in. And rather than be embarrassed for me, which he had every right to be, he came and knelt down in front of me and brought my head to his shoulder. He patted my back just the way he patted Angelique's when he tried to burp her—too gently to be effective.

"Sorry," I murmured at last and took a deep breath to calm myself.

Dr. Biddle handed me a box of tissues.

I'd left two black splotches on Jonathan's shirt where my mascara had washed off with my tears. They looked like little hula skirts. Right there on Jonathan's shoulder. One for me, one for Dee. I brushed at the spots with my fingers. "It's water soluble." That's all I could think to say.

He looked at the spots and nodded as if I'd made a wise observation. Then he went back to his seat. "Anyway, when DeeDee finally did remember what I was talking about, there was relief in her face for a moment. Then came the fear that I see when something like this happens." He kept his eyes averted from mine, as if he didn't trust himself or me with a visual exchange.

"Have you talked to her about it? Asked her what happens in those moments?"

He shook his head. "I know I should, but she seems so

flustered and embarrassed that it seems, I don't know, kinder not to."

I nodded in agreement.

"You'll have to talk about it," he said with a seriousness I didn't anticipate. "I'll schedule the MRI for the first week in January." He lifted the top page of DeeDee's chart. "I see her mother is in good health. What about her father? Is he still living?"

"We presume so," Jonathan said.

"But there hasn't been any contact in years," I added.

"They're permanently estranged," Jonathan said.

"Is there a way to find out his medical history? It could be important."

Jonathan and I exchanged an *I-doubt-it-but-we-can-try* look. "I'll ask DeeDee's mother. Maybe she can make a phone call."

Inwardly I groaned. Poor Linda. She had never really gotten over the divorce, in spite of the fact that it had been thirty years, and she had definitely not adjusted to the fact that there was a new Mrs. McAllister on the scene. I think she still held out hope it wouldn't last. This would not be an easy call for her to make.

"The sooner the better," Dr. Biddle said. "So we at least have a complete picture."

"What do you think it is?" I was not really sure I wanted to hear his reply.

"Let's see what the MRI shows," he said. "It would help if you would begin to document these incidents. Anything out of the ordinary, just jot it down. No matter how seemingly insignificant." He handed Jonathan the lab slip, shook both our hands, and gave us a smile meant to encourage.

We left his office with identical mixed emotions and drove back to WordWorks in near silence. On one hand, we were relieved that Dr. Biddle had finally taken us seriously. On the other, we were now convinced that our observations were not imagined. And if the urgency with which he was prepared to act was any indication, fear wasn't an unjustified response.

I left Jonathan at the office and drove to their house. As I made my way up the sidewalk to the front door, I heard laughter coming from inside. Ordinarily this would have set me to giggling, helplessly unable to stop myself. But not today. Today there wasn't much that could buoy my spirits. Still, I forced myself to put on, if not a happy face, at least the illusion of one.

I set my purse and keys on the entryway table, slipped off my shoes, and followed the sounds of laughter into the front room. DeeDee, the dignified woman who continued to turn heads everywhere she went, was sprawled out on the living room carpet with Angelique straddled atop her, bouncing like a bull rider and laughing for all she was worth. DeeDee was laughing too, and the sight of them having so much fun together made me cry. Again. I couldn't help it.

I retraced my steps to the powder room, hoping DeeDee hadn't noticed my entrance, and silently closed and locked the door. "Get a grip," I whispered to the frazzled woman in the mirror. "Now!"

I washed the remaining smudges of makeup off my face and patted cold water on my red, puffy eyes. I couldn't let DeeDee see me this way. No matter what, I had to be the strong one now. I'd have laughed had the thought not been so terrifying.

Because I wasn't the strong one. Had never been. DeeDee had seen me through so many crises, to use the word loosely in light of what we were facing now. Like when we were juniors at Lodi High. Frank Smith sat next to me in American Literature. And he was gorgeous. His name was written on every page of my diary, at least the first fourteen weeks of that school year. The first time he passed me a note, I thought I'd hyperventilate. He'd written, "You and DeeDee McAllister, are you, like, Siamese twins or something?" I made sure Mrs. Looney wasn't looking, then passed him back the note on which I'd written, "BEST FRIENDS! 4-EVER!" Best was double underlined. He nodded, added something to the note, then passed it back again. It read, "So, you guys wanna, like, get a Coke after school?"

Frank Smith was asking me out? This was, like, the best day of my life! "Sure," I wrote and handed him back the note, hoping he didn't see how my hand trembled.

"Miss Whitaker," Mrs. Looney said, catching me in midpass. Frank let go of his side of the folded paper and turned a hurried eye to *The Red Badge of Courage* lying open on his desk. There I was, stuck with the note. Some of the kids in the class began to snicker as she motioned for me to bring it to her desk. But who cared? Frank Smith had asked me out! I handed her the note, proudly, and gave Frank a smile and a nod as I returned to my seat. How would I ever get through typing and World History without DeeDee in either class? She was going to die when I told her!

Our note passing and Coke dates went on for weeks, and I just knew Frank was going to ask me to the Christmas ball. He was so attentive, meeting our bus every morning, buying all three Cokes every afternoon. His best friend was Cecil Abbott, which was unfortunate, but, for the sake of my happiness, DeeDee told me she would go to the ball with Cecil if Frank wanted to double. It was a huge sacrifice since she desperately wanted to go with Cliff Davenport. I would owe her, that was for sure.

Ten days before the ball, Frank handed me a note. I could tell by the look on his face that this was it. My hands shook as I opened it. I had no idea that a full sheet of binder paper could be folded so many times. I was careful to make sure Mrs. Looney didn't get *this* note because it was going into my diary on the page where I'd written Mrs. Frank Smith over and over in all six colors from my Bic pens bonus pack.

I gave Frank my most alluring smile, though it still needed work, opened the final fold, and read, "Gab, do you think DeeDee would, like, go to the Christmas ball with me?"

With him?

"PS: Cecil said he wouldn't mind, like, going with you."

With me?

Frank's eyes were on me, so I bit my lip and blinked like crazy. No matter what, I couldn't cry. Not there. He looked and waited, and waited some more while I folded the note, slowly, painstakingly, exactly the way he had folded it. At last I turned and looked into his hopeful eyes and shrugged. Meekly. Pathetically.

And I still had to get through typing and World History.

When DeeDee saw my face that afternoon she said, "What?" without even a hello.

I handed her the note, which she read. And read again. Great drops were filling my eyes, the dam ready to burst. Then DeeDee slid onto the bus seat beside me and began to laugh. Like crazy. And she laughed until she cried. I was too stunned to say or do anything, and even my tears dried up.

"You're not going to believe this." I had to give her credit; she was honestly trying to regain herself. "Not five minutes ago Cliff asked me — "

"To the ball?" I'm ashamed to say it only added to my misery.

She continued to laugh as she shook her head. "If *you'd*, like, go to the ball with *him*!"

I gasped in my amazement, then fell to laughing with her. We practically howled all the way home.

The bus let us off a block from my house, and we strolled home arm in arm. I didn't even care about the French test I had to study for. DeeDee would make sure I aced it. Well, for me that meant a strong C minus. But who cared?

She followed me into the house. "What do you say we skip the Christmas ball this year? I can't quite see me in Frank's yellow Pinto."

That brought on a whole new wave of laughter.

Another year would pass before I learned the truth. Cliff had asked all right, but not about me. Yeah, I owed her. Big-time.

The tears that were squelched that day were streaming down my face now. Me, the strong one? Hardly. I looked at my pathetic self in the mirror again. My stomach was in turmoil, knotted and nauseated. "You can do this," I said, not believing a word of what I told myself. And then, in a voice as real to my spirit as my own voice was to my ears, I heard the Lord whisper, *Peace. Be still.*

I looked around, like I expected to see someone else in the powder room. All I saw was my own startled face looking back at me. "But the waves are so big," I whispered as I headed toward the living room.

Oh me of little faith.

"Hey, look who's here!" DeeDee lifted the baby up in the air so she could see me. "Auntie Gab! Can you say Auntie Gab?" Gelée kicked her hands and feet and showed me her milk-white teeth in a dimpled, nose-wrinkling grin.

"She could if she wanted to," I said. I took the baby from DeeDee and rubbed noses with Gelée. "Couldn't she?" She grabbed for my earring.

DeeDee sat down beside me. "Gotta stop wearing loops. I've put mine away for the duration."

I nodded as I disentangled Gelée's fingers from my silver earring.

DeeDee reached over and wiped something off my cheekbone. Mascara. It had to be. "You forgot to flush this time. And stealth isn't your forte."

"I just . . ." I pointed to the powder room. "Um . . ."

"Where have you been? I called over an hour ago and you weren't at home."

"Oh, well, I was—"

"We want to go to the mall, don't we, punkin'? For our last bit of C-h-r-i-s-t-m-a-s shopping," DeeDee added in a whisper, as if the baby would understand her if she spoke the C-word out loud.

"Did you call my cell phone?" I asked, knowing full well I had turned it off before going into Dr. Biddle's office.

Cell phone. DeeDee mouthed the words to herself. Her face took on a look of concentration as she bit at a fingernail. She turned away from me, as if to shield herself as she worked to compute the meaning of the words. I grew weak in the knees watching her.

"It's okay, Dee. I didn't have it anyway." I forced another smile, thinking my face felt like a plaster mold that I could step away from and hang on the wall like a comedy mask, right next to its tragedy counterpart. "Shall we get some lunch, then head for the mall?" I wasn't the least bit hungry. In fact, the thought of food made me queasy, but lunch was always a part of our shopping adventures. If there was ever a time to keep up appearances, it was now.

"Is it Tuesday?" DeeDee asked.

Ordinarily I would have laughed at such a question. "Well, no, but—"

"Then we shouldn't go to D'Angelo's." Her voice was adamant.

"Well, okay. Whatever you say. Do you have a suggestion?"

She thought for a moment, then said, "Holy Mackerel's for fish and chips. I haven't been there in ages. Doesn't that sound yummy?" she said to Gelée, who grabbed her mother's nose and attempted to bite it. "What?"

I realized I was staring at her, slack-jawed. "DeeDee, Holy Mackerel's burned down when we were in college."

The look she gave me was a mixture of embarrassment, disbelief, and suspicion, as if I were attempting to confuse her. "Well, then. No wonder." She retrieved Angelique's jacket from the hall closet, stepping past me to prepare the baby for the cold December day. Then she just stopped. "You know, it's really crummy outside. Why don't we make it another time?"

I nodded as nonchalantly as I could. "Whatever you say. Want me to heat up some soup?"

"I think I'll just put the baby down for a nap and take one myself. I'm feeling a little tired."

"Oh. Okay." I kissed the baby's cheeks, feeling awkward in DeeDee's presence for the first time since the day we met. Not only that, but I felt deceptive, as if I were keeping secrets. I guess because I *was* keeping secrets. "If you need anything, just call." I held up my cell phone. "It'll be on."

She turned and headed up the stairs without a farewell.

I watched her until she was out of sight. "I'll just let myself out," I whispered to the empty room.

I slammed my car door shut with all the force I could muster and banged the steering wheel. "Okay, God. Whatever you want, I'll do it. Anything. I swear. But this has to stop."

I rarely bargained with God, hadn't even the day my father

died. We were all in such a fog that night that, in truth, I never thought to bargain. Besides, I didn't think I needed to. God knew how much I needed my dad, and that Mother needed him, and the church, too. Right? Whatever was wrong, God would fix it. I just knew He would.

But God had other plans. I won't pretend that I understood them, but I had to accept that there were times when God was up to something beyond me. I liked things simple and straightforward. And easy. But life wasn't always easy.

I tried to rub away the headache that always comes with a genuine, heart-wrenching cry and looked up to heaven. "You're never here when I need you," I whispered like a spoiled child, referring not to God but to my dad. And, as if in reply, I could almost hear him say, *Gabby, sweetheart, pray without ceasing. And at the end of the day, remember that God is sovereign.*

27

That night a distraught Linda paced in my living room as we assembled for a meeting about what was coming to be known as DeeDee's condition. I grew exhausted just watching her. Finally, she stopped to rummage through her purse, uttered a primal groan as she remembered she no longer smoked, and went back to her pacing.

My mother brought a tray from the kitchen, laden with tea paraphernalia. Nothing as soothing as tea. "Linda, honey, come join us for a cup."

Like an obedient child, she took a seat next to my mother and accepted one of the mismatched mugs that came from my kitchen. If you opened Mother's cupboards, all of her dishes were grouped in matching sets, all the cup handles turned the same direction, saucers, bowls, and plates stacked neatly, with the patterns perfectly aligned. Her silverware drawer was neat and tidy, and even her cooking utensils were compartmentalized in handy little trays that kept everything going in the right direction.

And then there was me. I knew that my dishes matched for the most part. But they never came out of the dishwasher in sets. It was pieces of this pattern and pieces of that pattern, and that's how they got stacked in the cupboard. So when they came out again, they were doomed for the same mismatched cycle that seemed to define my life. And my mugs? I bought them as they struck my fancy. No two ever alike. As for my utensil drawer, enter at your own risk.

I was quietly amazed that such were my thoughts on an evening when we were addressing so grave a topic.

"Lemon, no sugar," Mother said to Linda, somehow always remembering how people liked their tea. Then she proceeded to prepare a cup for Jonathan, Sonny, and me, without one mistake.

"I wonder why no one puts lemon in coffee." I absently swished a spoon through my tea, though there was nothing in it to stir. "You put the same things in both tea and coffee, except lemon. Honey, sugar, milk. Why not lemon?"

Jonathan, who liked to provide answers to every question, gave an apologetic shrug, while Sonny looked into his cup, as if seeking a clue to the conundrum.

"Hmm." Mother brought her own cup to her lips. "I'm sure I don't know."

This was, no doubt, the epitome of small talk.

"Where did you tell DeeDee you were going?" I asked Jonathan, feeling like the criminal conspirator I was.

He looked as guilty as I felt. "When she asked where I was going, I just said, 'It's way too close to Christmas for questions.'"

"That always works," Sonny said, then looked as if he'd swallowed his spoon. "Well, not that I . . . well, you know what I mean."

It would have been funny if things weren't so serious. "Well, it wasn't a lie," I said to Jonathan.

"It felt like a lie. You should have seen her. She donned this sly little smile you women are so good at and said something to Sunshine in French. Probably reciting their letter to Santa."

"What exactly did Dr. Biddle say?" Mother asked. "Besides the part about DeeDee's family history," she added as delicately as possible in consideration of Linda, who immediately jumped up and resumed her pacing, mug in hand.

"He said he'd schedule the MRI for the first week of January," I said.

Jonathan grabbed his wallet and pulled out a slip of paper that he'd torn off an interoffice memo notepad. "January 7. Nine o'clock. They called this afternoon." He looked reluctantly at Linda. "It would help if we had the . . . *information* before then."

"We haven't spoken in so many years. . . ." Linda's voice trailed away. "I wouldn't know what to say to him. I'm not even sure how to reach him."

"I know it's difficult," Mother said, "but don't you think he'd want to know about DeeDee's condition?"

She stopped pacing. "What exactly *is* DeeDee's condition? What do I tell him? And what if *she* answers?"

Jonathan set down his cup. "I'll call. DeeDee's my wife. I'll handle it."

"You will?" Linda's question came out a combination of relief and remorse.

"When is the last time the two of you spoke?"

Linda stopped and sighed. "The time the girls made that unfortunate visit. Let's see, they were—"

"Fourteen." A grimace crossed my face, as if I'd tasted something bitter.

"Not since then?" Mother was astonished. "Not even once?"

She shrugged. "There was never a reason to."

Jonathan picked up the telephone and pushed the On button. "Do you think he and his wife still live in the same city? Where was it again?"

"Something Beach," I said. "Laguna, Newport—"

"Long Beach," Linda said.

"Yeah, that's it."

Jonathan found the area code for Long Beach, California, dialed information, and asked for a listing for Roger McAllister.

"Roger A.," Linda said. "He always uses his middle initial."

"Bingo." Jonathan gave us a thumbs-up. He scribbled down a number on the cable guide lying on my coffee table. "There's only one. It's got to be him." He dialed the number, and after what must have been six or seven rings, he said, "Hello? Is Mr. McAllister in?"

We all huddled around him, especially Linda, listening intently to his half of the conversation and filling in the blanks as best we could.

"Mr. Roger McAllister. A." Jonathan glanced at his mother-in-law. "Roger A. McAllister. That's right." He fidgeted with a pencil, filling in the *e*'s, *a*'s and *o*'s on the cable guide, as the conversation continued. "Well, this is, um . . . I guess I would be, well, his, uh, son-in-law. Yes. Son-in-law." He cringed, as if expecting the person to hang up. Then suddenly he smiled. "That's right. DeeDee McAllister. Yes. She's my wife." He gave us another thumbs-up. "Jonathan Kent. Right. I was hoping to speak with her father if he's available."

He listened, nodding occasionally, as his features turned from pleasant expectation to serious concentration. "I see," he said a half dozen times, and each time his face became more severe. He stopped doodling and let the pencil fall to the table with a hollow ping. "For how long?"

A little cry escaped Linda. "He's dead." She covered her face with a trembling hand. "I knew it. I could feel it in my soul."

Mother put an arm around her shoulder. "Let's not jump to conclusions."

I knew by the look on her face that she'd already jumped there herself.

"Gee, I'm awfully sorry," Jonathan said. "Yes. I will. Thank you. Good-bye."

He ended the call and placed the phone on the coffee table. He looked at me, then Mother, then Linda, and sighed heavily.

"He's dead," Linda said again. She crumpled onto the sofa and covered her face with her hands.

Jonathan closed his eyes and shook his head.

Not dead? Mother, Sonny, and I exchanged surprised looks. "Then what?" I asked. "What could be worse than dead?"

Linda uncovered her eyes and wiped at the tears trickling down her cheeks. "Jonathan?"

"That was . . ." Jonathan hesitated, no doubt wondering how, for Linda's sake, he should refer to the woman he had spoken to. *Mrs. McAllister* or *Roger's wife*?

"DeeDee's stepmonster?" I used the title DeeDee had given her father's new wife all those years ago.

Jonathan nodded. "Although she didn't sound like a monster. Quite the contrary, in fact. I couldn't help feeling sorry for her."

"Why? What is it?"

"She says he's—"

"What?" Mother asked. "What did she say?"

Jonathan seemed reluctant to relay the news he'd been given and appeared to be searching for the best way to give it. Finally, he drew a breath and just said it. "DeeDee's father has Alzheimer's." Jonathan's voice broke on the last word.

The interminable silence that followed his announcement was broken by a sob, which I realized was my own.

"Isn't that for *old* people?" Linda asked the question of no one in particular. "Roger isn't old."

"I know," Jonathan said. His face had lost its color. "He has what's called—" he looked down at the notes he'd scribbled— "early-onset Alzheimer's. He hasn't—" Jonathan cleared his throat— "hasn't been himself for some time. Years, in fact. According to Mrs. McAllister, it's a miracle he's still alive."

Linda looked as if she'd personally been given a death sentence. Even Mother went pale. Sonny shook his head back and forth, unable or unwilling to accept this report. Then, remembering Jonathan, he went and put a hand on his shoulder.

"It doesn't mean anything." The tone of my voice jarred everyone back to reality. "Nothing at all. What could that possibly have to do with DeeDee?" I was surprised by the anger I felt, but I just couldn't accept such a ridiculous diagnosis. "You all know her. She's intelligent, witty, *strong*."

And everything I've ever wanted to be. Since the day we met I had looked up to her, had wanted to be her in every way. I considered myself fortunate just to live in her shadow. And the fact that she called me not just *friend*, but *best* friend, well, I couldn't begin to place a value on that. DeeDee McAllister-Kent was the rest of me. I loved her, and I needed her. "She isn't sick."

"Sweetheart—"

"Mom! There's just no way! She's only seen him once since she was eleven years old, for crying out loud!" I talked as if the disease were communicable, which, of course, was completely unreasonable. But the whole thing was unreasonable.

"I'm going to make a trip to Long Beach," Jonathan said. "To see him. And I want to talk with his wife face-to-face."

"You can't take DeeDee," I said. "She can't know anything about this."

"I agree. At least for now."

"Forever," I said stubbornly.

Jonathan, suddenly weary, rubbed his forehead and sighed deeply, looking as if he saw DeeDee's—and his—future all too clearly. He looked to Sonny with the eyes of a man about to sink for the last time. *Won't somebody please help?* is what they said.

I softened my voice. "Jonathan, this doesn't mean anything. It's hormones. It's the change. It's, it's *something*. But it's not this. This couldn't happen to DeeDee. You'll see. Dr. Biddle will tell us how crazy we are. He'll laugh." I looked at all the anxious faces looking back at me and shook my head as I walked away. "He'll positively laugh."

I went upstairs and ran a hot bath, leaving Sonny to see everyone out. I poured in my favorite bath fragrance and watched the iridescent bubbles fill the tub as if life were perfectly normal. I lit two scented candles we kept on the windowsill and never used, turned off the harsh overhead light, and, on impulse, reached over and locked the door. I sank down in the tub until the water covered my body like a warm embrace. And I cried.

When Sonny tried the knob and asked me to let him in, I pretended he wasn't on the other side of a locked door for the first time in our marriage. I listened to him try the knob one more time, knowing he didn't understand my silence, then heard him turn and walk away. And I continued to cry. Because no matter how much I wanted not to, I had to admit that I was wrong. Roger McAllister's condition had everything to do with DeeDee.

Everything.

28

In spite of my humbug attitude, that Christmas was the best Christmas ever. Who knew one baby girl could take life to a whole new plateau? The answer, of course, is anyone who's ever been a parent. But this was new to us. And fun.

Gelée would rather have chewed on her packages, but once Jonathan and DeeDee helped her rip into them, she loved what came out of the boxes. Clothes being the exception.

"That'll change," an all-too-knowing Jonathan said.

But all the brightly colored, squishy, musical, and/or noise-making toys were a hit. Most especially because they could all go in the mouth. Then, to top it off, Gelée took her first unassisted steps on Christmas Day. She walked from DeeDee's arms to Jonathan's, a distance of maybe three feet, and, oh, was she proud of herself. She laughed and clapped, rocked on those chubby bow-legs, then turned around and went back.

Of course, it was all captured on our camcorders.

Then, when I asked DeeDee where the walking shoes were

that we bought for Gelée at Frills & Frocks the week before, her face took on that strained look, as if she wanted with everything in her to remember.

But she couldn't.

⬥

Jonathan didn't wait for the holidays to end. He scheduled an early-morning flight to Long Beach for December 28. I spent the day with DeeDee and Angelique. Later, Linda stopped by with Italian takeout for dinner. She'd stay with DeeDee until Jonathan got home that evening. Until we knew what was going on, it was apparent someone needed to be with her and the baby full-time.

Jonathan came straight to our house from the airport. The grim look on his face said more than I wanted to hear, but I poured three mugs of coffee and took my place at the dining room table, where the guys were already waiting. I gripped my mug between both palms. "So. How did it go?"

Jonathan scratched his eyebrow, cleared his throat. "Not so good, I'm afraid. Not good at all."

Sonny tapped the table. "Just say it, Jon, straight-out."

"Okay. I met Mrs. McAllister at the care facility DeeDee's dad has lived in for the past ten years."

"Care facility?" I didn't expect to hear that. "Ten years?"

He nodded. "We talked a half hour or more, she filling me in on his background, before she took me to his room. Thirteen years ago he began exhibiting odd behavior, saying strange things out of the blue, not being able to remember the names of people he'd known for years, forgetting things that had just happened. Almost exactly what's been happening with DeeDee."

"And it obviously wasn't postpartum depression," I said, not bothering to hide the sarcasm.

"No," Jonathan agreed. "They went through a battery of tests, scans, blood work, you name it. Ruled everything out they possibly could, till all they were left with was Alzheimer's. Early-onset. He was forty-eight when it all began."

Sonny gave a low whistle. "Forty-eight. Wow."

"Forty-eight is not forty," I said, which is how old DeeDee was when her symptoms began. "That should say something." As if eight years would make that much difference.

Jonathan gave me a look mixed with fear and sympathy. It stirred the anger that was building in me. "Things progressed slowly for a year or two, then, overnight, they seemed to escalate. His mood swings became unmanageable; his short-term memory was all but gone." Jonathan paused. "But he talked day and night . . . about Doris."

My head shot up. "Doris? You mean DeeDee?"

Jonathan nodded. "She's all he talked about. When she was born, where she went to school, her drawing. He'd ask over and over, 'Where's Doris? Why doesn't she come?'" Jonathan's eyes teared. He looked away and took a drink from his mug. "She was very nice, his wife."

I tried to remember the woman from the one time we'd met so long ago. The only thing I could truly recall was how hard she tried to win DeeDee over. How nice she tried to be. It jolted my conscience, having thought of her as DeeDee's stepmonster all these years.

"So you met him?" Sonny asked. "DeeDee's dad?"

"I wouldn't say I met him, but I saw him." Jonathan shook his head. "Iris showed me a picture of Roger when he was probably our age," he said to Sonny. "There's hardly anything left of the man."

I crossed my arms over my stomach and rocked, ignoring the tears that spilled onto my cheeks. "What do you mean?" My voice was a whisper.

"He's in the end stages, Gabby. The disease has taken its toll in every respect. He's thin as a twig; he doesn't know anyone, including his wife; he's unable to do anything for himself; he's incontinent; he just mumbles disjointed phrases." Jonathan paused for a moment. Clearly this was way past difficult for him.

"But Iris loves him," he continued. "She goes to see him every day. Reads to him, talks about their life together and about DeeDee. I gave her a picture of Angelique." Jonathan ignored his own tears. "She took it right over and showed him."

Sonny looked away and sniffed. "End stages. How long do they give him?"

"From what Iris said, it's amazing he's lived this long. I think it's because of her." Jonathan nodded. "I do."

"Are you going to take DeeDee to see him?"

The shake of Jonathan's head was adamant. "I don't want her to see that."

What he left off was, *not if that's her fate.*

I continued to rock, not caring that my tears were making a puddle on my dining room table. *Oh, God. Oh, God. Where are you? Do you not care?*

I have loved you with an everlasting love, I heard in my spirit. *An everlasting love.* It was Jeremiah 31:3, one of my favorite Scriptures.

I wiped an eye with my shoulder. *Then tell me, why doesn't it feel like it?*

∽

Dr. Biddle did not laugh. "This at least tells us where to start," he said.

And that meant a whole new battery of tests for DeeDee. As if she hadn't been through enough trying to get pregnant. Now it was MRIs, PET scans, neurological testing, psychological evaluation. Since there was no clinical test to diagnose Alzheimer's disease outright, all other illnesses that manifested the same type of symptoms had to be ruled out. Everything from depression, which was already checked off the list, to thyroid problems to a brain tumor.

After months of testing and countless visits to a variety of doctors, early-onset Alzheimer's was the diagnosis we were expected to live with. After exhausting our list of alternative medicine providers, we were out of options. Except for prayer. And we prayed as if our lives depended on it. Because DeeDee's did.

Jonathan was a different man after his visit to Long Beach. Not defeated exactly, but aware that today was probably as good as it gets. Every day would bring a diminished tomorrow in the life of this incredible person we knew as DeeDee McAllister-Kent. She was there in body, but in every other sense she was slipping away. To where? That, of course, was the million-dollar question. Trying to preserve the DeeDee we knew and desperately wanted to hang on to was like trying to clutch the hand of a ghost.

Jonathan made an executive decision, one with which I concurred. He would not tell DeeDee about her father's illness, nor of his visit to Long Beach. It was enough for her to sit in the doctors' offices and hear their diagnoses without us providing a living example of the horrific course her life was on. We didn't have the heart for that.

Sonny and I made an executive decision of our own. Eight months after ditching my pills, I still hadn't conceived. And we began to consider it a blessing.

29

Sometime before Angelique's second birthday, Jonathan had taken DeeDee's car keys away, surreptitiously, I have to admit, because facing this awful milestone—removing the most obvious token of her independence—was such a difficult task. But the last time DeeDee drove had been a frightening event. She was taking Linda to pick up her car from a tire shop and had come to a red light at a busy intersection, paused, then proceeded through, with angry drivers who had the right-of-way braking and honking furiously at her. Among other things.

The fact that she got through that intersection without a collision was proof that guardian angels are the real deal. Linda nearly had a coronary, but DeeDee just seemed confused, like she didn't understand why everyone was upset.

After retrieving her own car, Linda followed her daughter home to make sure she arrived safely, then got right on the phone and told Jonathan what had happened. That night he took her keys off the entry table, where she kept them in a ceramic bowl, a gift from one of her up-and-coming artists. She turned her house upside down when she thought no one was watching, trying to find the keys she thought she lost. And while she found many items she had, in fact, misplaced, the keys, of course, were not among them.

As hard as it was to witness, it was easier than telling her outright that she'd never drive again. After a few weeks, she stopped looking for the keys and, in time, forgot that she'd ever known how to drive.

Driving wasn't the only activity lost to her. She was no longer able to maintain her checkbook after Jonathan discovered she'd made a thorough and costly mess of it. She'd forget to enter checks she had written or withdrawals she had made through the ATM. And the subtraction . . . evidently she'd forgotten how to use a calculator.

DeeDee was unable to cook anymore because she'd leave things on the stove or in the oven until they burned up or someone else found them. In that regard she was becoming a danger to herself and everyone else. This wasn't a total disappointment to any of us, I must admit, for though she had learned to put together a few special dishes over the years, cooking had never been her strong suit. But these days, even putting together a salad or making a simple sandwich took great concentration, and most days she wasn't up to it.

When fatigued, DeeDee would slur her words as if she were intoxicated, her thoughts would become more fragmented, and she would lose track of where she was and what she was doing. Too much activity brought on confusion, and confusion brought on withdrawal. It was much easier for her to go upstairs and lie on her bed than try to function in a world she no longer understood. Even simple communication was too difficult at times. She groped for the most elementary of words, often in vain. And then her head would begin to hurt. She couldn't write very well anymore either. The artist who had once had such lovely penmanship couldn't remember how to hold a pencil.

These things occurred in what I call the angry stage. DeeDee was always strong-willed, self-reliant, opinionated, bold, unsympathetic for the most part, and crass on occasion. But she'd never been angry—except at her dad. Until now. And boy, was she angry. At all the words she was losing. At not understanding a sentence she'd read three times. At not being able to tie her shoes.

She'd get so frustrated she'd swear. At embarrassing times and in embarrassing places. But honestly, who could blame her? I wanted to swear myself.

One early spring day I'd barely walked through my front door, tired from my day with DeeDee and Gelée, when the phone rang. Sonny, just home from the office himself, reached for the phone while I began to dish up our half of the dinner I'd prepared at the Kents. It made no sense to cook one meal there and another one at home, so I prepared their dinner every day and brought the rest home for Sonny and me.

The look on Sonny's face caused me to stop what I was doing midscoop. From where I stood I could hear Jonathan's frantic voice loud and clear over the telephone.

"We'll be right there," Sonny said.

It took eight agonizing minutes to get from our driveway to theirs. En route, I threw out a diverse list of reasons for Jonathan's frantic call. DeeDee had locked herself in the bathroom again or set fire to the stove. Gelée had fallen off her swing. The possibilities and fears were endless, but to each of my what-ifs, Sonny replied, "Babe, I don't know. Just pray."

As if I wasn't.

I had steeled myself for any number of scenarios, but what I was not prepared for was pulling to a stop behind a police cruiser parked in front of their house. I did, however, find the teeniest relief in the fact that there wasn't an ambulance anywhere in sight. I bolted from the car and raced up the walkway with Sonny right behind me and nearly tripped over a bike lying half on the walk and half on the lawn.

I pushed the front door open. "Jonathan?"

A police officer, huge and intimidating, pivoted on one foot to include Sonny and me in his line of sight. His right hand rested on the butt of his pistol.

A young boy and a man I didn't recognize stood beside him. Both kept angry eyes on DeeDee.

"What in the world—" I began, but stopped when Sonny said, "Gabby" in a tone I wasn't accustomed to hearing.

"Hey, there," the officer said. "You folks the Nevins?"

Sonny nodded and I relaxed just a bit.

"Seems we have a little mix-up here."

DeeDee and Jonathan and the strange boy and man began talking all at once, but little of it was coherent. I caught snippets of words here and there. "Bike. Mine. Crazy lady. Lawyer."

"Hey, folks." The officer held up a hand, his voice rising above the others. "I said we'd get it figured out, and we will. Now, you two. Why don't you take a seat in here and we'll start at the beginning."

Sonny and I did just that.

Officer Baxter, his name tag said, rested a beefy hand on the boy's shoulder. "Okay, son, just tell us what happened if you don't mind."

He shot an accusing finger in DeeDee's direction and said, "That crazy lady—"

Crazy lady? My brilliant, incomparable DeeDee? I jumped to my feet, shaking with outrage. "She. Is. Not. Crazy!"

And then the ruckus began all over again.

"Hey now! I said we'd get it figured out, but we're going to do this one at a time." The officer wagged a finger at the boy. "No name calling. Now, try it again."

The boy tried to shrug off his hand, but the officer kept it right where it was. "I came to collect," he said.

Ah, yes, the paperboy.

"And when I rang the doorbell, he answered." The boy pointed at Jonathan. "He went to get some money, and that's when she went nuts."

Gelée sat on DeeDee's lap, her little face crinkled with confusion. DeeDee absently played with her little ponytails and turned a curious eye to the paperboy. She, of course, had no idea who he was or that he was talking about her. Because whatever had happened was already forgotten.

"She said something about my bike and then tried to get on and ride it. I told her, 'Hey, lady, that's my bike,' but she wouldn't listen. She said it was hers. How dumb is that?"

The boy's father shifted nervously from one foot to the other. "Didn't know we had a nutcase living here or I wouldn't let my boy deliver to this neighborhood."

Jonathan came out of his chair, knocking the end table in the process. "Hey, fella, you're talking about my wife!"

I jumped, and so did the boy and his dad. In all the years I'd known Jonathan I'd never seen him act like that. My respect for him soared.

"That's *your* problem, buddy," the man replied, though with less bravado.

To which Officer Baxter said, "Enough! You and the boy step

over there while I talk to Mr. Kent." He motioned for Jonathan to join him on the opposite side of the room.

DeeDee continued to play with Gelée's hair, while Jonathan turned a pleading eye to Sonny, who took a step in his direction. When the officer didn't hold up his stop-sign hand, Sonny joined their little circle. As they whispered in their huddle I knew what was being said without hearing the words.

Sick . . . Not herself . . . Doesn't know . . .

I wanted to scream. Because DeeDee, my beautiful, brilliant, more-than-a-sister friend, had tried to take the paperboy's bicycle, and only I knew why. It was exactly, down to the color and the banana seat, like the bike her father had given her as a replacement for himself.

And the paperboy was riding it.

I passed him and his father without a word on my way out the door. I felt like a balloon swelling with too much air, and if I popped, every curse word I'd ever tried not to hear was going to burst forth like confetti on New Year's Eve. I was so angry I didn't know what to do with myself. I kicked the bike, and it felt so good that I kicked it again.

And I walked. And as I walked I ranted. At God. The word would soon be out that there were two nutcases in town. But I didn't care who saw me or what they heard. I had something to say and I was going to say it.

"How could you do this to her?" I looked straight up at the clouds. "What did she ever do to deserve this? She's taught me more about what it is to be a Christian than any sermon I ever heard. Even from my dad. You promised not to give us more than we can bear. You promised!"

"Excuse me?" A lady watering her roses eyed me curiously, but I walked by without so much as a sideways glance.

"First Corinthians 10:13," I continued, my finger poking the air. "Sixth grade Sunday school. Mrs. Kellerman wrote it on the board, and DeeDee and I learned it together. We *believed* you. John 14:14. Eighth grade Sunday school. *Ask me for anything in my name, and I will do it.* Well, I'm asking! And not just for me. But for DeeDee and Jonathan and, oh, Lord, for Gelée!"

John 11:25.

I stopped short and looked around. No one was there. But someone had spoken.

John 11:25. I heard it again.

And then I remembered. The voice from DeeDee's powder room. "John 11:25," I repeated. "John 11:25." I went through my litany of memorized verses. "John 11:25?" I knew I should know it. But I didn't.

I retraced my steps to DeeDee's house, where the commotion was finally breaking up. The paperboy sat astride his bike, trying to straighten the handlebars. No wonder I was limping. His dad waited in a Chevy pickup I would have needed a stepladder to get into, then honked impatiently. "Just put it in the back! We'll fix it at home."

Officer Baxter shook Jonathan's hand at the front door, then got into his patrol car and slowly pulled away from the curb.

The neighbors retreated back inside their houses with something new to talk about over dinner.

"There you are." Sonny looked relieved to see me. "You okay?"

I nodded and headed for the bookcase in the den. I pulled DeeDee's Bible—*the one she can no longer read*, I reminded God—off the shelf and turned to the gospel of John. Chapter eleven. Verses twenty-five and twenty-six were highlighted in yellow and double underlined in purple ink. Through eyes that instantly teared, I read, "I am the resurrection and the life. He who believes in me will live, even though he dies; and whoever lives and believes in me will never die. Do you believe this?"

"You betcha!" was written in the same purple ink in DeeDee's familiar print on one side of the column. "What else matters?!" was written on the other side.

I bent my head in humility, tears dripping onto the page. "I'm going to borrow this," I said to Jonathan.

He nodded, but I doubt he really heard me. He was leaning against the doorjamb watching his girls. DeeDee was curled up tightly in her chair, with Angelique still in her arms. DeeDee's eyes were fixed on some point far away, and I wondered if she wasn't reliving her memories while she still had some to relive. Jonathan looked broken. Unfixably so. I laid my hand on his arm. "I'll see you in the morning. Call if you need us."

The picture of the three of them just as they were stayed with me. When I climbed into our car, laid my head against the seat, and closed my eyes, clutching DeeDee's Bible to my stomach, there it was, a photograph in colorless tones. When I crawled into bed, weary and heartsick, it was there, just behind my eyelids. When I opened my eyes, it didn't go away. It was like a movie clip that had been paused, and now it waited for someone to push the right button to make it go again. Only it wouldn't.

The resurrection and the life. Do you believe this? Do you believe?

I rolled onto my side, away from Sonny, and let the tears flow. Did I believe?

I'm not the strong one, I reminded God. *I've never been the strong one.*

❧

DeeDee's appearance declined as her ability to manage the simplest personal care slipped away. Applying makeup or shaving her legs was more than she could handle. It was enough to brush her own teeth. She'd become dependent in almost every aspect of her life. So every weekday morning I arrived at the Kent home in time for Jonathan to leave for the office. I got DeeDee up, put her in the shower, saw that both of my girls were dressed and groomed, then went downstairs to fix their favorite breakfast: French toast with gobs of butter and powdered sugar, and bacon, extra-crisp.

Variety was out of the question.

My heart ached for Jonathan. He was overwhelmed by how rapidly the disease was claiming his wife, but Sonny said he put on a good face at the office, taking refuge in his workaday world. I was so lost in the *why* of what was happening that all I could do was go through the motions.

But Mother, bless her heart, kept us all focused on what was important and what was not. She stopped by one afternoon while DeeDee and Gelée were napping. I'd been staring at the blank screen of my laptop, hoping to do something productive while they slept, but I was unable to focus on anything except what I'd overheard at our small group the night before. "Someone actually implied that DeeDee wasn't getting better because Jonathan doesn't have enough faith. Honestly, Mother, I could have choked her with her own Bible."

"Sweetheart, you can't let people like that get to you. I decided long ago that those who think they have all the answers haven't yet lived through the questions."

Some of the tension left my body. "Then you don't agree that it's a lack of faith?"

"Of course not. There's no answer, Angel. Trying to find reasons to all the riddles of the universe isn't going to help DeeDee or you. She needs us to be brave and proactive on her behalf. And poor Linda. DeeDee has been her life. She's so lost right now. So we—you, Sonny, and I—have to step up to the plate. Sonny has to be there for Jonathan, at the office and away from the office. I'll do all I can for Linda, and I'll help you with DeeDee. But mostly, my love, you have to be there for that Sweet Baby Girl."

She was changing every day into a child with tons of personality and was largely dependent on me for her daily care. And that thrilled and terrified me all at the same time.

"What if I blow it?"

"Sometimes we have to roll up our sleeves and just dig in," Mother said matter-of-factly, which is obviously what she intended to do. But she was made of a different fabric than I. She was canvas; I was gauze.

"Mom, I've never been a mother. I don't know how."

"I know, sweetheart, but you *had* a mother—still do, in fact—and that's the next best thing. You know the basics. The rest isn't so hard. And you know I'll help." She added that last little phrase with gusto and a smile. "Angelique deserves everything we can give her."

"And DeeDee." My stomach dipped sharply when I thought about what lay ahead.

"One day at a time. That's how we get through." The pressure of her hand on mine brought only small comfort. "John 16:33."

I didn't have to look that one up. I knew it by heart. In the King James, no less. "These things I have spoken unto you, that in me ye might have peace. In the world ye shall have tribulation: but be of good cheer; I have overcome the world," I recited.

"Not just words about life, but words from the Giver of life."

I sank into a chair like a bag of beans, every bit of spiritual strength sucked right out of me. "I'd give anything to have your faith, Mom, but I know what's coming. And I'm so angry I could scream. I walk when I pray so no one I care about can hear my ranting, and my prayers turn to accusations. Because He could stop this with just a word. I know every promise about healing, and I've done all the spiritual aerobics to build my faith. Because if you have faith the size of a grain of mustard seed . . . that's what it says, the size of a grain of mustard seed. Do you know how small that is? And I think how pathetic my faith must be. Invisible to God's naked eye. Because if I had even just a little . . . And you must think everything you tried to teach me is bouncing off the stars because it sure didn't get in here." I pounded a finger into my chest. "And I'm terrified because I think she's still sick because I keep blowing it."

Mother let out a sigh smothered in compassion. "But then it would be about us. If we were good, bad things wouldn't happen. That's the Fall in a nutshell, my love. And the truth is, we can't be good enough. Not ever. We need grace to pick up the slack." She cupped my face in a hand tough and tender all at once. "I don't have the answers, Angel baby. I don't know why this horrible thing has happened to DeeDee. But I do know this isn't the final page. And as for your ranting, well, God has awfully big shoulders."

"I've disappointed Him."

"I think not."

The hollows beneath my eyes were raw from tears and tissues. "I want Gelée to know her mother."

"And you'll be just the one to tell her. About what a strong, beautiful, funny—"

"Auntie Gab?" Gelée ran into the kitchen, where Mother and I were finishing the last of our tea. "Mommy wants to watch *Aladdin*. But we watched it two times. I want to watch this."

Cats.

Cats?

Mother laughed, picked up her tote bag, and dug for her keys. "And cultured. Did I say cultured?"

30

Of all the toys Angelique had, and she had a truck-full, her favorite was the little cloth doll with the hand-drawn face I'd made to go along with the cradle before she was even born. She dragged that poor muslin creature everywhere she went. The sprouts of cloth hair that stood every which way on its little stuffed head, giving it a perpetually surprised appearance, had been gummed, chewed, and drooled on until they were hardly recognizable. Its daisy yellow dress was faded and stained, but Gelée loved that doll.

And on her fourth birthday, young as she was, she made what had to be the ultimate sacrifice for a four-year-old.

She dragged her doll from room to room of the home she shared with her mommy and daddy, laughing and singing about the party preparations, knowing they were all for her. I couldn't help but wish I'd paid more attention in Home Ec as I frosted a yellow cake with rainbow chip frosting. But I reminded myself that it's the taste that counts.

Mother and Linda blew up balloons and hung them from crepe paper streamers that stretched from one side of the dining room to the other. Jonathan and Sonny went shopping for a Cinderella tent with matching sleeping bag and fuzzy slippers in lieu of glass ones. It was the only thing Angelique had asked for.

It was certainly not the only thing she got.

I put four pink candles in the top of the cake, sprinkled candy confetti around the base of the plate, stuck the whole thing in the refrigerator, and went to see how the decorations were progressing.

I found DeeDee sitting at the dining room table, coloring a picture of Big Bird in one of Angelique's coloring books. Gelée climbed up into her mother's lap, clutching the doll between her arm and her chest, and began handing DeeDee crayons, one at a time as she needed them. DeeDee kissed the top of her little girl's head, then, just as sly as you please, took hold of the doll and eased it out of Angelique's grip. She brought it to her chest, slid her daughter off her lap, and went upstairs to her bedroom.

I stood outside the open bedroom door with Gelée clutching my finger. We watched as DeeDee curled up on her bed and began to rock herself to sleep. She hummed a lullaby and cradled the doll in the crook of her arm.

"It's okay, sweetheart," I whispered to Angelique. "I can make you a new one."

She looked up at me, bravely, with tears in her pretty gray eyes. "With a yellow dress?"

I nodded. "Absolutely."

❧

The day Angelique started kindergarten was an exciting day for all of us, except DeeDee, who didn't understand what all the fuss was about. Jonathan took the morning off so he could take his daughter to class that first day, and by the time I arrived to stay with DeeDee, he had already dressed Angelique in the new outfit he had picked out himself.

"You look like you just stepped out of a window display at Frills & Frocks," I said. And she did. Her hair, however, was a different story.

Jonathan handed me a comb and a ribbon. "I'm all thumbs. Could you do it in one of those French thingies you do so well? That'll keep it neat for the day."

I took Gelée's hand and led her off to the bathroom. "Don't you look gorgeous," I declared to her reflection in the mirror.

She smiled as she turned full circle to model her new outfit, drawing my attention to her new shoes and socks, then lifted her dress to show me her slip. "Daddy thought of everything," she said. "Even a backpack."

"What kind?"

"SpongeBob SquarePants."

Well, of course.

She stood patiently while I braided her hair, weaving a ribbon through it as I went, the way her mother used to do to her own hair in our college days. "Is Mommy going to kindergarten?" she asked all of a sudden.

"You mean going along with your daddy to take you to school? I don't see why not."

"No, not with Daddy. With me, so she can learn how to read."

"Well, sweetheart," I said, not sure where to go with this, "Mommy can read. She learned when she was little like you."

Angelique looked puzzled. "When I ask her to read *Amelia Bedelia* to me she just looks at the words and doesn't say anything. So Daddy reads it to me at night before I go to sleep."

I knelt down and looked into her eyes. "I think it's just that your mommy gets confused with the words sometimes."

"Like when I get confused with *saw* and *was*? That happens to grown-ups?" She looked surprised.

"Sometimes."

"What if my teacher gets confused? Who will teach me how to read the words I haven't learned yet?"

"Oh, honey, I wouldn't worry. I don't think your teacher will get confused."

She thought about that for a moment. "Does it only happen to mommies?"

I stood up and finished tying the ribbon at the bottom of her braid. "You know, punkin', we'd better finish your hair. You don't want to be late your first day of school." I admit it. I took the coward's way out. But there were some answers you couldn't simplify enough for a five-year-old.

"I'm ready, Daddy!" she hollered as she ran into the living room, where he waited for his little girl. She kissed DeeDee and then me, put her tiny hand into Jonathan's, and let him lead her to his waiting SUV.

The scent of her fresh-scrubbed self hung in the air like a bouquet, and I didn't want it to dissipate. As I stood there, lingering in the remains of her presence, DeeDee walked over and laid her head on my shoulder as if to say, *I'm here, don't be sad.*

What a day of joy.

And a day of sorrow.

The phone rang a little past noon as I helped DeeDee with her lunch. Iris McAllister was on the other end, telling me that

DeeDee's father had died that morning at a little past ten. He was sixty-six years old. I called Jonathan, knowing he would call Linda, then waited for DeeDee's daily nap to relieve myself of the emotion that had come with the news.

One of us had to grieve for him.

Jonathan and Linda flew to Long Beach for the funeral later that week. It was the first time Linda had met her rival face-to-face.

"She was actually nice," she said, on their return that night, "and so sad. I—"she stopped and swallowed back her tears—"I found myself feeling sorry for her."

DeeDee was forever hiding things, and while searching the house for the gift I'd purchased and wrapped for Gelée's second grade class Christmas party, I came across a journal tucked in DeeDee's nightstand drawer under some old magazines. I lifted it from its hiding place and opened it to the first entry.

"I want a baby!" it began. I forgot about the gift, took the journal to the kitchen, and made a fresh pot of coffee.

"What's that?" DeeDee took the journal out of my hands but didn't open it. Instead, she rubbed her hand over the leathery surface, enjoying the texture.

"Hmm. It's a story, I think. Maybe our favorite one, Dee."

She smiled and pushed two kitchen chairs together, then patted one, indicating I should sit. But I poured my coffee and took it and the journal into the living room instead, where a nice flame was dancing behind the glass doors of the gas fireplace. I pulled two pillows from the sofa, and DeeDee and I made ourselves comfortable in the warmth of the artificial fire.

A light rain pelted the windows, driven by a blustery December wind.

"Shall I read it?"

DeeDee nodded and turned onto her back with her head on her pillow.

Okay. I had the author's permission.

The journal was a red leather volume and had been tied closed with a satin ribbon when I found it in the nightstand. I opened it again to the first page. *"I want a baby!"* I began to read.

DeeDee turned and gave me a cryptic smile. I seldom knew anymore how much she understood, but this opening line had touched something inside.

"Never thought I'd say such words. Can't imagine why I put it off. Well, that's not entirely true. It's the whole divorce thing. I didn't want to risk having a child live through that. I know Jonathan and I would have tried to work out any problems . . . but what if we couldn't? It just hurts too much when you're a kid. And when you're not."

A pang of sorrow went through me for DeeDee, Linda, and the man I'd met only once. I paused in case DeeDee had something to say. But she continued to lie in silence beside me.

. . . .

"How will it feel to be pregnant? How will I look? Vanity, vanity, all is vanity! Oh well, I am who I am. Why fight it?!"

. . . .

"JONATHAN SAID YES!!! And not just yes, but YES! I know I don't deserve him—Gabby said as much at lunch on Tuesday. She knows me like no one else, the brat. Can't wait to get started!"

I raised to one elbow, took a sip of my coffee, and looked her in the eye. "I may have been wrong about that. I'm pretty sure I was."

She rolled onto her side to mirror me and reached out to touch the journal again. This time she ran her fingers down the ribbon, then slyly pulled the book out of my hand. She turned away from me, but I watched as she studied the open page.

"It's about Angelique," I said. "Would you like to hear more?"

She traced the words with her finger. She said something in French I could no longer interpret, then handed me the book.

· · · · · · · · ·

"Who knew mating could be such hard work?"

"Ooh, la la. This could get a little personal. What do you think, should I stop? No? Well, if it gets too juicy I'll whisper."

"It's wearing Jonathan out, poor boy . . . but nothing happens. Making the most of it."

"And probably without complaint from poor Jonathan, huh?"

· · · · · · · · ·

"No wonder. I may be out of eggs! I willfully opted out of mother-hood when I had my chance and now I'm getting what I deserve. No eggs!"

"Oh, Dee, that is *not* what you deserved. And it didn't even turn out to be true."

I sat up and crossed my legs Indian style and thought back on that day. "You surprised me, you know? I'd never seen you so willing to give up on a fight. But nothing ever surprised me like Sonny's announcement. Do you remember? Oh, Dee, do you remember any of this?"

364 | SHARON K. SOUZA

She began to hum "Twinkle, Twinkle, Little Star," which Gelée practiced on the piano every afternoon, then lay back on her pillow.

. . . .

"You won't believe . . . Gab . . . She's a saint. She was actually going to — But no need! WE'RE PREGNANT!!!"

"That was one of my best days ever, you know?" I shrugged to myself. "Of course you know. It was yours, too. And Sonny's and Jonathan's and everyone's. 'No room.' Leave it to you."

. . . .

"Tired, tired, tired, tired, tired."

. . . .

"She's alive in there and showed me so today. There are no words to express how it felt. Was it her tiny little fist or maybe her foot, pushing against my womb, saying, 'I'm here. Don't forget it!' She's got attitude. Can't wait to meet her!"

I laughed. "How could she not have attitude?"

But DeeDee's eyes were closed, and her breathing was slow and even. I glanced at my watch. Nap time. I pulled an afghan off the sofa and draped it over DeeDee, then filled my coffee cup and returned to my place by the fire.

"We're getting to the best part," I said to my sleeping companion. "I'm so glad you thought to do this, Dee." And I continued to read aloud.

"Everything's ready . . . but am I? Can I really do this? Be not just a mother, but a mommy? What if I just don't have it? Father God, don't let me fail."

"She *is* a mommy and she's missing it all, Lord."

Do you believe?

"It's not about me."

Do you believe?

You betcha!

Do you believe?

What else matters? What else matters!

Do you—

"Okay!"

DeeDee started beside me, turned a little, then settled back into a quiet sleep.

"Okay. It's just that I'm . . ." I stood and walked to the rain-streaked window.

I can take it.

". . . having this conversation with myself." I shook my confused head. "I'm losing it. I really am."

First Peter 5:7.

"That one I know!"

Cast all your—

"And I've tried! I've tried, Lord. But how?"

Do you believe?

I groaned. "It's going to keep coming back to that, isn't it?" I drew a circle on the foggy window, touched my first and middle fingers where eyes should go, then added a frown.

. . . .

"Oh!!! Why would anyone do this twice??? They say you forget the pain the moment you see the baby. Bet it was a daddy who said it!"

. . . .

"She's beyond perfect. Doesn't look at all like a joint effort!"

. . . .

"Tired, tired, tired, tired, tired."

. . . .

More than a year passed with hardly an entry.

"Did the strangest thing today . . . I can't—"

. . . .

"Who is everyone?! I know them. Don't I? Their names . . . what are their names?"

. . . .

The last entry said, *"Feel like the incredible shrinking woman. Where am I going?"*

"That is the question," I whispered. "I ask it a million times a day, Dee. Where are you? What are you thinking? Do you feel trapped inside—"

No! Don't go there! Seeing this from my side was bad enough.

But it would be worse to think this was all there was. I sighed deeply. "Yes, I believe." It was not a statement of faith but of surrender. "I've always believed. But I have to tell you, I hate this."

I tied the ribbon around the journal, wrapped it in Christmas paper, and placed it under the tree, a gift from DeeDee to Jonathan. And I had to smile. Gelée's class gift was there on a branch, the paper torn where DeeDee looked to see what was inside.

⁓

My life with Doris Day McAllister-Kent has been an adventure. She's my sister-friend, the half that makes me whole. I'd give my life *for* her in a heartbeat, but I am called upon to give my life *to* her instead. And she? She gave me identity and took the fear out of living.

Bittersweet? Oh yes. To see this vibrant, intelligent woman become lost inside herself is the most helpless feeling imaginable. She's there, somewhere. I see a glimmer of my spirited friend peeking out from those baby blue eyes once in a baby blue moon. And I desperately want to coax her out to stay, but she retreats, pulled away against her dwindling will.

But too hard? No. My life has taken on meaning I could not have imagined a few short years ago. I'm no longer just one of the self-absorbed elite, floating through life, having lunch at D'Angelo's because it's Tuesday. Now there are two special lives dependent on mine, and the knowledge of that both heartens and terrifies.

And my reward? It's the exquisite joy I derive from the priceless little girl DeeDee fought so hard to bring into a world that doesn't deserve her. To feel her sweet breath on my cheek as she climbs into my lap to give me a kiss is like feeling the breath of an angel. To hear her say, "I love you, Auntie Gab," well, what can beat that?

DeeDee once said that I should write about things that matter. That I should write about us, always and forever. And I promised that when we were old and toothless I would write the story of us—my masterpiece. Well, we aren't old, and we haven't lost our teeth, and I doubt I'll ever really write a masterpiece.

Instead, I'm content to live one.

etc.

bonus content includes:

- ► Reader's Guide

- ► An Interview with the Author

- ► About the Author

reader's guide

1. What would you say is the main theme of *Every Good and Perfect Gift*?

2. James 1:17 says, "Every good and perfect gift is from above, coming down from the Father of the heavenly lights." Discuss the various gifts revealed in the story. What are some gifts you have received from God?

3. Do you closely identify with any one character in this story? If so, which one and why?

4. What growth, if any, did you see in Gabby? In DeeDee?

5. Have you ever had a friend like Gabby? Like DeeDee? If so, how did that friendship influence your life?

6. Are a husband and wife truly a family when it's just the two of them?

7. Gabby asks the question, "Do you think it's a sin not to have kids on purpose?" How would you answer that?

8. How do you respond when things happen that are beyond your control and leave you feeling helpless?

9. When Gabby cried out to God in her frustration, she heard the still, small voice of God speak to her heart. Have you ever experienced a time when the Holy Spirit spoke into a situation you were going through?

10. Has infertility been an issue in any way in your life? If so, how did it affect you in the short term and in the long term?

11. Alzheimer's is a terrible disease, no matter at what age it strikes. What are some major differences and challenges between Alzheimer's and early-onset Alzheimer's?

12. What role did Gabby's faith play in the story? Did it decline or increase under fire?

13. Because of the terrible effects of DeeDee's disease, Jonathan's future as her husband is bleak. How should he proceed with his life once DeeDee requires full-time care? Does the fact that Jonathan is in his late forties and not his seventies or eighties make a difference in how you answer this question? Should it be any different for a person of faith than for a nonbeliever?

14. Was there a scene in this book that made you think, *So-and-so has to read this book*?

15. In the acknowledgments the author wrote, "This story is because of Evie. But the end will really be the beginning." What do you think she meant?

an interview with the author

What inspired you to write *Every Good and Perfect Gift*?

I wanted to write a book about a Jonathan-and-David-type friendship between two women, knowing that I was ultimately going to tell the story of a young woman who is diagnosed with early-onset Alzheimer's. I have a close friend who at the age of forty-two began to experience many of the symptoms that DeeDee exhibits. Since completing the book I've learned that another close friend has been diagnosed with early-onset Alzheimer's. What are the odds?

In determining what course the friendship between Gabby and DeeDee would take, I asked myself this question: What is the greatest way one of these women can express friendship to the other? The answer: by helping her conceive a child, which Gabby was willing to do if it came to that.

Why did you decide to use humor to tell a story with such serious issues?

It's exactly because the issues are so serious that I chose to inject some humor into the story. Our life experiences are heavy enough without adding to them as we read for pleasure. That's not to say there aren't serious moments in the book, but I hope the reader is buoyed by the lighter sections rather than overloaded with the weightier ones.

What do you want your readers to take away from this book?

I spent several years in my early adulthood without a close friend. When the first one came into my life, I realized what I had missed and truly saw her as a gift from the Lord. But beyond that, I've experienced the truth of Proverbs 18:24: "There is a friend who sticks closer than a brother." In her darkest moments, Gabby learned that the Lord reaches out to us in compassion, spanning the gap between our need and His provision. That's been the case in my life over and over. In fact, during the final edits of this book, my husband and I lost our son. Never have the promises in God's Word been more real. Never has His presence been so evident.

What is your purpose in writing inspirational fiction?

I've had well-meaning friends ask why I write fiction at all. If I want to share the gospel, why not write "the truth." Two answers come to mind. First, that burning "fire shut up in my bones" mentioned in Jeremiah 20:9 finds its release in fiction. Second, when Jesus wanted to get a heavenly truth across, He didn't deliver a three-point sermon. He told stories. My desire in writing inspirational fiction is that women who read my books will find them easy to share with other women who haven't yet come into relationship with Jesus and that those women will be directed to the One who loves them with an everlasting love.

What do you like to read, and who are your favorite authors?

Mostly I read contemporary Christian fiction, though I do read all things Grisham. Some of my favorite authors are Lisa Samson, Kathleen Popa, W. Dale Cramer, Charles Martin, and Ted Dekker. I also love all the old English literature classics: Charles Dickens, Jane Austen, the Brontës, and so on. My favorite book in the Bible is John, and I also enjoy all the prophetic books.

about the author

Sharon K. Souza has a passion for inspirational fiction, and *Every Good and Perfect Gift* is her debut novel. She and her husband, Rick, live in northern California. They have three grown children and six grandchildren. Rick travels the world building churches, Bible schools, and orphanages. Sharon travels with him on occasion, but while Rick lives the adventure, Sharon is more than happy to create her own through her fiction.

Visit Sharon's website at www.sharonksouza.com.

Check out these other great titles from the NavPress fiction line!

Storm Warriors

John Nappa
ISBN-13: 978-1-60006-172-1
ISBN-10: 1-60006-172-9

Storm Warriors is based on the amazing true story of a man inspired to save lives after losing everything he had. Filled with pulse-pounding action and crackling dialogue, this book will inspire readers of all ages to pursue a life that serves others.

The Restorer's Journey

Sharon Hinck
ISBN-13: 978-1-60006-133-2
ISBN-10: 1-60006-133-8

Back in our world with her teenage son, Jake, in tow, suburban mom Susan Mitchell is ready for life as usual. But when a foreign threat invades their comfortable home, Susan and Jake soon find themselves drawn back through the portal to the world of the People of the Verses. Make sure you read the first two in the series, *The Restorer* and *The Restorer's Son.*

The Reluctant Journey of David Connors

Don Locke
ISBN-13: 978-1-60006-152-3
ISBN-10: 1-60006-152-4

Family man David Connors is standing on the brink of suicide. One week before Christmas, he is burdened by a fractured marriage and a life disconnected from God and family. Yet in his darkest moment, he makes a surprising find: an old carpetbag buried under a snowy ledge. This is an extraordinary novel that features intriguing fantasy, lively dialogue, and a story of emotional power and unexpected humor.

To order copies, visit your local Christian bookstore, call NavPress at
1-800-366-7788, or log on to www.navpress.com.
To locate a Christian bookstore near you, call 1-800-991-7747.